THE MURDER OF
LALLA LEE

THE TELLTALE
TELEGRAM

Miss Helen Burnham

THE MURDER OF
LALLA LEE

THE TELLTALE
TELEGRAM

HELEN BURNHAM

COACHWHIP PUBLICATIONS
Greenville, Ohio

The Murder of Lalla Lee / The Telltale Telegram,
    by Helen Burnham
© 2022 Coachwhip Publications edition
Cover: *Jugend* (1897) edited by Grafissimo

Helen Burnham, 1896-?
The Murder of Lalla Lee published 1931
The Telltale Telegram published 1932
CoachwhipBooks.com

ISBN 1-61646-536-0
ISBN-13 978-1-61646-536-0

THE MURDER OF
LALLA LEE

1

Mr. Wimble looked up from the letter he had been reading and smiled across his desk at Corey Webb.

"You're thinking that I don't look much like a detective, aren't you, son?"

"Well," admitted the young man, "you don't look much as I expected you to."

Certainly no great actor, cast for the role of private detective, would have studied Mr. Wimble's portrait before making up for the part. Mr. Wimble was short and extremely round. He was almost bald and had two chins. His eyes were small and very blue and as merry as it is possible for eyes to be. His hands gave him his only claim to good looks; they were surprisingly well-shaped and delicate for so fat a man. But his careful grooming, a gift from Heaven in a plump person, and his engaging manner formed satisfactory substitutes for good looks.

Mr. Wimble chuckled.

"I suppose you thought I went around in a mouse-colored dressing gown with a hypodermic needle in my pocket?"

As Corey blushed, it struck the detective with a pang how closely the boy resembled his mother. Dolly Webb was the most beautiful woman Mr. Wimble had ever seen.

His resemblance to his mother was the bug in Corey's amber. When his enemies wished to be particularly obnoxious they said: "Webb looks enough like his mother to be her sister!" But, in regretting the bug, Corey did not fail to appreciate the amber. His shoulders measured one inch less in breadth than Gene Tunney's!

Of course the girls flocked. Corey, did not care for girls. In fact, Corey advertised himself as a woman-hater.

Corey's reason for disliking girls was excellent. As some girls cannot look upon a bachelor without trying to make a husband out of him, either their own or some girl friend's, neither could they look upon Corey Webb without trying to make a talkie star out of him.

"With your looks and voice, surely you're considering the talkies!" "But of course you intend going to Hollywood? It's your bounden duty to go!" Until he hardly knew which he hated the most: his good looks, the cinema or girls who saw in the talkies his métier.

Locking up Corey's college diploma in the secret drawer of her desk, along with his first tooth, his baby curls, his primary grade report card, and kindred treasures, Dolly had talked over with her son his future. In his detestation of his good looks, Corey yearned for a "he-man" job that in no wise would depend on his personal appearance. The talkies, he vehemently announced, were out! Whereupon his mother sighed. It had been Dolly's hope that Corey would outgrow his morbid aversion to the cinema. Now that talking films were being internationally distributed, Corey's ultimatum meant that actual millions would be denied the rare privilege of gazing upon and listening to her only son. However, if he really felt the screen to be impossible, there was her dear old friend O. W. she might send him to. O. W.'s sister Portia had told Dolly only yesterday that O. W. was working far too hard for a man of his years and reputation and really ought to employ an assistant.

Mr. Wimble had suspected from the first that his sister was behind the letter from Dolly. Portia had been harping lately on his need of an assistant. Portia was as tenacious as a tick: when she fastened on to an idea it was difficult to pry her loose. In suggesting his need to Dolly, Portia was incidentally procuring a job for her friend's boy, but her real purpose of course was to hoodwink O. W. into complying with her own wishes.

Portia had known he would not be able to refuse Dolly anything. He never had been able to refuse the delectable Dolly anything since the day, more years back than he cared to remember, when she had coaxed: "Now you won't go off and mope, will you O. W. dear, just because I want to marry Sim Webb instead of you?," and he had promised not to.

Apart from Dolly's hold on him, he decided that it would be agreeable to train young Webb—a decision that caused him a pang of self-derision as he recalled how elaborately he'd maneuvered all these years to avoid meeting this same young man. O. W.'s mind had never dwelt on the time he would retire from active business, and it did not now; but the thought did occur to him that it would be gratifying to know that his work would be carried on when he left off.

That was half of it. The other half was that, but for the little slip-up in his destiny that had brought Sim Webb on the scene, Corey might have been young Wimble instead of young Webb. It would be pleasant having the boy around.

"Your mother writes that you want a 'he-man' job, son."

"Yes, sir," replied Corey sternly, and hoped that Mr. Wimble wouldn't judge a fellow by the regularity of his features.

"If by a 'he-man' job you mean a job that entails blood-and-thunder methods, I'm afraid the detective profession will prove a disappointment to you. I've never disguised myself as a Chinese laundryman in the whole of my professional career. I have more respect for a criminal's eyesight than that. And I never go trailing around graveyards in the middle of the night in search of my man. I figure he doesn't care any more for graveyards in the middle of the night than I do."

His voice sobered. "Of course we sleuths have our exciting moments. But sewing-machine salesmen must have theirs, too."

The idea captured his fancy.

"I'd say there's a great similarity between a detective's job and a salesman's. Each meets a lot of persons, and all sorts; and each tries to get something out of the persons he meets. The salesman, orders. The detective, information. That's about what the detective game amounts to, son: getting information."

In concluding, he presented his detective philosophy: "I've found, as a rule, that the better a chap likes folks the more information he can get out of them."

In after years, Corey recalled this simple statement with the realization that it held the key to O. W.'s entire success. Mr. Wimble was successful as a man because he loved his fellow men, as a detective because he could get information from them.

At the moment, however, Corey's thoughts were on himself.

"I like people well enough," he stammered. "All except girls!"

Mr. Wimble sympathized with Corey. After all, the pursuit of her had provided much of the thrill of loving Dolly. Still, he wistfully reflected, Corey might be glad of his good looks some day. At least the boy'd be spared the anguish of seeing the girl he adored won by another because he hadn't any!

"Well, all right, son. You can have the job if you want it."

Corey Webb had been an assistant private detective for five days. These five days had not been without interest. Making the acquaintance of Willy O'Rourke, Mr. Wimble's office boy, alone was sufficient to insure one against boredom. Yet Corey felt the five days to have been wasted. For he had not as yet engaged in any professional duties. Mr. Wimble had, after thirty years' practice, arrived at the point where he could afford to choose his cases. Much that came into the office was turned down.

But at last, one Tuesday afternoon which Corey never in his life forgot, Willy O'Rourke announced the visit of Mr. John Hathaway.

As the District Attorney followed Willy into the detectives' private office, his eyes were twinkling with the amusement that contact with O. W.'s office boy never failed to arouse in him. Willy put him in mind of a jockey on holiday. The comparison was not inapt. Willy had been Mr. Wimble's office boy for thirty years. With his small boy body, he had always looked young; with his wizened, old-man face, he had always looked old. And he shared a jockey's predilection for checkered suitings, tan brogans and bowler hats.

What made Willy O'Rourke particularly amusing was his hobby: namely, the documenting of fictional criminal cases. Actual crime did not interest Willy in the slightest; but ask him anything concerning the criminal investigations of Messrs. Sherlock Holmes, Philo Vance, Arsène Lupin, et al., and he would turn to files as faultlessly kept as any official records.

Despite his idiosyncrasies, however, Willy O'Rourke was an exceptionally capable office boy.

The minute the newspapers get hold of a mystery story, the police and the private detective on the case, if there be one, are besieged by persons offering false clues, solutions, confessions, even. The ease with which Willy O'Rourke could get these spurious witnesses to write down and leave with him their testimony, instead of bothering Mr. Wimble with it orally, was nothing short of inspired.

Willy's high-handedness in the matter of visitors was another of the reasons he was so valuable. Interruptions are fatal to a detective. At times, being protected even from one's friends has its advantages. And no one stood the least chance of gaining audience with Mr. Wimble except by appointment.

Corey's eyes glowed as his chief introduced him to Mr. Hathaway. Corey had heard that the District Attorney often called upon his friend O. W. for advice. He knew, therefore, that a visit from John Hathaway held out some hope for his own professional debut.

As he was hanging on Mr. Hathaway's words, the District Attorney asked: "How would you like to take tea with a pretty lady this afternoon, O. W.?"

Corey's "Damn!" was soft but heartfelt.

Mr. Wimble made no sign that he had overheard the ejaculation. He appreciated the youngster's disappointment. This was hardly the time, however, to tell the lad that John Hathaway was not in the habit of sending him on wild-goose chases.

"Who is the pretty lady?" asked Mr. Wimble.

"I haven't had the pleasure of meeting her," returned Hathaway. "But her name is Lalla Lee. Mrs. Walter Lee. She rang me up about half an hour ago to invite me to tea at her house at four. I pleaded business, promising to send a proxy. . . . Oh," he broke off, "you know something about her?"

"Only that she is exceptionally beautiful. I have never heard of her before."

"Then how do you know she is beautiful?"

"From Webb's face. Look at the boy! Webb is a woman-hater," explained Mr. Wimble solemnly. "Therefore, it would take an exceptional woman to arouse his interest. I am safe in saying exceptionally beautiful, as young men don't care for much else in a woman."

Corey did not resent Mr. Wimble's teasing. "O. W.'ll tease you like the very dickens if he cares for you," Dolly had told him.

That Corey had admired Lalla Lee eight or ten months previously in no wise proved that he was not a misogynist. Because it was not the real girl he had liked; he had merely admired her pictures. At that time the papers had been full of photographs of Lalla Blair, a chorus girl who had become the bride of Walter Lee, a chain-store millionaire some thirty years her senior. A girl who could marry an old man for his money never could have appealed to Corey, of course, even if he had liked girls. But he had thought Lalla Blair Lee superlatively lovely to look at.

Mr. Wimble, it developed, had been abroad at the time of the Blair-Lee marriage. So Corey sketched for him the newspaper details.

"And now, finding herself bored, the fair Lalla has decided to carry on a little flirtation with my friend John," said Mr. Wimble, cocking a mischievous eye at the District Attorney.

She could not have picked out a handsomer man with whom to flirt. There was distinction in John Hathaway's tall, spare form; beauty in his clean-cut features, his crisp black hair that had begun, becomingly, to whiten at the temples.

"The woman doesn't know me from Adam!" retorted the District Attorney.

Mr. Wimble chuckled.

"Both your tone and your tint convince me that she flirted with you over the telephone."

"I'll admit that she was a bit—persuasive. But she assured me several times that she had something of great importance to tell me. As District Attorney," he hastily interposed. "She may be after excitement, of course, though a person with any intelligence at all must realize what it means to trifle with the law. At any rate, with the press and our political enemies hovering around like vultures, our office can't afford to ignore any such appeals as Mrs. Lee's."

"Did you invite her to call at your office?"

"I did not!" Mr. Hathaway was warmly emphatic. "I talked with her over the telephone, remember!"

He mopped his face with his handkerchief.

Mr. Wimble grinned.

"Wait till the woman begins on you!" snapped the District Attorney.

2

On his way to the clipping bureau, Corey Webb wondered if Mr. Wimble were not being just the least bit meticulous in his desire, before making the acquaintance of Lalla Lee, to be in possession of all the available facts concerning the girl.

Mr. Wimble had proffered an explanation.

"I never like to start out on a job without taking some tools along. In the present instance, we lack time. Making use of a clipping agency is about the quickest way I know of to get a line on a person. Not," with a grimace, "that I believe everything I read in the papers!"

Despite O. W.'s broad hint that the District Attorney never called for detective assistance unless at bay, Corey simply could not look upon having tea with the lovely Lalla as a "job." Hence his faint antagonism to investigating her.

The newspaper accounts of the Blair-Lee marriage were generously embellished with photographs of Lalla Blair, the majority of which were professional. In looking them over, Webb was again impressed by the remarkable beauty of the girl.

She wore her blonde hair like a boy's, the severity of its cut relieved by a little curl flattened, freakishly perhaps, but most charmingly, against the middle of her forehead.

Her eyes were wide, judging from the photographs, blue, and thickly surrounded by curling black lashes, enchantingly in contrast to her fair hair. Her mouth in shape was a small, slightly-horizontal heart, the space between her short straight nose and her upper lip brief and dimpled. She appeared to be of medium height; was slender and long-limbed.

Something curious about the photographs was that in none, of them were her hands or her feet in evidence. In busts, furs or bouquets hid her hands. In full-lengths, a long-feathered fan or the end of a shawl trailed across her feet.

Webb attributed this to coincidence.

The newspaper items were more or less alike. The following, dated April 7th, was representative of the rest:

> Miss Lalla Blair, returning yesterday from a short vacation at Colorado Springs, astonished her friends by the announcement that during her Western visit she had married Walter Lee, chain grocery store magnate of this city.
>
> Miss Blair will be remembered as one of the most beautiful show girls connected with the Starlight Follies, recently closed after enjoying a long and successful run on Broadway.
>
> Mr. Lee was one of the pioneers of the so-called "cash-and-carry" system of self-service in stores, the system successfully operating at the present time in all of his shops.
>
> In an interview with Mr. Lee this morning, it was learned that he is negotiating the purchase of the old Gayley property on

Park Avenue, where the couple plan to establish their home.

Mr. Lee's gift to his bride on their wedding day was a handsome pear-shaped
Colombia emerald, strung on a platinum
chain.

Mr. Lee is fifty-seven years old. His wife
is twenty-six.

All accounts of Lalla Lee ended with her marriage. For
that matter, except that her beauty was mentioned in one
or two reviews of the Starlight Follies, she had not been
of interest to newspaper subscribers before her marriage.

Upon leaving the clipping bureau, Corey rejoined his
chief. He felt that he had little of value to communicate.

"On the contrary," said Mr. Wimble, "I find your report most interesting."

His blue eyes twinkled.

"From her choice of a husband, it would appear that
the fair Lalla prefers old codgers like me to lads like you!
I am looking forward to the tea party."

Shortly before four o'clock they set out for Mrs. Lee's.

The Lee house on Park Avenue, since torn down to
make way for an apartment house, was at that time conspicuous as the only private dwelling in a neighborhood
of apartment houses. It was a three-story brownstone
building occupying a comer of the block. The front of the
house lay flush with the sidewalk of the Avenue, a narrow
garden running around the other three sides. Enclosing
the property was a seven-foot stone wall, intact save for a
servants' and tradesmen's entrance which opened on to the
side street.

The front doorbell was answered by a rheumy-eyed old
negro who informed the two men that his mistress was
not at home. He had no idea when she would return.

Sometimes when she went out in the afternoon it was late at night before she came back. Although he did not in so many words request the detectives to remove their persons from the premises, his attitude amply atoned for the omission.

"We were invited by Mrs. Lee to take tea with her this afternoon," said Mr. Wimble pleasantly.

The darky's manner testified to his alarm. Had Mr. Wimble not resorted to the old foot trick, the door most certainly would have slammed on Mrs. Lee's visitors.

Frustrated in his attempt, the negro, swallowing vigorously, put a question to Mr. Wimble.

"W-what name yo'-all call yourself, sir?"

That the reply to this question was of the utmost importance to him the detectives could not doubt.

"My name is Wimble. This young man is Mr. Webb."

The old man's alarm visibly lifted, though as yet he evinced no trace of that geniality for which his race is renowned.

"I's Sharl, sir."

"Well, Sharl, suppose you let Mr. Webb and me in to wait for Mrs. Lee?"

With a gesture of resignation, the darky admitted them.

The front door opened on to a wide hall. Here Sharl took their overcoats, afterward leading the detectives into a reception room where, without cordiality, he expressed the hope that they would make themselves comfortable.

As he went out he left the door ajar, which was the one thing he could have done to insure Corey, at least, against being comfortable. That young man had the feeling that everything he said was being overheard, which made whatever he said sound stentorian and rather silly. At the same time he admired the servant's vigilance. After all, Mr. Wimble and he were total strangers to the old man; and there were many movable objects of value in view.

The room was beautifully furnished and, with a single exception, in good taste. The furniture was Louis Seize, pure of line, simple of construction. Mulberry-colored velvet drapes hung at the window; the carpet was a handsome Aubusson. Besides several etchings, there was an admirable Prud'hon on the wall.

The incongruity was a modern, and exceedingly ugly, roll-top desk of fumed oak.

After about ten minutes Sharl re-entered the room.

"I could give you gentlemen your tea, now, Mr. Wimble, sir, jus' as well as not."

It was clear that his suspicion of the detectives was not completely dissipated.

"No, thank you, Sharl. We'll wait for the others."

The servant's eyes dilated.

"W-what others?"

"Weren't other guests expected?"

"No, sir! Mrs. Lee didn't say nothing to me about no tea party, sir. No, sir, she didn't! Nothing at all!"

"We'll wait for Mrs. Lee, then."

The old man, the epitome of gloom, shuffled out of the room.

After an hour Corey began to fidget.

"The whole thing may be a joke, sir," he whispered. Mr. Wimble acknowledged the possibility by a shrug, but made no move to depart.

Shortly before five o'clock the colored servitor again put in his appearance. When he spoke, his attempt at subtlety was offset by the anxiety with which he awaited Mr. Wimble's reply.

"If you was in a hurry to get back to some big office, sir, I don't guess Mrs. Lee'd 'xpect you to wait."

"Mr. Webb and I run a little business of our own. Nobody is waiting for us."

Suddenly, from somewhere at the back of the house, a shrill cry rang out: a woman's scream of terror. The old negro hurried out of the room, this time slamming the door behind him.

Corey had sprung to his feet.

"Sit down, son," laughed Mr. Wimble. "One of the servant girls probably saw a mouse."

Corey moistened his dry lips.

"I'm not enjoying our call very much!"

"No; I don't believe you are. You've been looking as if this were a dentist's waiting room ever since we arrived."

A few minutes later the detectives were favored by another visit from Sharl.

"One of the maids was scared by a fur coat hanging on the newel post of the back stairway," he briefly informed them, and disappeared.

This time Corey joined in O. W.'s laughter.

Again they settled down to await Mrs. Lee's coming.

Corey's watch showed it to be six o'clock when sounds of activity reached them from the front hall.

"A great time for a hostess to be coming to her own tea party!" remarked Corey under his breath.

"Pretty ladies are always privileged," said Mr. Wimble.

Corey told himself that it was his relief at Lalla Lee's arrival that was responsible for the eagerness with which he faced the hall door. Of course, in view of his misogynous principles, it couldn't very well have been otherwise.

But Corey was to be disappointed. It was Mr. Lee who entered the reception room, not his comely young wife.

Walter Lee was not in the least the type one usually pictures as the husband of a girl thirty years his junior. He was almost sixty; and there were no cosmetics, dandyisms or affectations about him to try to make any one believe he was younger than almost sixty. He was short and slight, but the steadfastness of his dark gray eyes and the firmness of his mouth and chin lent him an appearance of strength. He was reserved, rather formally polite. He did not seem to be a man possessing a great sense of humor. His prevailing facial expression was sad. He was modestly dressed in a dark business suit.

"Sharl, here, says you two gentlemen have been waiting quite a long time for my wife."

"Yes," replied Mr. Wimble. "And I'm beginning to feel the way I did once when I was a boy." He smiled. "I went to a dance the night before it took place!"

He introduced Corey to Mr. Lee.

"And my name is Wimble."

Mr. Lee shook hands with a stilted courtliness that immediately stamped him as a self-made man,

"The name of Wimble sounds familiar, though I don't seem to recall having heard the young man's."

"No doubt you have come across my name in the papers," said Mr. Wimble. "I have been a private detective for a number of years. Webb's my 'man Friday'."

At O. W.'s mention of his calling, again an expression of alarm crossed the old negro's features.

Mr. Lee showed some surprise.

"May I inquire whether or not you are here in an official capacity?"

"We were invited to take tea with Mrs. Lee."

"And, as so often happens with these popular young ladies, she's forgotten all about you! But which of you will be able to scold her for her cruelty?" One would have said that Mr. Lee was speaking of a favorite daughter rather than of his wife.

"You shall have your tea, though! We'll be drinking it when Lalla comes in. That will shame her. Fetch us up some tea, Sharl, please."

Though six o'clock was rather late for tea, Mr. Wimble did not remonstrate. Sharl departed kitchenward, and Mr.

Lee, inviting his appropriated guests to be seated, offered
them cigars.

After several minutes of casual small-talk, Mr. Wimble
inclined his head toward the Prud'hon.

"That's a capital painting you have there, Mr. Lee.
How—one might say—poetic Prud'hon seems at times!"

"Does he?" countered Mr. Lee simply. "I don't know
much about pictures, myself. I've always been too busy
to go in for Art. That painting came with the rest of this
stuff." He glanced around the room.

"My wife didn't care for the looks of the house when we
took it, so she called in one of these interior decorators."
He smiled reminiscently. "Queer-looking chap he was,
too! When he finished the room Lalla considered a gift in
order and asked me for a suggestion. I said I thought a silk
petticoat would be appropriate, if you get my mean—"

"Lord God in Heaven!"

Corey Webb had always scoffed at nerves, and he always would scoff at nerves. Yet, afterward, in reviewing
that scene, the only way he could account for the phenomenon was by attributing it to his nerves.

It was a crazy idea, of course: a smile turning pale! And
yet that's the way it looked to him. There had been a smile
on Mr. Lee's face as he spoke of the long-haired decorator.
Then, in the middle of the anecdote, from the living room
adjoining the room in which they sat, had come that sobbing scream: *"Lord God in Heaven!"* And Mr. Lee's face had
turned dead-white. With the smile still on it!

"It's Sharl!" gasped Mr. Lee. "He must have thought
we meant to have our tea in there. W-what can have happened?"

"Thank God," thought Corey, "speech has removed that
white smile from Mr. Lee's face!"

Mr. Lee made swiftly for the door of the living room.

"Sharl, old man, what is the matter?"

The door was locked. Mr. Lee pounded, frantically.

"Sharl! Sharl! Unlock the door— Oh, God! How do I know he *can* unlock the door?"

However, through the closed door they heard the old fellow's shuffling footsteps, his agitated fumbling with the key.

The door opened.

Normally, Sharl's complexion was a pale brown, the color of coffee and cream; but, in his fright, his face had taken on a lavender hue. His rheumy eyes were distended, and he was shaking in every limb.

"Sharl, old boy! What is it? What has happened?" There was a wealth of tenderness in Mr. Lee's voice, as his arms went out to steady his old retainer. Sharl seemed incapable of answering. He muttered incoherently, making feeble gestures the while over his shoulder.

The others peered into the living room. Someone was sitting in a corner of the high-backed davenport that fronted the fireplace. Only the back of a blonde head was visible, a head that, by virtue of a present-day whim of Fashion, might have been either male or female.

"Why, it's Lalla!" Unmistakable relief showed in Mr. Lee's face as he affectionately shook Sharl by the shoulders.

"You old donkey, you! Is it necessary to frighten us all to death just because you see your mistress when you suppose she's out?"

Sharl swallowed spasmodically, but was still incapable of conversation. Mr. Lee brushed him gently aside.

"Lalla!" he laughed, though his voice had not yet regained its habitual steadiness. "Sharl thinks he's seen your ghost!"

The woman on the davenport made no move.

"Lalla!" Mr. Lee raised his voice slightly, though he did speak sharply. "We have guests."

As she continued to ignore him, with a puzzled frown
he stepped across the threshold. It was then that speech
and action returned to the old darky.

"No!" he cried, catching hold of Mr. Lee. "Don't go
in! *Don't go in!*" His voice approached hysteria as Mr. Lee
endeavored to pull away from him.

"Permit me?" said Mr. Wimble quietly.

Clearly bewildered, Mr. Lee stepped back, allowing the
detective to pass into the living room.

O. W. went over to the davenport. A tremor crossed his
face as he looked down at Lalla Lee.

After a moment he rejoined the others.

"My wife is dead?" asked Mr. Lee softly.

"Yes."

At this juncture Sharl miraculously recovered control
of himself. It was as if his master's need of him had given
him strength. He stood beside Mr. Lee, calm, protective,
devoted.

"Come away now, Mr. Lee," he begged. "Do come away!"

"Unlike you, old fellow," said Mr. Lee, with a sad smile,
"I am not afraid of Death."

Pleadingly, Sharl rolled his eyes toward O. W.

"I fear her present state will be a great shock to you,
Mr. Lee," said Mr. Wimble.

"I don't believe even Death could rob Lalla of her beauty,"
returned Lee. But, as he stepped forward, the detective
placed a restraining hand on his arm.

"I must advise you, Mr. Lee, that your wife's condition
is—quite horrible."

For a moment Mr. Lee appeared uncomprehending.
Then the full significance of Mr. Wimble's words dawned
on him.

"You mean— Good God, Mr. Wimble! Lalla's not *murdered?*"

Mr. Wimble nodded.

3

"Mr. Wimble," asked Mr. Lee gravely, "will you find the murderer for me?"

"I shall be glad to handle the case. I assume, since you wish to retain the services of a detective, that you suspect no one."

"As far as I know, my wife hadn't an enemy in the world. And I am certain that she had no serious worries. She was in excellent spirits the last time I saw her."

"When was that?"

"At about half-past one this afternoon. She left the house, laughing." His voice faltered. "Lalla's laughter was—music."

Abruptly he turned away, Sharl trotting behind like a faithful dog.

The detective looked commiseratively after the bereaved man.

"If you care to retire to your room now, Mr. Lee, we can continue our discussion tomorrow."

"Pardon my weakness," said Mr. Lee, his emotion once more under control. "I am quite ready to go on."

"Were you aware of your wife's plans for the afternoon?"

"Only that she left the house to go to see her friend Myrtle. Myrtle Dale, a girl Lalla was on the stage with.

"My wife and I lunched here today as usual. After luncheon, Lalla asked me for five hundred dollars in cash. She had no bank account of her own. It was one of my pleasures, in which she graciously indulged me, that she should depend on me for spending money. I hadn't as much as five hundred dollars on me; so I sent Patterson, our chauffeur, to the bank to cash a check."

"Did Mrs. Lee say why she wanted the money?"

"No. Probably she and Myrtle were going on a shopping tour. She seemed in quite a hurry to get to Myrtle's. Usually she didn't care to leave the house until after Patterson had driven me to my office; but today she expressed a desire to use the car before I took it."

He smiled faintly. "She said that if I'd play solitaire without cheating for a change there'd be time for Patterson to take her to Myrtle's and get back before I was ready to leave. I always play solitaire for fifteen minutes or so after luncheon, getting back to my office around two o'clock. It is my old-fashioned conviction that sitting still after meals aids digestion."

"A notion," interrupted Mr. Wimble, "that was booed by Mrs. Lee, I take it?"

Mr. Lee stiffened. "Natural enough when you consider her youth, I think!"

"I intended no criticism of your wife, Mr. Lee," said Mr. Wimble.

He smiled. "I'm afraid I was merely trying to show off before Webb. You can see he's wondering how I knew Mrs. Lee had called your idea old-fashioned."

Mr. Lee relaxed; but he, as well as Corey, looked puzzled.

"I, too, am wondering," he confessed.

"You *quoted* the adjective. Please continue, Mr. Lee."

"Of course I agreed to let her take the car. She went upstairs to get ready. When Patterson returned from the bank, I told him that Lalla wished to use the car before I went back to the office, so he went out to wait for her. A moment later she came down, took the bills—there were five one-hundred-dollar bills—and, as far as I know, drove to her friend's. Patterson returned for me at two. It did not occur to me to question him about Lalla."

"Did you overhear Mrs. Lee telephoning before she left?"

"No. But that doesn't signify anything. There is a phone in her sitting room at the back of the house. I couldn't have heard her from the front of the house."

"Did you happen to notice whether or not she were wearing any jewelry when she went out?"

"I distinctly remember that she was wearing the emerald I gave her when we were married."

"Valuable?"

"I paid ten thousand dollars for the stone."

"Where did she keep her jewelry when not wearing it?"

"In a strong box at the bank. The Safe Deposit Department maintains a twenty-four-hour service. As we have no safe in the house, Lalla always left her jewelry there before coming home for the night."

"She is not wearing her emerald now, Mr. Lee. Before retiring, would you mind seeing if the emerald is in her room?"

"Not at all. But I shall be surprised if I find it there. It was a set rule with Lalla never to leave her jewels lying around."

"In case the emerald is not found in the house, will you kindly inquire of the bank if it is in her safe deposit box?"

"Willingly."

"How was your wife dressed when she went out?"

"She was wearing her sable coat and a small black hat—I think it was black; dark at any rate. Her head was covered by a heavy black veil."

"Mrs. Lee was in mourning?"

"Oh, no!"

"Your car is open?"

"I have an open car; but it's the closed limousine that's in use in weather like this."

"Then why did Mrs. Lee consider a heavy veil necessary?"

Mr. Lee shrugged. "Can a man ever account for the way a woman dresses?" He smiled slightly. "Perhaps I'd better give you Lalla's own reason for wearing it. I made some remark about her funereal-looking veil, and she said, laughing: 'I'm wearing it because I'm going to meet a Dead One at Myrt's this afternoon.'"

"Whom, exactly, had she in mind? Do you know?"

"No. And I didn't inquire. She and Myrtle had their girlish secrets." He eyed Mr. Wimble rather sternly. "I trusted Lalla implicitly, Mr. Wimble."

Mr. Wimble arose.

"That'll be all for the present, Mr. Lee. If you don't mind, before sending for the police, I'd like to examine the living room and interview the servants. You'll be kind enough to request the help not to leave the house without my permission?"

"And Lalla's—?"

"I think we'd better leave her as we found her until after the police have arrived. I'll see to it that you're left undisturbed tonight, Mr. Lee."

Leaning on the arm of Sharl, who had remained in the background during the interview on the anxious lookout for signs of collapse on the part of his master, Mr. Lee left the room.

"Well, my boy," said Mr. Wimble to Corey, as he led the way to the living room, "you're embarked on your first case. From now on, keep your eyes and ears and mind open, and your mouth shut."

The pretty head rising above the davenport, its smooth hair gleaming like gold under the lights, made Webb forget for the moment that Mr. Wimble had described Lalla Lee's condition as "quite horrible." He stepped rather confidently in front of the davenport. . . .

"Steady, son!" cried Mr. Wimble sharply.

It was hideous! The fore part of Lalla Lee's skull had been crushed in. Almost her entire face was bathed in blood. Blood had dripped down on her dress.

Later, when the body was moved, a short scratch, from which a faint stream of blood had trickled and dried, was discovered at the nape of her neck.

A most unprofessional hatred for the person who so brutally had cut off the life of this beautiful girl filled the heart of Mr. Wimble's assistant. He longed personally, immediately, to feel his fingers tightening around the murderer's neck.

"Mr. Wimble! Oughtn't we first to search the premises? The murderer may be concealed somewhere in the house."

"You will observe that the blood is dry," replied Mr. Wimble. "Just how long Mrs. Lee has been dead, will be for a medical examiner to determine. The crime certainly did not take place within the past hour, however. The assailant has had more than ample time to make his escape."

Beside the fireplace was a metal container holding, among other implements, an iron poker. From the condition of her skull, Lalla Lee had been struck by some heavy instrument. It occurred to Corey that this poker might have been the weapon used.

Mr. Wimble was not in accord with Corey's view.

"No," he said. "I believe that Lalla Lee was killed by the statue on the table behind her."

Apart from its possible connection with the crime, the statue in question appeared a sinister-looking object to Corey. It was a bronze, two feet high, representing a raven perched on a bust of Pallas—the subject having been inspired, of course, by Poe's immortal poem.

"There are probably fingerprints, so we won't touch it," said Mr. Wimble. "But can't you imagine someone using that statue as a hammer?"

Corey could. Especially when Mr. Wimble pointed out some blood stains at its base.

"Clearly she was attacked without warning," said Mr. Wimble, "either by someone who crept up on her unawares or by someone in the room whom she had no reason to fear. Her pose is too tranquil for it to have been otherwise: the supporting cushions; the open book on her lap; the footstool beneath her feet."

Corey glanced down at the footstool. Anywhere but at that frightful, blood-washed face!

Feet on footstools are always conspicuous. Yet, giving her the benefit of the doubt, Lalla Lee's feet were decidedly large for so otherwise perfectly proportioned a girl.

Her hands, too, were large. Perhaps, in life, they had not been altogether white.

Corey recalled the clipping bureau photographs. There had been a reason, then, for consistently hiding her hands and feet.

And yet she had been on the stage! Like Lady Hamilton, she had triumphed over her handicap. How beautiful Lalla Lee must have been in real life! Corey felt a wild desire to wipe the blood from her face. . . .

"Webb!" called Mr. Wimble abruptly. "You come over here and draw a plan of the room while I examine it."

Mr. Wimble's examination of the room was a bit desultory until, out of the corner of his eye, he saw the color returning to his young assistant's face. He then began his examination in earnest.

Normally, Mr. Wimble possessed that lightness of foot typical of fat persons; and as he now moved about the living room there was a quality almost catlike in his tread. And there was something suggestive, too, of a cat in a strange house in his manner of making his examination: he scrutinized everything, but rarely touched anything.

Corey later added to his sketch of the living room until finally he had the floor plan of the entire first story, which is presented below.

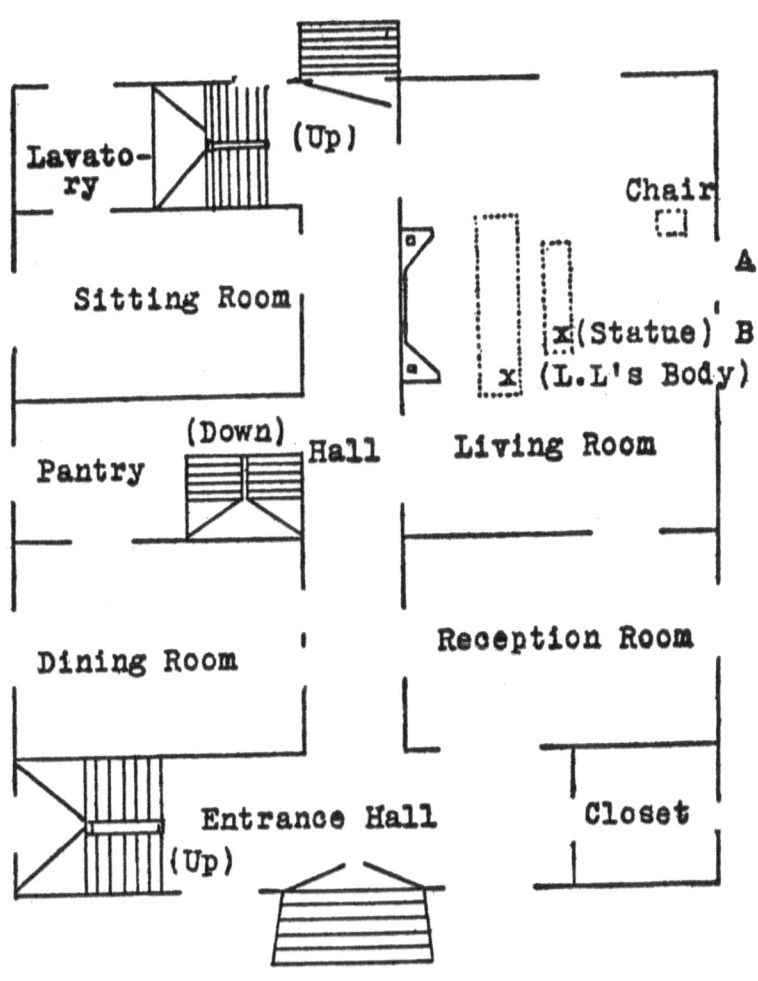

The living room was beautifully furnished, but it is the placing of the furniture, the position of the doors and windows, rather than the interior decorator's artistry, that have to do with this tale. On the map are indicated those pieces of living room furniture relevant to the investigation.

His sketch of the room finished, Corey joined Mr. Wimble, who was intently eyeing an armchair upholstered in the same beige brocade as the davenport. The back and arms of the chair were smudged with what looked like brown dye, as if someone wearing a poorly dyed garment had sat there, and recently; for when Mr. Wimble lightly touched one of the smudges he brought away a dirty fingertip to show for it.

There were some cigarette ashes on the floor beside the chair, fresh, one would judge in view of the general cleanliness of the room.

Mr. Wimble gave considerable attention to the window marked "A" on the plan. Unlike the other windows in the room, this one was unlocked.

"Unfortunately," said Mr. Wimble, "it is too dark now to look around outside. That will have to wait till the morning."

At this point Corey was startled to see his chief suddenly wheel toward the door connecting the living room with the reception room. It was on the jar.

"Yes?" he called sharply.

The door opened, revealing Sharl.

"Mr. Lee says the em'rald's not in Mrs. Lee's room, sir."

"Thank you, Sharl."

"Mr. Lee has ordered some supper laid out for you two gentlemen in the dining room, sir."

Mr. Wimble showed his pleasure.

"That's mighty considerate of Mr. Lee! Please thank him for us, Sharl. I don't believe a little food would do us any harm, eh, Webb?"

But before conducting the detectives to the dining room, Sharl had something further to say.

"Please, sir, when you begin questioning the help, will you take me first? There's a little private business I got to 'tend to uptown. I'd like to go early, sir, so's I can get back to Mr. Lee."

"I'll be glad to take you first, Sharl."

"Thank you, sir."

The old negro then led the way to the dining room.

4

It is a moot point whether or not oral testimony is of value in the investigation of crime. Of course, though a fact itself cannot be altered, the testimony of a dozen witnesses can give it as many aspects. The greatest danger lies in the propensity of witnesses for putting their own interpretation on what they have seen. Very often, too, their overwrought emotions conjure up for them incidents that have occurred nowhere but in their own imaginations. And, unfortunately, the glamor of the limelight frequently blinds witnesses to the truth.

But, if the inquisitor be anything of a student of human nature, by patient and adroit questioning he can dig out a fact from his witness' version of it. He will know when the witness is holding back something, when he is fabricating, when he is dramatizing. He can guess the truth from a witness' reception of a question, from his very lies.

The Lee domestic staff consisted of five servants, whose names and occupations were as follows:

1. Sharl—Mr. Lee's valet, also acting informally as butler.
2. Patterson—Chauffeur.

    3. Annie—Mrs. Lee's personal maid and up-
        stairs housemaid.
    4. Jules—Cook.
    5. Marie—Waitress and downstairs house-
        maid.

The day on which Lalla Lee was murdered happened to be Annie's day off, a servant's "day off" extending from noon till midnight. Mr. Wimble, however, interviewed the other four domestics.

True to his promise, he called for Sharl first.

He began by asking the old darky for a brief outline of his life. Though Sharl spoke without hesitancy, at times there was a lack of clarity in his testimony, due no doubt to the fact that blacks regard vital statistics rather more casually than whites.

Sharl did not know his own surname, for instance; he had always called himself Lee, after his master. Though he spoke with little trace of a Southern accent, he said that he had been born "in the South." More definitely he could not say, but submitted Vineville near Warrenton, Virginia, Mr. Lee's birthplace, as the probable locale of his own. He was not even sure of his age; "reckoned" he was about as old as Mr. Lee. He had been Walter Lee's body servant as far back as he could remember.

When about thirty years ago young Lee had decided to go north to make his fortune, Sharl as a matter of course had accompanied him. The pair had settled in New York; later had drifted westward, finally reaching California, where they had lived until about five years ago when a business opportunity had called Mr. Lee back to New York. Neither Lee nor Sharl had ever returned to Vineville.

Mr. Wimble interrupted Sharl to inquire how a young man just starting out in the world could afford the luxury of a body servant. Sharl replied with some asperity that money had never been mentioned between Mr. Lee and himself. Mr. Wimble pursued the subject, however; and it developed that, as Lee had prospered, he had deposited certain sums to Sharl's credit at the bank, until at the present time the negro's aggregate salary represented a considerable fortune.

Sharl admitted that, as Mr. Lee had never been a "dressy" man and went out but rarely, his duties as valet did not weigh on him very heavily. Neither did his duties as butler. The house appeared to be run in more or less of a haphazard fashion. Mrs. Lee's friends had come in the afternoons sometimes; but there was rarely company at night. Mrs. Lee had preferred entertaining in public places where it was gay. Sharl answered the doorbell and the telephone. He did odd jobs for the other servants, but spent most of his time, weather permitting, puttering about the small garden.

His position in the household was rather that of a beloved pensioner than of a servant.

When questioned about his actions on the day of the murder, Sharl's replies became more definite.

That morning, he said, he was helping Marie with the downstairs work when a young man called who, refusing to give his name, demanded to see Mrs. Lee. Sharl informed him that his mistress never got up before noon. It was then ten o'clock. The young man became so insistent, however, that although he knew it would displease her to be disturbed so early Sharl finally agreed to deliver a message to his mistress.

"He wrote a note."

"We have arrived," thought Corey, "at an impasse. O. W.'ll never get him to admit he read that note!"

Mr. Wimble merely asked: "Did you see anything in it to account for the young man's excitement?" But his tone implied: "Naturally you read the note. I'd have read it myself."

"Well," said Sharl, "he'd had a wonderful offer of some kind. He wanted to tell her about it right bad."

"How did he sign himself?"

"'R'." No name. Just 'R'."

"That *seemed* easy!" thought Corey.

"Did Mrs. Lee answer the note?"

"She started to; then she shut up her writing case and told me to go down and tell him she'd see him that afternoon at Myrtle's."

"Can you describe him?"

Sharl not only could, but seemed delighted to do so.

"Mr. R" was tall, thin, about twenty-seven or -eight. He was foreign-looking, with big brown eyes and a little moustache. He had on a hard hat, a dark fur coat, a red necktie and light spats.

Sharl eagerly vouchsafed: "I could tell him again, easy as not!"

"Where was he standing when you came downstairs?"

"Leaning up against the front door. He couldn't very well've got the lay of the land, though," said Sharl regretfully, "'cause Marie was in the entry the whole time scrubbing the floor."

"When did you last see Mrs. Lee alive?"

"'Bout half-past one. She went off in the car. I saw her through the dining room window."

"You heard her return?"

"No, sir. I was down in the help's sitting room in the basement till you come."

"She had no other callers today?"

"No, sir. No, *sir!*" he repeated, with undue emphasis. "She didn't have no other callers today but him. That 'Mr. R.' was abs'lutely the only caller she had today 'sides you and the young gentleman."

"How about the doors to the house? They are kept locked?"

"Yes, sir. The wall door is kept unlocked in the daytime, though, so as tradesmen can get in."

"Which one of the maids was it who was frightened by the fur coat on the newel post this afternoon?"

"Annie. It's her day off; but she come home after the movies to leave something."

"Thank you, Sharl. That'll be all for the present."

"Then I'll be off uptown, sir." He left the room.

Corey waxed enthusiastic. "We have a clue!"

"Namely?" inquired Mr. Wimble suavely.

"Why, 'Mr. R.'!"

Suddenly, with an agility remarkable in one of his rotundity, Mr. Wimble darted to the door through which Sharl had disappeared and flung it open.

Sharl was standing across the threshold.

"I come back to ask if I was to send in one of the others," he said, his aplomb perfect.

Mr. Wimble was not to be outdone in poise by the negro.

"Oh, Sharl! I was about to call you back to tell you that the front door is unlatched. I noticed it when we were removing our coats in the vestibule this afternoon. I wondered at it, the house being so near the sidewalk."

The negro was genuinely alarmed.

"Glory be! Who could've done that? I'll 'tend to it before I go out."

"You'll send Jules in, please?"

"Yes, sir."

Mr. Wimble looked thoughtful as he closed the door behind Sharl's retreating figure.

"That old fellow has a habit of lingering about doorways. So you think we have a clue, son?"

Corey hedged. "Sharl seems to suspect 'Mr. R'."

"He most certainly is eager for us to," said Mr. Wimble.

A discreet knock announced Jules, chef for the Lee household.

Jules Durand was a typical Frenchman. He had emigrated to America when a lad of sixteen, twenty-five years ago, had married a girl from New York's French colony, had earned and saved a tidy fortune—and was still a typical Frenchman. For in his heart a Frenchman never expatriates himself. Having made his money in America, Jules would return to France to spend it. He would buy a piece of land in the country and erect a house built as far as possible according to American standards of comfort. And forever after be loud in his endorsement of the popular European opinion that America has no soul, it never dawning on him that, had he been less intent on getting all he could out of America's pocketbook, he might have realized her soul.

Jules was a short, stout little fellow, with rather protruding eyes, the Frenchman's usual exquisitely shaped nose, and, of course, the inevitable moustache.

He said that he had not seen Mrs. Lee at all that day. This was not unusual. During his employment at the Lees', for days at a time he had not set eyes on her. She had rarely consulted him about meals, leaving them to his own discretion or sending down desultory orders by Annie or by Marie, Jules' wife.

"Mrs. Lee was the sort of woman who makes a good mistress and a bad wife," he observed, with Gallic openness.

Mr. Wimble became confidential.

"I've heard that Mrs. Lee was very—er—ah—"

Jules confirmed Mr. Wimble's innuendoes by an expressive rolling ceilingward of his round black eyes.

"'Oh, Jules!'" he aped, with that inimitable gift of mimicry possessed by the French. "'You will teach me how to make a Welsh rarebit, won't you, Jules?' 'Oh, Patterson! You will teach me how to drive, won't you, Patterson?'"

He broke off with a frown.

"There isn't a finer man living than Mr. Lee. I can't help but feel that perhaps someone who cared for Mr. Lee did it to save him from a terrible awakening."

"You don't think Mr. Lee suspected the sort of thing Mrs. Lee was up to, then?"

"No, sir. He treated her like his wife. It's usually the wife," he naively observed, "who keeps an eye on the husband."

There being nothing further to be learned from Jules pertinent to the investigation, Mr. Wimble dismissed him, calling for Marie, the chef's wife.

Marie was a plump little woman of thirty-five, strong, capable and serious-minded. Except when speaking of her children, she answered Mr. Wimble's questions without proffering any irrelevant information.

"It was you who cleaned the living room this morning, wasn't it, Marie?"

"Yes, sir."

"You left a window open?"

"Yes, sir."

"Which one?"

"The one near the big armchair. I always aired the living room a couple of hours each day, on account of there being so much cigarette smoke. I'd go in and close the window before setting the table for lunch, so the room would warm up before Mrs. Lee came down."

"You recall shutting it today?"

"Yes, sir. Oh, no!" she corrected herself. "I remember now. When I went in to do it, I found it already shut. I asked Sharl when I went back into the dining room if Mrs. Lee had been down; and he said that he had closed the window himself because the wind was coming in and blowing things about."

In describing "Mr. R.," Marie went a step farther than Sharl by declaring the young man to be either Italian or of Italian parentage.

At noon she had waited on the table as usual. Nothing untoward had occurred during the meal. Mrs. Lee had spoken abusively to Mr. Lee once or twice, but that was nothing unusual.

"You did not care for your mistress, did you, Marie?"

"I'm sorry she had to die so horribly, of course; but Mrs. Lee was not the sort of woman women care for. Jules and I stayed because our pay was good and because we like Mr. Lee. Mr. Lee's wonderful to Pierre. Takes him riding all the time."

"Pierre's our little boy. He lives with my mother. We had a little girl, too." The tears welled in her eyes. "Every time Mr. Lee goes to the cemetery he lays flowers on Berthe's grave."

"I wonder if I might take Pierre out driving some time?" said Mr. Wimble. "I *like* kids!"

"It will be kind of you to take him," said Marie, showing her pleasure. "But no popcorn!" she warned him. "Popcorn makes that child deathly sick."

"No popcorn!" promised Mr. Wimble.

Patterson, the chauffeur, was the next member of the Lee personnel to be interviewed. He entered the room with a swagger.

"Make this snappy!" he said. "I got a date."

Patterson, a chap in the early thirties, had the build of a third-rate prize fighter. He was good-looking in rather a brutal way, with the exception of his mouth, which was small and loose-lipped. He was conceited and insolent; and unable to bear unflinchingly anyone's direct gaze. His manner at present was aggressive; undoubtedly he felt that he was being detained on suspicion.

"Hoping to come across some clues that will help us find the murderer," explained Mr. Wimble. "We are interviewing those persons who associated with Mrs. Lee."

"I didn't associate with Mrs. Lee," retorted Patterson impudently, "I worked for her!"

The French chef had as much as said that there had existed a flirtation between Mrs. Lee and her chauffeur. Mr. Wimble chose to let this ride for the present, however, continuing with his inquiry.

Patterson, according to his own evidence, had entered the Lees' employ the preceding June, a week after they had moved into the house. Prior to that time, he had driven a taxicab.

Mr. Lee owned three cars: a limousine, a touring car and a small coupé. Mr. Lee used the cars very little. In summer, he preferred walking to and from his office. And he rarely went out at night. But Mrs. Lee had used the cars a great deal.

"Did she use one today?"

"Yes. I drove her in the limousine to Miss Dale's, some time around half-past one."

"What conversation took place between you and Mrs. Lee?"

Patterson's flabby lips slid into a sneer.

"You're hell bent on making out there was something between me and Mrs. Lee, ain't you?"

"A mistress sometimes gives orders to her driver," returned Mr. Wimble complacently.

"Well," said Patterson, with decidedly more triumph in his voice than the occasion warranted, "Lal—Mrs. Lee didn't say a single word to me today. See? I knew where I was to go because old man Lee had given me my orders

when I came back from an errand he'd sent me on down to
the bank. Mrs. Lee got into the car without saying a word.
I drove to Miss Dale's, and when we got there she got out
of the car without saying anything. See?"

"Are you familiar with Mrs. Lee's emerald?"

"What's her emerald got to do with me?"

"The stone is worth ten thousand dollars. Of course,
some people don't admire emeralds; still, circumstances
alter a fellow's taste sometimes. If a man happened to be
badly in need of money, for instance, he might find an
emerald worth that much mighty attractive. Shall I repeat
my question?"

"I recognized the emerald when I saw it," said Patterson sullenly.

"Did you see it today?"

The kind of look you find on a practical joker's face on
April Fool's Day flitted across Patterson's features.

"Yes, I did. When she got into the car."

"Where did you go after driving Mr. Lee to his office?'

"I went to a pool hall I go to sometimes. A place called
Tiny's, downtown."

"How long did you stay?"

Patterson's eyes shifted uneasily, as he struggled to
make his tone sound casual.

"Till a little before six, when it was time to drive to his
office to bring Mr. Lee home. I was shooting pool."

"Did you win?" It seemed as if Mr. Wimble were deliberately trying to antagonize the fellow.

"Now, look here!" cried Patterson peevishly. "Don't try
to get funny with me. See? I answered your questions because it seemed the decent thing to do by the little lady.
But according to the law I didn't have to. See?"

"So you've had some experience with the law before?"
observed Mr. Wimble urbanely.

Patterson scowled. "Say! It won't do to get fresh with me. See? I never did like dicks a Hell of a lot."

"A sentiment shared by most criminals."

Patterson ominously assumed a fighter's pose.

"Say, you!" he blustered. "It ain't safe to accuse a guy of being a crook. See?"

Mr. Wimble yawned.

"That will be all for the present, Patterson."

Corey had been ready to spring to his chief's assistance in case Patterson got rough; but the chauffeur was a coward at heart. He contented himself with muttering vague threats as he swaggered out of the room.

"I'm willing to bet that Patterson's 'date' won't be kept till he's been to Tiny's to establish his alibi," remarked Mr. Wimble.

5

MYSTERIOUS MURDER
OF THE BEAUTIFUL LALLA LEE

WIFE OF CHAIN-STORE MILLIONAIRE
SLAIN BY UNKNOWN ASSASSIN
Horrible Fate of Ex-Chorus Girl

Newspaper headlines thrive on crime mysteries. Newsboys
swarmed the streets the next morning crying extras.

At the time the articles had gone to press, no suspicion as to the identity of the slayer had been advanced by
the police. Several papers presented various hypotheses,
frankly admitting, however, that no clues had been discovered to substantiate them.

And yet, when Mr. Wimble and Corey reached the Lee
house, almost the first news that greeted them was that
Horace Pickering, police detective, had dug up a description of the murderer, had discovered how he had entered
the house and had established the criminal's motive.

It was Chief Detective Callahan, representing the police in the Lalla Lee affair, who reported his subordinate's
discoveries.

It rather shocked Corey to find the Chief Detective in a jovial mood. Still, he reflected, Callahan was of a race that holds festive wakes for the dead.

Callahan was delighted to have O. W. working with him.

"It's duck soup for me when your boss is on the job," he told Corey. "All I need to do is delegate him a few messenger boys."

"Cal means," explained Mr. Wimble, "that because his department is so short-handed he's always glad of an extra man."

Mr. Wimble shrank from praise. When possible he worked in conjunction with the police. If he were asked to solve a mystery that the police had given up, he always called them back on the case in time to come in for the glory.

"Oh, I just drew the attention of the police to a minor point here and there," he would deprecate.

"If your boss cared anything for the grandstand, young feller," said Callahan, "the department would sure be in one Hell of a mess! And yet what he says is partly true." The Irishman sighed, with a wistfulness that plainly told where his heart lay. "If we only had twice as many men as we've got now we might get somewhere."

"Your man Pickering seems to be getting somewhere," Mr. Wimble reminded him.

"Hell, Mr. Wimble! I'm looking forward to the fun when you send Horace Pickering's theories up in smoke!" He added apologetically: "Pickering's a new man or he wouldn't be so ready to spout his ideas, knowing 'One Week' Wimble's on the case."

Dolly Webb was the only one outside of Mr. Wimble's immediate family acquainted with his Christian name. O. W.'s mother had been a staunch admirer of Mr. Shakespeare, and when her son was born had named him Oberon, after her favorite character in "A Midsummer-Night's Dream."

Dolly Webb had once expressed her sympathy, which O. W. had countered with the dry remark that he was thankful his mother had preferred King Oberon to Mustard-seed.

He signed himself O. Wimble and was called by his friends O. W. In the profession he was alluded to as "One Week" Wimble, seven days being the maximum time it took him to unravel a crime mystery.

"Your man Pickering may be right, Callahan," said Mr. Wimble.

"'Tain't likely. Horace's the Chief's brother-in-law, or I'd hand him a net and tell him to go chase butterflies." He grinned in Corey's direction. "Seeing you've turned schoolmaster, Mr. Wimble, I thought I'd put Pickering on the job to see if he couldn't learn something too."

Horace Pickering was a young man with a head proportionately large for his frail trunk, no hair to speak of, a high forehead and small pale blue eyes that looked out restlessly from behind horned-rimmed spectacles. His movements were quick and jerky like a sparrow's. His hats always looked too small or too large as if he had picked up some other man's by mistake, which very often he had. Pickering acknowledged his introduction to Mr. Wimble and Corey Webb in a manner indicating that he saw no particular reason for their existence.

"The criminal's practically found, you know," he crisply informed the detectives. "Practically found! A large tall man—a foreigner. He got in through one of the living room windows. Motive: theft of Mrs. Lee's emerald."

Mr. Wimble stroked his chin.

"So you have discovered footprints outside the living room window that was found unlocked yesterday?"

"Precisely! Precisely!"

"Suppose you show us the footprints." Mr. Wimble made this suggestion much in the tone of one humoring a small boy who has just announced that he has dug a hole to China.

"Not at all necessary!" snapped Horace. "Not at all necessary!" He chanced to glance in the direction of Chief Detective Callahan. "However, you may follow me."

The three men followed him into the garden.

Fortunately for Pickering's clue it had neither rained nor snowed the night before. On the ground beneath the living room window marked "A" on the plan were embedded two prints of a man's shoe, one pointing toward the house, the other away from it. The shoeprints were large, with ridiculously acute toes.

"Whether the man was prowling around the grounds and happened to see Mrs. Lee's emerald through the window, or whether the robbery was premeditated, remains to be proved," said Pickering. "At any rate, you can tell that the murderer was a big man by the size of the footprints and by the fact that the window is six feet from the ground. That he was a foreigner you can see by the shape of his shoes.

"And a child," he pompously concluded, "could guess that he got in through the window!"

Callahan was eyeing Mr. Wimble as eagerly as if the latter were a Houdini on the point of bursting his chains.

"Yes," said Mr. Wimble, "that's about what a child would guess."

Gleefully Callahan rubbed his hands together. It dawned on Pickering that all was not well. In some bewilderment he addressed Mr. Wimble.

"You don't think that the murderer climbed in through the window?"

"Why should he have taken the trouble with the front door so handy?"

"But the footprints? The footprints?"

"What makes you think they're footprints?"

"I have eyes in my head!" returned Pickering.

"Eyes, at least," agreed Mr. Wimble softly. "Now, Pickering," he went on, "you're not a very large young man, are you? Suppose you stand beside those shoeprints for a moment."

A bit sulkily, Pickering obeyed.

"That will do," said Mr. Wimble, and Pickering stepped back on to the walk.

There ensued a chorus of gasps. Pickering's feet had sunk almost an inch into the soft earth. The original footprints, supposedly made by the feet of a man obviously twice the size of Pickering, lay barely a quarter of an inch deep!

"Someone standing on the walk might have made those prints with his foot," said Mr. Wimble. "But, even in that event, I believe the impressions would have sunk more deeply. They look to me as if they had been put there by hand."

"Do you think it's an inside job, sir?" asked Pickering. Horace was by no means daunted. The belated "sir," however, showed that at last he was beginning to see some reason for at least Mr. Wimble's existence.

"Perhaps," replied Mr. Wimble inscrutably.

"Before springing anything more on the public, Pickering," advised Detective Callahan, "I suggest that you talk over any theories that pop into your head with Mr. Wimble."

"I shall be delighted to confer with Mr. Wimble. Delighted."

He bobbed his head to indicate that he was quitting their presence.

"Good morning, gentlemen! Good morning!" As he darted around the house, Horace indeed looked far more like an entomologist on the trail of a butterfly than a detective in pursuit of a clue.

"Well, Mr. Wimble," asked Callahan, "what do you think of the Chief's brother-in-law as a detective?"

"Horace has his qualities."

"So do I!" grinned Callahan.

6

Corey Webb was a cub detective, which no doubt was the
reason it disturbed him to find so many occasions for
laughter during the investigation of a murder.

He almost disgraced himself the first time he saw the
maid, Annie Robinson. This was not due to the girl's personal appearance, for Annie was exceptionally pretty. She
was large, a bit above average height and fully developed,
which made her look older than her nineteen years. She
had curly brown hair, wide, slightly bovine brown eyes,
and a fresh complexion. Her hands and feet were surprisingly small for a big girl.

It was Annie's entrance that floored Corey. Such an
entrance he had never witnessed outside of an amateur
theatrical.

An arresting cough from the doorway proclaimed the
girl's presence.

Having thus gained the attention of her audience, she
advanced slowly into the room, her gait suggestive of a
leisurely camel's. Halting suddenly, her clasped hands
clamped to her bosom, in a broken voice she demanded:

"You—wished—to *see*—muh?"

Corey dared not glance in Mr. Wimble's direction. A
single twinkle in his chief's eye would token his own undoing.

The eye of Mr. Wimble, however, registered naught save admiration.

"An excellent performance, Annie! Superb! Did your mistress teach you that entrance?"

"Who? Her?" returned Annie scornfully. "Nobody with feet the size of Mrs. Lee's could float into a room!"

Recollecting that her mistress was dead, she flushed.

"I didn't mean to say anything against the—the departed!"

"That's all right, Annie. I practically forced you to say what you did."

His forehead wrinkled into a puzzled frown.

"I'm wondering who it is you put me in mind of?"

"Your friend ought to know," was Annie's surprising rejoinder.

Mr. Wimble thumped his thigh.

"To be sure! Someone in the talkies. Let's see. The name seems to have escaped me for the moment."

"I'm said to resemble Norma Neale," supplied Annie self-consciously.

"Norma Neale! Of course!" Corey was convinced that O. W. had never heard the name of Norma Neale before in his life. "Oh! The way Norma floats into a room!"

Annie scented a fellow addict.

"Say! Did you see her in 'The Bandit's Bride'?"

"Missed that one," admitted Mr. Wimble regretfully. "But I certainly don't intend letting her next picture get by me!"

"'The Runaway Wife'!" announced Annie eagerly. "Opening tomorrow night at the Globe."

"But, say!" she broke off, doubtfully eyeing Mr. Wimble. "I was told there was a detective in here who wanted to get some information out of me." The girl was naively unaware, of course, that Mr. Wimble had been on duty since her cough from the doorway.

"I'm Wimble."

"Are you? You look something like Pop Pearson of the Q. P. Comedies," said Annie approvingly.

The detectives found Annie more than willing to talk about herself. In fact, to her Miss Annie Robinson afford-ed an absorbing topic of conversation.

Until a year ago Annie had lived in a small Iowa town, occupying the envied position of village belle. Unfortu-nately for the girl's own good, she had won a beauty con-test conducted by the county newspaper. Her friends as-suring her that beauty like hers was not born to blush unseen, she had decided to make the stage her career. Her prize money had been spent on a ticket to New York.

Being under the popular misconception that prettiness alone suffices to get a girl on the stage, Annie's attempts to join the choruses of various musical comedies had met with failure. That she had no singing voice, was absolutely lacking in grace and a sense of rhythm, and, worst of all, was subject to the chorus girl's curse, avoirdupois, had counted for nothing in her young mind.

After hounding booking offices until her money ran out, she had found a situation in the wardrobe room of the Starlight Follies. Here, one of the chorus girls either actually had seen or, in a spirit of fun, had pretended to see in Annie a resemblance to Miss Norma Neale, where-upon Annie's ambition had switched over to the screen.

Answering an advertisement of a certain Mr. Goldstein, who claimed that but for him many a Hollywood satellite would still be clerking in a store, Annie had learned that the only thing between her and a dressing room with a star on the door was the paltry sum of a thousand dollars. This had been pretty much of a blow. Annie had not been able to save anything from her salary; and, now that the show had closed, was without employment.

It was about this time that she had learned, through one of the Starlight girls, that Lalla Blair had married a rich man and might be in need of a lady's maid. She had applied for the position and got it.

Of course, Annie informed the detectives, she was far above her present station. But, striking a pose, she was willing to make sacrifices for Art's sake! Nobody back home knew she was "maiding." Her mail came in care of a girl friend. Her salary as Lalla's maid had been good; and she had already saved eight hundred dollars toward the needed thousand.

Annie's face clouded as she mentioned her savings.

"Now I suppose I'll be out of a job again, and have to use some of my hard-earned cash before landing another."

Up to this point Annie had chatted along naturally enough. But, as Mr. Wimble's questioning approached the crime, nervousness crept into her manner.

She stated that she had last seen Mrs. Lee alive at noon the day before. She had helped her mistress dress for luncheon, tidying up the room before going down to the servants' dining room for her own meal.

"Did you notice anything unusual in Mrs. Lee's manner?"

"No. She found fault with everything and snapped me up several times over nothing at all, same as usual."

"Did you hold any conversation?"

"A little. I was fastening the clasp of the chain her em'rald's on for her, and I said: 'Gee!' I said, 'I'd like to have an em'rald like yours!' And she said: Well, why don't you marry an old man, then?' And all of a sudden her lips curled up the way they did when she was going to say something mean. 'As for myself,' she said, 'I'd rather have an imitation em'rald than an imitation husband!' That's about all the conversation we had."

"How did you spend your day off?"

"I went out after lunch, about one o'clock. I called on a girl friend of mine, and then I took in a show. After that

I went to see another girl friend. I got home about midnight."

"Then you weren't home between one o'clock and midnight?"

"No, sir."

"By the way, Annie," Mr. Wimble filled his assistant with consternation by asking, "will you do Mr. Webb and me the honor of coming to the Globe with us tomorrow evening?"

Annie flushed with delight.

"Say! On the level? You'd take a lady's maid out? Well, all I can say is, detectives aren't like . . ." She broke off sharply.

"Like whom?"

"Nothing. I forget what I started to say," said Annie lamely. "It's awf'ly nice of you to want to take me to the show."

"I *like* you, Annie," replied Mr. Wimble warmly. "I believe I'm safe in assuming that Mr. Webb shares my feeling." He beamed at Corey. Heroically taking his cue, Corey beamed at Annie.

"In fact," continued Mr. Wimble, "I feel as if the three of us were already real good friends!"

Whereupon he sighed. It would have been pleasant to terminate the interview on this note. But duty called.

"Have you ever heard of an 'accessory after the fact,' Annie?" he asked.

"No, sir," returned Annie chattily. "What is it?"

"A person who knows or suspects who a criminal is, but keeps silent. That makes him guilty, too, and punishable by law."

"I don't know anything more'n I've told you," declared Annie; but her tone lacked conviction.

Mr. Wimble said quietly: "We were in the house yesterday when you screamed."

A certain heaviness settled over the girl's face.

"Oh, that! I came back for a minute to leave some packages; that's all. I went right out again. I didn't mention it because I didn't think it mattered. Mrs. Lee's fur coat was hanging on the banister, and it looked kind of like an animal and scared me. That's why I screamed. You ought to've heard me scream last night when they told me Mrs. Lee had been murdered," she proudly added, the memory of her success somewhat restoring her poise.

"Who told you?"

"Pat. Mr. Patterson, the chauffeur. All of the help. Everybody was up when I got home."

"Patterson's certainly good looking," remarked Mr. Wimble. Annie acquiesced in this opinion by an enthusiastic:

"He sure is! Pure cave man."

"Anything between you and Patterson?"

"No!" emphatically.

"Was there once?"

"We ran around some when I first came; but it didn't amount to anything." Then she added arrogantly: "I can get all the men I want. I don't need him!"

"Was there anything between Mrs. Lee and Patterson?"

A furtive look stole over Annie's face.

"Of course I didn't follow Mrs. Lee around when she rode in the car; but I don't think so."

"Come, Annie! You know Mrs. Lee's reputation for liking men!"

An expression of fear crossed Annie's face.

"No, there wasn't!" she said quickly. "I'm sure of it!"

"Did Mrs. Lee confide in you?"

"Oh, she'd tell me once in a while how different men had fallen for her down in the Vamp Room—my name for her little private sitting room on the first floor," Annie pertly explained. "But you couldn't say she ever really confided in me. I didn't see much of her. She slept till noon; then she'd usually go out somewhere in the afternoon, rush home to dress and go out again; and that'd be the last I'd see of her till late at night, when she'd come in too tired to talk. I had a soft enough job all right, except that. . . ."

"Yes?"

"Well, it was like this." The girl was obviously sparring for time. "She had a rotten temper. I guess ladies' maids always do get picked on, though," she added philosophically.

"Did you ever hear her speak of a man whose name began with 'R'?"

"'R'? Maybe. I don't remember."

Mr. Wimble smiled broadly.

"How is your memory, by the way, Annie? Pretty good?"

"Trying to trip me up again?"

"No. Just trying to make sure you won't forget our date for tomorrow night."

"No hard feelings then?" asked Annie archly. Mr. Wimble replied to her satisfaction.

"I trust you haven't any beaux who'll object to your going out with us," he said, with mock anxiety. "Not that I'm worried on my own account!" And his glance in his assistant's direction was so significant that Corey felt his collar beginning to melt.

"No," said Annie gloomily. "Nobody around here cares what I do!"

"I'll warrant you couldn't say that if you were home in—in—?"

"Fieldtown."

She brightened slightly. "No, there'd be plenty of fellows there to object, all right. Chad Rucker. And others."

"Very well; it's settled, then. Now, will you please go ask Mr. Lee if we may examine Mrs. Lee's private rooms?"

Annie departed with reluctance. Despite its pitfalls, she had enjoyed the interview.

"So Annie's passion for the stage accounts for her blood-curdling yell of yesterday afternoon," observed Corey.

Mr. Wimble reminded him: "You were startled, remember. Do you believe that any of Annie's acting could genuinely move you?"

Which gave Corey food for thought.

7

The intimate apartments of Lalla Lee did not add to one's respect for that fair lady.

Her private sitting room on the first floor was an abomination in flesh pink. The dominating piece of furniture was a low, square divan covered with flesh-colored *velours* and banked with innumerable lace and silken cushions. A floor lamp, wearing a shade as ornate as the hats of the Floradora Sextette, cast a rose glow over the room. The wall, tinted pink, was thick with photographs of men. Among them, at intervals, and producing an extremely revolting effect, were hung prints of Henner's nudes.

Altogether it was a wicked place, adequately described by Annie's term: the "Vamp Room."

Besides learning much about the personality of the woman who had occupied the room, Mr. Wimble discovered in it two important clues.

The police having ordered the servants to keep clear of the downstairs rooms, housework in that quarter had been temporarily suspended. Everything remained presumably as it had been at the time of the murder.

A black cloche hat, as conspicuous as a bruise, lay on the flesh-colored divan. Partly clinging to it, and badly torn, as if the hat had been removed in a hurry or by someone greatly agitated, was a heavy black veil of the mourning type.

And a pair of shoes had been carelessly flung into a corner of the room.

"Women!" lamented Mr. Wimble to Corey as he examined these shoes. "Why, if Lalla Lee were in such a hurry, did she bother to change into shoes almost identical with the ones she took off?"

Mr. Wimble summoned Annie to identify the hat, veil and shoes.

"They're Mrs. Lee's all right," she said. "Though this is the first time I've seen a pair of her shoes without shoe-trees in them. Mrs. Lee knew she had ugly feet, so she always had her shoes made to order. She was awf'ly particular about them being put on trees the minute she took them off. She told me when she hired me that if I forgot about her shoes even once, she'd fire me. She would've, too!" she succinctly averred.

Upon Mr. Wimble's request to be shown Mrs. Lee's bedroom, Annie led the detectives up the back stairway.

After the Vamp Room, it was not surprising to find Lalla Lee's bedroom furnished like the sleeping chamber of a king's favorite. Annie ushered in the men with a certain air of pride. Of course she admired the room. It smacked sufficiently of a movie interior to guarantee her full approval.

The waste paper basket first engaged Mr. Wimble's attention. He found it empty. Annie said that, in straightening the room the day before, she had burned the contents of the basket.

"Was there anything in it when you came up later with Mrs. Lee's coat?"

"I don't know. I didn't look."

"Have you been in here since?"

"No, sir."

Mr. Wimble smiled. "Please show us the beast that frightened you yesterday."

Annie colored as she produced the coat in question. It was a handsome sable coat, full-length, with a broad shawl collar.

In the pocket of the coat Mr. Wimble found a small piece of paper which, without comment, he transferred to a pocket of his own.

In another he found a key.

Annie thought she recognized this as the back door key.

"But it's easy enough to tell for sure," she said, taking a key ring out of her sweater pocket. "Here's mine."

The keys were identical.

"Have all the help their own back door keys?"

"Yes, sir."

The writing desk revealed nothing of interest beyond a locked drawer. The lock was not very complicated. It was the kind that could be manipulated with a hairpin without being put out of commission. In fact, several scratches around the keyhole indicated that the drawer had already been pried open at least once. Mr. Wimble, however, preferred opening it with its key. But the key was missing. And Annie disclaimed knowledge of its whereabouts.

Mr. Wimble questioned Annie about the scratches around the keyhole.

"I never noticed 'em specially. Still, they might have been there all the time I worked for Mrs. Lee."

"Do you know what the drawer contains?"

"Dead Ones!" was Annie's amazing answer. "Photographs of 'has beens.' As soon as Mrs. Lee threw a man over, she took his picture out of the Vamp Room and put it in that drawer."

For the next few moments Mr. Wimble devoted his time to wandering with apparent aimlessness about the room.

Suddenly a low exclamation escaped him. He held up a finger to the light.

"Jove! A sliver! Run out into the hall, will you, Annie, like a good girl, and ask Sharl for his knife?"

"A needle's best for slivers, Mr. Wimble!"

"A man with a needle!"

"I could take the sliver out, maybe," said Annie doubtfully.

"And go off in a faint at the sight of blood? No thanks!"

"I am kind of funny that way," admitted Annie proudly.

"So it's the knife from Sharl." Mr. Wimble's patience was still intact.

"All right. I'll get his knife for you, sir. Only Sharl's in the basement; not up on this floor." However, when she had left the bedroom, the sound of their voices told the detectives that Annie had encountered the negro in the hallway.

Mr. Wimble chuckled. "A minute ago in the mirror I saw the door handle turning."

During the brief interval that Annie was absent, Mr. Wimble quickly dug down into a jar of dried rose petals that graced the chiffonier and brought forth two keys. For a bachelor he displayed an amazing knowledge of the habits of women.

At that moment it was the larger key that claimed his attention. Upon comparison, it proved to be another back door key.

Hearing Annie returning, he slipped this key into his pocket.

"Sharl was in the hall, after all," said Annie. "He hasn't got a knife, though. So I've brought a needle."

"Thanks just the same, Annie," returned Mr. Wimble serenely, "but Webb got the sliver out with the scissors.

"By the way," he said, "I've found a key that looks as if it might open that desk drawer."

The key did open the drawer, which, as Annie had testified, was full of men's photographs.

Mr. Wimble invited Annie to look these photographs
over.

"Any missing?"

Annie indulged in her favorite reply.

"I don't know. It's been a long time since I last saw
them. Wait a minute, though!" she reflected. "I don't see
that blond one. There was a good-looking blond fellow on
horseback, I remember. He looked like a society man."

"What did Mrs. Lee call him?"

"She called him Billy G—" She broke off sharply. "Or
Dicky, or Jimmy," she went on hastily. "Some pet name
like that. I don't remember exactly."

Mr. Wimble replaced the photographs and relocked the
drawer.

"That's all for now, Annie. About tomorrow night: I
don't believe I'd say anything to Mr. Lee if I were you
about going to the talkies with us. He might not like it
that you'd care to go out and have a good time so soon
after your mistress' death. Suppose you meet us in front of
the Globe at eight o'clock."

"I'll be there with bells on!" Annie assured him, and
took her departure.

Upon leaving the bedroom, the two detectives found
Mr. Lee waiting for them in the upstairs hallway. He
seemed to have aged ten years over night.

There was something pitiful, Corey thought, in the
grief of this man for a woman whom investigation was
proving to have been unworthy.

Mr. Lee greeted the detectives with his customary grave
courtesy.

"I have communicated with the bank," he said. "It
seems that my wife gave up her safe deposit box several

weeks ago. She told the manager that she intended keeping her jewels here. I can't understand it. We have no safe. And Lalla feared losing her jewels. That was always her excuse for not wearing them more often."

"You are sure they are not somewhere in the house?"

"One of Mr. Callahan's men and I made a thorough search this morning," he said wearily. "They are not here."

"This invasion of your home will soon be over, I hope," said Mr. Wimble.

"You have discovered something, then?" asked Mr. Lee eagerly.

The big thou-shalt-not in detective work is: Tell nothing! Not even for the sake of the person most concerned would Mr. Wimble modify this dictum.

"I meant, rather," he compromised, "that what clues we have point to investigation outside of the house."

"Mr. Callahan has assured me that the case will be cleared up in a week," said Mr. Lee pointedly.

"Cal is a loyal old braggart!" returned Mr. Wimble in some confusion. "By the way," he asked, anxious to get off the subject of his professional skill, "had Mrs. Lee a key to the back door?"

"There was an extra back door key. I don't know whether Lalla had it, or whether it is in my possession. We never used the back door. If I have a key, it will be in my desk. Shall I look?"

"Please."

Mr. Lee went into his room, returning after a moment or two.

"The key is not there; so I suppose Lalla must have had it."

"Who has access to your room?"

"Only Sharl, who keeps it in order. And, of course," his face twitching, "Lalla made free use of it."

When Mr. Wimble and Corey went downstairs, Sharl was in the vestibule, waiting to show them out. Judging by the zeal with which he helped them into their overcoats, the performance of this office afforded him extreme pleasure.

"Let me see your back door key, will you, Sharl?" asked Mr. Wimble.

"I haven't got none," replied Sharl. "Quite a spell back, Mrs. Lee lost her back door key, so I give her mine."

"Looks as if Mrs. Lee had entered the house by the back way yesterday," ventured Corey, as the detectives drove away from the house.

"I have hopes for your success as a detective, my boy," said Mr. Wimble congratulatorily. "Your contemporary, Pickering, would have said that, as a back door key was found in Lalla Lee's coat pocket, she *did* enter by the back way."

8

The inquest was held on Thursday morning.

A medical examiner testified that, to the best of his knowledge, Mrs. Lee had been murdered not later than three o'clock on Tuesday afternoon. A fingerprint expert in turn gave the information that the murderer either had worn gloves or had carefully wiped off whatever he had handled, for no incriminating marks could be found.

The verdict was that Lalla Lee had been willfully murdered by a person or persons unknown.

Horace Pickering attended the inquest. Throughout the proceedings he kept thinking of those shoe prints he had found beneath the living room window. He looked upon them, by right of discovery, as his own private property. As he'd already suggested to Mr. Wimble, in his opinion they pointed to an inside job.

The inquest was about half over when Horace arrived at the conclusion that, whereas they had been so lightly embedded, the shoe prints must have been the work of a woman. Therefore: Find the woman!

There were, of course, but two women to choose from: Marie and Annie.

Horace had spent the entire day at Mr. Lee's on Wednesday, the major part of his detective energy being vented in the vicinity of the shoe prints. Unfortunately, in a fit of

absentmindedness, Horace had left his overcoat at home.
Marie, investigating a peculiar wheezing in the garden,
very kindly had lent him Jules'.

During the afternoon, Horace had tried climbing
through the living room window. His object of course was
to learn what success a smaller man than the one he'd
originally described as the murderer would have had in an
approach by that route to Mrs. Lee's emerald. Athletic
feats not being his long suit, half-way up to the window
he had lost his footing and fallen on his face. Marie,
investigating a peculiar grunting in the garden, very kindly had rubbed arnica on Horace's bruises.

Moreover, at mealtime Marie had gone into the garden
looking for him with an offer of food.

So, all in all, Horace had acquired quite a fondness for
Marie.

On the other hand, he detested Annie. Annie had not
only failed to take Horace's detective activities seriously,
but had actually laughed at Horace's detective person.

It came naturally to Horace to suspect Annie Robinson
of crime.

No doubt the girl was an accomplice of the "person
unknown" referred to in the verdict. Horace had an idea
that, if he trailed Annie, she would eventually lead him to
the murderer.

Recalling certain advice given him by Chief Detective
Callahan, at the conclusion of the inquest Horace sought
out Mr. Wimble. But, in the midst of confiding his plan
to that gentleman, Annie, who had been present at the
inquest, showed signs of being present no longer; so, with
the hasty promise that later in the day he'd call at Mr. Wimble's office, Horace, with his customary air of a man on his
way to catch a train, bade his confrere good morning.

Despite Horace's nearsightedness, he did not find it
difficult to keep Annie in view. She was a figure that

commanded notice. Horace did, however, find it difficult
to follow her, and the process did not augment his affection for Miss Robinson. Annie liked to window-shop, and
Horace—well, in that respect at least, Horace was no different from other men. Besides, it was too cold a day for
strolling; and Horace's face felt stiff and painful from his
fall.

However, Annie finally came to a building minus show
windows, and went in. This building housed the Merchants' Bank.

As he saw Annie headed for one of the receiving windows, Horace proceeded to install himself behind a nearby
pillar where, undetected by her, he could watch the girl.
His antics in effecting this maneuver rather disconcerted
several of the Bank guards; but, fortunately, Pickering was
wearing his official badge, so managed to rout the guards
in time to see Annie depositing five one-hundred-dollar
bills.

In the meantime, O. W. was initiating Corey into the
routine of crime detection. Before the day was over Corey
agreed with Mr. Wimble that there was something tanta-
mount to being a house-to-house salesman in the activities
of a private detective.

"It's facts I rely on," Mr. Wimble told his associate.
"Having the facts at my fingertips ready to call on when
I want to prove something. That's why I get everybody to
talk who might possibly let fall even the most trivial fact
bearing on the case.

"Of course," he grinned, "that method lets me in for a
lot of life histories. But," with a touch of naïveté, "I *like*
folks, and as a rule I find their stories mighty entertaining."

Having remarked that, from certain of the windows of
the apartment building opposite the Lee house, it might
be possible to see into the Lee living room, Mr. Wimble's

investigation included probing this possibility. Explaining his business to the manager of the building in question, he learned that the windows of interest to him were those of the kitchen and servant's room of an apartment occupied by a young couple named Barton.

Mr. Wimble and Corey were admitted to the pertinent apartment by a sweet young thing with blue eyes and a round chin, looking very much like a little girl masquerading in adult clothes, who informed them, with a charming blush, that she was Mrs. George Barton.

"And, of course, you're the gentlemen from the office with the papers for my husband to sign," she babbled. "I'm sorry, but George is in bed. He has a bad cold."

"We're not from Mr. Barton's office," Mr. Wimble corrected her. "We're detectives."

This information had a startling effect on the sweet young thing. She emitted a shriek that brought George post-haste, in sky-blue pajamas, from his sick bed. With his hair rumpled, and the rather unintelligent look on his face of a person who is frightened, he in turn gave the impression of being a small boy playing papa.

It did not require a detective to pronounce the pair newly married.

"B-B-Betty? W-what you hollering for?"

"These men are detectives!" wailed Betty. "Now see what your breaking the law's brought us to!"

At which point George sneezed.

"See here, my boy," said Mr. Wimble. "You'd best put some clothes on."

"A chap wouldn't look so well going to jail in these, would he, sir?" agreed George, with a sickly grin.

In view of the recent rage for pajamas as appropriate street garb, it was probably not the thought of her spouse going to jail in sky-blue pajamas, but merely the thought of him going to jail at all, that caused Betty Barton to swoon; but swoon she did.

There comes a time in a man's married life when his wife's swoons leave him cold. But George had been a husband for a very short time. Betty's gesture utterly demoralized him.

Mr. Wimble felt it incumbent on himself to take charge. His motive was not purely humanitarian. He had an ulterior reason, purely professional: drawing water from the kitchen tap with which to revive Betty would afford him an excellent opportunity for making a survey of the rear of the flat.

Making a sign to Corey to follow, he proceeded kitchenward.

The kitchen was deserted, except for a clock.

"A place never seems wholly deserted to me when I hear a clock ticking," said Mr. Wimble.

He took out his watch.

"By the way, that clock's three-quarters of an hour fast."

It was impossible to see into the Lee living room from the Bartons' kitchen window.

Mr. Wimble's rap on the door of the servant's room adjoining the kitchen being unanswered, he went in. From this room, Mr. Wimble decided, it would be possible to see a few feet into the Lee living room, but certainly not on a dull December afternoon, unless the room were brilliantly lighted. This finding, therefore, did not prove a particularly valuable one.

The servant's room window did, however, command an unhampered view of the rear entrance of the house across the street.

Their survey over, the detectives returned to the Bartons.

Corey sprinkled the water over little Mrs. Barton while Mr. Wimble, still solicitous about Barton's cold, rummaged around for some additional clothing, finally unearthing a pair of trousers.

"Here, George," he said. "Slip into these."

Betty instantly revived.

"Oh!" she cried in the voice of a calf being removed from its mother. "You're not going to put *handcuffs* on him!"

This was too much for Corey. With incredible speed he carried the empty glass back into the kitchen.

When he returned, the young Bartons were wantonly attempting to bribe the man they thought was a representative of the law.

"With that cold, George'd die in jail!" from Betty.

"You saw what a weak heart Betty has!" from George.

"Well," said Mr. Wimble, "if George—"

"George'd love to!" declared Betty.

"I'll turn 'em over," promised George, a shade less rapturously than his bride.

"All right," agreed Mr. Wimble. "You go turn them over to Webb, George, while I have a little talk with Mrs. Barton."

George led Corey into his bedroom, where his behavior waxed extraordinary, to say the least. Prostrating himself on the floor before his bed, young Barton gave utterance to an incantation familiar enough to Corey under certain circumstances, but rather mystifying under the present.

"Come, Seven! Come, Eleven!"

Beneath the bed, somewhat scuffled. In another moment, to Corey's astonishment, two blinking guinea pigs put in a timid appearance. George clucked, whereupon the pigs scampered over to him, nuzzling with undisguised affection against his neck.

George eyed Corey with bitterness.

"Seven and Eleven are no trouble to anyone! Not half the nuisance that some of the kids in this building are!"

Corey rightly guessed, to his credit with a straight face, that the presence of the guinea pigs was against the rules of the apartment house.

"You'll find a good home for Seven and Eleven, won't you, Mr. Webb?" begged young Barton as Corey pocketed his pets. As Corey replied in the affirmative, he thought he detected tears; still, George really did have a bad cold!

Not until they were downstairs in the lobby could Corey trust himself to exhibit Seven and Eleven.

Mr. Wimble laughed. "Betty's farewell whisper is explained. 'I'm glad!' she said. 'I was jealous of Seven and Eleven!' I thought that perhaps George had been staying out nights with the boys."

The Lee house being conveniently near, the pigs were deposited with Marie as a gift to her son Pierre.

O. W. was pleased with the result of their visit to the apartment house. Although Betty had been too busy nursing George's cold to pay heed to any goings-on across the street herself, through her Mr. Wimble had learned of someone who might have.

"Was it that hateful Hilda Hanson who gave George away?" Betty had wrathfully demanded of Mr. Wimble.

Hilda Hanson was the Barton's former domestic, discharged only the day before for incompetency.

"Hilda didn't do a stitch of work!" Betty had indignantly informed Mr. Wimble. "She was always in her room. Reading novels, or something. I don't know what she was doing; but whatever it was it certainly wasn't what we were paying her to do!"

Betty did not know where Hilda lived, but it was easy enough to trace the girl. Hobson's, the employment bureau through which Mrs. Barton had hired her, obligingly submitted a number in the Bronx as Hilda's address, and the detectives drove there, by a piece of good luck finding the young woman at home.

Hilda was a raw-boned Swedish girl with thin straw-colored hair, loose features and red hands. It was not difficult to elicit information from her. In fact, Hilda was the type from whom Willy O'Rourke obtained most of his written interviews.

During her two months at the Bartons', Hilda had been highly entertained by the "doin's" across the street, her bedroom window being quite as good as a seat at the "theayter." Discretion not having been numbered among Lalla's virtues, new dance steps and new flirtations had often been practiced in front of the living room windows, the curtains of which had rarely been drawn. Hilda saw nothing amiss in her espionage, even shamelessly confessing to the purchase of a pair of opera glasses.

"Gawd! She vas purty!" sighed Hilda. "No vonder all dose men vas crazy apout her!"

There was something pathetic in Hilda's indirect participation in the "doin's" across the street. After all, it is not only the Cleopatras, the Helens, the Guineveres, who crave Adventure and Romance. Even a Swedish servant girl, with features as formless as a mud lump, may hanker after those amorous adventures that follow physical beauty as surely as seagulls follow a ship.

Hilda had not heard of the murder. The crisis in her own affairs had kept her from the papers.

"No!" she ecstatically ejaculated, when Mr. Wimble told her that Lalla Lee had been murdered.

"You're a witness in a murder case!" said Mr. Wimble impressively,

"*No!*"

"That is, if you happened to be looking out of your window on Tuesday."

Hilda's features became the least bit more determinate as reminiscent excitement gripped her.

"Toosdy's day 'she' raise Hal!" she began. Hilda consistently referred to her mistresses as "she."

"Ay vas vatchin' for 'doin's' 'cross de street ven ay seen de purty lady vat lives dere drive up to de pack door in a yaller taxi an' sneak into de house."

"Perhaps it was one of the maids you saw?"

"No; she haf on svell brown fur coat."

However, Hilda was out for thrills.

"Gawd!" she remembered. "Dere vas t'ick black veil on top her face. Perhaps vas maid vearing purty lady's clo'es!"

Hilda was busily elaborating this theory when O. W. interrupted her to inquire what next had taken place.

"'She' come, poundin' on my door fit to bust it down. 'Hilder! Hilder!'" the girl spitefully mimicked little Mrs. Barton, "half past two an' no dishes done yat! Vat yuh doin'?'"

If Hilda could be relied upon, Betty's tirade had not stopped here; but Mr. Wimble stemmed the flow of her account by another inquiry as to what then had occurred.

"Ay vash dishes!" said Hilda disgustedly.

"But ven ay t'rough, ay go pack to vindow, an' ay seen a gent runnin' out pack door lak devil vas after him."

"Had you ever seen the man who ran out the back door before?"

"No. He vas vun svell looker, dough. He haf on moustache an' spats an' fur coat."

To Hilda's intense regret, she had witnessed nothing further.

When Horace Pickering first saw Willy O'Rourke, he had no idea that he was encountering Damon. Nor did Willy, upon making the acquaintance of Horace, realize that he was meeting Pythias.

And yet that's how it was.

Horace had dropped in to report to Mr. Wimble his trailing of Annie to the bank that morning. Willy informed Horace that Mr. Wimble was out, inviting him to wait. It was monumental of Willy to ask Horace to wait. He didn't usually encourage anyone's lingering about for Mr. Wimble.

While waiting, Horace described the Lalla Lee case to Willy. Willy listened. This, also, was monumental. Willy had been filing a Disher success when interrupted by Horace.

Horace's description simmered down to his suspicion of Annie Robinson.

"The girl of course stole the five one-hundred-dollar bills from Mrs. Lee. Probably at the same time she or her confederate stole the emerald."

And then Horace Pickering asked Willy O'Rourke for advice. This was more than monumental. It was miraculous!

Willy consulted a card index on his desk. Finding the reference he was after, he went to a filing cabinet and removed therefrom a neat cardboard folder.

"I have before me," he told Horace, "a file covering 'The Mystery of the Marked Bank Note' case handled by the illustrious criminal investigator, Septimus Doolittle. Suspicion in the Bank Note case, as in the one you have just mentioned, centered around a housemaid. But, though circumstantial evidence pointed to the girl's guilt, Mr. Doolittle proved that a director of the bank was the guilty party."

Willy cleared his throat.

"You have been so flattering as to ask me for advice, Mr. Pickering. I quote a remark of Mr. Doolittle's that you might find beneficial. Septimus Doolittle said: 'Circumstantial evidence is the mirage on the desert of detection'."

"A keen mind!" said Horace. "A keen mind!"

"I felt sure," said Willy, "that the epigram would not be lost on you."

Solemnly, urged by they knew not what, Horace Pickering and Willy O'Rourke shook hands.

Later, in making his report to Mr. Wimble, Horace said: "It may be, of course, that Mrs. Lee gave Annie the bills. I consider Miss Robinson worth watching, however."

"An opinion you would have little difficulty in getting other young men to share, I am sure," replied Mr. Wimble, his eyes twinkling.

9

Resplendent Annie awaited Mr. Wimble and Corey that evening in front of the Globe Theatre. She was not, as she had promised, "there with bells on," but she certainly was in gala attire. Though the weather demanded concessions in the way of wraps, Annie was arrayed as if for a garden party.

She greeted her escorts eagerly. Whatever the secrets that troubled her in connection with the murder of her mistress, her devotion to the foundling Muse Cinema was sufficient, temporarily at least, to take her mind off of them.

"Well," Mr. Wimble asked her, "all set to see 'The Happy Husband'?"

"The picture's 'The Runaway Wife'."

"Analogous!" grinned Mr. Wimble. But Annie lost the witticism in impatiently steering her host toward the ticket window.

They were early. Corey made the fatal mistake of admitting that he had never seen the star; so, before the lights were dimmed, Annie repeated to him in detail the public version of the private history of Miss Norma Neale. And Annie was highly entertained by the recital.

The film was not much more banal than most. Miss Neale in beautiful clothes, with a stage presence like an animated doll's, was the runaway wife. It was not made clear what she was running away for. At any rate, she was pursued through several reels of film by a young man with shellacked hair who might have caught up with her sooner had he not at intervals abandoned the chase to burst into the play's theme song.

During the performance, somewhat to Corey's dismay, because he knew that it was his chief's object to make himself agreeable to Annie Robinson, he saw the senior detective napping. Corey should have realized that the attention of so enthusiastic a fan as Annie would not waver an instant from the screen. To his relief, during the final closeup in which Norma and the young man with the shellacked hair fell into the inevitable clinch, Mr. Wimble awoke. Perhaps he had depended on Annie's gasp of rapture at the final fade-out to serve as his alarm clock.

After the performance Mr. Wimble invited his guests to supper. He chose Tate's, a place brave in gilt and candelabra, no doubt to obviate any let-down after the sumptuousness depicted on the screen.

"Some day, Webb," remarked Mr. Wimble, when the waiter had taken their order, "you and I'll be going to the Globe to see Miss Annie, here, in a picture."

"Miss Diane Adair!" corrected Annie dreamily.

Her eyes clouded.

"Believe me, when I'm known as Diane Adair the fellows'll be falling all over themselves to take me out!"

"I know a couple of fellows who were just as pleased to take out Miss Annie as Miss Diane," Mr. Wimble reminded her.

"Oh, I didn't mean you and Mr. Webb! You're all right. And I'm not one to forget my friends when I'm famous, either."

To Corey's consternation and Mr. Wimble's delight, she said: "I'll bet I could get Mr. Webb a job on the screen easy!"

When the waiter switched Annie's thoughts from this track by arriving with a chafing-dish of lobster a la Newburg, Corey supposed the worst was over. Corey was deceived. The worst was yet to come!

There exists a class of persons who believe that two pills will double the efficacy of the one pill prescribed by the doctor. Annie proceeded to demonstrate her fealty to this class. There had been a supper scene in "The Runaway Wife" during which Norma Neale's fingers as she handled her knife and fork had resembled so many shorthand characters. As Annie supped, her table manners were twice as affected as the doll-like Neale's!

The diners at adjoining tables were beginning to look as if they thought Annie's performance explained the excessive cover charge when her table tricks succumbed to her healthy appetite, and the spectacle terminated.

"Annie," said Mr. Wimble, as Corey mopped his brow, "I'd like to see you earn the other two hundred dollars you need for Mr. Goldstein."

"We're going to get the sack at the house, once they find out who killed Mrs. Lee," said Annie gloomily.

"Then it's up to you to earn the two hundred dollars before they find out!"

"No chance! Half my income's cut off, now that Mrs. Lee's dead. I mean," she went on quickly to explain, "the tips I got from the men she went out with. That was the best money I earned. Naturally I can't count on tips any more."

Mr. Wimble appeared lost in reflection.

"I have it!" he said at last. "Why not help Mr. Webb and me on this case? You could earn a good slice of that two hundred."

The idea brought a sparkle to Annie's eyes, which disappeared however as a disconcerting thought smote her.

"No, thanks. I'm not a girl to squeal on my friends!"

"It isn't a question of squealing on anybody. We ask you to find out something for us. If you do, we pay for the information. If you don't—well, the deal's off. That is, as far as you're concerned. We'll never ask you for information that we couldn't get ourselves."

"Sounds fair enough," admitted Annie.

Mr. Wimble pressed his advantage.

"There are several things we'll be wanting to know from time to time. The position of certain pieces of furniture, for instance. With someone on the ground, we'll be saving time, that's all."

"You'll pay me for stuff like that?"

"Gladly. The only thing we ask is that you tell no one. Not even your girl friends. If you weren't an actress, of course I'd never suggest it."

Annie swallowed the bait. "Well, all right!"

She said importantly: "I know a thing or two about detective work. Only you can't force me to tell something if I don't want to."

"Why should you wish to hide anything?" inquired Mr. Wimble suavely.

"I said *if!*"

Mr. Wimble consulted Corey.

"How about starting Annie out on a test job, Webb? Let's see," he mused. "Well, here's something, Annie. I'll give you ten dollars for finding out where Sharl buys his shoes."

"I bite!" jeered Annie.

"I'm serious! If you're a good enough actress to find out where Sharl buys his shoes without him becoming any the wiser, then I'll make you our assistant and pay you ten dollars for every bit of information you give us. Who cleans Sharl's room?"

"He sleeps in a little room off Mr. Lee's. He cleans it himself. And I'd catch old Ned if he found me in his room and complained to Mr. Lee. Mr. Lee treats Sharl like a twin brother."

"Well, that wouldn't exhibit your talent as an actress, anyhow. I have a better scheme. Have you a pair of felt-soled slippers?"

"I have a pair of moccasins."

"Well, tomorrow morning put them on. Find something from which a small nail has come loose: a picture, a box; you can find something. Wait till Sharl appears. Then be very busy trying to replace the nail. When you see Sharl, ask him to lend you his shoe for a hammer. He wears those shoes with elastic sides that slip off easily. When you get the shoe, look for a name inside. And don't forget to do your hammering!"

"What's the idea of the moccasins?"

"Sharl might suggest that you use your own shoe."

"Suppose there's no name in his shoe?"

"Then I'm in ten dollars!"

Later, when they had seen Annie home, Mr. Wimble asked Corey:

"Do you suspect me of borrowing ideas from Willy, son?"

"My thoughts are pretty much tied up in a Gordian knot," admitted Corey.

"I don't want Sharl to know I suspect him of anything."

After a short silence, Mr. Wimble said: "I *like* Annie!" His smile became a bit wistful. "Annie is a piece of putty, if you will; but you can make some mighty attractive things out of putty. If Annie were back in Iowa she'd probably marry some nice young farmer, buy a radio and a Ford and raise half a dozen kids; in fact, be a very pretty little segment of what is called the Backbone of our Nation. As it is, she's in love with the wrong man."

"Patterson?"

"Not hard to guess, is it? Queer about women. No matter how weak they are otherwise, they'd go to the stake for

the men they love. Annie is obviously shielding Patterson.
I do hope she hasn't been up to anything more serious. I'd
like to send her back to Iowa."

"And Miss Diane Adair?" Corey wickedly inquired.

"*What I Might Have Been If!* Our only illusion that
grows to old age. I'll save Annie that!"

His eyes twinkled.

"And, in keeping her out of the pictures, I'll be the
unsung hero of the talkie-going public."

The success of Annie's first detective venture was announced in green ink on a pink billhead:

> For discovering that Sharl buys his shoes at
> Jones' Harlem Emporium. . . . $10.00

Judging from his chuckling while making out a check
in the name of Miss Annie Robinson, the pink bill afford-
ed Mr. Wimble considerable amusement.

The detectives' subsequent call at Jones' Harlem Emporium, however, did not prove especially fruitful.

The Emporium was a small shoe store located in that
section of the city inhabited by its colored residents. The
proprietor himself was in charge, an obliging little negro
called Hiawatha Jones. Jones did not know Sharl by name
but, when Mr. Wimble described the old man, placed Sharl
as a customer he had been serving for several years. Like
the majority of the shops in the quarter, the Emporium
remained open nights till nine o'clock. Jones particularly
recalled Sharl's purchase of Tuesday evening as, much to
his surprise, instead of his customary elastic-sided "Kum-
fy Kuts," the old man had called for the "bigges' an' for-
eignes' lookin' shoes" Hiawatha had in stock.

Nothing further could be learned from Jones about
Sharl for the simple reason that Sharl had never discussed
his personal affairs with his shoe dealer.

10

Pertinacious inquiry on the part of the police disclosed the fact that Miss Myrtle Dale had been Lalla Lee's only close woman friend, while among the scores of men in her train a professional dancer by the name of Lorenzo Panella seemed to have been the most favored.

It was noticeable that marriage had done nothing for Lalla socially. Most of her acquaintances had come from the seamy side of society: professionals whose mode of living so little corresponded with their salaries as to make it obvious that their wits formed the major portion of their stock in trade; self-styled "art students," that convenient alias for Work's conscientious objectors; and the inevitable "camp followers" of a wealthy hostess who cares little for the social credentials of her guests if only their parlor tricks be entertaining. Several men from socially prominent families had numbered among Lalla's acquaintances; but there was no indication that any of these had ever introduced her to their womenfolk.

Lorenzo Panella was one of a number of exhibition dancers at Gianni's, a fashionable Italian restaurant on upper Broadway. There seemed to be a diversity of opinion as to where Panella's affections lay. According to some accounts, the dancer was practically engaged to Myrtle Dale; and to others, he had been "mad about" Lalla Lee.

There was no indication that Lalla had been mad about him. There was no proof that she had been mad about anyone. She certainly had made no pretense of caring for her husband. In fact, it was said of Lalla that she hadn't been a girl who "fell easy."

There were, however, several rather indefinite references to "a chap out West" with whom Lalla had been in love. Nobody interviewed had ever seen this Westerner; nor could it be learned whether Lalla had fallen in love with him before or after her marriage. But the fact that it was repeated a number of times lent importance to the rumor.

There was no trace of a "Mr. R."

It was learned through several of the former Starlight girls that Myrtle Dale had left the stage about the same time as Lalla Blair. In showgirl terminology, "Dale," a "gold digger" like the rest, had "struck it rich."

Miss Dale's address was ascertained, and on Friday morning Mr. Wimble and Corey called on her. She lived on that superbly situated, but no longer smart, thoroughfare, Riverside Drive.

Before going up to Miss Dale's apartment, Mr. Wimble made a few inquiries of the manager, a Mrs. Blackmore, who also owned the building. Mrs. Blackmore was not surprised to learn that detectives were calling on her tenant. She had read of the murder in the papers, and had been anticipating such a visit.

"Miss Dale's the kind that gets mixed up in unsavory affairs," she gloomily pronounced. "I've known for some time she was no better than she should be. But she's always paid her rent regularly and hasn't caused any serious complaints; so I've shut my eyes to a lot of things. With this neighborhood going downhill and apartments getting harder and harder to rent every day, it doesn't pay to be too particular."

Mrs. Blackmore knew Lorenzo Panella by sight; asserted that he was a constant visitor at Miss Dale's. And she had been on speaking terms with Mrs. Lee, for whom she had cared even less than she cared for Myrtle.

"She had no dignity, that one! I've seen her time and time again going up to Miss Dale's arm-in-arm with her chauffeur!"

Mrs. Blackmore distinctly remembered seeing Lalla entering the apartment house on Tuesday.

At about half-past one, Mrs. Blackmore had been out front getting into the taxi that was to take her to her doctor's when Mrs. Lee had driven up, jumped excitedly out of her car and run into the building. Mrs. Blackmore thought maybe Mrs. Lee had just come from a funeral, because she was wearing a heavy black veil, just the sort Mrs. Blackmore herself kept on hand for funerals.

"I mightn't have recognized her except for her coat." Mrs. Blackmore lapsed into self-pity. "Every time I saw her fur coat I'd think: 'If only I had a fur coat like Mrs. Lee's, with a big warm collar I could snuggle my head into, maybe my neuralgia wouldn't be so bad!'"

It was characteristic of Mr. Wimble that he then listened with the utmost interest and sympathy to a full ten-minute discourse on the subject of Mrs. Blackmore's neuralgic headaches.

Miss Dale's apartment was No. 46 on the fourth floor. A narrow corridor about twenty feet deep connected No. 46 with the main hallway. As they turned on to this corridor, the detectives came upon a woman huddled up against the wall, bitterly though not noisily weeping.

She was a small woman, modestly dressed, perhaps forty-five years of age. Her features had been rendered slightly bulbous by crying; ordinarily she was probably pretty in a quiet way.

"Pardon our intrusion," said Mr. Wimble. "We are looking for Miss Myrtle Dale's apartment."

"You needn't apologize. Serves me right for picking such a public place to cry in as the entrance to Myrtle Dale's apartment!" A remark, judging from her tone, not entirely without malice aforethought. "Her apartment is at the end of this hallway."

"Is there anything we can do?" suggested Mr. Wimble.

"I guess I've already done it."

She smiled a bit ruefully. "It seems that women just *have* to cry sometimes."

"At least I can show you to the elevator."

The little woman gave him a searching look. Her eyes were surprisingly intelligent.

"You are very kind," she returned civilly, "but I'm all right now. I've interrupted your call long enough as it is."

Bidding the men good-bye, she hurried down the corridor.

11

The door of No. 46 was opened by a female servant of uncertain age whose features looked fused together like those of a snowman in the process of melting. As it was the custom for visitors before coming up to announce themselves through the telephone at the downstairs entrance, she showed a disinclination to admit the two men until learning that they were detectives. She then threw open the door without further discussion, a gesture which no doubt proclaimed respect for the detective profession, though nothing in the woman's facial expression indicated as much.

The detectives waited in a small entrance hall while the servant went to present Mr. Wimble's card to her mistress.

A long hat rack in the hall with a row of hooks beneath indicated that Miss Dale did not lack for callers. The wall below the hooks was smudged in several places with what looked like brown dye, as if a poorly dyed garment had rubbed against it, and recently; for, when Mr. Wimble lightly touched one of the smudges, he brought away a dirty fingertip to show for it.

Presently the sodden-featured servant returned with the announcement that Miss Dale would receive them in the "lib'ary," showing them into a comfortably furnished room commanding a picturesque view of the Hudson. The reason for the room's designation was obscure; for though one or two popular magazines garnished the center table not a book was in evidence.

Myrtle Dale was a large, well-formed woman between thirty-five and forty. She would closely have approached being a real beauty if she had left her looks to Nature instead of taking matters into her own hands. Her hair was too yellow, for one thing; her makeup, instead of producing the desired effect of youthfulness, merely coarsened her face; and the various hollows about her cheeks and neck indicated that rigid dieting had reduced a more becoming weight by at least fifteen pounds.

She greeted the detectives with some annoyance, though a woman of Myrtle Dale's type could never be definitely antagonistic toward anyone male.

"More police investigators, I suppose?"

"Investigators," returned Mr. Wimble, "but not police. We're private detectives employed by Mr. Lee."

Myrtle Dale regarded him with an equivocal smile. Perhaps no one knew so well as she just how unworthy Lalla Lee had been of any efforts of Walter Lee to avenge his wife's death.

"We saw a woman weeping in your corridor as we came in," remarked Mr. Wimble irrelevantly.

Miss Dale tilted her eyebrows interrogatively.

"A little woman, dressed in navy blue."

"Oh, yes!" One would have said from Miss Dale's smile that she was recalling something extremely agreeable. "A clerk from—my lawyer's office. I wonder what she was crying about."

"She didn't say."

Again Mr. Wimble abruptly changed the subject.

"Have you taken your fur coat out of storage yet?"

Miss Dale laughed gaily.

"You sound like a 'How do you rate?' questionnaire. As a matter of fact, I took it out two months ago and sent it to one of my nieces in Cabell, Colorado."

"What color was it?"

"Gray. Squirrel."

"You have a new one?"

Miss Dale nodded.

"A mink," she said, with undisguised gratification.

"Real?"

"Sure! What did you think it was, dyed cat?"

"Mr. Panella hardly earns enough to pay for genuine mink coats," observed Mr. Wimble.

"I consider that a most objectionable remark, Mr. Wimble," said Myrtle, a bit too indolently, however, for the stricture to carry much weight.

From beneath the couch, with his foot Mr. Wimble shoved out a pair of bedroom slippers, obviously masculine.

Myrtle's reproof disappeared in a burst of laughter.

"Detectives enjoy their little jokes, I see. You're right. Those are Renzo's. He's a dancer, you know, and his feet get so dead beat he always changes into slippers when he comes to see me."

"Renzo?" inquired Mr. Wimble offhandedly. Corey had all but sung out: "Mr. R!"

"Short for Lorenzo."

"I paid for my coat myself," Myrtle virtuously confided. "I'd been saving up since spring."

"Naturally," said Mr. Wimble blandly, "Mr. Panella wasn't buying mink coats for you when he was in love with Lalla Lee."

Myrtle's eyes blazed.

"That's a lie! Renzo is my fiancé!"

"Once a detective discovers a plausible motive for a crime," explained Mr. Wimble, "the capture of the culprit follows more easily. Your jealousy of Lalla Lee provides an excellent motive, Miss Dale."

At this several emotions played over Myrtle's face; but among them no fear showed itself.

"You think I killed Lalla?" she gasped. "Well, if that isn't—*funny!*"

Throwing back her head, she laughed uproariously. The astonishing thing about the performance was that her amusement sounded genuine.

"Being a detective, Miss Dale, suspecting persons is my job. At present I suspect everyone who came in contact with Lalla Lee on the day of the murder, including yourself."

"I didn't set eyes on Lalla the day of the murder. That's God's truth!"

"Did Mr. Panella?"

"No!" snapped Myrtle.

"How do you know?"

"I have a friend who— That's my business!"

"Mr. Panella called on Lalla Lee at ten o'clock Tuesday morning," said Mr. Wimble quietly. "He was seen by two of the servants. He had on a brown fur coat, a hard hat, a red cravat and tan gaiters."

Myrtle paled beneath her rouge.

"My word's as good as any servant's!" she said with open hostility. "I'm willing to swear on the Bible that Renzo Panella was in this flat all morning."

"You're a good fellow, Myrtle," said Mr. Wimble gently. "I'm glad the little woman in blue brought you such good news."

Myrtle stared.

"How in Hell—?"

"You were smiling with happiness when Webb and I came in. And you fairly purred with it when I mentioned the weeping little clerk." He made a little grimace. "If your news weren't exceptionally good, one would wonder at such cheerfulness in the face of your best friend's death."

"You won't find many women wearing mourning for Lalla Lee," said Myrtle bluntly. "Of course it's rotten about the murder; but you won't get very far if you expect me to tell you that either Renzo or I did it."

"I might get a little further if you'd refrain from telling me any more fairy tales."

Myrtle smiled good-naturedly.

"All right. I'm willing to help all I can. Shoot! If I don't like your questions I'll look out of the window."

"Did Mrs. Lee care for Mr. Panella?"

"Lalla didn't care for any man."

"Not even for the chap out West?"

Myrtle darted him a swift glance; then deliberately turned and looked out of the window. Mr. Wimble laughed.

"Thanks for not lying. What time was Mr. Panella here on Tuesday afternoon?"

"Between two and four; again between six and eight. His off time between shifts, the same as usual. Doesn't look as if he'd been very crazy about Lalla, does it? The only thing he saw in Lalla was her money."

With a smile of contentment, she leaned back in her chair, stretching like a lazy cat.

"That Pollyanna look you saw on my face was because I'd just learned I'd been named in a will."

"Was it Mrs. Lee who left you the money?"

Myrtle Dale was seized by another paroxysm of laughter.

"Your questions sure beat Hell, Wimble!" she said, wiping her eyes. "No, it wasn't Lalla."

"Mr. Panella's fondness for money supplies another motive," said Mr. Wimble. "He was seen leaving the Lee house very hurriedly at the time the murder is supposed to have been committed. When Mrs. Lee's body was discovered, the emerald pendant she was wearing that day was missing."

This news did not in the least disturb Myrtle.

"I'm afraid you're on the wrong track again, Wimble. Crazy as I am about Renzo, I'll admit he has his faults like another. He might even do a murder if hard put to it. But to accuse Renzo Panella of murdering a woman for a piece of jewelry! Why, good Lord, man!" she exploded, with a short laugh in which pride and vexation, intermingled, "when Renzo Panella does his stuff, there isn't a woman in ten thousand who isn't falling all over herself to give him her jewelry!"

"You'll never be happy with Renzo," observed Mr. Wimble softly.

For a moment Myrtle Dale looked her full age.

"I know it. But I'd never be happy without him, either."

12

"Have you any cigarettes, son?"

Corey handed Mr. Wimble a package which, to the younger man's mystification, O. W. dropped into one of his desk drawers. However, being of the opinion that assistant detectives should be seen and not heard, Corey asked no questions.

"Lorenzo Panella's calling this afternoon," said Mr. Wimble. "As he's the only foreigner we've encountered, he may be responsible for the Gitane cigarette butt I picked up the other day when we were examining the shoeprints. At any rate, I'm going to try to find out."

At the conclusion of this speech Corey was feeling, to say nothing of looking, decidedly sheepish. He had neither seen the cigarette butt nor noticed O. W. picking up anything.

Mr. Wimble laughed. "Don't look so distressed, son. There are two good reasons why you didn't. In the first place, I knew how to pick up the butt without any of you noticing. A friend of mine named Brady put me on to that trick. Brady's a chap I was instrumental in sending up for pickpocketing once. He has a great sense of humor, that lad. After his conviction, he asked if he might shake hands with me. 'You caught me square, boss.' he said."

Mr. Wimble chuckled softly as he recalled the incident.

"Half an hour later someone asked me the time—and my watch was gone!

"I called on Brady at the prison. I told him how much I admired his sleight-of-hand performance and said I'd be willing to pay him to teach me how to get my watch back the way I'd lost it. So when he got out he gave me some lessons. Put me through all sorts of stunts. Mighty interesting, some of them; and difficult, too. For instance, I had to take a handkerchief, to which some little bells had been fastened, out of an inside coat pocket without making a single sound.

"It took me some time to get my watch back." His eyes sparkled. "Though Brady'd assured me, the minute he looked at my hands, that I was a born pickpocket!"

It was for Tim Brady, later, to expound for Corey Mr. Wimble's anecdote.

As his choice of a profession exemplified, there was nothing of the soppy sentimentalist about O. W. in his attitude toward criminals. He was not the sort of citizen to sign a petition demanding after-dinner mints for the poor dear prisoners. On the other hand, let Mr. Wimble discover a spark of something worth while in a criminal, and, in so far as so doing fell within the bounds of sane common sense, he would be the first to kindle it. Such a spark he had recognized in Tim Brady.

No doubt pickpocketing brings you close to a person in more ways than one. At any rate, by the time Mr. Wimble was efficient enough to retrieve his watch, Brady had found himself not only with some new economic ideas but, for the first time in his life, with some money he had procured other than from a dealer in stolen goods.

"It took me some time to get my watch back," Mr. Wimble put it.

"Till he'd paid me enough jack for lessons to set myself up in business," interpreted Brady, adding softly: "I'd go down singin' 'Nearer My God to Thee' for O. W. . . ."

"And the reason I didn't see the cigarette butt?" Corey asked his chief.

Mr. Wimble grinned. "I was standing on it!"

Shortly after two, Willy announced Mr. Panella.

Lorenzo Panella was Italian born, though he spoke English without an accent. He was a tall, supple young man with sleek black hair and warm brown eyes. He wore his hat at a rakish angle, and when he lazily peeled off his gloves, one saw several rings adorning his carefully manicured fingers. His shoes were long and narrow, but not, as were the shoeprints beneath the window, exaggeratedly pointed at the toe. Not even the dancer's heavy chocolate-brown fur coat could hide the grace that characterized his every movement. Though probably languid at all times, at present Panella was affecting a profound despondency.

Mr. Wimble made a great show of hospitality.

"It was kind of you to come, Mr. Panella," he said, helping the dancer off with his coat.

Panella shrugged.

"If I had not, as you suggested over the telephone, you would have called at Gianni's. And that would have been bad. Gianni likes fame for his dancers, yes," he said, with an air of self-esteem, "but notoriety, no!"

Mr. Wimble mentioned cigarettes; but, to his well-acted chagrin, upon feeling in his pockets, he discovered he had run out. Corey, of course, made the same discovery.

"Allow me," said Panella, producing a package.

Mr. Wimble helped himself to a cigarette.

"Gitanes! So you import your smokes?"

Panella regarded the package curiously.

"Gitanes? Oh, yes. A friend of mine—gave me these."

"I dare say you've been too upset since the murder to take much heed of what you smoke, eh?"

"That's it," agreed Panella cheerlessly. He had winced at the word "murder."

Suddenly he moaned tragically.

"I have just come from dancing. The sacrilege! The only woman in my life lying dead, while I dance! Not even for a few days will that pig of a Gianni let me off. Tonight I must dance again. And tomorrow, my three dances as usual. *Gallabres!*" he cursed in his native tongue.

"So you cared for Lalla Lee?"

Panella regarded Mr. Wimble with sorrowful eyes.

"Until I met Lalla my life was like a garden without flowers!" Lorenzo Panella was either a great lover or a great liar.

"Poor Myrtle!" exclaimed Mr. Wimble softly.

"Poor Myrtle!" echoed Panella, a trace of malevolence in his voice. "Myrtle, with her jealousies! Myrtle, with her threats— But one is rather shy of recalling threats just after a crime has been committed," he said, with a self-conscious smirk. "Poor Myrtle! Naturally a man feels sorry for the women who care for him!"

"Certain matrimonial views sponsored by the Mohammedans may not be so stupid after all," observed Mr. Wimble.

"If you're referring to harems, I don't imagine the idea works out satisfactorily. From my experience with women, each wife in the harem would clamor to be the favorite."

Corey cursed the conventions that kept a fellow from punching another fellow's head.

Mr. Wimble changed the subject. No doubt he was entertaining the same regrets as Corey.

"Mr. Panella, when you saw the murdered body of Lalla Lee, why did you not immediately notify the police?"

"I was afraid of incriminating someone," Panella promptly replied. A little too promptly.

"Myrtle Dale?"

"The sight of Lalla dead, dripping blood, unnerved me." The Italian shivered exquisitely. "I became mad. I was afraid that if the police questioned me while I was in such a state I might let fall something thoughtless. To be frank with you, Mr. Wimble, I did suspect Myrtle. You know what a demon a woman can be when her jealousy is aroused; and Myrtle was exceedingly jealous of Lalla. She had even threatened to kill any woman who came between us. Had I gone direct to the police, I probably would have accused her."

"Your temporary insanity has passed?"

"Quite. I am desolate, but no longer mad."

"Then what is your present excuse for insinuating that Miss Dale committed the crime?"

Panella bit his lips.

"You are taking unfair advantage of my frankness in telling you why I did not go to the police," he said, in a hurt voice.

"I *like* Miss Dale!"

"I have often told Myrtle that a woman of her age should try to attract older men," remarked the Italian smoothly.

"Now, Mr. Panella," suggested Mr. Wimble, "suppose I give an account of your actions on the day of the murder, so far as I am aware of them, leaving you to supply the rest."

Panella agreed. "For Lalla's sake!"

"Also for Myrtle's!" said Mr. Wimble, none too gently.

"At ten o'clock on Tuesday, Mr. Panella, you called at the Lee house, demanding to see Mrs. Lee. Upon being informed by the butler that she was not yet up, you sent her a note. I found your note in Mrs. Lee's coat pocket. It reads: 'Have had a wonderful offer. If you can't come down now, tell me that you'll see me later—at the same place. R.'

"Mrs. Lee refused to come down, but sent word by the servant that she would see you that afternoon at Myrtle's. Whereupon you left the house.

"But," continued Mr. Wimble, "while Sharl was upstairs, you backed up against the front door, for the purpose of surreptitiously unlatching it. This you managed successfully to do without being observed by Marie, who at the time was scrubbing the vestibule floor. The dye from your coat left a smudge on the front door. Whoever dyed your coonskin did rather a poor job, I'm afraid. Quite a bit of the dye rubbed off on my hands while I was helping you remove your coat."

Panella's eyes narrowed, but he offered no comment.

"Mr. Gianni tells me that you reported for duty as usual on Tuesday at noon, leaving at two. You called on Miss Dale later in the afternoon. But, before doing so, you called on Lalla Lee, entering by the front door. It was an oversight on your part not to relatch the door. You went into the living room, either sitting in one of the armchairs or placing your coat there. The same dye that stained the front door, the wall in Miss Dale's hall and my hands also smudged the armchair. And you were seen leaving the house very hurriedly by the rear entrance.

"Now, Mr. Panella, will you kindly fill in the gaps?"

"There are few to fill in," said the Italian, flatteringly. "However, there are one or two inaccuracies which I shall correct as I come to them.

"I knew Lalla would be angry with me for calling at her house. She had forbidden me to do so, for fear of Myrtle learning of our affair. But I was very anxious to see her. She hadn't been to Gianni's for days."

"It was her habit to meet you there?"

"Every day, between four and six. There is floor dancing at Gianni's, as well as exhibition work; and when Lalla
was being kind to me she'd come there for tea and we'd
dance together. She danced divinely. It was my dream that
she would become my professional partner. In fact, it was
an offer from a Parisian music hall that I referred to in my
note."

He sighed. "We could have made a fortune!"

"Does Miss Dale ever go to Gianni's for the tea dances?"

Panella smiled oilily.

"Myrtle understands that it is forbidden by Gianni for
the exhibition dancers to dance with the patrons of the
restaurant."

Mr. Wimble motioned for him to continue.

"While the negro servant was upstairs, the idea of unlatching the door occurred to me. I was afraid Lalla would
tell him not to admit me again. And I was determined to
see her!"

"The fact that she promised to meet you at Myrtle's
made no change in your plans?"

"I didn't believe her. She'd been promising for days to
come to Gianni's, but hadn't kept her word."

"Is it not possible that, to punish you for disobeying
her, she intended confessing to Myrtle that you and she
had been carrying on an affair?"

"Possible, yes."

"Is it not likewise possible that your return to the house
in the afternoon was to prevent her from pursuing such a
course?"

"My dear sir," cooed Panella, "if you're trying to fas-
ten a motive on me for the killing of Lalla Lee, I'm afraid
you'll have to do better than that. In the first place, I'd
unlatched the door before learning that Lalla was going
to Myrtle's. And, in the second, I shouldn't have cared a

damn if she had told Myrtle! Shall I continue my story?" Mr. Wimble nodded assent. That gentleman was enjoying himself. As he would have put it, he *liked* a worthy opponent!

"I got through work at Gianni's at two and walked to Lalla's before going to Myrtle's. There was a chance that Lalla'd really go to Myrtle's, of course; there was also a chance that I'd find her at home."

His lips worked convulsively. "I found her at home. But, *Madonna mia,* in what a condition!

"My one idea was to get out of the house. I started back the way I had entered; but as I neared the door I heard the sound of footsteps in an outer room. Fearing someone might enter the living room before I had left it, I had the presence of mind to lock the door. Then I went out by the back way.

"I had been in the room no longer than three minutes at the outside; and, contrary to your theory, Mr. Wimble, I neither sat in one of the living room chairs nor put my coat on it.

"I then went to Myrtle's."

"For the purpose of accusing her of the crime?"

Panella looked abused.

"That suspicion left me the moment I saw Myrtle," he said with dignity. "She had a girl friend with her. When I saw Myrtle and Annie sitting there, gossiping so lightly together, I realized that my suspicion was absurd. I did not even mention the crime until Annie had left."

"Annie, Mrs. Lee's maid?"

"Yes."

"Didn't it occur to you that Annie might be interested in your news?"

"Hysterical women annoy me."

"It is believed that Mrs. Lee was murdered for her pear-shaped emerald," said Mr. Wimble.

"If that theory is correct," returned Panella in a voice vibrant with bitterness, "then the Almighty has a sardonic sense of humor!"

Mr. Wimble sat up briskly, indicating that the interview was over. But, as Panella prepared gracefully to go, he shot the question:

"What about Mrs. Lee's friend out West?"

The Italian had turned to pick up his gloves. On his countenance appeared the look of a man who is scheming, and scheming fast. And yet, as he leisurely faced Mr. Wimble, it seemed as if he might be on the point of yawning.

"I am afraid, my dear Mr. Wimble, that your knowledge of women is scant. 'Mrs. Lee's friend out West' was a myth invented by Myrtle to kill any hopes I might have had of winning Lalla."

For some moments after the dancer's graceful exit, Mr. Wimble sat silently at his desk, drawing little designs on a writing tablet as was his wont when thinking deeply.

Finally he spoke.

"Someone wearing Panella's fur coat sat in that armchair at the Lees'! Panella's no fool. He must have appreciated that with all we had on him it wouldn't be worth his while to lie too much. And he looked genuinely surprised to find the Gitanes in his fur coat pocket. I'm of the opinion that he lent his coat on Tuesday to a friend. I've been wondering who Lalla's other caller was ever since Sharl eagerly informed us that there'd been none."

13

"If you ever want any help from me, O. W.," Tim Brady once had told his friend, "just say the word and you'll get it!"

A promise is a debt. So, when Mr. Wimble rang up Tim and asked him to keep an eye on Patterson, he knew that whenever the chauffeur visited Tiny's he'd be watched and that whatever Tim learned of importance would be reported to his office.

For Tiny's Pool Room, which Patterson had told Mr. Wimble he was in the habit of frequenting, was Tim's.

Tim Brady was six feet tall. When he had asked his friend O. W. for an appropriate name for his place, Mr. Wimble had suggested "Tiny Tim's." The habitués of the pool room rarely got the literary allusion, but the pseudonym usually registered.

It was Friday before Tim had anything to report. But when it came his information was juicy.

"The shofer's meeting Manheim here tonight after supper," he told Mr. Wimble. They were speaking over the telephone.

"If by any chance they arrive before I do, keep them apart till I get there, will you, Tim? I should like to see Manheim first."

As he replaced the receiver on the hook, Mr. Wimble sighed.

"I'm sorry Felix Manheim's mixed up in this. Manheim's a—second-hand dealer. Interested chiefly in precious stones. His appointment with Patterson can mean but one thing, of course."

Neither Patterson nor Manheim had yet arrived when Mr. Wimble and Corey reached Tiny's. Brady invited the detectives to wait in his private office.

"Tiny" Tim was a regular giant of a man, with a rough-hewn, good-natured face and a deep rumbling laugh that sounded like distant thunder. Only his beautifully shaped, agile-fingered hands pointed to his former profession.

"I got a waiter on the lookout for your men," he said. "The minute Manheim shows up, Gus'll bring him in here. If the shofer's first, I've told Gus to fake up a phone call for him so he'll be in the booth and out of the way when Manheim passes through. While you're waiting, how about a swig of near beer?"

The beer was so "near" as almost to hit the mark; but Mr. Wimble offered no comment.

"Did you learn what it is that Patterson has to sell?" he asked.

"Yeh. This afternoon he hints around he's got something to peddle, so I gets into a real chummy confab with him."

He glanced obliquely down at his hands.

"I finds out he has a big emerald he wants to get rid of," he demurely announced.

Mr. Wimble laughed.

"I trust he still has it!"

"You know he has!" replied Brady feelingly. "I'm off that old gag!"

Mr. Wimble teased: "Why? Not so good any more?"

"Quit it!" returned Brady good-naturedly.

"A little later I sees the shofer gassing with Abe Fox, one of Manheim's running mates. I asks Fox what's up and he tells me that Patterson's meeting Manheim here tonight after supper."

Mr. Wimble took out his watch.

"They ought to be along pretty soon now."

The most extraordinary change came over Brady. A moment before he had been leaning back in his chair, genially beaming upon his friend O. W. Now, with a startled jerk, he sat up and began pounding on his hips and stomach.

"I told you you weren't so good any more," said Mr. Wimble blandly.

Tim regarded O. W. blankly for a moment. Then the room fairly reverberated with his thunderous laughter.

Through the din Mr. Wimble explained to Corey:

"When I accused Tim of being stale, to get even, he nipped my watch. I nipped it back again!"

A knock on the door interrupted the thunderstorm. It was the waiter, Gus, with Manheim in tow.

Tim got to his feet.

"While you're having your little talk fest, O. W.," he said, with a last rumble of thunder, "I'll run along and lock up my joolry in the safe!"

14

Felix Manheim was a wiry little Jew of about thirty. He wore his black derby pulled so far down over his head that it had the appearance of being supported by his ears. His eyes were small and shining like black beads. He had a habit of every now and then darting a nervous glance behind him. It was as if he feared at any moment being pounced upon.

To Webb, the man was repulsively rat-like.

When he saw Mr. Wimble Manheim burst into an enraptured sing-song.

"Well, by golly, if it ain't Mr. Wimble! How do you feel, Mr. Wimble?" Mr. Wimble shook hands with the little fellow as warmly as if he actually liked him.

Greetings accomplished, Manheim stood with his arms folded across his abdomen, rocking back and forth.

"If it ain't only yesterday Momma was saying: 'How I wish that nice Mr. Wimble was here to have some of this noodle pudding!'"

He confided in Corey:

"Momma thinks Mr. Wimble is the finest man in the world."

He smiled self-consciously. "Next to me!"

"How is that little mother of yours, by the way?" asked Mr. Wimble.

"Spry as a bird, Momma is! What you know, Mr. Wimble? Momma still refuses to have help! 'No, Felix,' she says, 'save your money. I couldn't stand to see it a servant girl should eat us out of house and home when I'm perfectly able to do the work myself!' That's Momma for you, Mr. Wimble, by golly!"

All at once his thin shoulders sagged.

"Momma don't get no better, Mr. Wimble. I have the most expensive doctors. They pull and they poke and then they say there ain't nothing to do. Nothing to do but send in a big bill, by golly!"

During Felix's childhood, his mother had met with a railroad accident. Manheim Senior had sued the railroad company, won the case, and decamped with the money. Mrs. Manheim had raised her child from a wheel chair.

"It's marvelous how she gets around in it," Mr. Wimble told Corey. "Felix has every reason to be proud of his mother. She's a remarkable little person, brave and true."

He put his arm about the little Jew.

"And she has every reason to be proud of Felix. He's a good son!"

Manheim's small eyes blinked; and an extraordinarily large Adam's apple appeared above his collar.

With his usual tact, Mr. Wimble mentioned the one subject likely to take Manheim's mind off his troubles.

"Let's talk business," he said.

"You came here tonight, Felix, to buy an emerald from a man named Patterson."

This statement had the immediate effect of accentuating the wariness of Manheim's beady eyes, the rigidity of his sharp features. Once more his resemblance to a rat forced itself upon Corey. Moved by the little Jew's sweetness of manner while speaking of his mother, Corey had repented his first impression. "Still," thought Corey, "there is no reason for supposing that a rodent doesn't care for its mother."

Manheim corrected Mr. Wimble's statement.

"I come to look at an emerald Patterson's got to sell."

"With the intention of buying it, if you liked the looks of it."

"Now, Mr. Wimble," whined the little Jew placatingly, "I'm only an agent."

"Of a 'fence'!" retorted Mr. Wimble.

His voice grew wistful.

"With your knowledge of stones, Felix, there's no need of you having a job that entails such risk."

"It pays," said Manheim briefly. "Besides," cajolingly, "you got my job all wrong, Mr. Wimble. There's lots of people like to get rid of their jewelry private. They think there's some disgrace attached to selling their personal belongings, so they come to us on the quiet. We don't handle dirty stuff, Mr. Wimble. Not if we know it, we don't."

"Haven't you connected this emerald Patterson's offering you with the Lee murder?"

"My job's to appraise the stuff people got to sell," replied Manheim evasively. "My boss does all the investigating."

Mr. Wimble laughed dryly.

"Precious little he does, I'll wager, when he comes upon a stone that the holder finds burning a hole in his pocket and is willing to let go at a bargain."

"You looking for someone who's supposed to have stole the Lee emerald, Mr. Wimble?"

"I'm looking for the murderer of Lalla Lee!"

Mr. Wimble's voice softened. "And I'd like you to help me, Felix."

Manheim's greasy face lit up with affection.

"I'd take it like a personal favor if you was to let me help you out, Mr. Wimble."

He snickered. "Remember them postcards?"

One summer Felix had got into petty larceny difficulties. Fortunately for the little Jew, Mr. Wimble happened to be in court the day Manheim's case was tried. In Felix's agony lest his mother learn that he was going to "the Island," the detective had discerned that divine spark for which he was invariably on the lookout.

Mr. Wimble had taken it upon himself personally to inform Mrs. Manheim of her son's departure for Atlantic City where he was to appraise some jewelry. Postcards in Felix' handwriting subsequently arriving from that seaside resort, there had been no reason for the little Jewish woman to doubt Mr. Wimble's word.

O. W. of course had indulged in subterfuge. The postcards were indeed written by Felix. At Mr. Wimble's direction, on the eve of his going to "the Island," Felix had prepared for the post some two dozen postcards bearing colored views of Atlantic City's show places. But it was Mr. Wimble who at proper intervals had mailed the cards to Mrs. Manheim from Atlantic City.

If the price of the subterfuge were a change in his vacation plans, at least O. W. was never heard to complain about it. He afterwards assured Felix that he had enjoyed his vacation in Atlantic City as fully as if, following his original intention, he had spent it in Palestine. After all, O. W. *liked* people; he was primarily interested in the inhabitants of foreign lands. And there is a marked racial similarity between the populace of Atlantic City and Palestine.

"Them postcards!" giggled Felix, in reviewing the episode. "All the time Momma keeps asking me about some boardwalk or something, and when I look dumb she totes out a picture postcard of the place with my writing on it, saying there I was and wishing she was the same!

"Help you, Mr. Wimble? Well, say! You know me, by golly!

"I don't believe my boss'd care to handle anything 'One Week' Wimble was after, anyhow," he flatteringly appended.

"I'm anxious to learn just how Patterson comes to have the emerald in his possession," said Mr. Wimble. "He won't take it amiss if you question him?"

"I often do a little preliminary investigating for my boss," said Manheim guardedly.

"I suggest that you gain his confidence by promising him right off that you'll take the stone. After that, tell him that for your own protection you'd like to know just how he got hold of the emerald. Finally, I think it will be wise to make another appointment with him; say, here, tomorrow night. Tell him you'll bring your boss along to make the last arrangements."

A knock sounded on the door, and Gus poked his head into the room.

"The shofer's here, Mr. Wimble."

"Thanks, Gus. Mr. Manheim will let himself out by the back way presently and will arrive by the front entrance. Patterson is waiting where he'll see Manheim come in?"

"Yes, sir," said Gus, and withdrew.

"Where do you do your talking, Felix?"

"In one of the private card rooms."

"Well, Webb and I'll be waiting for you here."

"Very good, Mr. Wimble."

"By the way, Felix," asked Mr. Wimble, as Manheim prepared to go, "know anything about a dancer up at Gianni's called Lorenzo Panella?"

A snort of disgust escaped the little Jew.

"Lives off women, that guy! Abe Fox bought something from him once, I think. As for myself, I'm too busy to deal with that sort!"

The social distinction among crooks is one of the most interesting and most inexplicable phases of the underworld. A man may take money from a woman without her knowledge, and he's considered a fine fellow. But let him take it with her knowledge, and he's a social outcast.

Manheim led Patterson into one of the small card rooms connected with Brady's establishment. The chauffeur was clearly out of sorts.

"You ain't so prompt keeping dates!" he grumbled.

"To tell you the honest truth, Mr. Patterson," returned Manheim suavely, "I usually wait till the police are looking the other way before I meet my customers."

"Is that so?" snapped Patterson. "Well, there's nothing crooked about this little customer. See!"

Manheim coughed discreetly.

"I thought, since you come to me—"

"Well, you can take it from me that everything about this transaction is open and aboveboard. See? I have my own reasons for putting the deal over on the Q. T. The question is: Are you prepared to take the emerald I got, or ain't you?"

"Of course I am, Mr. Patterson! Naturally, for my own protection, I'd like to know just how you come by the stone."

"That's my business!"

"I ain't insinuating that you come by it dishonest," said Manheim artfully, "that you—stole it, or nothing like that."

"Say! You shut your trap. See! I didn't lift the emerald. The sooner you get that through your nut, the better. I told you once this deal was open and aboveboard, didn't I?"

"It ain't for myself, Mr. Patterson," persisted the little Jew propitiatingly. "It's my boss who's so cautious. After all, he pays so good he has a right to be."

This last remark bore fruit.

"If I tell you I have proof I got the emerald on the level, will that be enough?"

"I guess it will have to be," sighed Manheim. "Of course, Mr. Patterson, you are prepared to produce the proof—that is," he wheedlingly added, "if my boss offers you a big enough price for the stone?"

"We'll see about that later."

"Suppose I take a look at the emerald?" suggested Manheim.

There followed a short silence, split suddenly by the high-pitched voice of Manheim, shrill with anger.

"Really, Mr. Patterson, I'm too busy a man to spend my time playing child games!"

"Say, you kike! What's eating you, anyway?"

"Surely you don't think this here's an *emerald?*" retorted Manheim witheringly. "Why, by golly, a babe in arms could tell the stone's a fake!"

15

Part of Corey's job was to operate Mr. Wimble's car. He took it as a reflection on his driving ability, therefore, when on Saturday morning O. W. announced that they were going to Mr. Lee's by taxi, giving as his reason:

"We'll save time."

"At the expense of our lives," thought Corey, with the usual contempt of a driver for the other fellow's driving.

O. W., enjoying his jokes only till they began to sting, explained:

"We're taking Hilda's 'yaller' taxi—the one that drove Lalla Lee home from Myrtle's on Tuesday."

On his way to the office that morning, Mr. Wimble had stopped at the taxicab rank in front of Miss Dale's apartment house. Upon making himself known, a series of laughs had gone down the line. The laughs had varied in degree of mirth, for the reason that there had been a bet on among the drivers as to whether or not "One Week" Wimble would show up.

One of their co-workers by the name of Jenks, knew something about the Lalla Lee case.

Jenks had discussed with his companions the advisability of going to the police with his story. Some had thought it Jenks' duty to go; others had advised him to mind his own business. One of his comrades, seeing in the paper that "One Week" Wimble was handling the investigation, had declared that all Jenks need do was sit tight till "One Week" came looking for him.

Just before Mr. Wimble's arrival at the stand, however, Jenks had driven off with a fare. The others had promised to send him to the detective's office the minute he returned.

"I thought hearing Jenks' story on our way to Mr. Lee's would save time," said Mr. Wimble. It was at such moments as this that Corey wondered if his chief were not the least bit vain of his sobriquet "One Week."

A few minutes later Willy announced that the taxicab driver was waiting downstairs.

"I hope you're one of the winners, Jenks?" smiled Mr. Wimble as he greeted the chauffeur.

"Fifteen bucks!" replied Jenks with a grin.

"I want you to drive us to the house you drove the veiled lady to on Tuesday," Mr. Wimble directed him. "We'll listen to your story as we go along."

Jenks' story did little but corroborate a part of Hilda Hanson's. Or so it seemed to Corey. Perhaps O. W. wasn't quite used to working with an assistant; or perhaps he wanted Corey to do his own thinking.

Tuesday afternoon, Jenks had been hailed by a woman wearing a brown fur coat and a heavy black veil.

"She was holding a handkerchief up to her face and was crying so hard she couldn't tell me where she wanted to go." Instead, she had handed him a calling card.

"I still got it," said Jenks. "When I saw the murdered dame's address in the paper, it sounded sort of familiar, so I hunted up the card and found they were the same."

Upon nearing the house, Jenks' fare had tapped on the window and called out: "Back door!"

"She was still crying. I felt sorry for her and tried not to stare. I guess she was thankful to me, because just before she got out she reached through the window and dropped five dollars into my lap, and ran into the house without waiting for any change."

Jenks' testimony completed, Mr. Wimble's fingers sought his pencil pocket; but, before he could get to work on some designs, the taxi had pulled up before the Lee house. Mr. Wimble tipped the chauffeur liberally and dismissed him.

When Sharl opened the door to them, the detectives found Mr. Lee in the entry, on the point of leaving the house. Marie was with him.

Mr. Lee greeted Mr. Wimble and Corey with apparent pleasure. Marie eyed them with a friendly smile. Sharl, on the other hand, had no welcome for the detectives. His manner was conspicuously ill at ease, and the gaze he fixed on Mr. Wimble was hostile.

"You came to bring us some news?" asked Mr. Lee.

"To get some," said Mr. Wimble. "We'd like to interview Annie and Patterson again."

At these words, Sharl recovered his composure. Abandoning his watchfulness over Mr. Wimble, he began brushing Mr. Lee's hat.

Mr. Lee said: "Sharl and I have a special reason for hoping that the mystery will be cleared up right soon.

"Don't go, Marie!" he said, as Marie turned quietly to slip out of the vestibule. "I'd like Mr. Wimble and Mr. Webb to hear of your kindness.

"You gentlemen already knew, I believe, that Marie and her husband intended retiring to France. Well, they've just heard through Jules' parents of a place available near Agon, in Normandy. They've offered to take Sharl and me along as boarders. Sharl will help in the garden. And I—"

He smiled faintly. "I'll have my solitaire and—" the smile faded, "and my memories."

His eyes were suspiciously bright.

"I'll be getting along to my office now, if you gentle-men don't need me. My secretary, Miss Martin, is most able; still I like to keep an eye on things myself. If you'll interview Annie first, I'll send Patterson right back."

"Your muffler, Mr. Lee!" Marie reminded him, as he started for the door. Sharl took the muffler from Marie, arranging it around his master's neck with a solicitude that was almost paternal.

It was evident from Annie's face that she had been crying.

"What's the matter with Miss Diane Adair this morn-ing?" asked Mr. Wimble.

"Nothin'," said Annie dejectedly. "Thanks for the check."

"You must expect to be treated rough if you fall in love with a cave man," said Mr. Wimble imperturbably.

"To hear Pat tell it," she retorted, "you'd think he was the King of Sheba!"

Mr. Wimble regarded her kindly.

"Won't anyone but Patterson do, child?"

Whether Annie feared that unwittingly she had impli-cated Patterson, or whether she were incapable of pro-longed grief, at Mr. Wimble's question she recaptured her wonted archness.

"Proposing to me, Mr. Wimble?"

Mr. Wimble replied, with uncustomary severity: "I'm proposing to take care of you, Annie Robinson!"

His voice softened.

"Don't you ever get tired of Easterners, child? Don't you long to go home, out West where—er—men are men?"

Annie sniffed disdainfully.

"The men are all farmers in Iowa!"

16

Patterson came in with his habitual show of bravado. When he saw Annie, he threw her a look so full of rancor that she cringed. And yet it was obvious that her apprehension was tempered with admiration of the fellow. After all, the ability to inspire fear is probably one of the major charms of a "cave man".

"Say!" he blustered. "I'm tired of all this questioning. See? I'm just about ready to pack up and clear out."

"I shouldn't advise you to do that, Patterson," replied Mr. Wimble gravely. "Though you may not know it, you're under police surveillance."

"What int'rest the cops got in me?" He put the question indifferently; but it was noticeable that he hung on the detective's reply.

"Perhaps you arouse their curiosity."

"I ain't good at riddles!" growled Patterson.

"Don't you think a chap who'd run over an old gentleman, without having even the common decency to stop his car and offer a little first-aid, is curious?"

"Oh!" said Patterson, the interjection riding on a sigh of relief, "so that's what's eating you, is it?"

"It's maintained in some quarters," said Mr. Wimble softly, "that Mr. Peters would have lived if he'd reached the hospital sooner."

"I was acquitted, don't forget!" snapped Patterson.

"You were happy in your choice of Benny Lazarus as your lawyer. It was fortunate, too, that the only witness of the accident happened to be poor Mrs. Peters."

"There were three witnesses testified the old man deliberately stepped in front of my car!"

"Benny has a gift for producing witnesses," said Mr. Wimble dryly.

He watched Patterson closely.

"They say Benny's prices are exorbitant. I'll wager a man like Benny is none too indulgent in the matter of payments, either."

"Cut it! All that's ancient history. You haven't got anything on me now; and you can call off the cops. See?"

"On the contrary, Patterson, I have several things on you. For instance: Mr. Lee was kind enough to give you a job when you'd been out of work for weeks and were badly down on your luck. You repaid that kindness by making love to his wife."

"Say!" snarled Patterson, "you keep your damn mouth shut! See?"

"There's a lady present," said Mr. Wimble pleasantly.

Annie knew considerable about Patterson's private life. The more Mr. Wimble had tormented him, the more firmly convinced Patterson had become that Annie had been disclosing some of this knowledge to the detective. To be expected to treat her with respect, therefore, was a little too much.

"Lady!" he spat. "That —!"

No doubt his blasphemy would have been worthy of the classification, had he been permitted to continue. As there was but a single report, the two detectives must have hit him simultaneously.

From the floor, Patterson first went over his jaw with gingerly pats, and then nursed his wounded vanity with trite remarks about two-against-one.

Annie gazed down on her fallen idol.

"You're a Hell of a cave man!"

Mr. Wimble did not remind her that there were gentlemen present.

"Before we continue," said Mr. Wimble, puffing a little, "I want you to know that our information was not supplied us by Annie. I believe it is unnecessary for me to add that you will find it most unhealthy to persecute her in any way from now on.

"Now that we understand each other, suppose you tell me how you came by Mrs. Lee's imitation emerald?"

"She gave it to me."

"You have proof?"

Patterson extracted a piece of paper from his wallet.

"She handed it to me with this note just as she was getting into the car Tuesday."

Without in the slightest degree showing the surprise he felt, Mr. Wimble read the note:

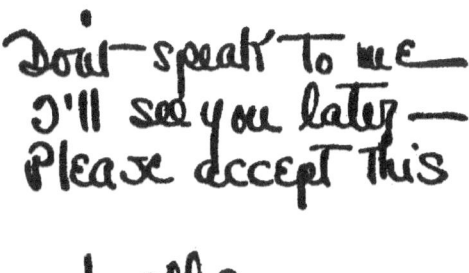

That afternoon, a handwriting expert, shown this with other specimens of Mrs. Lee's penmanship, declared them all written by the same person.

The note explained Patterson's smart-aleck look of Tuesday evening when asked if he had seen the emerald. He had seen it, though not, as Mr. Wimble naturally had supposed, adorning Lalla Lee's comely person. It also accounted for his childlike triumph when able truthfully to deny having held conversation with his mistress on that day.

"Did the note surprise you?" asked Mr. Wimble.

"It had me guessing, all right. The swell present, specially." He gave a short, bitter laugh. "I didn't know then that she'd only slipped me a hunk of green glass! But she said she'd see me later; so I figured she'd explain everything to me then. See?"

"And did she explain when you saw her later?"

Strangely enough, audiences often feel sorry for the "bad man" of the piece. It is said that the fan mail of the movie villains rivals that of the heroes. Patterson was a figure almost to sympathize with at that moment. He was so in need of relieving his feelings. And Mr. Wimble had imposed an embargo on the only way he knew how.

"What's eating you?" he inquired, rather feebly.

"Didn't you have an appointment with Mrs. Lee, at, let us say, five o'clock?"

"Well, what about it?"

"Suppose you do a little talking."

"Well, when Lalla went into Myrtle's, she held up her hand. That meant she expected me at five. See? She always signaled the time to me like that, with her fingers. So at five I went home and looked for her in the pink room. I saw her hat and coat, but she wasn't there herself."

"Just a moment, Patterson. I wish to make sure that Annie got your last remark. Did you hear Patterson say that he saw Mrs. Lee's hat and coat in the pink room, Annie?"

"Yes, sir," gulped Annie.

"So, Patterson," prompted Mr. Wimble, "finding that Mrs. Lee had not kept her appointment, you went into the living room looking for her."

"You got it straight!" admitted Patterson surlily. "I knew she was expecting me, so I went in. The room was dark. I thought I saw her sitting on the couch, so I spoke to her. When she didn't answer, I switched on the light. See?"

He swallowed hard.

"When I saw what had happened, I put out the light and beat it."

"Why didn't you notify the police?"

"I didn't want to get mixed up in it. See?"

"The way you felt when you left Mr. Peters for dead?"

"Quit rubbing that in!"

"In the meantime," continued Mr. Wimble complacently, "for some reason which she will explain later, Annie had returned."

Annie jerked to attention like a Judy on a string.

"She, too, saw Mrs. Lee's coat; but unlike you she saw some money sticking out of one of the pockets."

Annie gave a little squeak as she turned on Patterson.

"You squealed, you big stiff!"

Mr. Wimble said quietly to Annie: "You were seen banking five one-hundred-dollar bills at the Merchants' Bank on Thursday. Of course, Patterson, you came out of the living room in time to see Annie acquiring five hundred dollars in a way that she shouldn't. Naturally you didn't want her to tell she'd seen you leaving the room where the crime was committed. But you had something on her, too. I wonder you didn't make a bargain with her: you'd hold your tongue if she'd hold hers. That would have been far less stupid on your part than to have risked bringing everyone in the house on the scene by getting her consent in a manner that caused her to scream. Perhaps at the time, believing yourself in possession of Lalla Lee's emerald, you felt you could afford to be generous."

"You haven't any proof I saw her take the money!"

"Suppose you hand over the check Annie made out for you last night?"

Patterson's eyes kindled with hatred for Annie. "Oh, no! *Miss Robinson* didn't do any talking!"

"I'm familiar with Annie's handwriting," said Mr. Wimble. "Also with the green ink she uses. I saw the check in your wallet when you took out Mrs. Lee's note. Hand it over, please."

Though with bad grace, Patterson obeyed.

"The whole five hundred!" said Mr. Wimble, so softly that his voice could hardly be heard; but Patterson backed away from the look in his eyes.

"Blackmail," observed Mr. Wimble, "besides being so filthy a profession that most crooks won't touch it, is a criminal offense."

Patterson's self-possession was almost shattered, but he still held out.

"How you going to prove Annie didn't give me the money of her own accord?"

"Last night when you parted from Manheim, Patterson, Mr. Webb followed you. He witnessed the meeting of you and Annie. He heard you telling her you'd seen her take the five hundred dollars and demanding your share of the loot."

What semblance of spirit Patterson had maintained, shabby as it was, succumbed without further struggle.

"You don't suspect me of doing Lalla in, do you, Mr. Wimble?" he whined.

"We have not yet discovered any reliable witness to establish your alibi," replied Mr. Wimble coldly.

17

When Patterson, wearing the air of a whipped dog, had slunk out of the room, Mr. Wimble turned his attention to Annie. The girl looked as if she might be sitting in a bed of thistles.

She said in a thin, far-away voice: "It's been haunting me—what you said about me being an 'accessory after the fact'."

"Annie," said Mr. Wimble kindly, "I told you the first day I met you that I *liked* you. If you liked me, perhaps you'd trust me a little more than you do now."

Annie's round countenance assumed a more hopeful expression.

"I do like you, Mr. Wimble! I can prove that I do! You asked me not to tell Myrtle I was your assistant; and I haven't! There! Doesn't that prove I like you?"

"I've realized all along that you're good at keeping secrets," smiled Mr. Wimble.

Annie blushed. "The reason I didn't say anything about Pat was because I was scared to." Lapsing into the Diane Adair manner: "He thr-r-reatened me!"

"I wonder if it wouldn't be a good idea for you to tell us your story all over again?"

Annie thought it would.

"I appreciate all your kindness to me, Mr. Wimble. Honest, I do! I haven't been any too happy in this house, believe me, watching Mrs. Lee playing with Pat like a cat plays with a mouse, and having him breaking dates with me time and time again just because she raised her little finger, and all."

Extreme satisfaction showed in her face.

"I sure was wild about that man!"

Annie's youth and adaptability were already coming to her aid. Though its protagonist had proved a disappointment, Annie would never regret her affair with Patterson. It would be something thrilling to look back on as long as she lived.

"I left the house Tuesday at one-thirty like I told you. I went to a girl friend's."

"Myrtle Dale's, to be exact."

Annie eyed Mr. Wimble with admiration.

"I guess a person's a fool to try to hide anything from you!"

"I can be deceived for a time, but I usually find out the truth in the end."

"I met Myrt when I was working at the theatre. She got me my job with Mrs. Lee. We're good pals."

"Do you know her friend Renzo?"

"Renzo!" Annie repeated the name with disgust. "I wonder why she doesn't buy herself a real lap dog. Myrt's crazy about him, though. And jealous! Say! She turns green if she catches him looking at a girl on a magazine cover!"

"Was there anything between Mrs. Lee and Renzo?"

"That's something I'd like to know myself," replied Annie eagerly. "I think Myrt suspected there was. She made me promise that if I ever saw Renzo at the house I'd tell her."

"So you called on Miss Dale Tuesday to make a report?"

Annie looked startled.

"Why—what do you *mean*, Mr. Wimble?"

"You went to tell her that Mr. Panella had visited here on Tuesday morning?"

"Oh! That! No, I didn't know he'd been here Tuesday morning. For that matter, I never saw him here, though once I heard Mrs. Lee phoning him to come."

"You saw Mr. Panella at Miss Dale's on Tuesday?"

"Yes, sir. He came in while I was there. When he saw me, he kind of acted like the place was crowded, so I left."

"What time was that, do you remember?"

"It must have been a little after two, because I went from Myrtle's to the Palladium and got there in time for the two-thirty show.

"I came home about five. You know; you heard me yell. I'd been noticing that Mrs. Lee didn't seem quite so crazy about Pat as she used to, and I thought if I could find him around anywhere, maybe I could coax him to go to a dance with me that evening. It was his day off, too.

"Just as I opened the back door, I heard him say: 'Lal-la!'" She burlesqued Patterson's voice. "Just like that. All pie and cake. Enough to make you sick. I thought they were in the Vamp Room, so I tiptoed up to the door to listen. I found the door open a little ways, but when I peeked in there was nobody there."

She hung her head.

"I don't know what struck me to take the money, Mr. Wimble. Honest, I don't! Just my crazy jealousy, I guess, and wanting to get into the pictures so bad. I always thought, if I had the clothes and jewelry and things Mrs. Lee had, Pat'd like me as well as her.

"Anyhow, when I saw the money it seemed like an answer to a prayer. It was easy to take it. I knew by that time, of course, that Mrs. Lee and Pat were in the living room. Besides, I figured that if either of them came out and saw me I could easy enough slip the money back in the pocket and say I was taking the coat upstairs to put it away.

"But when Pat came rushing out of the living room, the look on his face paralyzed me. I just stood there holding the money and staring at him. When he saw me, he rushed into the Vamp Room and grabbed me by the throat. 'If you let on you saw me coming out of that room, there'll be another murder. See?' he said. I guess you can't blame me for hollering, Mr. Wimble."

Mr. Wimble guessed that he couldn't.

"Pat didn't say a word about the money. I didn't think he saw it.

"Then I went upstairs with Mrs. Lee's coat. She was always wild if I didn't hang her things up. I mightn't have taken the trouble on my day off, though," she naively confessed, "if I hadn't wanted an excuse to get away from Pat.

"After that I went out again. I really did go to another girl friend's, like I told you. I didn't hear about the murder till I got home that night."

Mr. Wimble smiled.

"And did yourself proud at screaming again?"

"I sure did! I screamed when I remembered what Pat had said about there being another murder if I told on him.

"Of course that five hundred dollars had been on my mind ever since I took it. When I heard that Mrs. Lee was dead, I thought. 'What's the dif' if I keep the money? She won't need it now, and it'll do me so much good.' Besides, I'd hated her. It sort of gave me satisfaction to think I was getting away with her money. But when I got to thinking of Mr. Lee, and how kind he always was to me—well, I knew I couldn't keep the money!"

"So, apparently, did Patterson," observed Mr. Wimble.

Annie eyed him reproachfully.

"Oh, I know you think I was pretty easy, handing money over to Pat like that. But say! You don't argue when a fellow's got his fingers 'round your throat!"

She shuddered. "That's a rotten habit Pat's got into! Besides," and her large, soft eyes begged for understanding, "I kind of thought if I gave him the money he'd be nice to me again like he used to.

"But that check was for my own money. I'd already given the five hundred dollars back to Mrs. Lee."

Corey, at least, eyed the girl with astonishment. In appreciation of the bomb she had just thrown, Annie grinned.

"Sounds sort of spooky, doesn't it? Of course I didn't actually give the money back. But I did the next best thing. I deposited it to Mrs. Lee's credit at the bank."

"You deposited it after Mrs. Lee's death. You weren't questioned at the bank?"

"Well, you see, she was going by the name of Lily Blake at the bank. That made it easy for me."

"Annie," said Mr. Wimble softly, "I humbly beg your pardon."

Annie's teeth flashed in a good-natured smile.

"Oh, that's all right, Mr. Wimble. I don't blame you for thinking I stole the money. After all, I did steal it. It's just that I had the gumption to give it back."

"You had deposited for Mrs. Lee before?"

"No, sir. Until last Monday I didn't even know she had an account. Monday, thinking she was out, I went into her room without knocking and caught her looking at a bank book. I knew what it was, because I have one just like it. 'Oh, do you bank at the Merchants', too?' I said. Say! I thought she was going to hit me, she was so mad. 'You tell a soul that I have a private bank account,' she said, 'and I'll make it hotter'n Hell for you. Understand?'"

"I suppose you mentioned it to Myrtle?" smiled Mr. Wimble.

"Oh, well, say! We're pals. Myrt said it was like Lalla Lee to bleed her husband and then cache away the money to spend on some other fellow. I said I'd try to find out how much she had."

"Miss Dale asked you to find out?"

The girl's face screwed up in distress.

"Why—what do you *mean*, Mr. Wimble?"

"Nothing in particular. It's just a detective's habit to be precise."

Annie's concern lifted. It was obvious that her trust of Mr. Wimble was nearing full bloom.

"I forget whether Myrt asked me to, or whether I just said I would. We were only curious. You know how girls are. It was while I was at Myrtle's Tuesday that I mentioned it.

"I lied to you, of course, about not being in Mrs. Lee's room again after hanging up her coat. When I decided to bank the money, I went there to get her pass book. I had a good idea where to look for it, because I remembered seeing her trying to hide it Monday in a magazine with a red cover."

"Does Miss Dale think you make a good detective?"

Again anxiety twisted Annie's features. She pressed forward in her chair.

"Why—what do you *mean?*"

"You told your friend you'd find out how much money Mrs. Lee had in the bank."

"Oh, that!" Annie leaned back with a sigh of relief. "I haven't seen Myrt since then."

"It didn't occur to you to turn Mrs. Lee's pass book over to her husband?"

"Yes, sir. But, if Mrs. Lee was really getting money from him to spend on other men—well, you know how hard Mr. Lee's taking her death. I didn't want to be the one to tell him about her secret bank account."

"I see. I'd like you to turn the bank book over to me, Annie. You may present your bill for ten dollars."

"Say! Thanks! You want me to get it now?"

"Please. And you might dispose of this at the same time."

He handed her the check he had taken from Patterson.

When she was beyond earshot, Mr. Wimble said: "So Annie is in the employ of Myrtle Dale."

Corey nodded, gratified that he too had arrived at this conclusion. Not that the girl's distress at Mr. Wimble's probing in that direction had not fairly shouted out the fact! Something in the affairs of the late Lalla Lee had been of paramount interest to her friend Myrtle Dale. How would O. W. go about finding out what this was?

When Annie returned with the pass book, Mr. Wimble made no effort to glean this information from her. Perhaps he felt that the limit of the girl's veracity had been reached.

The bank book recorded twenty-five deposits. The first amount, one thousand dollars, had been entered seven months previously; the last, five hundred dollars, on Thursday, the day Horace had seen Annie at the bank. The largest sum entered was five thousand dollars deposited on July seventh. The deposits totaled some thirty thousand dollars.

"Have you any recollection of what happened on July seventh, Annie?"

"Yes, sir; I have. For two reasons. In the first place it was my birthday. In the second, that was the last happy day I spent with Pat. It was our day off. Mrs. Lee knew it was my birthday and asked me how I was going to celebrate. I said I guessed Pat would take me out somewhere. You see, I didn't realize then just how far things had gone between them. She burst out laughing in the nasty way she had when she was up to something, and sent for Pat. She told him, as long as he had a previous engagement, she'd get Mr. Panella to help her with her business.

"Pat was mad, but I thought it was only because of the way she'd snapped at him. I didn't dream he was jealous. He made me believe Mrs. Lee had been chasing him, inviting him to parties at Myrtle's, and everything. Myrt hadn't told me he'd ever been to her place. That made me sore; so to get even with her I never said a word about Renzo going out with Mrs. Lee."

"You're sure he did go out with her?"

"Well, I heard her ring him up and invite him to help her transact a little piece of business downtown."

"Do you know what the business was?"

"Not exactly. I kind of remember something about 'traveling expenses,' though. I don't know just what; but I'm sure when she was talking to Renzo over the phone she used the words 'traveling expenses'."

18

Mr. Wimble being the sort of gentleman he was, his next call on Myrtle Dale was bound to be preceded by a short visit with Mrs. Blackmore, the tristful manager of the apartment house.

In reply to his inquiry, Mrs. Blackmore dismally assured him that since last seeing the detectives her neuralgia had kept her "walking the floor".

Mr. Wimble produced a drug store package.

"I've had a prescription duplicated for you that my sister once found helpful."

Mrs. Blackmore's mournful countenance momentarily brightened.

"Why, how kind of you!"

Mr. Wimble made a gesture deprecatory of her gratitude.

"I only hope it proves beneficial."

The mere fact that he had been so thoughtful as to bring the medicine had already reduced Mrs. Blackmore's pain.

Upstairs, Miss Dale's unlovely servant, whose name was Dorcas, informed the detectives that her mistress was not yet up, but that if they wished they could wait in the "lib'ary." Mr. Wimble replied that they had come early expressly in order to have a little talk with Dorcas herself before seeing Miss Dale.

"You only wasted your time, then. I have nothing to say."

Dorcas had a peculiar way of speaking. She would run along at a fairly good clip until reaching a period, when she would stop an exceptionally long time before continuing. Her conversation put Corey in mind of an accommodation train with its tiresome waits at innumerable way stations.

"Well, I'll leave you my card, anyhow," said Mr. Wimble. "You girls sometimes change your minds."

Corey reflected that Dorcas must have been a girl about the same time that Mr. Wimble had been a boy.

Obviously activity did not begin early in Miss Dale's household. The library was in a state of disorder. Corey noticed particularly that the waste paper basket was full to overflowing. Apparently Myrtle's desk had undergone a spring cleaning the night before.

The detectives had been waiting several minutes when something in the waste paper basket caught Corey's eye. He stooped over and extracted from the basket a piece of pink paper.

Mr. Wimble gave a warning cough. Without stopping to consider whether or not appropriating something out of a waste paper basket constituted theft, Corey plunged the pink slip into his pocket.

A moment later Miss Dale, charming in a mauve lace *peignoir,* entered the library.

"I trust we didn't get you up," said Mr. Wimble.

"Time I was getting up. Lolling in bed makes a person fat!"

Mr. Wimble grinned.

"I'm never up later than six in the morning myself!"

"After this I sleep till noon!" laughed Myrtle. "Well, commence! I always enjoy looking out of the window."

Mr. Wimble chuckled. He really *liked* Myrtle.

Though habitually Mr. Wimble interrogated in an easy, complacent manner, occasionally he shot out a question so abruptly that it seemed to come as an entire sentence rather than as a series of words. The first question he put to Myrtle produced this effect.

"How did Mrs. Lee and Sharl get along?"

"Like a couple of strange—"

Mr. Wimble laughed.

"You didn't look out of the window quickly enough, Miss Dale. 'Like a couple of strange bulldogs', eh?"

Myrtle pouted prettily.

"You have a way of making every innocent remark I utter sound so serious that I'm afraid to open my mouth!

"Naturally Sharl was a little jealous of Lalla. He'd always come first with Mr. Lee before. As for Lalla, to begin with she didn't like niggers; and then, you see, we used to tease her about her domestic staff. We said she didn't keep very stylish servants for a 'multi-millionaire's' wife. Of course, Walt's not exactly in the multi-millionaire class, and he hasn't any social position to live up to; but for fun she decided to make Sharl wear butler's livery. And he refused. They had a regular set-to about it. Needless to say Sharl won. Mr. Lee always gave in to her in everything except when it came to Sharl. Naturally Sharl and Lalla weren't on any too friendly terms after that."

"Why didn't you tell me Annie'd been here on Tuesday?"

Myrtle smiled tauntingly.

"Why didn't you ask?"

"I'd like to speak to you about Annie sometime," said Mr. Wimble. "As a friend, not as a detective. Right at present Annie's not looking upon Patterson any too favorably; but Annie's a girl who changes her mind easily. I don't want Annie to marry Patterson."

"I don't think there's much danger. Pat thinks he's miles above Annie since Lalla took him up."

"But there won't be another Lalla to take him up in a hurry, and he might reconsider Annie."

"Well," promised Myrtle, "I'll meet you halfway on any subject that doesn't concern Renzo."

The buzzer in the entrance hall, sounding three times, interrupted the conversation.

Myrtle eyed Mr. Wimble a bit doubtfully.

"That's Renzo, now," she said.

"Quite opportune for us. There's something I want to ask him. Shall I interview him in or out of your presence?"

"In, if you don't mind. It'd be interesting to hear something that concerns Renzo first-hand for a change, instead of getting his interpretation of it later."

Renzo, perfumed and, despite his protestations of grief for Lalla, gaily accoutered, was shown into the library. As he bent over Myrtle's hand, the look of devotion on her face was rather pitiful.

"Miss Dale," said Mr. Wimble, "we came here this morning to get you to tell us what happened on July seventh."

"July seventh! Lord, man! I can't remember that far back."

"It was Annie's birthday, if that recalls anything to your mind."

Apparently it did.

"Oh, yes! That's the day I found all that money in your pocket, Renzo. Remember?"

"That's the day you went through my pockets like a fishwife," amended Renzo malevolently.

Myrtle bit her lip, but she did not lose her temper. Evidently she wished Renzo to appear in as favorable a light as possible.

"He'd played the races, the naughty boy!"

Mr. Wimble turned to the Italian.

"Did Mrs. Lee win, too?"

Myrtle glared suspiciously at Renzo.

"I wasn't with Lalla," said the dancer.

"I believe I must refresh your memory, Mr. Panella."

Panella asked rather more hastily than he habitually spoke: "Hadn't we better retire to another room? I'm afraid all this discussion is painful to Miss Dale."

"Damn considerate all of a sudden!" was that lady's pert comment. "Miss Dale listens in!"

Panella shrugged.

"As you will. But don't blame me if you get hurt."

O. W. continued his inquiry.

"Then you admit being in Mrs. Lee's company on July seventh, Mr. Panella?"

The dancer yawned.

"I understood that you were about to refresh my memory, Mr. Wimble."

"Very well. On July seventh Mrs. Lee asked your advice about some business she wished to transact."

"Well?" queried Panella lazily.

Mr. Wimble turned to Myrtle.

"Did you know that Mrs. Lee had been converting her jewels into cash?"

"Why, no!"

"Then of course you couldn't have known that Mr. Panella got a handsome commission out of the sale of her emerald to Mr. Fox. I dare say Mrs. Lee would have received more than five thousand dollars for her emerald if it had not been for the size of Mr. Panella's commission."

"Business is business," retorted Panella, his eyes glittering. "Gianni pays poorly. Abe Fox was grateful to me for bringing him a customer. Lalla lost nothing."

"So that's where you got all that money!" snapped Myrtle. "Races, my eye!"

"Naturally, Mr. Panella had to tell you some specious story to keep you from learning about his and Mrs. Lee's—traveling expenses," said Mr. Wimble quietly.

Myrtle, her face distorted by rage, wheeled toward Panella.

"You lollipop!" she screamed. Her fury was at such a high degree of temperature that it did not occur to anyone to laugh. "You'd go week-ending with Lalla, would you? After I'd been paying your bills for months!"

"The day Lalla sold her emerald was the happiest day of my life," drawled Panella.

He became very drowsy.

"It was the first time she had ever kissed me."

Myrtle sprang forward, as if propelled by some mechanism.

"I'll exterminate the bug!" she shrilled. If her metaphors were becoming mixed, at least her fury remained unadulterated.

Mr. Wimble stepped between them. He said something in a low voice to Myrtle which calmed her. He afterwards told Corey what it was he had said.

"Lalla wasn't the kissing kind, Myrtle. You know it. Panella is only trying to punish you for putting him in a false position before us."

The Italian addressed Mr. Wimble.

"I have already told you that Lalla and I were perfect dancing partners. For months I had been trying to persuade her to join me on a European tour."

He glanced mockingly toward Myrtle.

"But for the fact that she—met with an accident, Lalla would have gone to Paris with me."

Myrtle, since her outburst, had been quietly weeping into her folded arms. But, at Panella's last words, she reared back her head like a snake's.

"You fool!" she cried bitterly. "Do you imagine that Lalla cached away all that money in the bank so she could run off with *you?* Why, you were nothing but her catspaw! She intended going off with—"

With a rapidity one would not have dreamed him capable of, Panella leaped out of his chair and sprang at Myrtle. Covering her mouth with his hand, he fairly spat out the command:

"*Corpo di Cristo!* Keep your mouth *shut!*"

"Whew!" breathed Corey, as the detectives drove away from Miss Dale's. "I'm glad to be out of there!"

"Yet by going we learned of 'Mr. G'."

Myrtle of course had been on the point of mentioning somebody's name when Panella had clamped his hand down on her mouth. But how O. W. had made out the name as beginning with "G" was beyond Corey.

"I take it you didn't read the pink slip you filched from the waste paper basket," said Mr. Wimble.

So that was the answer to the enigma! Corey reached into his pocket. The paper was gone!

"I considered it wiser to leave the paper where you found it," said Mr. Wimble. "So, during the fracas, I took it out of your pocket, read it, and dropped it back into the basket. You will be interested to learn that it was a bill from Annie on a form similar to those she sends us, for a 'telegram from G., L. A. . . . $5.00.' Undoubtedly it was to keep herself informed as to what was going on between Lalla and this 'Mr. G.' that Myrtle had hired Annie's detective services. I think I'm safe in saying '*Mr. G*', as the fair Lalla doesn't seem to have wasted much time on women."

"You think it was this 'Mr. G.' Miss Dale was about to mention when Panella stopped her?"

"No. I *hope* it was!"

Corey realized that he was being warned not to let his imagination run away with him. At the same time, O. W. was giving him to understand that a valuable clue had been unearthed.

19

Corey Webb, leaving the booking agency with two airplane tickets to Warrenton, Virginia, in his pocket, wondered how Mr. Wimble had managed to expedite matters in the old days before hopping off in a 'plane was almost as commonplace as boarding a train. No doubt he had transacted some of his investigations by wire. Which must have entailed considerable regret on O. W.'s part, thought Corey with a smile more tender than he realized, his chief doting so on the personal contact.

When he reached the office, Corey found a young man waiting in Willy's anteroom. Upon seeing Corey, the young man sprang to his feet with the exuberant announcement:

"Well, here I am, Mr. Wimble! Chad Rucker!"

Corey was more used to being hailed by the gushing query: "Oh, I say! You are Dixon Dalyrymple of Hollywood, aren't you?" than being mistaken for a real man. Needless to remark, he was immediately prejudiced in Rucker's favor.

And at first sight there was considerable prejudice to overcome!

Chadwick Rucker was the living example of what a mail order house will do to you if you don't watch out. His clothes were the color of a tin roof gone rusty. His collar was the kind lighted matches send up in smoke. Only a catalog complex could account for his doughnut-colored buttoned shoes. And the least said about his tie the better!

Yet Rucker's badly cut clothes could not wholly conceal the muscular strength of his body, its vitality and perfect health. His eyes looked as if his thoughts were clean; and he did not stint in his smile.

Corey liked Rucker's firm handclasp, the humorous twinkling of his eyes upon learning of his mistake.

As Corey passed into the inner office, he wondered who Rucker was and why he had come.

A few minutes later Mr. Wimble entered.

"You don't realize who the boy is, son?"

"I seem to remember hearing his name somewhere."

"Your memory needs a wet nurse," teased Mr. Wimble. Simultaneously with the gibe, Corey recalled where he had heard Rucker's name.

"Annie's country beau!"

"Exactly. I *like* him. Don't you?"

"I certainly don't see how she could have tolerated Patterson after Rucker!"

"There's no accounting for tastes," sighed Mr. Wimble. "I understand that trepangs are esteemed by the Chinese for making soup. However, I've felt all along that Annie was all right underneath. When she mentioned his name, I sent young Rucker a wire: 'What's Annie worth to you?' He answered: 'Fighting for.'"

"You don't think he's too good for her?"

"No. I *like* Annie!"

Mr. Wimble had followed his first wire with another, briefly explaining the situation, and asking Rucker to come on. And now the lad was actually sitting in Willy's office, waiting to hear from Mr. Wimble how he best could serve the girl he loved.

"Myrtle has agreed to take him in hand," Mr. Wimble told Corey.

"Myrtle?" O. W. certainly moved in mysterious ways!

"Why not? She's really fond of Annie—hates to see her riding for a fall as badly as we do."

He chuckled.

"Myrtle says: leave it to her and we'll be sleeping with wedding cake under our pillows."

Later, when Chad Rucker had joined the detectives in their private office, he was quite open about his love affair.

"I've always aimed to marry Annie. I've been opposed all along to this acting bee she's got in her bonnet; but I thought she'd better sow her wild oats now 'stead of later. Seems to 've taken a littler longer'n I s'posed it would," and a tinge of yearning in his voice told how much he had missed the girl. "It's high time now she was coming to her senses."

But Chad had a perfect understanding of Miss Robinson. He was quite willing to listen to Mr. Wimble's suggestions as to the proper method of procedure. Which is why, greatly against his inclination, he agreed to make no attempt to see Annie until given permission by Miss Myrtle Dale.

20

Mr. Wimble was not so fatuous as to discount the element of chance. In fact it always entered into his calculations. At the conclusion of the Lalla Lee murder case, however, he denied that chance had been accountable for the ease with which he and Corey had learned the thirty-year-old story of Sally Eugénie Randall and her servant, the young black Charlies—Charlies Randall he was then, though later, before being nicknamed Sharl, he called himself Charlie Lee.

"For," said Mr. Wimble, "the bigger the town you live in, the less you know about your neighbors. Inversely, in a place like Vineville, that's so small it isn't even on the map, everybody knows about everybody else. Most people like to talk and," making a little *moue,* "I like to listen. What more do you need for educing information?"

The two detectives left Saturday afternoon by air for Warrenton, Virginia, the closest landing field to Vineville being located at that point. As the 'plane took off, Mr. Wimble looked as calm as the picture on an airplane company's advertising folder of a gentleman traveling by air. Corey looked less so. He'd forgotten his Mothersill's!

By the time they reached Warrenton, Corey was beginning to think that the detective game wasn't everything it was cracked up to be. His relief was intense, therefore,

when O. W. said there'd be no sense in pressing on to
Vineville at that late hour, only to return to Warrenton
to sleep. He'd do some "paper work" tonight, he said, and
they'd run over to Vineville in the morning. He advised
his assistant to have a bowl of soup and go to bed. Corey,
turning a little green, declined the soup. But he went to
bed.

The next morning he felt fit again. Looking down from
his hotel window to the railroad station labeled WARREN-
TON across the street, he decided that being an assistant
private detective was great stuff after all.

Beside the station stood a line of taxicabs. From his
window Corey saw Mr. Wimble in earnest conversation
with an ancient negro occupying the driver's seat of a
dilapidated surrey at the end of the line. Both the horse
and the driver were wrapped in tattered gray blankets.
Corey had been told at the airplane booking office in New
York that there was no public conveyance from Warrenton
to Vineville, so had been prepared for some other means of
transportation. But why on earth, when there were plenty
of automobiles handy, did O. W. select such an antedilu-
vian equipage as the surrey?

However, the antiquated rig was hired; and when Corey
went down to breakfast he found O. W. ordering a cup of
warming coffee for its driver, whom he addressed as Uncle
Joe.

Mr. Wimble's small attention delighted the old darky.
Only those who understand why some Americans stand up
when they hear "Dixie" will be able to gauge the measure
of Uncle Joe's appreciation by his query: "Is yo'-all f'om
de South, suh?"

Before starting for Vineville, Uncle Joe removed his
horse's blanket. The poor nag looked as if he had one foot
in the grave, displaying more bones than Corey had realized a horse possessed.

But the old negro felt no qualms as to the beast's ability.

"White Foot ain't no Fyord, but he gits thar! Step in, gen'l'men. Mah name ain't Uncle Joe ef White Foot don't have yo'-all in Vineville in an houah!"

In thus boasting of the animal's ability to cover the five miles to Vineville in an hour, Uncle Joe was displaying optimism of the first water. However, in the solving of the murder mystery, the information gleaned by Mr. Wimble during the ride proved of such value that he did not regret the time consumed in making it.

The detective had been wise in his choice of so ancient a Jehu. According to Sharl, Walter Lee and his body servant had left Vineville thirty years ago and had not returned since. None of the younger drivers, from among whom Mr. Wimble had selected Uncle Joe, would be likely to know, or to remember if ever they had heard, anything about the pair.

Although Uncle Joe at present resided in Warrenton, he had lived the greater part of his life in Vineville. He assured the detectives that nothing of any importance had happened in Vineville that he didn't know about.

And yet, at the very outset, when O. W. asked him if he recalled a young negro there by the name of Sharl Lee, the old man discouragingly announced that to his knowledge no family called Lee had ever settled in Vineville. Considering the horde of Lees inhabiting the State of Virginia, this was a bit of hard luck.

It evolved that the leading citizen of Vineville was one "Colonel" James Randall, married, with three grown daughters. When asked if he had ever worked for the Colonel, Uncle Joe laughed nervously.

"Ev'y cullid pusson 'roun' hyah has wukked fo' Cunnel Ran'all!"

It seemed that the Colonel was a severe taskmaster, and his employees rarely stayed long. According to Uncle

Joe, Randall considered the Emancipation Proclamation a myth.

Uncle Joe possessed a sunny disposition. A discussion of Colonel Randall was not conducive to cheerful conversation. The old negro was about to change the subject when a distressing incident took place.

White Foot habitually obeyed his impulses. When it occurred to him that it would be pleasant to stop for a little rest, he stopped. He was at present in the grip of such an impulse. That he had chosen for his resting place the center of the road near a sharp turn was not in itself alarming, as so far during the journey the surrey had not met a single vehicle. But, simultaneously with White Foot's determination, an automobile swung around the curve.

Later, Corey remembered that the only thought occurring to him at the time was that White Foot was the bravest steed he had ever seen. Most horses, under like circumstances, would have considered Doom upon them. White Foot did not so much as flop an ear! It was on the return journey, while passing this same spot in the road, that Uncle Joe vouchsafed the information that White Foot was a sound sleeper.

Fortunately the machine had slowed up at the turn, and was able to stop within a few inches of White Foot's nose.

The driver flung himself out of his car.

"You damned old nigger!" he thundered. "How dare you block the road with your damned old wagon?"

Uncle Joe quaked in his blanket as, pacifyingly, he quavered:

"Ise gwine git out of de way imeejit, Cunnel Ran'all! Mah name ain't Uncle Joe ef I isn't! Giddyap, thar, White Foot!"

But terror muffled the old man's voice, and the surrey did not budge.

James Randall was a huge man, past fifty, although his hair was still coal black. He was no doubt handsome in a heavy way when not mad with fury. He had a voice that boomed like a cannon. And at present he was bearing down on the trembling Uncle Joe with the ferocity of an angry bull.

Upon reaching the surrey, Randall, utterly disregarding its passengers, tore the horsewhip out of its rack.

At that moment there flashed a streak of gray between the car and the surrey. A timid-looking little woman stood beside the big man, her hand placed restrainingly on his arm.

"James!" she implored.

For a moment the Colonel stared down at her in amazement. Then his face reddened to such a degree it looked ready to burst. Freeing his arm, he faced the little woman. Menacingly, he raised the whip. The expression in his eyes was diabolical. Whether or not he intended punishing Uncle Joe later, his present intention was to deal with this frail woman who had dared defy him.

Corey leaped from the carriage. But the honors went to Mr. Wimble.

The tip of the raised whip, flung backward over the Colonel's shoulder, came within easy reaching distance of Mr. Wimble's hand. O. W. took hold of it and pulled. In his rage, the Colonel had gripped the whip as if he meant never to let go. When O. W. pulled on it, Randall had time neither to release his grasp nor to resist.

In another minute he was experiencing the indignity of lying flat on his back on the Vineville road.

A gasp issued from the automobile. Three young women peered from the back seat, their faces livid with fear. Uncle Joe had sunk into his blanket up to his battered headgear. And the little woman, whom Mr. Wimble had saved from a public horsewhipping, looked so on the point of collapse that Corey hastened to her side.

The rescuer himself sat quizzically gazing down at the fallen giant who, by this time, was struggling to a more dignified position.

When his eyes fell on the benevolent-looking little gentleman who had thrown him, Randall regarded Mr. Wimble much as the Giant of Gath must have looked at David, before the latter arranged it that Goliath never should look at all.

The trembling little woman made several attempts to speak. She finally managed it.

"Oh, James! You're covered with mud and you've left your hat in the road."

It required real bravery for her to try to divert his attention from Mr. Wimble. But James ignored her. He was intent on the man who had felled him.

"How dared you?" There was a great deal of wrath in his voice and some curiosity.

"It doesn't take much courage to attack a man who fights women and old men," said Mr. Wimble.

Randall's hand shot out. It was his intention to throttle the man who had just insulted him. But Mr. Wimble, who had been toying with one of his business cards, calmly placed the small square of cardboard in the Colonel's outstretched hand. So simple a cause as fleeting curiosity may prove the downfall of a warrior. The moment he read Mr. Wimble's card, Colonel Randall was defeated.

"Detective?" he glowered suspiciously. "What's a detective heading toward Vineville for?" It was obvious that the man immediately connected the visit of a detective with himself, if only for the reason that he considered himself the sole person of importance in Vineville.

Mr. Wimble glanced significantly at the little woman in gray.

"Perhaps to investigate charges against a certain Colonel Randall for cruelty toward his wife. Or perhaps," he
hesitated slightly, "for an entirely different reason. At any
rate, he is heading toward Vineville, and if Colonel Randall will kindly move his car to one side, he will proceed."

The Colonel was alarmed, and his fear induced him
to pocket his indignities. Taking his wife by the arm, he
returned to the automobile. As with affected gallantry he
helped Mrs. Randall into the car, a faint scream escaped
her. Mr. Wimble's compressed lips told Corey that the
same suspicion he was entertaining had occurred to O. W.
—that the Colonel's mock courtesy had masked a nasty
pinch on Mrs. Randall's arm.

No doubt fearing that her rescuers might act on such a
suspicion, the little woman hopped out of the car.

"Oh!" she cried, trying to repeat the scream. "You've
forgotten your hat, James!" A little package of the real
thing, Mrs. Randall!

Randall's hat was lying near the surrey. As Corey handed it to her, Mrs. Randall directed a swift, beseeching
whisper in Mr. Wimble's direction:

"Don't judge him too harshly, sir! He had a terrible
sorrow in his youth."

Uncle Joe was so shaken by the encounter that Corey
offered to take the reins.

"Don't trouble, suh! White Foot goes by hisself."

Nevertheless, as it required some manipulation to pass
the Colonel's car, Corey forced his services upon the old
man until the curve was rounded.

Jogging along on the last lap to Vineville, Uncle Joe
gazed at his surroundings with new interest, sniffed the air
with enjoyment, eyed White Foot as proudly as if the nag
were one of Ben Hur's fiery steeds. In a word, Uncle Joe
acted exactly as he would have acted had he recently risen
from the dead.

21

When Uncle Joe had fully regained his calm, Mr. Wimble asked him for the story of Colonel Randall's early tragedy. Uncle Joe would sooner have talked about Beelzebub himself; but one does not question the whims, morbid though they be, of one's deliverer. And Uncle Joe firmly believed that, but for the intervention of Mr. Wimble, he would have met his death that day on the Vineville road.

So he told the story.

Jim Randall inherited too young. Or perhaps it was in his destiny to come a cropper, no matter what the circumstances. At any rate, upon succeeding to his father's property, he changed from a gay, lovable lad, whose worst traits seemed only a youthful recklessness and a greediness for fun, into a young demon.

"The Vines," the stately, pillared mansion of the Randalls, became the scene of orgy after orgy. Young James Randall was rarely sober and during his short intervals of sobriety was sullen and ill-tempered. Dogs snarled when he approached. Children ran.

Of course he neglected the property. But what was worse in the eyes of those who had known his father's pride, as the squandering of his inheritance reduced him financially, he began to sell portions of the estate. The first sale records the birth of Vineville.

With one accord the negroes who worked on the place had adored "ol' Marse Ran'all," Jim's father. They stayed with young Randall as long as they could bear his ill treatment of them. Among the last to leave was a young darky called Charlie.

Charlie, on his knees, used to pray that something would happen to drive the "debil outen Marse Jim."

When one day Jim brought the lovely Sally Eugénie home from Creole New Orleans as his bride, it seemed as if this prayer had been answered. No one had ever seen young Randall so charming, not even before the advent of the devil. All of the servants adored Sally Eugénie, not only for having brought about the change in Jim, but for her own sweet, shy loveliness.

But Sally Eugénie had only cast a spell over the devil; she had not driven him away. One day the spell was broken. Debauchery became the word used to describe the daily life of James Randall.

And on Sally Eugénie's face appeared the wistful expression of a girl whose dreams are broken.

Of course all the negroes saw and sympathized. But it was the young black Charlie who, learning that the old plantation songs entertained her, found a hundred chores to do within singing distance of Sally Eugénie. Charlie who, seeing a smile curve her lips when he laid some young thing in her arms, borrowed every new puppy and every new pickaninny on the place to take up to the "big house." Charlie, who always knew of a dogwood tree in blossom somewhere to show her, of a bird building its nest.

Charlie's was the devotion of a faithful dog. But Jim Randall chose to misunderstand.

One day agonizing screams sent Sally Eugénie racing into the orchard. There she saw something that killed the last vestige, if not of the love—for strange is the heart of woman—at least of the respect, she had borne her husband. Lashed to a tree was young Charlie, stripped to the waist. And, ruthlessly beating him, was Jim Randall.

A cry: "No, no, Jim! No!"—and the girl was at the tree, her soft white body acting as a shield for the screaming negro. And never was Charlie Randall—Charlie Lee—Sharl—to forget the pressure of Sally Eugénie's soft white body, as blow after blow from her husband's whip across her tender shoulders flattened it against his own bleeding back.

The girl's silence shamed Charlie into stifling his own terrified whimpering, so that he heard when Randall went away, hurriedly, as if frightened by the ghost of his dead conscience.

When Charlie felt Sally Eugénie's body slip to the ground, it seemed hours before he could free himself, secured hand and foot as he was. But he managed it, and at last got Sally Eugénie back to a fluttering sort of consciousness. Had he been a dog, he would have licked her poor torn back. Being a man, he did better than that.

James Randall never saw his wife or his servant again.

At this point Uncle Joe's narrative ceased.

"Reckon he he'ped her 'scape." And that was all.

No; he had never heard of a Walter Lee. Warrenton, unlike Vineville, harbored Lees. There was a Jefferson Davis Lee, an Ezekiel Lee, an Obidiah Lee, an Alexander Lee, a Robert E. Lee—Lees white and black—but no Walter Lee. There might be someone by that name among the "po' white trash" of the town, but certainly not among the "fine" or the "cullid" folks. Strange how feeble a hold Democracy, in the true sense of the word, has on the human imagination!

By this time, Uncle Joe's rickety conveyance had reached Vineville.

Vineville had never become a real town. Doubtlessly Warrenton would some day spread in that direction and incorporate it. The town was made up of small farms, each an early sale of young Jim Randall's. A General Store, including a post office, comprised Vineville's business district. Warrenton offered the nearest school and church. Corey remarked with pleasure that there was no picture palace in Vineville.

Uncle Joe of course had many cronies in the negro section of the settlement. Assuring his passengers that, after a little nap, White Foot would be perfectly able to carry them back to Warrenton, he went off in search of his friends.

The detectives entered the General Store.

They found the proprietor a simple, easy-tempered fellow in the late thirties by the name of Herb Dorsey. Herb's eyes fairly popped out of his head upon learning that he was in the presence of private detectives. Lowering his voice, he inquired if their business had anything to do with Colonel Randall.

"It's always the detective who asks for information," said Mr. Wimble, in reply to which observation Herb drawled:

"Reckon it's the Colonel you're after, all right!"

Apparently Randall was the big frog in the small puddle of Vineville.

"I'd like to know who was skunk enough to put you wise to that still, though," frowned Herb. He would have been the most surprised individual on earth if Mr. Wimble had been cruel enough to enlighten him.

"Is your indignation due to the fact that liquor is so rare around here," smiled Mr. Wimble, "or are you so fond of Colonel Randall you hate to see him get into trouble?"

"As for your first question," replied Herb, his eyes alight with fun, "what you don't know can't hurt you."

His fists clenched.

"I'd see the Colonel to Hell an' gone if it wasn't for Mrs. Randall and the girls."

An anxious note crept into his voice.

"I don't guess he has any income except what he makes out of that still. I believe Mrs. Randall brought him right smart of money when she married him; but he must have got through that long ago. Lawdy! I hate to think of what'll become of Mrs. Randall and the girls if you run the old man in. Unless—"

The facial expression most difficult for a man to disguise is the one that accompanies his thoughts of "her." It is a look at once as beautiful as Notre Dame in the moonlight and as pathetic as a moulting hen. Herb's face now wore it.

"One of the Misses Randall?" inquired Mr. Wimble softly.

"Yes, sir, Miss Grace. She's a—a peach, sir! But I'm only the son of a grocer. What's the use of dreaming?"

The South is truly the Kingdom of America!

"To tell the truth, Dorsey," said Mr. Wimble, "we're down here on an entirely different matter, something that perhaps you can help us with. As far as we're concerned, the Colonel's source of income is safe."

So it turned out to be Herb Dorsey, as an expression of his gratitude to Mr. Wimble, who finished Uncle Joe's story.

With that hospitality for which the South is famed, Herb invited the detectives to luncheon. During the meal he told them what he knew about Sally Eugénie and the young black, Charlie.

When Herb was a child, his father owned a grocery store in Warrenton, employing one clerk, a young man called

Walter Lee. Walter, unlike most Virginians, at least
according to their own accounts, was not an F. F. V., but
of lowly origin, of meager education. He occupied two
tiny rooms above a drug store, earning a little extra money
by answering the druggist's emergency bell at night.

Walter was a quiet, unassuming chap, not a general
favorite. But he had a way with children, and young Herb
adored him.

Suddenly, even to the child, it was noticeable that a
change had come over Walter. Herb said he had often
thought about it since. Walter's nature had been like a
dark, quiet room. All at once it became gay and bright,
as if someone had come along and flung up the shade and
opened the window, letting in laughter and sunshine.

One day, shortly after Herb had remarked this change,
a woman customer stayed after closing time to speak to
the boy's father. When Herb heard Walter's name mentioned, he hid behind a molasses barrel and listened. The
woman voiced a vile insinuation against Walter, which the
boy was old enough to understand. Of course he didn't
believe it, but thought it best to caution his friend. He
went to Walter's rooms. . . .

He found a young woman living in Walter's flat!

Dorsey had stopped talking.

Mr. Wimble said: "That must have been a large shock
for a small boy."

"The next day I asked my dad to put me in long pants.
I felt too old to be wearing knickerbockers any longer. Of
course there wasn't a grain of truth in the story the gossip
had told my father. Walter and Sally Eugénie explained the
whole thing to me. I remember how proud I was to be tak-
en into their confidence, how solemnly I swore to guard
their secret from Colonel Randall."

One night a colored boy knocked at the door of Walter's little flat, begging him to open the pharmacy. His young mistress was sick, he said, and needed immediate attention.

When Walter got downstairs, he found Sally Eugénie in a deplorable condition. He suggested a hospital, but the idea so terrorized her that he did not insist. The girl even refused to have a doctor. Walter administered to her as well as he could. As there were no conveniences whatever in the drug store, he offered her one of his rooms. He and Charlie arranged beds for themselves on the floor of the adjoining room. The girl's gratitude was pitiful, and very beautiful.

Walter felt as if an angel had dropped through Heaven into his humble flat.

The next morning Sally Eugénie was delirious. Charlie came out with the whole story, begging Walter to aid them. Walter believed himself chosen by God for the very purpose. He knew a doctor whom he could trust. By changing shifts, he and Charlie managed to give Sally Eugénie what care she needed. After a severe illness, she pulled through.

Had Jim Randall wished to get Sally Eugénie back, she might have been traced to Walter Lee's flat. But a perverted sense of pride prevented him from pursuing a woman who had "eloped with a damned nigger." So Sally Eugénie was left unmolested.

The trio had planned, of course, to leave Warrenton as soon as Sally Eugénie regained her strength. Upon learning through Herb that they were attracting notice, they considered the time propitious.

So a few days later Sally Eugénie and her two squires left for New York.

Herb had neither seen nor heard of them again. But the whole thing had made such an impression on his mind that he remembered it as if it had happened yesterday. He could even tell the day of his friend's departure, because Walter had left the boy his copy of "Robin Hood," in which he had inscribed the date. Next April third it would be thirty years since Walter Lee had gone away.

He did not know whether Sally Eugénie still lived or not. Colonel Randall's second marriage had taken place a sufficient number of years after her disappearance to render it legal.

Why the present Mrs. Randall had ever married the Colonel was a mystery to Herb Dorsey. Perhaps she had entered matrimony in the same spirit that prompts a person to become a missionary or a lion tamer: an inborn desire to effect reform.

As far as Herb could make out, the Colonel had married Mrs. Randall in order to have someone to bear the brunt of Sally Eugénie's infidelity.

The doctor who had attended Sally Eugénie being dead, Herb believed himself to be the only person who knew that Walter Lee had sheltered her. The Colonel didn't appear to know that such a person as Walter Lee had ever existed. Occasionally, when in his cups, Randall would make some reference to the elopement of his first wife with her "nigger paramour." But, respecting his promise of secrecy to Walter, Herb never entered into the conversation.

A gray blanket appeared in the doorway.

"Bettah git stahted, boss, ef we's to git to Wa'enton befo' dahk."

"All right, Uncle Joe," said Mr. Wimble. "We'll be right along."

As he shook hands with Dorsey, he said kindly: "If I were you, I'd speak to Mrs. Randall about Miss Grace. She must know by this time that a girl'd be far better off married to a son of a grocer than to a son of a gun.

"And now we must be off." He smiled. "White Foot can't see in the dark."

The detectives caught the week-end special back to New York. Travel by air is not conducive to conversation. Noise and, in the case of some junior detectives, nausea interfere. Mr. Wimble referred but once to the Lalla Lee affair.

"You will recall Marie's mentioning Mr. Lee's habit of laying flowers on her daughter's grave every time he goes to the cemetery. I shall not be surprised if we learn that the name on the headstone of the grave Mr. Lee goes to visit is Sally Eugénie's."

22

On his way to the office the next morning, Corey was feeling decidedly blue-Monday-ish. His few hours' sleep the night before had been fitful, broken by dreams appertaining to the Lalla Lee murder. In his dreams the case had assumed the form of a drop of Lalla's blood which he was examining through a magnifying glass for facts, the facts appearing as hideous wriggling bacteria.

With only two more days remaining, Corey wondered how "One Week" Wimble meant to justify his reputation. He longed in some way to help. And yet in verity, as in his dreams, he was confronted by a conglomeration of baffling facts, baffling not because out of them he could construct no tenable theory but because he could construct several.

When Corey reached the office, he saw that Mr. Wimble's desk was littered with scratch paper covered with penciled zigzags, chevrons and lozenges. O. W. probably had been there at daybreak, no doubt was out now getting a bite of breakfast. His sister claimed that during a case O. W. slept at the office. This was not precisely true. Mr. Wimble often spent the night there but not for the purpose of sleeping.

When Mr. Wimble returned he was accompanied by Dorcas, Miss Dale's maid, whom he had overtaken on the way up. Nothing in Dorcas' expression indicated to Corey what her business was. In fact, facial expression had little chance of fair play on a physiognomy like Dorcas'.

"Hello, son!" Mr. Wimble greeted his associate. "Bad dreams get you up early?"

At Corey's start, he laughed.

"It was your own paleness around the gills and not my perspicacity that prompted my question. Sit down, Dorcas. Dorcas has changed her mind about making a statement," he told Corey.

Dorcas explained: "Miss Dale was quarreling with Mr. Panella about his carrying on with Mrs. Lee behind her back.—'Lord!' she said,—'I bet you make love to *Dorcas!*'—'No,' said Mr. Panella,—'I draw the line at totem poles!'—And then they laughed."

So wounded vanity accounted for Dorcas' change of heart! Perhaps nobody in the world but O. W. had ever guessed that Dorcas possessed any vanity to be wounded.

"I'm sorry we're getting your evidence at the price of your happiness," said Mr. Wimble.

"I'm glad to give it to you, Mr. Wimble.—You've always been polite to me."

"Both times you showed us into Miss Dale's library, you left the door slightly ajar. I presume you were listening behind it?"

"Miss Dale told me to, sir."

"Well, it'll save time now. Just skip the facts and confine your remarks to correcting Miss Dale's flights of fancy. You can tell us, for instance, whose slippers those were I found under the couch."

Corey stared at his chief. O. W. grinned back elfishly.

"The moment you set eyes on Panella you realized, of course, that the slippers that Miss Dale claimed were his were much too small for him?"

Corey hoped he didn't look as big a fool as he felt.

So, religiously observing her sentential pauses, Dorcas gave her account of what had transpired at Miss Dale's on the day of the murder.

Early Tuesday morning, Dorcas, who had always profited by her mistress' late rising to get in a few extra winks herself, was awakened by the doorbell. Not fully awake, under the impression that she was hearing Panella's signal, she answered it. Miss Dale's caller turned out to be a young man Dorcas had never seen before. He was carrying a suitcase.

He was rather an effeminate-looking young man, though perhaps the fact that he was pale and nervous made him appear more so than he actually was. He was about twenty-eight or thirty, had curly blond hair and wore stylish clothes. And he had exceedingly pleasant manners.

When Dorcas informed the young man that she certainly had no intention of calling her mistress at such an unearthly hour—it was then nine o'clock—he was most affable.

"All right, Cherry. Suppose you just let me stretch out on the sofa till she gets up."

Dorcas admitted wearing a cherry-colored dressing gown at the time, repeating that the young man had very agreeable manners.

However, as Dorcas was not the sort to leave strange young men lying around on sofas, she decided to risk Myrtle's displeasure by announcing the visitor.

When Myrtle saw the young man she looked ready to faint.

"'Goatie'! Why have you come to New York?"

"Goatie" was the only name Dorcas heard the young man called during his visit.

"To keep Lalla from coming to Los Angeles," said "Goatie."

Miss Dale warned him against saying anything further in the presence of the servant.

"Goatie" was shivering, and as they went out of the room Miss Dale teased him about wearing such a lightweight overcoat at that time of the year.

"I suppose nobody owns such a thing as a fur coat in 'Sunny' California?"

"A fellow doesn't need a fur coat when he's in Hell," replied "Goatie" gloomily.

And then the door shut behind them.

When Dorcas got dressed, she went into the library, where Miss Dale and "Goatie" were "talking a blue streak," to ask them when they wanted breakfast. She overheard a scrap of their conversation.

"I think I ought to see Lalla!" said "Goatie."

"Well, I don't! Walt's the person to see. He's the only one who can manage Lalla, and you know it!"

The young man declined food. He was stretched out on the sofa; Myrtle advised rest.

"You look all in. Why don't you take a snooze, 'Goatie'? I'll go see Walt."

"O. K. by me!"

So Miss Dale got dressed and left the house. When she had gone, Dorcas took the young man a cup of hot coffee.

"Thanks, Cherry. You're a darn good scout. I seem to have caught cold on the train. I catch colds easily since the time in France my gas mask didn't work."

There was a polite young man for you! Not at all like Mr. Panella, who arrived a little later in a very bad humor demanding breakfast.

Dorcas, who disliked Mr. Panella, saw no reason for confiding in him. She therefore did not enlighten him when he made some remark about it being unnecessary to disturb Myrtle; nor did she mention the presence of the young man in the library. She merely laid a place for Mr. Panella in the dining room and served him breakfast.

While he was eating she went to see how the polite young man was getting along. To her dismay, he was nowhere to be found.

After awhile Miss Dale returned. She was furious upon finding "Goatie" absent.

"The fool! He's gone to Lalla's! He'll ruin everything!"

Renzo, hearing Myrtle's voice, came out of the dining room. Whatever explanations Myrtle favored Renzo with later, all that was said in Dorcas' presence was that "Lalla's friend from out West" had arrived.

In about an hour "Goatie" returned. He had been to see Lalla, he said, but unfortunately she had gone away for the week-end and had not yet returned. "Goatie" was wearing Panella's fur coat. He had seen it hanging in the hall and, hearing enough of Panella's and Dorcas' conversation through the dining room door to know that the coat would not be needed before his return, had borrowed it. He apologized most charmingly to Mr. Panella for his "taking ways."

Myrtle told "Goatie" that Mr. Lee wished to see him at his office. As Renzo had a dance number to rehearse at Gianni's, the two men left the apartment together. Dorcas did not see Panella again till the afternoon, but "Goatie" returned for luncheon. He seemed less nervous than he had been earlier in the forenoon.

After luncheon he took his suitcase and left the house. Miss Dale accompanied him.

They had been gone a quarter of an hour or so when Panella's signal sounded. Dorcas pressed the button that automatically opened the entrance door of the apartment house, but nobody came up. As Mr. Panella was supposed to be at Gianni's at that hour, Dorcas assumed that somebody with the same signal had pressed the wrong doorbell, and thought nothing further about it.

One thing more. That evening she overheard Mr. Panella and Miss Dale discussing the murder.

"With Lalla dead," lamented Panella, "I'll be out a lot of sugar!"

"Sugar!" cried Myrtle bitterly. "My God! Suppose it was your *daily bread?*"

When O. W., with the gallantry of a Raleigh piloting his Queen across a mud puddle, had shown Dorcas out of his office, he made a bee line for a scratch pad. It was well filled with geometrical designs before he spoke.

"I wonder what Lalla Lee was up to Tuesday that she took such elaborate pains to make Patterson and her husband believe she was calling on Miss Dale? For, without doubt, it was she who rang Myrtle's bell, knowing that Panella's signal would insure her a speedy opening of the door. Entering the building, she must have remained in the lobby long enough to allow Patterson a few minutes' leeway so that Mr. Lee would be out of the way when she reached home. Then, slipping out, she hailed Jenks and drove to her back door. Her appointment with John Hathaway was not until four o'clock. Obviously she had some important and mysterious plan for the early afternoon. Did all her cunning, all her secretiveness, merely result in making things easier for her murderer?"

23

Mr. Wimble and Corey lunched on Saturday at Gianni's.

Mr. Gianni ran a very smart establishment. With its shaded lights, soft music and predominance of tables for two, it smacked of *rendezvous*. Its cabaret was entertaining. Its cuisine was excellent.

But what guaranteed the restaurant's success was that Gianni personally superintended its operations. He was a veritable Argus in his ability to see what was happening in several places at once, a trait by the way that did not endear him to his employees.

As a rule, more for business reasons than by temperament, Gianni was a genial host. He would stand in the foyer welcoming his guests, bowing to some, jollying others—always with just the right word for each.

But on Saturday, when Mr. Wimble and Corey arrived at the restaurant, Gianni's customary cheer was sadly lacking. Distress marked him for its own. Indeed, if it had not been for the fact that he was entirely bald, one would have said that the little man was on the point of tearing his hair.

As Corey once told his mother, beauty parlors had no monopoly on face lifting. O. W. was a past master in the art of shortening long faces.

Gianni's certainly called for treatment on Saturday.

Mr. Wimble began by introducing himself.

"I'm the detective who called you up the other day. And this is my assistant, Mr. Webb."

If possible, Gianni's face fell still farther. And his hands actually did soar to his head; though, for want of hair, he had to content himself with beating his scalp.

"Oh! Oh! Oh! Oh!" he bleated.

Gianni's boast, he finally stopped bleating, excitedly and with many gestures to explain, was that not once during his career, either before or after the passing of the Eighteenth Amendment, had the finger of scandal so much as pointed in the direction of his restaurant.

A Pagliaccian laugh escaped him.

"But *now!*" Never could an Anglo-Saxon infuse a word of his own tongue with so much desperation as the little Latin introduced into that borrowed adverb.

Passionately he invoked all of the Roman saints whose names he could recall on the spur of the moment to look down and see for themselves the policemen infesting his once respectable restaurant.

Mr. Wimble saw a glimmer of light. Of course, under normal conditions, a lunching copper, if he remember his table manners, is not scandalous. But O. W. recalled what Panella had said about Gianni's detestation of notoriety attaching itself to his employees. The telephone inquiry no doubt had filled his mind with dire forebodings. And now the thing he dreaded most was upon him: an arrest within the sacred confines of his restaurant.

Mr. Wimble did his best to placate the little Italian.

"We're not policemen, Mr. Gianni. Our visit here today is unofficial. Having made the acquaintance of Mr. Panella, we were desirous of seeing him dance; that's all. We certainly shall not force our patronage upon you if you find it in any way distasteful!"

But Signore Gianni had had his say and was feeling better. Besides, Mr. Wimble's gracious manner, his sympathetic smile, were soothing. The Signore calmed down.

"It's that young man from the Police Department who upset me," he confided. "About half an hour ago he came hopping into my restaurant like a grasshopper. From the first, I did not like that young man's looks. 'A table near the door,' I thought, 'so that if anything happens . . .' But no! 'I must have a table near the exhibition stage,' he said, and brought out an official badge larger than himself. But come," once more the host, "I shall point him out to you as I show you to your table. You will agree with me that such a figure mars the appearance of any well-ordered establishment."

As O. W. and Corey had guessed from Gianni's description, the police detective in question turned out to be Horace Pickering.

"Hello, Pickering!" Mr. Wimble greeted his confrere. "So you, too, are lunching among the gourmets?"

Horace's nearsighted eyes peered in the direction of the platform, and he lowered his voice.

"I have come to watch Lorenzo Panella."

"Oh! You're fond of dancing?"

Horace looked as painted as his memory of Chief Detective Callahan's eye on him would permit.

"I'm investigating Lorenzo Panella," he said stiffly.

"You've lost interest in Annie Robinson, then?"

"Not at all! Not at all! It is because of Annie Robinson, precisely, that I'm studying the dancer.

"Mr. O'Rourke invited me to his boarding house for luncheon yesterday. We spent the afternoon discussing crime. From Mr. O'Rourke's observations he has come to the conclusion that, for the most part, crimes committed by women are motivated by jealousy. Lorenzo Panella is the type of man a girl like Annie Robinson would admire. It is possible that she killed Lalla Lee through jealousy."

Mr. Wimble permitted himself a slight smile. After all, Horace was very nearsighted.

"Then you've relinquished your theory that Annie stole the emerald?"

"Not at all! Not at all! But I have sufficient respect for Mr. O'Rourke's opinions to investigate the jealousy motive."

He solemnly concluded: "A jealous woman makes the Devil green with envy."

"Another view held by the illustrious Mr. Doolittle?"

"No, sir. That remark may be credited to me." He modestly added: "I flatter myself that I turn a neat phrase."

"Neat," said Mr. Wimble, as he indicated to Corey, who by this time was on the verge of convulsions, that they would now proceed to the table Gianni had reserved for them, "is hardly the word!"

When Panella came on, his appearance was greeted by an extravagant burst of applause, though it was noticeable that most of the handclapping was done by women. Panella's performance was indifferent, but his popularity among the women patrons was unmistakable. No doubt it was for the latter reason that Gianni kept him.

When he saw the detectives, the dancer's spineless body momentarily tautened. At the conclusion of his dance he glided to their table.

"Still finding smudges?"

"No," replied Mr. Wimble pleasantly, "we're finding smudgers, now,"

Alarm flickered for an instant in Panella's somnolent eyes. Then, with a shrug, he made his languid way to the next table.

Mr. Wimble and Corey were beginning an exceptionally well prepared meal when O. W. directed the latter's attention to the doorway. Myrtle Dale, escorted by Chad Rucker, was entering the restaurant.

An up-to-date haircut and a fairly good-looking ready-made suit had effected a vast improvement in Rucker's appearance. Corey noticed that not a few feminine glances followed Myrtle's companion.

With gratification, Myrtle, in turn, noticed that the dancer's eyes were also on young Rucker. Renzo's eyes had become a bit jaundiced lately. Not that Myrtle deceived herself as to the reason for this phenomenon. Renzo's jealousy dated from the moment he had learned that she was an heiress. Myrtle knew that it was her money, not her charms, that Renzo feared she might bestow on some other gallant. But even left-handed jealousy was an agreeable change from the old order of things.

Myrtle's scheme for the reconciliation of Annie and Rucker was to make Annie jealous, with herself in the role of seductress. She knew, however, that Chad was far too straightforward a chap to be able to play his part convincingly without some rehearsals. He and Myrtle, Saturday afternoon in the Dale library, had been in the midst of one of these rehearsals when Panella had walked in.

Myrtle, with quite the most delightful sensation of her entire affair with the Italian, had looked into Renzo's eyes and seen jaundice setting in.

Myrtle was fond of Mr. Wimble and fully intended helping him make a match between Annie and Rucker. But, until it was necessary to turn Chad over to Annie, she saw no reason why she shouldn't make use of him in playing up to Renzo's jealousy. So she had not revealed to Panella Rucker's identity.

Myrtle was in a radiant frame of mind as, in the wake of Gianni's head waiter, she passed the detectives' table.

"Don't forget that I'm giving a fancy dress party at my place tonight!" she reminded them.

As Chad came abreast of the table, he made a wry face.

"I need air!" he said, sotto voce.

The service at Gianni's was such that you could "eat"
or dine. In other words, you could consider your meal as
so much food to keep the machinery going; or, like a foreigner, you could look upon it as a rite to be performed
with all due ceremony.

The detectives "ate" and, a little after one o'clock,
found themselves outside the restaurant.

Corey was becoming accustomed to the apparently random way in which his chief went about collecting clues.
But, when Mr. Wimble announced that they were next to
visit Mr. Lee's office for the purpose of picking up some
information concerning "Goatie's" identity, it did seem as
if O. W. were rather overworking the theory of Probabili-
ties. According to Corey's reasoning, Walter Lee would be
the last man on earth likely to know anything about the
man with whom his wife had planned to run away.

However, it was with great interest that he accompanied Mr. Wimble to Mr. Lee's office.

Mr. Lee maintained two small rooms on the third floor
of a downtown office building. The door to one of the
rooms was marked: THE LEE STORES—PRIVATE, the
other bearing the legend: THE LEE STORES—ENTER.

As they approached the latter, the sound of muffled
sobbing reached the detectives. An extraordinary sound to
emanate from a business office, to say the least!

Mr. Wimble pushed open the door, motioning Corey
to follow.

At a desk, her fists pressed against her eyes, sat a woman
weeping.

"I beg your pardon," said Mr. Wimble, "are you Mr.
Lee's secretary, Miss Martin?

The woman raised her head. To their surprise the detectives recognized the little woman they had discovered a
few days ago weeping in Miss Dale's corridor.

24

"It is our misfortune again to intrude upon your grief," said Mr. Wimble contritely.

"Mr. Lee will not be back for an hour." Miss Martin's tone plainly embodied their dismissal.

Sometimes during the investigation of a crime Opportunity knocks at the investigator's door. This was such an occasion. Mr. Wimble took advantage of it.

"We're aware of Mr. Lee's habit of playing a game of solitaire after his luncheon and arriving here at two. We did not expect to find him. It was you we came to see, Miss Martin. My name is Wimble. Mr. Webb is my assistant. We're private detectives."

Miss Martin received this news in a surprising fashion.

"If you don't mind," she said, "I think I'll powder my nose. Crying does unbecoming things to noses."

Her grief had been real. The rapidity with which she recovered her poise, therefore, was rather remarkable. Still, a person amounts to little in the business world unless he possesses self-control. And Mr. Lee had vouchsafed the information that Miss Martin was an able secretary.

Corey glanced toward Mr. Wimble; but the face of that gentleman wore an unfathomable expression.

"Well," said Miss Martin briskly, "that's finished. Now, what is it you want to see me about?"

"I want you to tell us everything you know about Miss Myrtle Dale."

"I haven't the least intention of betraying my employer's confidence."

"Mr. Lee is our employer, too, at the present moment, Miss Martin."

"He did tell me he had detectives working on the case," she admitted.

"So he surely wouldn't wish you to withhold any information from us?"

"He might if he realized just what information it is that I possess," she retorted bluntly.

"We found no such punctilio in Myrtle," observed Mr. Wimble.

A short, bitter laugh escaped the secretary.

"After all, with Mrs. Lee no longer here to learn of it, Mr. Lee probably doesn't care if his affair with Miss Dale leaks out or not."

Her voice grew tense.

"I'd give my right hand to be able to wipe this past week out of my life!"

Her lips trembled piteously.

"It was cruel of Mr. Lee to send me to Miss Dale's! He might at least have spared me that."

"Are you sure he knows you care for him?" asked Mr. Wimble softly.

Miss Martin flushed. "He couldn't have been around me for ten years without sensing at least the respect I had for him."

"Didn't your respect for him get a bit of a jolt when he married Lalla Blair?"

"No. I was surprised at the type of woman he chose; but, though his marriage was sudden—he went off on a business trip and returned with a wife—that was honorable. This other thing is not."

"You had never seen Miss Dale before her visit here on Tuesday?"

"No. Mr. Lee's women come into my life very suddenly," she said, with a twisted smile. "Of course, I knew vaguely that Mrs. Lee had a friend named Myrtle Dale, but I'd never dreamed there was anything between her and Mr. Lee."

"Miss Dale was agitated when you saw her?"

"Very. I told her I'd find out if Mr. Lee could receive her. She said: 'Oh, he'll receive Myrtle Dale all right!' Something in the proprietary way she said it told me that she had a stronger hold over Mr. Lee than was warranted by the fact of her being his wife's friend. And of course everything she said in Mr. Lee's office backed up my suspicion."

"Will you please repeat what she said in Mr. Lee's office?"

"Mr. Wimble! Is that necessary? You must realize what a painful subject it is to me!"

"Please, Miss Martin."

"I don't recall all of her words verbatim. But their meaning is burnt into my brain. Of course I eavesdropped. It seemed that there was some man willing to marry her, a man with an Italian name—it's slipped my mind just now. But unfortunately it was her money that was Miss Dale's chief attraction in the Italian's eyes. And Mr. Lee was supplying the money! Naturally, her allowance from him would stop if she married another man.

"'You're rich, Walt,' she said. 'You'll never miss it!' She told him he didn't know what it would mean to her to have a husband of her own instead of some other woman's for a change. And: 'I'm not getting any younger,' she said. 'I'll never have another chance.'

"She swore she'd never disclose what their relationship had been. 'I'll never squeal, even if you don't give me another cent. I swear it! But be good to me, Walt! Be good to me!'

"That's all I heard. All I could bear to hear. I went out into the dressing room and remained there till Miss Dale left."

"Then you didn't hear Mr. Lee mention his will to Miss Dale?"

"No. After Mrs. Lee's death he drew up a codicil to his will transferring to Miss Dale what he had intended leaving to his wife. He sent me to Miss Dale's apartment with a copy to show her."

"Did Mr. Lee have any other callers on Tuesday?"

"Before he went out to luncheon some man came, but I don't know who it was. Callers who have definite appointments with him often enter Mr. Lee's private office directly from the hallway, without passing through my office."

"Did you ever hear of a chap called 'Goatie'?"

"'Goatie'? No, not that I remember."

"Now, Miss Martin," said Mr. Wimble pleasantly, "will you please show us what you slipped into your desk drawer when you so cleverly got Webb at least, if not me, to turn his head politely while you powdered your nose?"

Miss Martin flushed to the roots of her hair. "Oh, please, Mr. Wimble! My—affection for Mr. Lee entails some loyalty!"

"After all, those stockings might have belonged to his wife," said Mr. Wimble quietly.

"You saw them! Yes, they might have belonged to Mrs. Lee," returned Miss Martin truculently, "but it's hardly likely."

Opening her desk drawer, she took out a pair of crumpled beige silk hose and tossed them over to Mr. Wimble, who stuffed them into his pocket.

Miss Martin said: "I found the stockings in a box of receipts I was looking through." Her voice quavered. "I guess he'd forgotten they were there."

"I've tired you, Miss Martin!" said Mr. Wimble contritely.

The little secretary smiled wanly. "It's just that I haven't been sleeping well lately."

A sound in the inner office announced that Mr. Lee had returned.

"I'll tell him you're here," said Miss Martin, turning to her desk phone.

The detectives were invited to step into Mr. Lee's private office. The furnishings of this room, as of that occupied by Miss Martin, were on the order of the roll-top desk in Mr. Lee's home, plain and practicable. Apparently Lalla had been Walter Lee's only luxury.

"You haven't come to report success!" said Mr. Lee.

"Unfortunately, no," replied Mr. Wimble. "We just dropped in to get a little information. We're endeavoring to learn the name of a chap who is called 'Goatie'."

"I'm afraid I can't help you," replied Mr. Lee regretfully. He smiled faintly. "I'm sure I'd remember such a name if I'd ever heard it before."

Mr. Wimble shrugged, as if the matter were of scant importance.

"By the way, Mr. Lee, have you examined Mrs. Lee's desk since Tuesday?"

"Yes. When you asked me to search for the missing emerald, I forced open one of the drawers with my pocket knife. I found nothing but some photographs, however, which I left as they were."

With a glance at his watch, Mr. Wimble arose.

Mr. Lee accompanied the detectives to the door. He said to Mr. Wimble: "I cannot begin to tell you how eagerly I shall be waiting the news of your success tomorrow."

Mr. Wimble looked uncomfortable, as always when the conversation touched on his professional skill.

"You shall be the first to know," he promised.

"Just why," asked Corey, as he and O. W. drove back to the office, "are women so prone to doubt the men they love?"

"Usually because the men are unworthy of their trust," retorted Mr. Wimble. "However, I feel as you do about Mr. Lee. Miss Martin no doubt reported in good faith what she overheard; but I see no grounds whatsoever for her assumption. Myrtle is confessedly in love with Panella; and absolutely nothing in Mr. Lee's simple mode of living points to 'another woman' in his life."

As they entered the office, Willy greeted them with the announcement that Annie Robinson was on the wire, demanding Mr. Wimble.

There was not the faintest trace of Diane Adair in the voice that reached Mr. Wimble over the telephone. It was that of a badly frightened little girl calling for help.

"Oh, Mr. Wimble, come quick! Mr. Pickering's taking me to prison!"

25

Horace Pickering envied Willy O'Rourke his job. Waiting outside Gianni's for Renzo to appear, Horace pictured his friend comfortably writing at his desk in a warm, quiet office. Willy, in the performance of his duties, thought Horace bitterly, was never exposed to cabarets and cold weather.

Horace had not enjoyed his luncheon. In the first place Gianni, an enormous napkin slung over his arm, had stationed himself beside Horace's table from which spot he had not budged till Horace's departure. The idea of the napkin was that if the police detective sprang into action Gianni could screen the ignominious spectacle from his guests. Its effect on Horace was the feeling that, if he made the slightest move foreign to the requisites of eating luncheon, he would be instantaneously bagged.

In the second place, Horace had never cared for music with his meals. Especially jazz. If Hell could be set to music, Horace imagined that jazz would be the result.

Despite these drawbacks, however, the luncheon had not proved a total loss. Horace had visited Gianni's for the purpose of learning something about Lorenzo Panella, and during his meal he had learned considerable. He had witnessed the ovation accorded the dancer by the women.

And his waiter had told him that Panella's weekly gifts from the ladies far exceeded the salary Gianni paid him.

Assuming Annie to be in love with Lorenzo—and from the carryings-on of the females about him it appeared to Horace that every woman who came in contact with the dancer straightway began casting sheep's eyes at him—perhaps she had stolen the emerald as a love offering to lay at Panella's feet. Maybe the dancer had actually forced the girl to crime in order to gain possession of the jewel. From all appearances the creature certainly wielded an astonishing power over women.

At any rate, Horace decided, if he were sufficiently diligent in his sleuthing, Lorenzo, like a honey guide to a bees' nest, would eventually lead him to the emerald.

So at two o'clock, which was the hour he had learned from his waiter that Panella got off duty, Horace was shivering outside Gianni's, prepared to trail the dancer.

Shortly after two Panella appeared. He had lingered a few minutes beyond quitting time to make a telephone call. Apropos of this telephone call, he now headed toward Park Avenue. Horace followed.

It seemed at first as if the Italian intended going to the Lee house. But, one or two blocks this side, he turned off of the Avenue on to a side street. Half-way up this byway, to Horace's subsequent dismay, his quarry entered an ice cream parlor.

Horace's dismay lay in the fact that, when he had followed Panella into the interior of the shop, he felt it incumbent on him to order something, and he had already eaten a great deal more than was good for him.

Panella seated himself at a table in one of a number of booths lining the rear wall. Pickering stationed himself in a booth adjoining. His elaborate maneuvers to effect this move unnoticed by Panella focused the attention on him of everyone in the place, including the dancer. There was no danger of Renzo recognizing his shadower, however. Though Horace did not realize it, Gianni's vigilance at the restaurant had served him well. For Renzo, of late having discovered a distinctly hostile look therein, had been avoiding his employer's eye as much as possible. Thus at luncheon, in averting his gaze from Gianni, he had also overlooked Pickering.

Over a strawberry ice cream soda, Horace heard Panella in the next booth telling the waitress that he expected a friend. Horace felt in his bones that this friend would turn out to be Annie Robinson, so hiding behind his newspaper he awaited her coming.

It is well known, of course, that the Fates sometimes play practical jokes. Be that as it may, in a few minutes Miss Robinson entered the ice cream parlor and joined Mr. Panella.

Although Horace had been expecting the girl, Annie's actual arrival so excited him that instead of sucking he blew through his straw. He therefore missed the opening words of the couple in the next booth. So sure was he of the business that had brought them together, however, that this loss counted as nothing in his mind.

"So that's the 'important business' you wanted to see me about!" Annie was saying when Horace had finished removing strawberry ice cream soda from his face. "Well, I haven't got it!"

"Naturally not on your person!" replied the dancer scathingly, "but you can lay your hands on it all right, and the sooner you give it to me the better. Don't try any foolishness with me, my girl! And remember, Annie! I don't want Myrtle in on this. Understand?"

Pickering's ensuing history shows what is liable to happen if you take the wrong cue.

Curiosity alone had brought Annie to the sweet shop in response to Panella's telephone summons. She had never liked Renzo and at this moment was liking him rather less than usual. She was accordingly about to take her leave when Police Detective Pickering hopped around the partition and changed her plans.

When she saw Horace, Annie screamed. Or, to be more accurate, she screamed when she saw the revolver he was brandishing. For Horace had decided that the occasion demanded firearms.

The occasion, in Horace's mind at least, was the capture of two murderers. Several customers of the ice cream parlor never did get it through their heads just what it was that Horace was up to.

As usual, something happened the moment Annie screamed. In this instance, the store became bedlam. Some of the patrons, most of whom were women, when they saw the revolver, rushed to the street. Others decided to stay at least till it went off. Somebody said: "They're taking talkies!" And somebody else suggested summoning the police.

Horace barked: "I'm the police!" And the dignity of the law, if not of Horace personally, caused the uproar somewhat to subside.

"You two are under arrest!"

Someone looked at Annie and called for water.

"What are we arrested for?" inquired Panella lazily. So long as he was surrounded by women Panella could enjoy himself.

"We'll discuss that at Headquarters!" snapped Horace.

Annie suddenly became loquacious in her own defense.

"I don't know about Renzo, Mr. Pickering, but you're certainly making a mistake about me. Honest you are! You may not know it, but I'm Mr. Wimble's assistant. I can prove it!"

She opened her handbag and drew out a check.

"Look at this! It's a check I got from Mr. Wimble this morning. See? It says: 'For professional services rendered'."

Horace was nonplussed. Also a little uneasy. For, at mention of O. W., had recurred to him Chief Detective Callahan's admonition that before taking any decisive step he confer with Mr. Wimble.

Panella, who sensed the little man's misgivings, smiled. Which did not add to Pickering's complacency.

"As we are in the neighborhood," said Horace grandly, "we shall repair to Mr. Lee's, there to confer with my worthy colleague, Mr. Wimble."

"But I must warn you," he sternly advised Annie and the dancer, "that you are in my custody. Any attempt at resistance"—he blinked in an endeavor to capture the phrase—"will be used against you!"

Corey took charge of Annie and Panella, while Mr. Wimble, closeted with the hero in the living room, got Horace to tell him the story of the capture. Mr. Wimble listened quietly until the tale was unfolded, and then proceeded to clear up a few of Horace's misconceptions.

After which O. W. had a heart-to-heart talk with Horace. When it was over, Horace, picking up Mr. Wimble's hat under the mistaken idea that it was his own, said hollowly:

"I should like to bid Marie goodbye."

Gently O. W. substituted Horace's hat for his own.

"After you've spoken to Marie," he said kindly, "won't you go down to my office and see Willy? I believe he has a suggestion to make to you."

Rejoining the others in the reception room, O. W. first addressed Panella.

"We don't need you—yet!"

Panella yawned; then arose and lazily took his departure.

Annie by this time was putting on a more cheerful front. The arrival of Mr. Wimble had done a great deal toward restoring her *sang-froid*. And now, with the dismissal of Panella, it looked to her as if the worst were over. However, she had received a bad scare, and was in consequence in a tractable mood.

"Your holding back information got you into this mess," said Mr. Wimble.

"What I've kept to myself hasn't a thing to do with the case. It has to do with a private matter. Honest it has, Mr. Wimble!"

"Unfortunately, the private matter you mention does have a bearing on the case, Annie. Suspicion surrounds the persons you're trying to shield."

"Gosh! Am I Myrt's 'accessory after the fact,' too?"

"Well, you've been supplying her information about 'Goatie'."

Annie could not have looked more astonished if Mr. Wimble had pulled a rabbit out of her sweater pocket.

"I'll never keep anything from you again as long as I live!" she said. And meant it.

All evasions in her former statements were now dissipated.

Annie had been in Lalla Lee's employ but a short time before realizing that Myrtle had installed her there for a specific purpose. One day Myrtle had offered to pay her for "keeping an eye on" Lalla's correspondence. As Annie had cared but little for her employer and had been badly in need of money, she had agreed. The job had entailed intercepting and turning over to Myrtle outgoing letters written by her mistress and copying for Myrtle all of Lalla's incoming mail.

The espionage had proved simple. Lalla hating letter writing, the bulk of her correspondence had been done by telegraph. Annie had not been able to read the outgoing wires, as usually Lalla had sent them herself from some telegraph office. But, like most persons believing that a paper is safe from prying eyes once it is torn up, she had thrown most of the replies into her waste basket.

Myrtle had never confided in Annie whom of Lalla Lee's correspondents she was so interested in; but in the course of time Annie had guessed and, by tacit agreement with Myrtle, after a few weeks had stopped submitting anything unless signed "G" or "Goatie."

"Did you ever learn 'Goatie's' right name?"

"Yes, sir. Once I found a telegram reading: 'Address me William G. Dorn, General Delivery, Los Angeles.' I took Mr. Dorn to be 'Goatie'."

"Also the 'Billy Goat' whose photograph was missing from among the 'Dead ones'?"

Annie colored, remembering her former loss of memory.

"I lied that time to protect Myrtle!"

She went on: "I figured that Mrs. Lee was in love with 'Goatie', but that he was poor, so she married Mr. Lee for his money."

Annie knew her scenarios!

"Mr. Lee prob'ly didn't know anything about 'Goatie'. Mrs. Lee used to get her mail from him General Delivery under a false name: Miss Lily Blake, the same as she used at the bank. Perhaps the young fellow didn't even know she was married!"

"You gathered all that from their correspondence?"

"Not exactly. You can't tell much from telegrams. But I doped it out, as best I could. He'd keep saying he loved her but couldn't come to New York. That's how I got it into my head he was poor. Then she'd say, come or she'd invite John Hathaway to tea. That puzzled me a lot, until one day I saw Mr. Hathaway's picture in the paper. The paper called him the handsomest man in New York. Then I understood. I knew how she was always playing one man against another, so I figured she was trying to make 'Goatie'

jealous. She succeeded, too, because every time she threatened to invite Mr. Hathaway to tea, 'Goatie'd' come back
with a lot of pie and cake!"

"Did you remove anything from Mrs. Lee's waste paper
basket the day of the murder?"

"Yes, sir."

Annie blushed, remembering her previous falsehood.

"There was nothing in it when I straightened up the
room; but, when I went upstairs later with Mrs. Lee's coat,
I found some scraps of paper. I'd looked in the basket on
purpose, because when I was at her house earlier in the day
Myrtle had given me the dickens for being careless. She
said if I'd found a certain telegram from 'Goatie' I'd have
saved her a lot of trouble.

"The scraps I found didn't make any sense, though.
I have them yet, if you want to see them. I've been too
jumpy lately to clean up my room."

"Please give them to me before we leave. And, now,
suppose you tell us what it was Panella asked you to hand
over to him at the ice cream store?"

"Say! Is that how Horace got it into his head I had the
em'rald? Renzo was trying to get 'Goatie's' address out of
me." She bridled. "But he got fooled! I didn't give it to
him.

"I wonder why he wanted it?" she asked curiously.

To Corey's astonishment, as O. W. rarely favored those
he was interrogating with information, Mr. Wimble answered Annie's question. Corey noticed that he enunciated
very clearly, and spoke simply, as if explaining a lesson to
a child.

"'Goatie' borrowed Mr. Panella's fur coat on Tuesday.
Mr. Webb and I found a sizable smudge of the dye from
that coat on one of the living room chairs. Mr. Panella
knows about the smudge, and it is his belief that 'Goatie'
visited this house on Tuesday, sat in the chair and later

committed the murder. His reason for wanting 'Goatie's' address is—"

Mr. Wimble was interrupted by a crash in the next room. Annie screamed, and Corey, greatly startled, jumped to his feet. But O. W. looked as if he had been expecting something of the kind.

He opened the door into the living room. Across the threshold, where obviously he again had been eavesdropping, in a dead faint lay Sharl.

26

Some time elapsed before the old man could be brought back to consciousness; in fact, Corey was on the verge of summoning a doctor when Sharl's eyelids fluttered. Upon realizing what had happened, frantically the negro's eyes sought Mr. Wimble, his mouth twisting in a painful effort to speak.

"Take it easy, old fellow," said Mr. Wimble. "There's plenty of time for us to hear what you have to say when you're feeling better. Let Annie help you to your room now."

Annie assisted the darky to his feet.

"Mr. Wimble is right, Sharl. Come on." She added, with no sense of being funny: "You're looking quite pale."

"Take him right into his room, Annie," said Mr. Wimble. "See that he lies down."

Propelled by the girl's strong arms, the servant had no alternative but to leave the room.

What remarks O. W. intended addressing to his assistant concerning the negro's seizure were suspended by the entrance of Marie.

The look she fixed on O. W. was reproachful. No doubt she had passed Sharl and Annie in the hallway and suspected the detective of having hectored the old man. It would have conflicted with Marie's ideas as to her proper place, however, to have presumed to criticize.

"You came for Pierre, sir? He's downstairs, all ready."

"Just a word before you bring him up, Marie. Why didn't you tell me that Mrs. Lee and Sharl got along like a couple of strange bulldogs?"

"Mrs. Lee didn't get on well with anybody."

"But she was more unfriendly toward Sharl than anyone else?"

"She didn't like blacks."

"Come, Marie," said Mr. Wimble pleasantly, "surely you care enough for Mr. Lee to want to see the murderer of his wife brought to justice?"

"You don't suspect Sharl, Mr. Wimble!" She was really indignant. "Why, Sharl's a dear old man!"

It was evident that there was a warm spot in her heart for the negro. There is no racial prejudice among the peasantry of France. Sharl would have a happy time on the Durands' Continental farm—if he got there!

"Please, Marie! It will help me a lot in finding the murderer of your employer's wife if you'll try to recall what quarrels you overheard between the two; what threats."

Marie was of a race whose women deferred to men. So she told him what she knew, not without reluctance, however.

"Mrs. Lee hated Sharl. At first, I thought it was because she was jealous of the attention Mr. Lee gave the old man. But it couldn't have been that. Mrs. Lee didn't care for her husband. Sharl avoided her as much as possible. He knew she hated him. When he spoke to her, he was always civil; but she never was to him. She was always thinking up unkind things to say to him. The worse she ever got was one time when he refused to wear a butler's uniform she'd bought him. She was almost beside herself with rage that day. Besides insulting him, she screamed: 'I'll get even with you! You see if I don't! I'll tell! That's what I'll do! I'll tell!'"

"What reply did Sharl make?"

Marie looked troubled.

"He—he threatened her."

"What were his exact words?"

"He said: 'The day you tell you'll die!' I think she was frightened. She never quarreled with him after that; though she kept up her dirty remarks till the end. Remarks about niggers smelling like skunks, and things like that."

"Thank you, Marie."

He smiled: "You'll trust me with Pierre?"

"Why, of course! Why shouldn't I, Mr. Wimble?"

"When you came in just now, you looked as if I were a small boy you'd caught at the jam pot."

"Well, I thought you'd been pestering Sharl needlessly."

"But your better sense now tells you that I was only performing my duty?"

She said, with a flash of wisdom: "I guess, even in the detective business, it's sometimes hard to do one's duty."

While Marie was downstairs getting the boy ready, Annie returned. Her eyes were shining.

"I'll be sending you another bill this afternoon, Mr. Wimble!"

She paused dramatically.

"For discovering 'Goatie's' picture in Sharl's room!"

Although to give Annie pleasure in her coup Mr. Wimble feigned astonishment, he felt none. He had already established a connection between William G. Dorn and Walter Lee's negro servant. And a very close connection. For you do not faint upon learning that someone you know is suspected of murder unless that person is dear to you.

"Better make out another bill for identifying these stockings," said Mr. Wimble, bringing out the beige silk hose he had surprised Miss Martin secreting in her desk drawer. Corey had imagined that Miss Dale's maid Dorcas would be the one called upon for this information.

"They're the kind Mrs. Lee always wore," said Annie, adding with unconscious malice: "Judging from the size of them, they belonged to her, all right!"

Mr. Wimble replaced the stockings in his pocket as Marie, holding a little boy by the hand, appeared in the doorway.

Pierre Durand was a sturdy lad of seven years, with a mop of curly brown hair and large, shining brown eyes. He was French in type though he proved American enough in deportment. Or is it that small boys have no nationality?

Corey believed Mr. Wimble too conscientious a workman to go on a pleasure excursion in the midst of a job. Beyond doubt he hoped to learn something helpful during the ride. Sharl was on friendly terms with the boy's parents. Perhaps, relying on a child's lack of tact, O. W. was counting on young Pierre to let fall something of value to the investigation about the negro.

From his incessant chatter during the hour and a half he was the detectives' guest, it seemed as if the youngster were telling everything he knew. Amusedly Corey recalled O. W.'s favorite injunction:

"Get everyone who is even remotely concerned in the case to talk. The more statements the better. Some stray remark may pop up to help establish the truth."

There was no difficulty in getting the child to talk. Corey felt that Pierre's tongue would be ready for splints by the time the ride was over.

". . . I certain'y like to go out riding, Mr. Wimble. Mr. Lee's going to take one of his cars over to France with him, and when I grow up he's going to teach me to drive. I 'xpect I'll have an airplane by that time, though. I can steer an automobile now. Sharl says I'm smarter'n him. He can't even steer. Mr. Lee can drive, though he gen'rally lets Patterson do it when we go out riding. He says he can answer my questions better when he isn't driving. He says

I certain'y ask a pow'ful lot of questions, more'n anybody he ever knew 'cept one little boy friend he had once. . . .

"What did you say, Mr. Wimble? . . . No, he didn't tell me what his little boy friend's name was. I asked him once and he acted kind of funny. My mother said I wasn't to ask Mr. Lee that question any more. She thinks p'r'aps his little boy friend is dead.

"I'm glad I'm not dead, aren't you? My puppy'd, feel awful if I was dead. Have you got a puppy? My puppy's name is Hans Brinker. He comes from Holland, where they use dogs 'stead of horses to pull the wagons. Do they say an automobile is eight-dog-power 'stead of eight-horse-power in Holland, do you s'pose?

"Mr. Webb's prettier'n you, Mr. Wimble, but you're just as nice as him. What's your face so red for, Mr. Webb? It's the color of my goldfish. Why do they call goldfish gold when they're red? I like the guinea pigs you gave me, Mr. Webb. Only I didn't like the names they had. I call them Mr. Wimble and Mr. Webb instead. My Uncle Goatie says—I'll help you steer if you're tired, Mr. Webb."

This last as Corey brought the car to a full stop.

"I 'xpect with two of us steering we can keep going now!" said Pierre, as he squirmed on to Corey's lap and placed his little hands on the wheel.

The junior detective was red to the ears. Later his chief told him: "I'd have run into a telegraph pole, no less." But at present he addressed his remarks to his guest.

"It's kind of you to help Mr. Webb drive, Pierre. Who did you say your Uncle 'Goatie' was?"

"Uncle Goatie's Mr. Lee. But I don't call him that 'cept in private, only when I forget. My mother says it isn't 'spectful. Goatie is the French for Mr. Lee's front name."

Of course! *Gautier!* Walter, in French, sounding to unfamiliar ears like "Goatie"! Having studied French in college, Corey wondered why he had not guessed as much before.

Could "Goatie", the chap from out West, be related to Mr. Walter Lee?

Corey was bursting to compare his thoughts with O. W.'s, but, recalling the adage concerning "little pitchers", desisted.

Pierre, unaware of what a plum of a clue he had offered his hosts, continued to chatter. Corey relieved O. W. by answering the boy's questions, which now were leading up to a definite goal.

"Did my mother tell you not to buy me any popcorn? Mr. Lee bought me some popcorn once, and it certain'y made me sick. But I can eat lots of other things that don't make me sick 't all. I can eat meat an' 'tatoes. An' ice cream cones. I never get sick when I eat ice cream cones. Mr. Lee always buys me an ice cream cone when we go out riding. That's because he likes little boys. P'raps you don't like little boys?" he anxiously inquired.

Corey assured him that both Mr. Wimble and he liked little boys and, furthermore, that he knew of an excellent ice cream cone stall a short distance along the road.

Pierre did himself gastronomically proud at the ice cream stand; so much so, in fact, that like a healthy young animal, he fell asleep on the way home. He had been "steering", and when Corey felt his body relax and saw his little hands slide off the wheel, he whispered to Mr. Wimble to take the boy.

Instead of sandwiching him between them, Mr. Wimble held the little chap in his arms. Once, glancing toward the pair, Corey saw O. W. looking down at the sleeping boy and wondered why, among so many paintings of Mother and Child, one never saw a Father and Child.

There comes a moment in the solving of a crossword puzzle when so many of the words have been guessed that the filling in of the remaining spaces becomes mere form. As he left the Department of Health, Corey felt that a like moment in the solving of the Lalla Lee mystery was near at hand.

As he was eager to report to his chief, he was annoyed upon reaching the office to find O. W. in conference with Horace Pickering.

"Pickering feels that he can do better for himself in some other walk of life than criminal investigation," said Mr. Wimble. He fixed a stern eye on Corey. "Horace has decided to become an author of detective tales."

"Mr. O'Rourke deserves the credit for my decision," said Horace. "It was he who suggested the idea to me."

"Willy says that the minute he set eyes on Pickering he thought: 'There stands the creator of a second Septimus Doolittle!'"

"I have no doubt," said Horace, "but that the detective springing from my brain will prove as brilliant as Mr. Doolittle."

"Nor have I," said Mr. Wimble gravely.

"Hey!" said Corey, as Horace prepared to go, "that's my hat you have on!"

"And I'm afraid," said Mr. Wimble when Horace had made a second choice, "that the one you now have on is mine."

When Horace, wearing his own hat—that is to say: the one he had brought in with him—had left the office, Mr. Wimble turned with interest to his assistant.

"So Sally Eugénie did have a son!"

Corey eyed his chief in amazement.

"My dear boy," laughed O. W., "I'm only putting two and two together. I sent you to the Department of Health

Building to get a piece of news. You came back looking as pleased as Punch. Could I possibly make anything but four out of that?"

Corey's visit to the Department of Health, of course, had been the outgrowth of the ride with Pierre. And the records had divulged another chapter in the life of Sally Eugénie Randall. Thirty years ago, six months after her flight from Warrenton, Sally Eugénie had died. A few hours before her death, she had given birth to a son. This boy had been christened Walter Lee Randall.

"I think we were both a trifle dense in not identifying 'Goatie' sooner," said Mr. Wimble. "We both know enough French to have recognized 'Sharl' as the French pronunciation of Charles, and from that to have inferred that 'Goatie' stood for Gautier."

"Sally Eugénie was a Creole," Corey remembered.

"I think that 'Goatie' conferred the nicknames," said Mr. Wimble. "We know he went to War. And he was young enough to have brought home some affectations. The Gitanes, for instance. And you will recall that he dubbed Dorcas 'Chérie,' which she took for 'Cherry' as a compliment to her cherry-colored wrapper."

"Look here son!" he broke off, indicating some bits of paper on his desk. "These are the scraps Annie removed from Lalla's waste-paper basket Tuesday afternoon."

Over his shoulder Corey read the note O. W. had pieced together.

You have a nerve coming here! Don't speak to me about offers again that's off. I'll see you later — like Hell! I'm through Please accept this as final

Lalla

"You remember the note Panella sent up to the fair Lalla on Tuesday morning? 'Have had a wonderful offer. If you can't come down now, tell me that you'll see me later—at the same place.'

"This no doubt was the reply she first intended sending down to him before deciding to give him a verbal message through Sharl.

"Now, look at this!"

Mr. Wimble covered the left half of the note, so that what remained was:

Don't speak to me—
I'll see you later—
Please accept this

Lalla

"The note she gave to Patterson with the emerald!" exclaimed Corey.

"Exactly. Half of Lalla's original note was used. Half was torn up.

"Leaving in Mrs. Lee's waste basket the scraps of the half of the note that was torn up was one of those mistakes even the most accomplished criminals are sometimes guilty of."

27

Corey could never afterwards recall Myrtle Dale's party without getting shivers along his spine.

It had been arranged that the two detectives were to escort Annie to the party Monday evening. As O. W. had some business to attend to before going, it so happened that it was Corey who called for her.

In a spirit of deviltry he presented himself at Mr. Lee's back door. He found Patterson lingering disconsolately in the hallway. Patterson had asked Annie to a dance and had been refused on the plea that she had accepted an earlier invitation. He was waiting around, curious to see from whom the invitation had come. It piqued him not a little to learn that Corey Webb was his rival.

When Annie appeared, Corey sustained a slight shock. The girl was wearing a kimono!

"Madame Butterfly!" she characterized herself.

Corey remembered with a guilty pang that Miss Dale's party was to be a fancy dress affair. Myrtle had probably taken one look at Chad's mail order suit and issued her invitations accordingly.

Corey thought Annie a bit buxom for the role she had chosen. However, the color of the kimono, a rich butter yellow, was most becoming to her, as were the yellow chrysanthemums she had stuck into her hair above each ear.

Besides, if the fattest prima donnas undertook "Butter-fly", why not Annie?

Annie criticized Corey for not dressing up.

"I don't think it's very compliment'ry to Myrtle!"

"Can't I say I'm a Gentleman who Prefers Blondes?"

Patterson had been listening to the discussion.

"Why don't you dress your friend up in some of your clothes, Annie? He'd win the prize sure!"

Discretion being the better part of valor, before speaking Patterson had curled his fingers around the door knob. The moment his dart was thrown he slid through the back door and vanished into the night. Annie saw no connection between Pat's unceremonious departure and the fact that Corey was busily engaged in removing his gloves. She was engrossed in the chauffeur's suggestion.

"That's a wonderful idea, Mr. Webb! You can wear my green georgette; and, with a little rouge and powder, you'll look too cute for anything!"

Corey gritted his teeth. But it was not his to reason why. Though having a talk with Rucker would be pleasant, attending Myrtle's party was a matter of duty. He must, of course, go properly accoutered.

So Annie brought down her green georgette, and Corey retired to the pink sitting room to put it on. It was a dress rich in ruffles, a garment Annie with her *embonpoint* would have been wiser to have left in the shop.

As he had his car, Annie insisted on making up Corey's face. Annie had been a lady's maid for a year; to boot, a lady's maid to an actress. When she had finished with Corey, she had done a good job.

She stood back admiring her handiwork.

Corey saw a familiar look dawning in her eyes.

"If you ask me why I don't go to Hollywood," he threatened, "I won't take you to the party!"

They arrived at Myrtle's a little before ten. Dorcas informed them, rather superfluously in view of the clamor issuing therefrom, that the others were in the "lib'ary."

Annie, familiar with her friend's apartment, went off somewhere to divest herself of her wrap. While Corey waited, to his surprise, as he knew Panella's evening shift at Gianni's to be from eight to ten, the Italian sauntered into the hall. In deference to the occasion he was dressed as Bacchus, though to Corey he looked as usual more like a sleepwalker than anything else.

Panella had given up his work at Gianni's—by request. For the strain of entertaining Police Detective Pickering at luncheon had proved too much for the little Signore.

Panella informed Corey that he need not wait for Annie. As he had something of a private nature to say to the girl, he would take her in.

"We'll let Miss Robinson decide who'll take her in," said Corey.

"You don't look much like a bodyguard!" observed Panella.

Corey advanced a step.

"You are referring, of course, to my masquerade?"

"Of course," said Panella, rather hastily.

At this point Annie entered. To Corey's gratification she moved to his side.

"May I have a word with you, Annie?" asked Panella.

Annie eyed him coldly.

"I don't know 'Goatie's' address, I told you!"

There is a South African reptile which when irritated ejects venom from its mouth. Had Panella been one of these snakes, he would have been "spitting fire" at that moment. As it was, the "Shut up, fool!" he spat at Annie adequately served to suggest the analogy.

"Corey Webb and I haven't any secrets from each other," the girl flippantly returned.

"Then no doubt he has told you about Chad Rucker's lunching with Myrtle at Gianni's today."

"Give us a good one while you're about it!" jeered Annie. "Chad's in Iowa!"

"Chad's in the library with Myrtle," corrected Panella.

Annie turned inquiringly toward Corey.

"I believe Rucker is in town," stammered Corey. "But he can explain, I'm sure," he lamely concluded.

Panella laughed mockingly.

"It will be interesting to hear Rucker trying to explain how the provocative Miss Dale swept all thought of—" He took in Annie's Japanese costume. "Of Madame Butter Ball out of his head!"

Corey sprang forward, but before he could lay hands on Panella the latter had slithered out of the room.

"Don't get mussed up killing that!" Annie enjoined her escort.

"Does Mr. Wimble know Chad's here?" she asked.

"I—I think so." It was not for Corey to put his finger in Mr. Wimble's pie.

"Do you know," said Annie, "I believe O. W. had an idea in the back of his head when he sent us to this party together."

"Nonsense! O. W. would have come with us if he hadn't been busy."

Instead of thus dismissing the subject, Corey would have done better to have paid some attention to the card Annie had up her kimono sleeve.

To one end of the library had been rolled a tea wagon. There was as much rapport between tea and this wagon as between books and Myrtle's library; but it appeared to be an exceedingly popular article of furniture.

Myrtle's guests, for the most part, were of the chorus. They were not a bad-looking lot—from the standpoint of pulchritude. They wore, rather unconventionally, the conventional fancy dress costumes seen at every party of the sort. And everybody took particular pains to seem gay.

Somewhat apart from the others sat Myrtle and Chad. Myrtle was dressed alluringly, and somewhat scantily, as Cleopatra. Around one upper arm she wore a wide black sequin band. Throughout the evening there were frequent references to this band as "Dale's mourning band for Blair". The attitude of the late Lalla Blair Lee's associates seemed hard, to say the least. But no doubt their regret was commensurate to her deserts.

Corey, who had not been apprised of Myrtle's *modus operandi,* experienced a slight sensation of distaste upon remarking that Chad was costumed to represent Mark Antony.

The boy made a splendid Roman in his royal purple toga. Moreover, his portrayal of Mark in the presence of the Queen of the Nile was superb. Without an exception, Myrtle's guests believed young Rucker to be madly infatuated with his hostess.

Chad had suggested postponing this part of the act until the arrival of Annie, but Myrtle had insisted that success would be more assured if her other guests were likewise deceived.

Chad was not happy. He did not like Myrtle. In plain, Middle-Western idiom, he considered the woman "fast". And he did not care for her methods—thought her too theatrical. He was beginning to think it would have been the better policy if upon his arrival he had gone straight to Miss Robinson and said: "Now, look here, Annie! It's time you came home!" However, as he had started this monkey business, he might as well go on with it.

He was going on with it when Annie and Corey entered the library. Had Chad been less amorously occupied, Annie in the joy of seeing him again might have forgiven him his luncheon with Myrtle, even if Chad had remembered

Myrtle's instructions to greet the girl without warmth. But unfortunately Annie witnessed a good ten seconds' of Chad's "going on with it" before he saw her, by which time it was just ten seconds too late for his radiant smile upon recognizing the girl he loved to take.

Corey was also a witness to Rucker's attentions to Miss Dale; and, unaware of Myrtle's scheme for killing two birds with one stone, was dumfounded. But remarking Rucker's smile upon seeing Annie, he decided that Chad's gallantry toward Myrtle was merely a gesture authenticating his fancy dress costume.

Corey moved aside in order to facilitate Annie's rush into Rucker's arms. Simultaneously he got his first inkling that something was wrong.

Annie grasped Corey's arm with a grip that made him suspect her of having assisted with the ploughing back home.

"Mr. Wimble'll be furious if you let me down!" she whispered.

What happened next Corey always referred to as "the events leading up to the tragedy". Annie extravagantly greeted Myrtle, complimented her on her costume, admired the decorations, commented on the cold weather they were having,—in passing, noticed Chad: "Oh, h'lo, Chad! What you doing in New York? How's everybody back home?"—and then let loose the thunderbolt!

"You don't seem to recognize my lady friend, Myrt!" she giggled. She turned to Rucker. "This is my fiancé, Chad, Mr. Webb." Nothing worse could ever befall a woman hater!

Corey, in need of a handkerchief, fumbled in a place where there should have been a pocket and found only ruffles.

"I say!" he protested feebly, with an entreating glance at Rucker.

Rucker turned to Miss Robinson.

"What did you say your fiancé's Christian name was, Annie?"

"Corey!"

"Oh! I thought it was Judas!" He hadn't the least notion he'd been anything but sarcastic.

"Which remark settles his hash!" said Corey to himself. And followed Annie to the tea wagon where she had discovered some friends. He was in such a state of nerves that he thought he was staggering; but it was only that he was unused to walking in skirts.

Myrtle of course was under the impression that Cupid had beaten her at matchmaking. Having lost this game, she went on with the one so much more to her liking.

Unfortunately for the maintenance of her own good sense, Myrtle had been too successful in arousing Panella's jealousy. Renzo was in a cold sweat lest the one woman he had felt absolutely certain of slip away from him. And he showed it. Her triumph went to Myrtle's head. Women are extremists. Having made the man jealous, Myrtle now determined to drive him frantic.

Myrtle Dale was an attractive woman. An attractive, experienced woman. Chad Rucker was an inexperienced, clean-minded boy. At present, a very unhappy boy. It sickened Corey to see Chad falling for Myrtle's wiles. . . .

And then Myrtle crossed the Rubicon! Waiting until Panella's smouldering eyes were upon her, she leaned over and kissed young Rucker full on the mouth.

"Oh, *Chad!*" Annie's cry silenced the room. The child probably had never really suffered until that moment.

Her pretty face snow-white, her mouth twitching, she rushed from the room.

Whereupon Corey Webb got rid of some of his pent-up resentment by informing Mr. Rucker in a single breath that only a thick-skulled hayseed, blind in one eye and unable to see out of the other, would have swallowed Annie's bait, hook, line and sinker, the way one Chadwick Rucker had, the poor sap! After which he went in search of Annie.

He found her in the front hall, a yellow heap in a corner.

"I wish I was dead!" she sobbed.

To Corey's relief Rucker arrived on the scene, shame in his eye, apology in the handclasp he silently offered the girl's champion.

Gently Chad raised the weeping girl from the floor.

"Now, look here, Annie!" he said, "it's time you came home!"

Corey decided that, as the real business of the evening was over, there was no longer any need for the green georgette, He started for his car to get the clothes he had left there. As he turned off of Miss Dale's corridor on to the main hallway, he saw Mr. Wimble approaching.

O. W. looked tired; his footsteps lagged a little. This was the eve of the day on which Mr. Wimble was to make known the name of Lalla Lee's murderer; yet there was no elation in his manner. With an odd sense of disappointment, Corey wondered if, for the first time in his career, "One Week" would require an extension of time.

"Great Scott, son!" Mr. Wimble's gasp stopped Corey in his tracks.

"Great Scott!" Corey mentally echoed as he regarded his chief. Had he thought, a minute ago, that O. W. seemed fagged, discouraged? Why, the little man was looking as fresh as a daisy!

With an accompanying feeling of tenderness, it came to Corey what had caused this metamorphosis. For a moment he had forgotten that he was dressed as a girl. He must be looking very much as his mother had looked when young. And O. W. had been in love with Dolly.

"I was on my way to the party, son," said Mr. Wimble. "But I've just changed my mind. Will you please extend my apologies to Myrtle? I have some important work to do!"

"I'm afraid I haven't been much of a help to you, sir."

"My boy," returned Mr. Wimble earnestly, "you've helped me tremendously. This evening, particularly."

28

It was the seventh day of the investigation, the day on which, if he were to preserve his nickname of "One Week", Mr. Wimble must disclose the name of Lalla Lee's murderer.

On his way to the office, Corey encountered Mr. Hathaway.

"Well," asked the District Attorney, "have you two sleuths settled on the Lee murderer yet?"

Corey had to confess that, whatever views Mr. Wimble held on the subject, the assassin's identity was still a mystery to him.

"Mr. Wimble says he doesn't intend doing my thinking for me."

Mr. Hathaway laughed.

"I wonder if O. W. doesn't rather enjoy his little seventh-day surprises?" But the affection in his voice precluded ridicule.

"I'll be around this afternoon to hear the news," he told Corey at parting.

Corey found his chief at the office.

"There'll be a number of surprises for you today, son," said Mr. Wimble, indicating a pile of telegrams on his desk. If the telegrams in question embraced Mr. Wimble's solution of the mystery, his manner, Corey thought, was curiously lacking in exultation.

The first surprise proved to be an early morning visit from Myrtle Dale.

"Well, I made it!" she cried, as shortly after half-past eight she followed Willy into the inner office. Though officially Willy's working day began at nine, a visitor before that hour had yet to be announced by anyone else.

"Bet you're wondering how I did it," laughed Myrtle. "The secret is that I didn't go to bed last night at all. After Webb left, the rest of us went to a night club and then motored down to a roadhouse for breakfast. I stopped in at my place for a shower and a change of duds, and here I am! What do you want to see me for?"

"To have you give your evidence without looking out of the window."

Corey did not appreciate until later just how gingerly Mr. Wimble conducted the ensuing interview. Of course, Miss Dale and O. W. were sympathetically inclined toward each other, which helped. Then, too, Mr. Wimble was not beyond employing a little bluff to further his ends. For instance, the complacent air with which he kept shuffling the heap of telegrams on his desk inferred that they contained everything he wished to know, that Myrtle's statements were merely corroborative.

Myrtle smiled. Then her mouth tightened.

"If it's anything about Renzo you're after, I'll look out of the window till Hell freezes over!"

"Your friend Renzo's been mighty anxious to learn 'Goatie's' address, hasn't he?" inquired Mr. Wimble lightly.

Instinctively, Myrtle's fingers went to her arm where, the night before, she had worn the black sequin band. Evidently, Renzo had been a bit rougher with Myrtle than with Annie.

"Well, what of it?"

"Renzo knows, of course, that 'Goatie' wearing his coat called at Lalla's on Tuesday. From something we let fall in his presence about a smudge on one of the chairs in the Lee living room, Renzo believes that 'Goatie' was in that room on the day of the murder. It is my opinion that Renzo intends blackmailing 'Goatie'.

"Myrtle, the worst kind of crooks look down on blackmailers."

Myrtle eyed him meditatively.

"I don't get you, Wimble. You'd break a leg rather than let your sister meet me; and yet you actually sound as if you care what happens to me."

Mr. Wimble contemplated the telegrams.

"When you let drop that you'd sent your fur coat to a niece in Cabell, Colorado, I had your relatives out there looked up. What I've learned about your sister Nell and her children makes me proud to know you, Myrtle."

He regarded her wistfully.

"I'm sorry about your allowance from Mr. Lee."

Myrtle was startled. But after all she had some ability as an actress.

"I admit it," she returned evenly. "Mr. Lee has been 'protecting' me."

Mr. Wimble toyed with the telegrams.

"Wouldn't it perhaps be more accurate to say that Mr. Lee has been protecting himself?"

Myrtle gasped.

"Now, Myrtle," said Mr. Wimble briskly, "suspicion is strong against you. It is known that Lalla Lee's death made you potentially a wealthy woman. You were absent from your apartment Tuesday at the time the crime was committed. A woman in a brown fur coat was seen entering the Lee house by the rear entrance. According to our witness, this woman was Mrs. Lee in sable. It might easily have been you in mink."

"I realize when the game's up," said Myrtle dully. "What is it you want me to tell you?"

"Everything. Suppose you begin with the allowance Mr. Lee made you?"

"I guess you think my taking money from Mr. Lee to keep my mouth shut about the wedding is next door to blackmail. But, believe it or not, I wouldn't have asked for it. He offered it to me of his own accord. Of course it was rotten of me to accept; but it came so like a godsend! It was a chance to send Nell to a sanatorium. And then, too, I was beginning to realize that I never could hold Renzo on a showgirl's salary."

"Tell us about the wedding."

"It was news that Nell was so sick that decided me to go out to Cabell. I happened to mention at the theatre that I was going; and Lalla asked if she could come along for a little vacation. I didn't know Lalla so very well then, as I was one of the principals in the show, she in the chorus; but I was glad of company. She didn't mention 'Goatie's' name the whole trip. Lalla never did talk the way most girls do.

"So I was surprised when a young fellow she introduced as Walter Lee, 'Goatie' for short, met her at Cabell.

"When I got to my sister's, I found old Nell in a bad way. She'd contracted lung trouble, and I was at my wits' end to know what to do. I was already sending all I could spare out of my salary. My brother-in-law is a preacher in Cabell. The pay he gets is a joke! Not that he does much to earn what he does get. Always burying his nose in some moth-eaten old book. Nell brags that Ben can think in Latin and Greek. If he could think in dollars and cents it would be a load off my chest!

"I didn't see much of Lalla and 'Goatie'; but I understood they'd gotten in with a speedy bunch over at the Springs—Colorado Springs, next door to Cabell—and were staging some wild parties.

"Well, one night I'd been wakened by Nell, who'd been taken with a terrible coughing spell, and had just gotten back to bed, when there came a banging at the front door that sounded as if all Hell had broke loose. I went downstairs; and there was Lalla and 'Goatie', saying they'd come to get Ben to marry them. 'Goatie' was drunk and looked as if he didn't know what he was doing; but nobody'd appointed me his guardian, so I let them in and went up to call Ben.

"Lord! Will I ever forget that wedding? I don't believe poor old Ben really woke up during the entire ceremony. Neither did 'Goatie', though not for the same reason. Nell, who'd come down to act as witness along with me, got another coughing fit in the middle of it. Great little celebration, all right!

"Well, Nell got so bad toward morning we had to send for the doctor, and I didn't think much more about Lalla and 'Goatie' until 'Goatie's' Dad arrived a few days later and made me his little business proposition."

"Just a moment! Did Mr. Lee actually say he was 'Goatie's' father?"

"Well, no; I don't believe he did. He just said he was Walter Lee, and his name being the same as 'Goatie's' I took it for granted."

Mr. Wimble chose one of the telegrams from the pile.

"I don't believe Webb is aware of the proposition Mr. Lee made to you."

"Well, 'Goatie' was wild when he woke up the day after the wedding and saw how he'd been taken in. Besides being sore, he didn't love Lalla. So he sent for his Dad to get him out of it.

"The old man didn't get very far with Lalla. Lalla was always hard at nails. Unfortunately 'Goatie' had written some pretty compromising letters, so he couldn't prove she'd tricked him. Lalla wouldn't hear of a divorce. And 'Goatie' swore he'd kill himself rather than take her back to Los Angeles with him as his wife. A sweet little mix-up!

"Lalla refused money. It was the old man who offered the money. He made it clear that 'Goatie' didn't have a cent above an ordinary salary except what his Dad gave him. What Lalla wanted, she said, was a husband and a home. Of course what she meant was that she wanted 'Goatie'. Lalla was simply bugs about 'Goatie'.

"So finally the old man came out with an offer. Clever in a way, but sort of damfool, too. Lalla was to go back to New York with Mr. Lee, Senior, and masquerade as his wife. That way she'd have her husband and her home and plenty of money— I'm sure Walt never looked on Lalla in any other light than as an adventuress out for all she could get—whereas if she refused she'd have nothing. So Lalla accepted.

"Not a soul caught on. Cabell being such a jerk-water place, and Lalla and 'Goatie' getting married in the rough-and-ready way they did, helped a lot. I was really the only one who had got a good look at 'Goatie'; and I was to be paid for holding my tongue. The local paper, which always lists the town's marriages without any trim-mings, simply stated that the week before Lalla Blair and Walter Lee, 'both over twenty-one', had applied for a marriage license. So when the item was copied by the big papers, it all fitted in."

"And now," said Mr. Wimble, "will you kindly continue the story from the arrival of 'Goatie' at your apartment on Tuesday morning? By the way, we know about Annie's pink bills."

Myrtle smiled gaminishly.

"Well, I kind of liked my monthly checks from Mr. Lee. I knew if Lalla played any tricks I'd lose them. That's why I hired Annie. I had an idea what was in the back of Lalla's head when she accepted Walt's offer. She'd won 'Goatie' once and she'd win him again! And in the meantime she'd have a soft berth.

"I nearly dropped dead when I saw 'Goatie' Tuesday morning. Annie hadn't brought over anything that had even hinted he was coming.

"'Goatie' said that Lalla had been making his life miserable—threatening to go to Los Angeles unless he came to see her.

"Somehow I felt he was holding something back. He'd been pretty lovesick over Lalla once; maybe he was suffering a relapse. He kept telling me how much he detested her, but on the other hand he seemed darn anxious to see her. I tried to dissuade him from going to Lalla's. In the bottom of my heart I'd always been hand and glove with Lalla's idea that, given time, she'd get 'Goatie' back. You can see, of course, what a mess I'd be in if they patched things up. My checks from Walt would stop." She made a face. "Also Renzo's affections!

"I thanked my lucky stars 'Goatie'd' come to my place for a wash-up and a rest before tackling Lalla. If I worked fast, I might be able to do something.

"I went down to Mr. Lee's office. Walt was a perfect brick! He told me not to worry about losing Renzo; that my allowance would go on even if Lalla did go back with 'Goatie'. He seemed to think he could persuade Lalla to leave 'Goatie' alone, though.

"And then, when I thought I was sitting pretty, Renzo brought me the news that Lalla'd been killed! I saw the end of everything!"

"Why? Even with Lalla dead, a word from you would have brought disgrace on the Lees."

"I'm not like that," said Myrtle simply.

"Well, I'd lost Renzo, but I still had poor old Nell to think of. So I wrote a note to Mr. Lee, explaining about

Nell and the kids. I begged him, if he could see his way clear to do it, to send me at least a part of my allowance till Nell got well. It was in answer to my note that he sent his secretary over to tell me about the will. The little woman you found weeping in my hall; remember? I don't know why she was crying. Envious about the money I was going to get, maybe. And, until I come into the inheritance, I have my allowance!" Again the face. "And Renzo!"

"How did Mr. Lee persuade 'Goatie' to return to California?"

"I don't know, exactly. On the way to the station I asked 'Goatie' about his call on his Dad; but he wasn't very communicative. 'Goatie' doesn't like Walt much. Kind of looks down on him for earning his money in grocery stores, I think; feels ashamed of him. 'Goatie's' a snob underneath. I've often thought if ever I get bored it'd be a great lark to call on 'Goatie' in his office in Los Angeles. He'd probably ring for the janitor!

"I suppose Walt convinced him that he could manage Lalla. The old man probably thought a few bank notes, or another piece of jewelry, would quiet her."

"You actually saw young Lee off?"

"Yes. Just my luck that his train left at the time Lalla was murdered. Of course I could have established an alibi easy; but I preferred being suspected of the crime to saying anything that might cut off my allowance—and Renzo's affections."

At this point the inter-office telephone rang.

"Yes, Willy," said Mr. Wimble. "Very well. I'll see him in just a moment."

Miss Dale arose.

"That's all you want of me?"

"Yes, except to thank you for the part you played in Annie Robinson's engagement."

Myrtle grinned.

"I almost gummed up the works, didn't I? Well, so long. I certainly feel as if I could use sleep."

At the doorway she turned. "All I can say, Wimble, is: I hope you've retired before I decide to commit a crime."

Throwing the detectives a kiss, she made her exit.

In response to Mr. Wimble's signal, Willy ushered Sharl into the office.

"Well, old fellow," asked Mr. Wimble, "what brings you here so early?"

The old man moistened his lips and gulped with great effort. Then, bravely raising his head, his rheumy old eyes looking into Mr. Wimble's, he said:

"I killed Lalla Lee!"

29

Mr. Wimble placed a chair for Sharl.

"Now, old fellow, suppose you tell us all about it?"

A change had come over the old negro. It was not only that his eyes had lost their furtive expression and that the antagonism toward the detectives had been replaced by an eager cordiality of manner. There seemed some subtle change in his spirit. With such an air as Sharl now manifested, Corey thought, the early Christians must have faced their martyrdom: a manner entailing calm, courage, a sense of right.

As he sat down, the ghost of a twinkle appeared in Sharl's rheumy old eyes.

"I reckon it'd 've been more to your credit as a detective to 've made me fess up."

"Perhaps that's why I wouldn't listen to your confession yesterday," smiled Mr. Wimble.

The fun left Sharl's face.

"Mr. Wimble, I been watching you. I can see it's your aim most gen'rally to help folks 'stead of harming 'em. Now, Mr. Wimble," he coaxed, "if it ain't no *use* telling Mr. Lee just *why* I killed Lalla Lee, I don't guess you'd go and tell him, would you?"

"I don't believe it will be necessary to tell Mr. Lee why you killed Lalla Lee."

Sharl brushed a feeble hand across his eyes.

"I didn't guess it'd be no *use!*

"I hated Lalla Lee! She made my life wretched. She insulted me every chance she got. She wanted to dress me up like a play actor. She tried to poison Mr. Lee's mind against me.

"I could've stood all that; but she found out something 'bout me I didn't want nobody to know. She threatened she'd tell it to the District Attorney, and I warned her if she did I'd kill her.

"Marie heard me warning Mrs. Lee, Mr. Wimble. You can ask her.

"Last Tuesday afternoon, just before you gentlemen come to tea, I went into the living room and there was Mrs. Lee sitting on the sofa reading a book. She said: 'Well, Snow White, this is your last day of liberty. The District Attorney is calling on me this afternoon!'

"So I— I did it!"

"When Webb and I came for tea, you feared I was Mr. Hathaway?"

"Yes, sir," returned Sharl eagerly.

"What was it Lalla Lee intended telling the District Attorney?"

There was a trace of melodrama in Sharl's voice, as the inborn love of his race for sensationalism asserted itself.

"That I am a fugitive from justice!"

Corey, at least, responded to the negro's bid for amazement.

"I am wanted for kidnapping!"

"So Sally Eugénie was a minor when you and Walter Lee took her away from Virginia."

Upon Mr. Wimble's observation Sharl did not, as Annie would have put it, turn pale; but he certainly did change color. His face took on the lavender hue it had worn the day of the murder.

"Strange that you should prefer the electric chair to a short prison term," said Mr. Wimble.

"I didn't calc'late they'd put you on to the case, sir," replied Sharl naively. "Everything was all fixed for me to go to France with Jules and Marie. I figgered nobody'd 'spect me."

Mr. Wimble arose from his chair. Gently he placed his hand on the old man's shoulder.

"Mr. Webb is going over now to tell Mr. Lee of your confession."

Sharl's woolly gray head sank till his chin was resting against his chest.

"Yes, sir. 'Course he's got to know."

Mr. Wimble patted the old man's shoulder before turning to give Corey his instructions.

In accordance with these instructions, a short time later Corey was speaking to Mr. Lee in that gentleman's private office.

"Sharl has confessed to the murder of your wife, Mr. Lee. The old fellow's at Mr. Wimble's office now."

"Sharl has confessed—" gasped Mr. Lee. "Why, he can't have! The thing's impossible!"

"Mr. Wimble thought you might like to come over."

Mr. Lee arose with alacrity.

"By all means! Let us go at once!"

When they arrived, Corey recognized two of Callahan's plainclothes men patrolling the corridor outside O. W.'s office. He pictured Sharl, frail and tottering, shortly being led away between these two Irish giants. But, when he and Mr. Lee entered the office, Sharl was nowhere in sight.

Even under the stress of his present discomposure Mr. Lee's courtesy did not forsake him. He bowed slightly in greeting Mr. Wimble before exclaiming:

"Mr. Wimble! Mr. Webb tells me that Sharl has confessed to the crime."

"Yes, curiously enough, he has."

"I can't imagine why he has done such a thing! Unless his confession has been forced," he said, looking troubled. "After all, Sharl's a very old man."

"He was not accused by us, Mr. Lee."

"Then you haven't taken his confession seriously?"

"I'll not go so far as to say I haven't taken it seriously. But I will say this: I do not believe that Sharl committed the crime. I think his terrified scream upon discovering the body of Lalla Lee was enough to clear him of all suspicion."

Mr. Lee sank into a chair.

"I'll admit I was startled. This came as a bolt out of the blue. By the way, where is Sharl? Mr. Webb told me he was here."

"I sent Sharl home. Before going, he gave me his solemn promise that he'd begin making definite arrangements for his trip to France."

"I have often remarked a strong imaginative tendency in Sharl," said Mr. Lee. "But I didn't dream it would ever extend so far. I wonder why he accused himself?"

"I am of the opinion that his confession was to shield a friend."

"Indeed?" queried Mr. Lee conversationally. "Most interesting. Have you any idea who his friend might be?"

"Sharl suspected 'Goatie' of committing the crime, Mr. Lee."

Lee's fingers tightened about the arms of his chair.

"We had a hard time identifying 'Goatie'," said Mr. Wimble. "Of course you were paying Miss Dale to remain silent on that subject. As we've seen, Sharl was ready to protect the boy with his life. And you no doubt cautioned Miss Martin to deny all knowledge of him."

He picked up one of the telegrams from his desk.

"But we have this wire from Los Angeles. It reads: 'William G. Dorn identified as Walter Lee, Junior, of this city. Is called by his associates "Goatie".' Was Sally Eugénie Randall's boy legally adopted by you, Mr. Lee?"

Mr. Lee gave a wan smile.

"Annie told me this morning that there was nothing you didn't know. I'm beginning to think she was right. No, I saw no necessity for a legal adoption. Randall had no knowledge of the boy's birth, as Sally Eugénie had not mentioned to him that she was *enceinte*. 'Goatie' has no idea he is not my own son. That will come out only when my will is read. I think he will be glad. There is not much in common between 'Goatie' and me."

"Has the boy inherited anything of the Colonel's viciousness?"

"Nothing!" cried Mr. Lee hotly. "Absolutely nothing! He is his mother all over again."

"And yet Sharl, who knows the young man as well as you, believed him capable of murdering his own wife," Mr. Wimble quietly reminded him.

"So you are also aware that Lalla was 'Goatie's' wife? Well, be that as it may," he said heavily, "Sharl has no grounds whatsoever for suspecting 'Goatie'."

"I have proved to the old fellow's satisfaction that 'Goatie' is not guilty. 'Goatie' made but one 'visit to your house on Tuesday. In the morning. The crime was committed in the afternoon. Sharl was in a very happy frame of mind when he left here."

He added quietly: "I didn't tell him that you will be unable to accompany him to France, Mr. Lee."

A tense silence filled the office. Even the street noises seemed momentarily to have abated, emphasizing the stillness of the room. Mr. Wimble finally broke it to say:

"I have seen through Lalla's veil, as it were."

For a few minutes, the accused man sat there gravely returning Mr. Wimble's gaze. When he spoke his voice was calm; he did not give the slightest impression of pleading his case.

"I was mad about my son's wife. I had an absorbing passion for the beautiful young thing Lalla was.

"Thinking 'Goatie' rich, she had inveigled him, while drunk, into marrying her. Afterwards, when he became sober, he went half out of his mind to think what he had done. 'Goatie' had got in with a very select social set in Los Angeles, a set that wouldn't have tolerated Lalla for an instant.

"I must impress on you what his social position means to my son, Mr. Wimble. As you perhaps have guessed, I myself have no social pretensions whatsoever. 'Goatie' has built up his own social status, which is perhaps the reason it is so precious to him. But precious it most certainly is.

"When Lalla learned that 'Goatie' had no money beyond a nominal salary, she threatened to divorce him. She pictured for us just how she'd proceed. It wasn't a pretty picture. So, you see, 'Goatie' was facing scandal both coming and going! He sent for me.

"I think I must have fallen in love with Lalla at first sight. They say all lovers are a little crazy. The far-fetched idea came to me of posing as Lalla's husband, taking her back to New York with me as my wife.

"When she accepted my offer, I did not flatter myself for a moment that it was for any other reason than that, because of my wealth, she could quit the stage which she hated and settle down to a life of ease.

"As time went on, however, I did flatter myself that she was becoming fond of me. And I lived in a Fool's Paradise!

"Then, all at once, last Tuesday, the blow fell! She told me that she had succeeded in getting 'Goatie' to acknowledge her as his wife, that he was coming for her that very day. It had never occurred to me that she had cared for 'Goatie' except for the money she had been under the impression he possessed. I had misjudged her motive in accepting my mad offer.

"I reasoned with her. I made extravagant promises. I pleaded. I sank so low as to weep! And she laughed. Laughed! Have you ever been laughed at when you've just bared your very soul?

"In a jealous frenzy I killed her!"

Mr. Wimble picked up a telegram from his desk.

"You are a fine actor, Mr. Lee; but I'm afraid this rather spoils your little piece."

He handed the telegram to Mr. Lee.

Mr. Lee's face blanched as he read it.

"God!" he groaned. "God!"

30

"Detective Callahan insisted that 'One Week' Wimble would triumph," said Mr. Lee. "I don't believe, from the moment I came home last Tuesday evening to find detectives in the house, that I really thought I'd escape. Premonition, perhaps; for I supposed I'd covered my trail.

"And yet, instead of taking our tea into the living room, if Sharl had brought it to us in the reception room, as I'd intended he should, my guilt might never have been discovered. For I don't believe the police would have accomplished what you have, Mr. Wimble.

"As there is no longer any need for subterfuge, here are the facts:

"'Goatie' came to New York in reply to a curt, decisive wire from Lalla: 'One chance more. Take it or leave it!' Lalla was not a girl to mince matters, and 'Goatie' knew it. He realized that things were nearing a crisis.

"After luncheon on Tuesday I had a serious, though brief, talk with Lalla. I said to her: '"Goatie" called at my office this morning. He is now on his way back to California. He wants me to tell you that he leaves it.'

"Of course, from my terse statement, Lalla assumed that 'Goatie' had made no effort to see her.

"You have heard of the fury of a woman scorned. . . . It was the malice in her eyes that put me on my guard. When she went into her pink sitting room to use the telephone, I followed and listened outside the door. I heard her telling the District Attorney that she had something important to see him about.

"It was then that I knew I was going to kill her.

"I returned to the reception room, seating myself at my roll-top desk, where automatically I began arranging the cards for my customary solitaire game. 'Homely and stupid looking, just like you', Lalla once described my desk. She used to point to it when her friends came and say: 'A woodcut of my husband!'

"I bore Lalla Blair no affection, Mr. Wimble!

"I was at my desk but a few minutes when Sharl entered, greatly perturbed, to tell me that Lalla had informed him she was entertaining the District Attorney at tea that afternoon. Sharl had no personal reason for fearing a visit from Mr. Hathaway. His agitation was on 'Goatie's' account. 'Goatie' that morning had warned Sharl that, short of bodily ejecting Mr. Hathaway if he called, the old fellow must do everything within his power to prevent a meeting between Lalla and the District Attorney. And, except when they conflicted with mine, "Goatie's' orders were Sharl's laws. It was because I'd warned Sharl that, if 'Goatie' ever came to the house asking for Lalla, he was to say she was out of town, that he had refused to let 'Goatie' see Lalla that morning.

"I scolded Sharl for taking Lalla's 'joking' seriously; assured him that John Hathaway was far too busy a man to go around making afternoon calls. Sharl knew the truth about my relationship with Lalla, of course; and I did not want him in any way to be involved in what I was going to do.

"God! When I heard him scream upon discovering Lalla's dead body, I feared for a moment that the shock had killed him—that I indirectly had caused the death of my best friend!

"I paid so much attention to my solitaire game that I more than half convinced him that Lalla had been joking about the District Attorney coming for tea. I told him to go about his business, that I'd call him when I was ready to leave for my office.

"I went into the living room. Lalla was sitting at the end of the davenport, just as you found her, reading.

"'Well,' she asked, without looking up from her book, 'how are you going to get "Goatie" out of the mess this time?'

"I remembered about fingerprints giving a person away. I took out my handkerchief, improvising a mitten for my hand. Then I picked up the statue behind Lalla's head. . . .

"It was simple. She had not moved. There was not even a cry.

"I saw her emerald. I had no idea she had substituted a false one for the original. I tore the chain from her neck, with an idea of making it appear that she had been robbed.

"Leaving the living room, I encountered Patterson in the hallway. Knowing my habit of playing solitaire, he had sneaked up to see Lalla. But, when I discovered him, he had a lie ready. 'I wanted to ask Mrs. Lee about driving her to Miss Dale's this afternoon,' he said. That was when my idea of *having Patterson drive Lalla to Myrtle's* first came to me!

"'I was just looking for you,' I said to Patterson. 'I want you to go down to the bank for me,' my idea in sending him on an errand naturally being to prevent him from discovering the body.

"Patterson out of the way, I hurried by the rear stairway up to Lalla's room. Lalla and I were about of a size. You may have remarked that she had large hands and feet for a woman. Her hair was cut like mine. I could easily get into her clothes, her shoes, her stockings, her hat. I knew she had an opaque veil. There had been times when it had been politic for Lalla to wear such a veil. A small hat pulled down over my head, the veil doubled over my features and her fur coat wrapped around me, its collar well up over my face—and my masquerade would be complete.

"I gathered together what clothes I needed.

"Then the disturbing thought smote me: 'But what of my voice?' I knew that Lalla and Patterson, being on familiar terms, were bound to converse. And, as it was my plan after leaving Myrtle's to taxi back to our house, what about instructions to the driver? I thought of passing a calling card to the driver; found one in Lalla's desk. But I was at my wit's end to know how to deal with Patterson.

"It was then that chance played into my hands. Looking for the calling card, I found a note in Lalla's writing case. If the note had appeared in its entirety, the thought of using it might not have occurred to me. But it was folded, and by a trick of Fate the half of it I saw made sense. You know about the note?"

Mr. Wimble nodded.

"The note called for a gift. I remembered the emerald. Patterson would surely take good care to keep it out of sight, and the robbery motive would hold.

"I placed Lalla's clothes in the little sitting room downstairs, and was back at my roll-top desk when Patterson returned from the bank. I told him that Lalla wanted him to drive her to Myrtle's before taking me to my office. He went out to wait for her; and I hurried into the sitting room to dress myself in the clothes I had brought down from Lalla's room.

"I left the house as Lalla!

"Patterson's seeing through my disguise had been my greatest worry. But it proved too easy! Women's present-day styles helped me. About all of my face that showed was my nose, and two thicknesses of veil hid that. Fortunately it was a dark, cloudy day. And Patterson's intimacy with

Lalla had bred contempt. He did not get down from the driver's seat to help Lalla into the car. I tossed him the note and the emerald, and he drove off.

"You know how I proceeded? How I gave Panella's signal at Miss Dale's? How I went inside, staying only long enough for Patterson to get out of sight? How I returned home, entering by the back door?

"The servants were downstairs at their luncheon. I got into the pink sitting room without being seen, where I quickly removed Lalla's clothes, for time's sake keeping on the hose until I reached my office. I hurried back to my roll-top desk. It was as if I had never left it!

"Sharl helped me on with my coat, and saw me to the car, unaware that it was my second departure from the house within the hour; and Patterson drove me to my office, also ignorant of my trick. As I would take care that afternoon to be seen by a number of persons, I wished the time of Lalla's murder to be set as late in the afternoon as possible. I feared that Patterson might return to the living room. That is why, when I was entering Miss Dale's building, I held up my hand, so that he should take it that Lalla would receive him at five. I had often seen her employ that sign. There was no danger of the other servants stumbling upon the body, as they dared not incur Lalla's wrath by entering the living room in the afternoon unless rung for.

"It seemed to me that I had covered my trail perfectly. But, apparently, I made some mistakes."

Later, when District Attorney Hathaway had presented himself at Mr. Wimble's office to learn the result of the investigation, O. W. said:

"Of course motive is the kernel of a crime. In this case, the motive was not very obscure. Lalla Lee possessed someone's secret. She intended disclosing this secret to the District Attorney, but was prevented from so doing by drastic, but most effective, means.

"The way to proceed with the investigation, therefore, was for us to poke into the cupboards of every possible suspect for family skeletons. I might add that we found quite a collection.

"And the way to discover such cupboards is by trailing clues. As I tell Webb, clues don't consist only of blood stains and fingerprints. Sometimes the best clue you can get is a stray remark. And if a detective doesn't follow up each of these clues as if his very life depended on it, well, it's another 'unsolved mystery' for the newspapers, that's all!

"The Sally Eugénie story led us, by devious ways, I'll admit, to a dark, dank cupboard. And there was the very skeleton we were looking for, down to the two-hundredth bone!

"I always start out on a case suspecting everyone connected with it. Therefore it's a little difficult for me to tell afterwards just when I began suspecting the guilty person.

"Lee's alibi seemed perfectly sound. It did strike me at first that he had been rather forward in establishing it. On the night of the murder, without waiting to be asked, he had made it very clear how he'd spent the afternoon. But as I could find no flaw in his alibi, I concluded that this had been mere coincidence.

"As the case developed, I met with little difficulty in eliminating suspects. Most of our clues served this purpose. Which, of course, is one way of arriving at a solution. But I had a lot of clues left over. A number of these pointed to Mr. Lee as the criminal; but always I came up against the blank wall of his alibi. He had left the house at two o'clock, *after* Lalla's departure. There were too many witnesses to corroborate these facts for them to have been otherwise.

"And then we discovered something that tightened the net about Lee. We learned from a servant girl across the street that Lalla had returned to the house, entering by the back way, at half-past two. But the clock in her kitchen was three-quarters of an hour fast! This timed Lalla's arrival at a *quarter to two*.

"Therefore, Lalla had been in the house when Lee had left it!

"However, I did not suspect then that it was Lee in Lalla's clothes who had entered by the back door. Last night Webb was dressed up as a girl for a masquerade. I looked at him for about ten seconds before recognizing him. It was then that it flashed over my mind that Walter Lee might have been posing as Lalla on Tuesday. And the suspicion used up absolutely every clue I had left!

"The torn veil, her clothes strewn all over the place, when according to Annie Lalla had always been most particular in that respect, were accounted for.

"I understood why the veiled lady had been so desirous of remaining *unheard* as well as *unseen*.

"Lalla Lee's tears while riding with Jenks were explained. She hadn't been crying at all; his fare's voice had sounded husky to Jenks because it had been masculine.

"I realized how Lee's back door key had happened to be in Lalla's coat pocket.

"I knew how Lalla's stockings had found their way to Lee's office. . . ."

"But just what," inquired John Hathaway, "was Lee's motive?"

"Walter Lee committed murder because he had given his promise to Sally Eugénie Randall that he would look after her son!"

"I knew Sally Eugénie less than a year," said Walter Lee, "and yet those few months have justified my existence.

"I cannot begin to tell you what the advent of Sally Eugénie into my life meant. I was born in a little shanty in the Blue Ridge Mountains, where my parents and their five children lived—existed is the better word—together in one room.

"The squalor of that room is unmentionable. My childhood was a nightmare—drunken brawls between my parents; hunger; beatings; terrifying occasions when the sheriff's posse came to fetch one of my older brothers or sisters. At sixteen I ran away to Warrenton.

"At Warrenton I struggled against great odds to earn my livelihood. I had no health; no education. Mine was an unfortunate disposition. Only in the presence of children could I be anything but shy and stupid. I lived within myself, making no friends. Even the blacks scorned me as 'po' white trash.'

"Then, all at once, everything changed. An angel came into my life: Sally Eugénie, white as magnolia blossoms, with hair of gold and eyes like patches of summer sky. Art? What pictures could interest me after having seen Sally Eugénie?

"How well I remember the day I reminded her that I was po' white trash! 'Po' white trash?' she replied. 'Nothing of the kind! You're Sally Eugénie's.'

"And I was! Body and soul I was, and am, Sally Eugénie's!

"Sally Eugénie's boy was three hours old when she died. Oh, God! The day she lay, poor little broken magnolia blossom, so white, so young, on her hospital bed, telling us of her plans for her boy!

"'He is to be called Walter Lee,' she said, 'and you and Charlie will look after him.' Sharl—we called him Charlie, then, before our young warrior returned from France to name him Sharl—sobbing his young heart out, stumbled from the room, so that I was alone with Sally Eugénie when she died.

"Just before she went she whispered: 'I wish you were the father of my boy.' That was when my life reached its crescendo! 'But you are not,' she said. 'Jim Randall is his father. My son will need looking after!' I gave Sally Eugénie my promise to look after her son.

"I killed Lalla Lee in keeping that promise."

"Mr. Lee," said Mr. Wimble, "this afternoon the District Attorney is coming here to learn the results of my investigation. The District Attorney is one of my closest friends. I am going to ask him to support me in a statement I presently intend making. I do not anticipate his refusal."

He arose.

"And now, Mr. Lee, it is my duty to turn you over to the police."

"Very well," replied Mr. Lee quietly.

Opening the door, O. W. summoned Callahan's men.

"Mr. Lee has confessed to the crime, gentlemen. His motive was jealousy of his wife."

Mr. Lee wheeled toward Mr. Wimble. For a moment his eyes glowed with the radiance of the midday sun.

Then, squaring his shoulders, he signified to the waiting officers that he was ready and, between them, passed out of the room.

O. W. sat down rather heavily in his chair.

"John'll blow me up for telling that one!"

After awhile he said: "I'd have *liked* Sally Eugénie!"

He became aware of his assistant's intent regard.

"You're wondering just what it was that Lee was saving 'Goatie' from, aren't you, son?"

He pushed the top telegram of the pile toward Corey. . . .

Walter Lee had murdered Lalla to prevent her from exposing Sally Eugénie's son as a bigamist! For last April, at the time of marrying Lalla Blair at Cabell, Colorado, "Goatie" Lee already had a wife and child in California.

THE TELLTALE
TELEGRAM

1

"The little blonde in the blue beret is on her way up," said Mr. Wimble, turning from the telephone to his young assistant.

His chief's assumption that he would recognize the description was not lost on Corey. It was complimentary in a way—O. W.'s taking it for granted that he had not failed to observe what was out of the ordinary.

He had seen the little blonde in the station upon arriving three days ago with O. W. on "The Lark" from Los Angeles. Corey felt that his noticing her in no way proved he was not a woman-hater. Even a misogynist could admire a beautiful picture, couldn't he? And the little blonde, in her smart blue coat and beret, her stylishly twisted scarf lending just the right note of color, most certainly had been that!

He wouldn't have given her a second thought but for the pink newspaper. It had seemed strange to see a young girl in the middle of a bustling railroad station smiling down at a newspaper. Stranger still, as he and O. W. came through the gate, to see the little blonde look up, spy the detectives and suddenly press the pink newspaper against her cheek. Of course, when the little blonde's eyes had met his, Corey had given her the dirty look he reserved for girls—not quite so dirty as usual, perhaps, but sufficiently soiled to make her understand he was not the least bit interested in girls.

The first thing Corey had done upon reaching their hotel was to purchase a pink newspaper. He found a photograph of Mr. Wimble and himself on the front page, with an accompanying article stating that "One Week" Wimble, famous New York criminal investigator, and his assistant Corey Webb were passing through San Francisco on their way home after a visit to Webb's mother in Hollywood.

From the first Corey had mistrusted his mother's sudden hankering after a winter in Hollywood.

It made a fellow proud to have the most beautiful mother in the state of New York, but it was pretty tough luck to resemble her. Especially when the result was the sort of looks that made people Pictures-conscious the minute they set eyes on him. "You're in the talkies, aren't you, Mr. Webb? *Not in Hollywood!* Oh, but Mr. Webb, you must go at once! It's your duty! No good will come of flying in the face of Providence!"

When the choice of a career for Corey was up before Dolly Webb and her handsome offspring, by looking out of the window so as to avoid the pleading in her gorgeous eyes, Corey had managed to specify that he would consider none but a "he-man" job. His present association with Dolly's lifelong friend, O. Wimble, was the outcome of this momentous decision. But Corey knew that despite her high esteem for the detective his mother wasn't wholly satisfied. In Dolly's mind there was only one real field for a youth of such faultless features as her son's, such a tall, well-knit frame, such a pleasing timbre of voice: the talking pictures!

Being a woman, Dolly was a strategist of the first water. What was more natural than that she should tire of Florida and Bermuda and manifest a wish to spend a winter in Hollywood? Or that once there everything should turn out to be so perfectly lovely she couldn't bear to tear herself away?

"She'll inveigle me out there!" wailed Corey into the sympathetic ear of his chief. "I know she will! She'll beguile some movie magnate into offering me a contract and, when I refuse to sign, go around sighing over me as if I were the sort of villain that robs kids of their lollipops. You wait and see! You know Dolly!"

Indeed O. W. did know Dolly! He'd never been able to refuse her anything. He remembered the day he'd almost cracked his skull keeping a promise to Dolly. Even as a youngster, O. W.'s figure had taken on the proportions of an Italian opera singer's. But when Dolly had coaxed him to walk a tight rope he'd got busy on the back yard clothes-line. He remembered another day when she'd made him promise not to mope because she'd decided to marry Sim Webb instead of him. It was O. W.'s heart that got cracked that day.

Fortunately for Corey's ambition to be a private detective, his resistance to the fair Dolly's coaxing was made of sterner stuff than his chief's.

Dolly had been in Hollywood but two months when she wrote her son:

> "They haven't boasted a bit about their climate. It *is* bigger and better! But I'm so lonesome I could die! If only I could see you and some of my old friends, I'd be ideally happy. *I can hardly wait till you get your vacation!*"

"I knew this Hollywood trip was a ruse!" groaned Corey. "All in the hope of making me fall for those terrible talkies!"

"Not such an unpleasant prospect," returned Mr. Wimble, and sighed. Corey knew O. W. wasn't referring to the talkies. Which gave Corey an idea. He'd indulge in a little coaxing. After all, he was Dolly's son.

"Of course I'd love to visit Dolly," he said. "Now if only you'd go along, O. W., as my moral support—"

"Dolly's letter did say she'd like to see some of her old friends." Corey caught the tinge of wistfulness in the senior detective's voice. He pressed his advantage.

"I wish you'd take the trip with me, O. W. You know you've been working mighty hard lately."

"Well, all right, son. I'll go out to Hollywood with you for a few weeks."

Aside from the pleasure of seeing his mother again Corey hadn't enjoyed his visit in Hollywood.

"He keeps looking as if the talkies 'll get him if he doesn't watch out," chuckled O. W. one day when he and Dolly were out walking together.

Dolly expressed exasperation that her son should prefer Life to Drama. "I can't see why Corey considers poking around for fingers-prints and spots of gore so much more enjoyable than—"

"Receiving mash notes?" teased O. W.

"Now, O. W., don't be like that!" pouted Dolly. "You know what I mean. Why on earth can't Corey get his thrills out of speed-boats and polo and things like other boys?"

"I don't believe Corey's in this game purely for excitement, Dolly," returned O. W. thoughtfully. "As a matter of fact our job's mighty tedious at times. Just as the countless laboratory tests were tiresome to the fellows trying to discover what germ carried yellow fever. Of course there's a thrill when you get the man you're after, but capture is only an incident of detective routine, just as the actual isolation of a germ is an incident. I think the big thrill in both instances is in realizing you've helped humanity. I'm sure the scientist stamping out one peril looks beyond and dreams of stamping out all Disease." Though Dolly

knew there was nothing of the soppy sentimentalist about
O. W., she recognized the look of the visionary in his eyes
as he added: "I know a true detective dreams of stamping
out all Crime."

Dolly cocked a reflective eye at her friend. "You're so
sweet outside, O. W., that it's hard to believe you have
such queer ideas inside."

"Dolly," retorted O. W., the twinkles in his small blue
eyes giving the lie to the reproof in his voice, "I object to
being called a sugar-coated old pill!"

Corey's sigh of relief upon kissing his mother good-by had
not been so hearty as if the detectives' train had been
heading for New York. At the request of Mr. Wimble's
sister Portia, O. W. and Corey were returning East via
San Francisco so that O. W. might call on a cousin there.
Corey would breathe in peace only when California, Kingdom of Kinema, was several states behind him.

Or so he had thought three days ago. Corey recalled
that in the advertising brochures the city by the Golden
Gate was always referred to as "fascinating San Francisco".
The lure of the city certainly must be accountable for his
sudden desire to view a bit of the San Francisco Bay region
before returning to New York.

If O. W. suspected that the little blonde in the blue
beret had anything to do with Corey's sudden change of
heart, he was too wise to say anything. He knew that what
the slamming of the oven door is to an angel cake, a matchmaker is to a romance.

Of course O. W. was too fond of Dolly and of the lad
himself to stand by and watch Corey get hurt. As "One
Week" Wimble happened to be one of the finest detectives
in the land, it was not odd that before being in San Francisco twenty-four hours he had learned enough about the
little blonde in the blue beret to make him look favorably

upon Corey's proposal that they stop over long enough to
see the sights.

Discovering that Miss Janet Hill was Assistant to the
Society Editor of the *Globe,* Mr. Wimble had taken it upon
himself to call at the editorial offices of that daily. Among
other things, he had found out that little Janet was not
the sort of girl to trump up excuses to call at almost nine
o'clock at night on a young man who had chanced to take
her fancy.

At O. W.'s announcement that the little blonde in the
blue beret was on her way up, Corey's visage burst into
flame.

"What do you suppose she wants?"

"She wants to see me," replied O. W. artlessly.

Amazement flooded the handsome face of Mr. Wimble's
assistant. Though O. W.'s unfailing kindliness, his good
humor and courtesy endeared him to all who knew him,
certainly there was nothing in his appearance to intrigue
a young girl. In stature Mr. Wimble was pudgy. He had
the merriest blue eyes in the world but they were set in
a round face that had an extra chin. And you had to get
behind him to see his hair.

Corey opened the door for the charming visitor. From
the way she regarded the lad, O. W. realized with some
wistfulness that little Janet's interest in him as a detective
would never reach her interest in Corey as a young man.
She stood looking up at Corey in breathless wonder, as
if this close-up of him were so much dearer than she had
dreamed it could be.

An unexpected sadness for old age settled over the
senior detective. "Those two young ones are happy just
standing there gaping at each other!" he thought.

Corey seemed bereft of speech. He was wondering how
eyes could be so blue without being violet, how lashes

could be so thick without obstructing a girl's vision, how it was that a little honey-colored curl hanging down a girl's forehead and making her face heart-shaped could do such queer things to a fellow.

O. W. coughed gently. The youngsters started as if a cannon had gone off.

The senior detective grinned. "Trying to make a liar out of me, son?" He said to Janet Hill: "I told my assistant that you had come to see me."

"I came to see you on business, Mr. Wimble," replied Janet briskly.

Amusedly the detective reflected that in his day little girls played house; nowadays they played business.

The little blonde told the detective what he already knew: "I'm Janet Hill, society reporter on the *Globe.*"

Her forehead puckered under the yellow curl. "I simply loathe society reporting! It's so—tame!" With a quick glance at her wrist-watch she went on hurriedly: "I want to be a real reporter, dealing with the vital things of life—battle, murder, sudden death!"

Again the little curl hid a frown. "Did you ever come up against a city editor? Stubborn as mules, city editors! Dunk—that's mine, Mr. Bancroft—takes the attitude that I'm just a kindergarten teacher he has to take care of till I come to my senses."

She clasped her hands in a wave of feeling. "I thought if I could write a story about something big, something important—the findings of a renowned detective working on a murder case, for instance—and lay the story on Dunk's desk, maybe he'd put me on as a real reporter."

She concluded humbly: "I didn't intend taking your time to talk about myself."

O. W. thought indulgently: "Only as much of it as was necessary to enlist my sympathy, you sly minx!"

"Who's been murdered?" he asked.

From her breathless manner, quick speech and constant glances at her wrist-watch, the detective knew that little Janet was in a hurry. He was pleased therefore that at his question she didn't take time out to be coy and complimentary and so astonished at his perspicacity.

Beyond a brief "Oh!" her voice was as businesslike as one can make a voice that sounds more like the tinkling of little silver bells than anything else.

"Gary Gilbert was murdered tonight at the home of Miss Marcia Allen who lives at Thousand Oaks across the Bay. Miss Allen was giving a fancy dress party. I was to have gone over sometime during the evening to write up the costumes. About half an hour ago my paper got news of the crime. I remembered that 'One Week' Wimble was in town. You see, I've been reading about you and," shyly, "Mr. Webb in the papers. I immediately telephoned to Miss Allen."

Janet's little hands clung together. "Miss Allen wants you to handle the case, Mr. Wimble."

"Well," deliberated Mr. Wimble with mock gravity, "my partner has been pretty anxious to leave California."

"I shouldn't think of allowing my personal wishes to stand in the way of my duty, sir!" hastily returned Corey, and wondered why he felt so hot around the collar.

"All right, Miss Hill," said Mr. Wimble. "We'll take the case."

2

In asking Janet Hill to accompany them to Miss Allen's residence in Thousand Oaks, Mr. Wimble's motives were threefold: he meant to supply Janet with leads for stories that would convince the adamantine Dunk of her value as a reporter; he thought it would be fun to explode Corey's misogynous principles; and he felt that Janet would be of aid to the investigation.

On the ferry-boat crossing the Bay he let the two youngsters get acquainted. It was only when they were in a taxi driving to Miss Allen's home that he put any professional questions to the heart-faced Janet.

"Miss Hill, was Gary Gilbert of any social prominence hereabouts?"

"Oh, yes! He was invited everywhere."

"Being a society reporter, you should be able to tell us something about him."

Janet nodded, "I have a notebook acquaintance with everyone of any social importance in San Francisco and the trans-Bay cities."

"I trust your memory's good. Unless you have a notebook hidden in that funny little blue hand-bag of yours, for the time being we'll have to rely on it."

Janet blushed. "I think you can bank on my memory, Mr. Wimble."

"A good memory's a fine recommendation for a reporter, isn't it, O. W.?" Mr. Wimble masked a smile upon hearing a self-styled "woman-hater" thus bestowing praise on a girl.

Janet said modestly: "It's about the only one I possess, I guess."

"Except the tenacity of a bulldog when you want something," teased O. W. And Corey glowed. Mr. Wimble never teased anyone he didn't like. Just why it was so important that his chief like Janet Hill it did not occur to Corey to analyze.

Mischievously Janet asked: "Shall I tell you what we printed about Gary Gilbert in the paper, Mr. Wimble, or what I thought of him personally?"

"Begin with what the *Globe* thought of him."

Janet gave a brief "who's who" account of the murdered man, substantially as follows:

Both the Garys—his mother was a Gary—and the Gilberts were prominent pioneer families of California. Gary's parents perished in the San Francisco fire of 1906 when he was a little boy, and Gary was taken abroad to live by an aunt. After this aunt's death he returned, some two years ago, to San Francisco. Though it was supposed that the Gilbert fortune disappeared in the disaster of 1906, Gary apparently had enough to live on without working. Perhaps he had inherited from his aunt. At any rate, upon returning to the city of his birth, he established his residence in a beautifully furnished penthouse on the roof of a luxurious downtown hotel. He was very much in demand for social affairs, being exceptionally good looking, of a fine family and apparently well off.

As Janet ceased talking Mr. Wimble smiled: "Now suppose you tell us why you didn't like him."

Janet wrinkled up her bud of a nose. "So I let spite edge my voice, did I?" She looked as fierce as it was possible for so adorable a creature to look. "I had plenty of reason for disliking Gary Gilbert!"

"Not enough for committing murder, I hope," said Mr. Wimble quietly.

Janet's gasp and Corey's "Good Heaven, O. W.!" came simultaneously. It occurred to the detective that it wasn't taking his young assistant long to succumb to the allure of Miss Janet Hill. After which reflection he sighed recalling how, more years ago than he cared to remembered, he had looked upon the cameolike face of Corey's mother and become hers.

"I can establish a perfect alibi!" retorted Janet. Thank the Lord, thought O. W., the girl possesses intelligence as well as charm!

"You know, then, the exact time the murder was committed?"

"The extras say around eight o'clock this evening."

"So you believe everything you read in the papers?"

Janet laughed. "No, sir. I write for them!"

O. W. chuckled. "Tell your story, child."

"In the first place," said Janet, "I hate 'pretty' men." As O. W. surreptitiously nudged her, breathlessly she interposed: "Unless they have big broad shoulders and strong masterful chins and—and glare at girls and—" O. W. had to nudge her again; he wasn't going to have Corey bursting his hat band. "And unless they're doing he-man work!" concluded Janet despite the second nudge. Whereupon Corey decided that God was in His heaven, all was right with the world.

Janet went on: "Gary Gilbert considered himself God's Gift to Women. I suppose that was largely the women's fault. I never saw him when some woman wasn't making a fool of herself over him.

"Then, too, I think he was a grafter.

"One day I was sent by my paper to interview him. By some mistake the hotel office failed to announce me. You leave the elevator on the roof and walk across to the penthouse. I knocked and Mr. Gilbert answered: 'Entrez!' He had an affected way of speaking. When I went in he was lunching on crackers and milk. They hadn't been sent up by the hotel dining room, either. I could see that. 'The wages of Prohibition gin is crackers and milk!' he said. 'Pain in the old tum today and all that sort of rot. Couldn't face a real luncheon.' But somehow I got the impression that he managed to get invited to most of his meals."

Janet hesitated slightly before going on. The detectives realized that she was now approaching the personal.

"When Mr. Gilbert learned I was the granddaughter of rich old Cyrus Hill he made a play for me. He didn't know of course that I wasn't friendly with Granddad." She paused, a catch in her voice. O. W. gave her hand a little pat. He already knew this part of her story, but if Corey were to become interested in the girl it was well that he should know it, too. He suspected that Janet shared his feeling and respected her for it. "When I got out of school Granddad told me the story of my mother. Dad was Granddad's son. He and mother were married when they were both quite young. Mother was a dancer. Granddad took Dad and me away from her."

Janet was looking at Mr. Wimble's assistant now. Corey longed to pat Janet's hand as O. W. had done. He chafed under the convention that permitted an old man a gesture denied a young man.

"Dad and Mother—died tragically." O. W. knew that they had killed themselves, those two, rather than be parted.

After a short interval of silence Janet said simply: "I told Granddad I'd like to earn my own living. My Declaration of Independence made quite a stir at the time. It was before Gary Gilbert came home, so he hadn't heard of it.

He thought I was just another of those rich girls who, on the strength of their social position, take jobs away from poor girls who need them. He began his siege by leaving a standing order with one of the leading florists to send me an orchid daily. The morning I rang up and explained that I was merely a 'poor relation', I'll bet he cancelled that order before he brushed his teeth!" "That ended Gilbert's attentions?" asked O. W.

"No, sir. One day I called on a Mrs. Padgett to get some information about her daughter's coming-out ball, and while I was waiting Gary Gilbert happened to drop in. As I wasn't a matrimonial prospect he felt perfectly free to get fresh." She said unsteadily: "I pushed him in the face. Of course that isn't the most ladylike way of getting rid of a man, but I was standing against the wall and if I hadn't he would have kissed me. I don't believe he got pushed in the face very often. The shove I gave him came as a surprise and knocked him over. He pulled down a vase as he fell. The crash brought a servant to the scene. 'Sorry I smashed Mrs. Padgett's gewgaw,' Mr. Gilbert said. 'The sight of this young woman startled me.'" Janet's voice shook. "He said: 'Janet reminds me of a dancing girl I lived with once in Tunis.' You see, by that time he'd heard about Mother. But, Mr. Wimble," she broke off in some embarrassment, "this seems to be developing into my Life History instead of a description of Gary Gilbert!"

"On the contrary I've learned a great deal about Mr. Gilbert from what you've told us. What a person says in anger very often gives one the key to his character. That's all you can tell us about him?"

"Except that he was unmarried. All the papers were on the lookout for an engagement, each paper favoring a different candidate."

"And the woman at whose house he was murdered—what's she like?"

"Miss Marcia Allen's a dear! I don't know her very well; she's older than I. I know her sister Roberta better. Marcia must be almost thirty; Roberta can't be of age yet. Rob entered boarding-school the semester before I graduated. In Hollywood. Hollywood's a town, you know, as well as a talkie colony. Rob's a large, rather masculine-looking girl; her nickname is not inept. Mr. and Mrs. Allen were divorced when Rob was a baby, I believe. Mrs. Allen married again and is living in Rome. The girls stayed with their father. Mr. Allen died just a year ago, leaving everything to Marcia, and there was a lot of money. Mr. Allen didn't care for Roberta, it seems; she is too much like her mother."

The taxi which had been steadily climbing finally reached Thousands Oaks, one of the several residential districts situated among the coastal hills bordering San Francisco Bay on the east. Raised in the East where hills this height meant hiking suits and accouterments for camping out, Corey was amazed that Californians took pitching their dwellings so high as a matter of course.

In the moonlight he could see the low spreading oaks that had given the suburb its name. What comfortable looking trees oaks were, he thought; and with their substantial, easily climbed branches what a temptation for small boys! Above the oak tops, a delicate silhouette of eucalyptus leaves trimmed the sky with lace. Below Thousand Oaks the university city of Berkeley, a pattern of sparkling lights and patches of darkness, looked to Corey like a black and silver Coptic shawl flung over the foothills.

The taxicab was stopped at the entrance of the Allen estate by a man waving a flashlight covered with a red cloth. Upon learning who its occupants were he explained that he was a plain-clothes man delegated to keep the guests Miss Allen had invited to her party from driving in at the gate. He said the red cloth over his flashlight was Miss Allen's idea.

As the taxi drove off, O. W., quietly conversing with the plain-clothes man who gave his name as Riley, entered the grounds, followed by Janet and Corey. Except for the sound of passing automobiles an almost rural stillness pervaded the scene. The shadows cast by the moonlight among the many trees, had not a murder recently been committed in the vicinity, would have seemed romantic to Corey and Janet. Now they appeared sinister.

Suddenly through the night was heard the sound of someone running. Immediately the little group at the gate showed signs of activity. Swiftly Mr. Wimble appropriated Riley's flashlight and extinguished it, at the same time ordering the men and the girl behind the bushes. Riley's hand sought his hip. It being an ill wind that blows nobody good, Corey was enjoying, for the present, the delectable sensation of holding Miss Janet Hill's little hand which had trustingly sought his at the first hint of danger.

The footsteps came nearer. From the shadows the watchers could distinguish the form of a woman, apparently heading for the gate. Gently, and even in that tense moment with consummate regret, Corey let go of Janet's soft fingers and got ready to intercept the runner. However, before reaching the gate the woman turned off to the right.

"The gardener's cottage is in that direction," whispered Janet.

"The rest of you stay here," ordered O. W. in a low voice. With an agility remarkable in a man of his rotundity he darted in pursuit of the runner.

The others heard the woman run up the cottage steps and rap smartly on the door; and then came the sound of her voice, muted but intense.

"Blanche! Blanche!"

A second feminine voice reached them, sleepily, through an open window.

"Who's there?"

"Marie. Open the door!"

"Marie! I thought you were going to stay all night at the house with Rosie."

"Something's happened. I got to go home tonight. Let me in!"

From inside Blanche apparently turned on the electric switch for in another moment light flooded the cottage porch. Peering around the bushes, Corey perceived a woman in a maid's conventional black and white impatiently marking time before the locked door. As there was no sign of O. W., he concluded that his chief was hiding in the nearby shrubbery.

However, Mr. Wimble was soon to be heard from. As a woman in a flannel wrapper opened the door he called out:

"I wonder if you happen to have a piece of red cloth in the house." Simultaneously he sprang up the steps.

The women were startled. Both uttered ejaculations. But O. W.'s voice was so cheery, his manner so amiable, that their alarm was more the faint shock one experiences upon being surprised by a Jumping Jack popping out of a box than real fear.

The woman called Blanche pulled her wrapper more securely around her and gave her untidy hair a swift pat.

"Sakes alive, Marie!" she exclaimed, half banteringly, half annoyed. "Why didn't you say you had a boy friend with you?"

"I never saw the man before in my life," returned Marie brusquely, and would have brushed past the detective into the house had not O. W. arranged his portly person so that she couldn't manage the maneuver.

"I'd really like to borrow a piece of red cloth, if you happen to have such a thing in the house," he repeated to Blanche.

Whereas a different type of man asking in the middle of the night for a piece of red cloth might be taken for an escaped lunatic, O. W.'s attitude was so friendly, his appearance so disarming, that the woman in the flannel wrapper immediately began racking her brains.

"Well," she said finally, "I have a strip of red bunting you might use."

Marie, however, though not afraid was suspicious.

"Cut it, Blanche! What's a man want a red rag this time of night for? To wave in front of a bull, maybe?"

To the astonishment of everyone listening, O. W. chuckled: "To tell the truth I did want it for a bull. For his flashlight. I've taken a liking to the cloth he had around it and am going to keep it." He turned to Blanche. "So will you be so kind as to get me the bunting?" Apparently Blanche would be so kind, as she disappeared from the doorway.

"Say, listen!" snapped the girl addressed as Marie. "What's your game? I got to cross the Bay tonight and I'm in a hurry."

"Didn't they tell you at the house you weren't to leave the grounds until given permission?"

"What if they did?" returned the girl morosely. "I got to go to Frisco."

"You're aware that a murder was committed here tonight?"

"What of it? I didn't do it. Say," she glowered suspiciously, "are you a detective?"

"Yes. How did you guess it?"

Despite the strain she was under the girl tittered. "By your gum shoes, I guess. I didn't hear you following me."

"Perhaps because you were making so much noise yourself."

"Why should I sneak?" demanded the girl belligerently. "I haven't anything to hide."

"Then surely you won't object to remaining until you're given leave to go?"

"Can't get out of it, I guess," replied the girl sullenly. "The place is alive with cops. I was only now able to get away from the house. I'd have left before the police came, only Rosie had to throw a fit when she heard of the murder."

At this point Blanche appeared with the red bunting. O. W. observed that she had stopped to tidy her hair and to powder her nose. His keen eyes confirmed his initial impression of Blanche. From the woman's assurance of manner, her slight air of coquetry, unless she were an inimitable actress she knew nothing of the crime. Although he felt satisfied on this score he ventured a leading question.

"Haven't you been disturbed by all the excitement tonight?"

"Oh, no! You see we live so near the road Michael and I are used to the noise of automobiles. Those coming to Miss Allen's party wouldn't make any difference. Here's your cloth. Hope it serves the purpose." Though obliging, Blanche was thrifty. "I'd like it back, sir, when you've finished with it."

"It's just what I wanted," replied O. W. graciously, "and I'll see to it myself that it's returned. Webb!" he called.

"That the bull?" sniffed Marie.

"No. My assistant."

Blanche was becoming bewildered. "Is there anything the matter?"

"One of Miss Allen's guests has met with an accident," the detective told her.

"Done in, that's what!" said Marie shortly.

Blanche's startled glance traveled from Mr. Wimble to Marie.

"I believe I better get Mike up," she said in a troubled voice. She broke off, her eyes distended. "Sakes alive, *look at Marie!*"

Corey had run up on to the porch and was awaiting his chief's orders. As O. W. turned toward Marie he saw that the girl was staring at his assistant as if transfixed. Her face wore an expression of abject terror. Her scream came in a series of gasps as though someone had her by the throat. When it was done she fell like dead on the front porch.

3

Upon being admitted to Miss Allen's, the detectives found Inspector Clancy in the entrance hall. Various police officers were moving through the downstairs rooms. Though Corey did not doubt that each was methodically performing his particular duty, as far as he was concerned the house was in the throes of utter confusion.

Clancy's manner was cordial.

As he shook hands with Corey his forehead puckered in a puzzled frown. "Your face seems vaguely familiar, young man."

"Ye Gods!" groaned Corey inwardly. "He's going to say I remind him of someone in the talkies!"

"They had our picture in the papers," said O. W.

"I guess that's it," decided Clancy.

To Corey's relief the Inspector transferred his attention to Mr. Wimble. "According to the papers, sir, we're lucky to have 'One Week' Wimble on the case."

"From the looks of things around here," Mr. Wimble put in quickly, anxious to get off the subject of his professional skill, "Webb and I are going to have a lot of help."

"The Force is as short-handed on the West Coast as everywhere else, Mr. Wimble. After these necessary formalities, I think you'll find Headquarters pretty willing to leave the heavy work to you. Of course we'll expect you to call on us for finger-prints, photographs, medical reports and so forth." He added with a touch of pride: "I don't believe you'll find us much behind the East in our methods!" A true Californiac!

It was O. W.'s habit to work in conjunction with the police. In fact, whenever possible he gave them the credit for his conclusions, for which reason as well as for his winning personality he was greatly beloved by the members of every police force with which he had ever collaborated. Too many private detectives are prone to mock at the tedious routine of the police—just as too many policemen are wont to ridicule the exotic methods of private detectives. Mr. Wimble possessed to a marked degree the gift of correlation, sensing the mutual relation between sedulity and speculation.

"Hard work and imagination! That's what it takes to be a detective," Mr. Wimble told Corey during the latter's first days as an assistant detective; "You've got to follow every clue as if your life depended on it. And that means work. Because a clue's like a rabbit. At any minute it's liable to give birth to a litter of little clues, all of which also must be followed. As for imagination—well, imagination's sort of a flashlight to help you when you're poking around in dark corners."

Clancy informed the two men that Miss Allen and what guests had been in the house at the time of the tragedy were upstairs in her private sitting room. He advised the detectives to view the corpse before presenting themselves to Miss Allen, as his men were waiting to remove it. Clancy thereupon led the way to the library where the crime had been committed. Not a little awed by the presence of so renowned a criminal investigator as Mr. Wimble, the few men who still lingered finished up their work and departed.

Ordinarily upon looking at the victim of a murder one expects to see something hideous. Corey, less hardened

than his chief to viewing mutilated bodies, stepped rather
timidly to the Persian rug were Clancy indicated the body
lay. But as he looked down upon the remains of Gary Gilbert, Corey was filled with admiration rather than horror.
With a single discrepancy, it was as if an exquisitely executed sculpture by Praxiteles lay there.

Furthering the illusion, the body of Gary Gilbert was
clothed in the garb of ancient Greece—explained of course
by the fact that Marcia Allen's guests had been invited
to a fancy dress ball. In life Gilbert's figure must have
been graceful and supple. Even in death the man's face was
handsome—perhaps more so than when he was alive, for
Death kindly removes from a face lines graven by temper
and self-indulgence. Crisp blond curls covered his beautifully shaped head. Judging by his full lips it was easy to
imagine that his eyes had been meltingly languorous.

The discrepant note was the thick-handled butcher
knife that had been plunged in Gary Gilbert's heart and
left there by the murderer. Considerable blood had flowed
from the wound; the body lay in such a position that most
of it had been soaked up by the Persian rug.

Suddenly Clancy and Corey saw Mr. Wimble drop
lightly to his knees. They thought his intent gaze was focused on the death wound. In reality what was claiming
the detective's attention was a small blood-flecked rent
in Gilbert's tunic above the butcher knife. Gingerly, with
fingers as sensitive as a safe-cracker's, O. W. pulled down
the loose, low-cut tunic. A short scratch on Gilbert's chest
was visible about three inches above the knife wound.

Without comment the detective arose.

"Nothing of course has been touched since the discovery of the crime?" he asked Clancy.

"Nothing. When they telephoned Headquarters that
Mr. Gilbert had been killed, we warned them not to handle anything."

"Who phoned, do you know?"

"Miss Allen's Chinese cook. They said, to have heard him over the phone, you'd have thought he was ordering groceries. Calm's a cucumber! He's the first one I questioned when I got here." The burly police detective grinned. "To tell the truth, that Chink rather got the best of me. I tried to bluff him, pretended we had the goods on him, said if he'd confess things would go easier for him. He just stood there like a stone image, letting me rave. I lost my temper finally. 'Why don't you say something?' I yelled. He said: 'A wise man does not reprove a fool.' I felt like a kid caught at the jam pot!

"But when I treated him civilly, cut out the wisecracks and asked sensible questions, I found him as willing and courteous as one could wish. He told me there was to have been a fancy dress dance here tonight; the murder happened before the guests arrived. There were several in to dinner, though. They began eating at six; finished around seven-thirty. We got news of the crime at Headquarters at about eight-thirty."

"You have a list of the dinner guests? And of the servants in the house?"

With an air of ill-acted nonchalance Clancy produced both lists.

"You're a man after my own heart!" O. W. commended him, a remark Clarence Clancy later confided to his wife he wished he had in writing.

Besides the murdered man, Miss Allen's dinner guests had numbered four:

1. John Dwight.
2. Chiquita Dwight, his wife.
3. Hugh Osborne.
4. Mrs. Katharine Wells.

Mr. Wimble handed the list to Corey. "Please make a copy of this, son. Later I want you to run up to the gardener's cottage and see if Miss Janet can tell us anything about the private lives of these persons."

"You're going to be our private reporter on this case," Mr. Wimble had promised little Janet, "but," sternly, "I'm not going to have you messing around with cadavers." So Janet had remained at the gardener's cottage.

"Webb *likes* running detective errands," the Senior detective remarked to Clancy, at which his assistant bent with considerable haste over the paper on which he was copying the names of Miss Allen's dinner guests.

Mr. Wimble scanned the list of servants. Janet Hill had mentioned the fact that Marcia Allen was a rich woman. The furnishings of her home testified to the truth of this assertion. According to the number of servants maintained by Miss Allen, however, she lived very simply. There were but four domestics listed:

1. Wing—Chinese cook.
2. Rosie Ryan—waitress and second girl.
3. Michael Maloney—gardener.
4. Blanche (Michael's wife)—laundress and downstairs maid.

Mr. Wimble told Clancy that he wished to make a survey of the room before the body was removed.

"O. K. I'll instruct my men accordingly. I'm going up to see Miss Allen before I leave. Shall I tell her you're here?"

"Please. I'll want to interview her dinner guests. You might suggest, however, that if they're tired and want to retire I can see them tomorrow morning just as well. Naturally Miss Allen will vouch for them."

When Clancy had left the library, O. W. entered upon his usual exhaustive examination of the scene of the crime, while Corey as was his custom began a sketch. As certain aspects of the case later carried the investigation outdoors, Corey's final drawing included a part of the grounds.

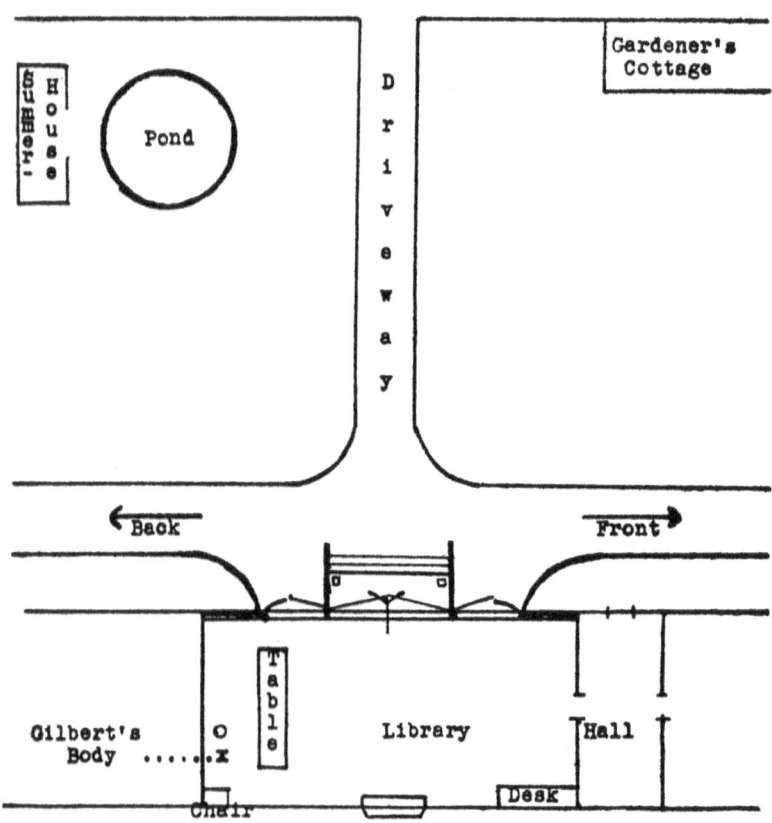

The library was a spacious room, oblong in shape, lined on three sides with well-stocked bookshelves of fine mahogany. As that side of the house commanded a gorgeous view, the west wall was sensibly devoted to tall French windows. Because of the many-colored books no single color scheme was maintained. Red, blue, green and yellow bindings predominated in Miss Allen's library, these colors being carried out in the rich Oriental rugs that strewed the hardwood floor. Maroon velvet drapes, which could

be drawn if desired, hung at the windows, with care taken
that they in no way obstructed the view. The furniture
consisted of a large mahogany table, a davenport and several inviting chairs with footstools and small tables bearing smoking paraphernalia within easy reach. There was
the bountiful display of cut flowers typical of a California
interior. Comfort was the keynote of the library; upon
entering the room one immediately longed to take down
a book and ensconce himself in one of the low, cushioned
chairs.

"The only pieces of furniture relevant to the investigation are one chair and a stool, I think," said Mr. Wimble
to his assistant, "though there's something mighty interesting about the lamp on the large table."

"That high-backed upholstered chair?" queried Corey
in reference to the one nearest the body.

Mr. Wimble nodded. "You noticed the bump on the
back of Gilbert's head, I suppose?" His smile indicated
that he supposed no such thing.

"S-sorry," stammered Corey.

"Needn't be!" returned Mr. Wimble. "I didn't either till
just now when I discovered a fleck of blood on the corner
of the high-backed chair and investigated."

Corey decided that he would learn for himself what
bearing the library table lamp had on the crime.

Out of the corner of his eye O. W. watched his assistant. After a moment he teased: "Getting warm?"

"There ought to be a red mat under the lamp. There's
one under everything else."

"Maybe the omission's the artistic touch."

"Without a pad of some sort, the metal base would
have made marks on the table," argued Corey. "Of course
the lamp may be a recent addition."

"My boy," said Mr. Wimble warmly, "I'm proud of you!"

"Don't be too lavish with your praise, O. W.!" retorted Corey with a grimace. "As far as I'm concerned my conclusion is an isolated little island in the middle of the ocean with no possible connection with the mainland."

"So I should be considering it myself if I hadn't chanced upon a bit of good luck at the front gate." To Corey's surprise his chief pulled out of his pocket a crimson silk doily similar to those on the table. "The red cloth Miss Allen gave Riley for his flashlight. Of course there would have been no particular reason for my substituting Blanche's red bunting for this doily except that, as I snatched the flashlight from Riley, I noticed what I thought might be a spot of blood on the doily."

It has become quiet in the house; it was quiet outside. As the library clock struck eleven, therefore, Corey was startled. In his interest in the crimson doily he had forgotten the dead body of Gary Gilbert. Mr. Wimble now saw his assistant back away somewhat warily from the corpse.

"Getting the willies, son?"

Corey countered, a bit tremulously: "I wonder why clocks always strike so solemnly?'

"Recording the passing of time's a solemn business."

Corey's smile froze on his face as three knocks sounded. Not if his life had depended on it could he have summoned the sang-froid with which his chief observed:

"Now all we need is for the lights to go out and a bat to fly past the window and we'll have the perfect setting."

"Glug!" was the only reply Corey could manage at the moment.

O. W. grinned. "Buck up, lad! All that's happened is that someone with a darn good dramatic sense has knocked on the library door."

Corey felt decidedly sheepish as O. W. opened the door in question, revealing a young servant girl standing over the threshold. She was a forlorn, unattractive figure as she stood there, due to her unkempt appearance and the fact that she had been weeping off and on for at least two hours.

"You must be Rosie Ryan," said Mr. Wimble kindly. Corey noticed that O. W. held the door in such a way as to prevent his assistant from being seen.

"Yes, sir," sniveled Rosie Ryan. "Miss Allen sent me down to speak to you. I didn't want to come." Her fearful peering into the library explained her reluctance. "Miss Allen says, will you please come up to her sitting room now?" Eagerness brightened Rosie's voice. "And she says prob'ly you'll want to stay all night in the house. There's loads of room, sir." This last the detective took to be Rosie's.

"You'd like me to stay?"

"I'll say!"

Mr. Wimble smiled. "You can't be afraid of anything with all these policemen on the premises!"

"My old man's a policeman," returned Rosie without enthusiasm.

"Very well; I'll stay. You may tell your mistress that I'll be up to see her in a few minutes."

Rosie departed with amusing dispatch.

Mr. Wimble returned to his young assistant. "I think you'd better bunk at the gardener's cottage tonight."

Corey said with dignity: "If you are under the impression, sir, that I am afraid of spooks—"

O. W. chuckled. "Stop sputtering, son, and come here!" Wonderingly, Corey obeyed. His chief's tone became professional. "I want you to examine Gilbert's face more closely than you did the first time. Does it resemble anyone's you've seen before?"

"It's a bit like Dolly's" decided Corey finally.

"Kneel down and try the profile." With increasing interest Corey did as his chief bade him.

"The image of Dolly's!"

Mr. Wimble bridled slightly. "Not the *image!*" he said.
No face could possibly be as beautiful as Dolly Webb's!
"But similar, especially in profile. Do you know now why
Marie fainted?"

It flashed over Corey's mind that he looked enough like
his mother to be her twin brother. "Because I reminded
her of the dead man!"

"Exactly. And you'll admit it must have startled the
poor girl suddenly to see standing beside her a man she
thought dead. Had you approached her in a good light
and full-face she might not have been so frightened. It's
only in profile your resemblance to Gilbert is so marked.
Clancy was on the right track when I switched him off by
referring to our newspaper photograph. Because of this
resemblance, son, though there'll be many ways you can
assist me, I've decided to keep you more or less in the
background on this case." The twinkles that were never
absent for long at a time reappeared in the senior detective's eyes. "When you see little Janet home tonight you
might ask her if she'll take you in tow for a week."

As delightful as was the prospect of spending a week in
the company of Miss Janet Hill, the emotion that welled
up in Corey's heart at that moment was due to another
cause. Curiously enough the weaknesses of those we love
arouse our tenderness. O. W.'s one vanity was his reputation for completing the investigation of a crime within
seven days. In suggesting to Corey that he spend the ensuing week with Janet, Mr. Wimble unwittingly had exposed
this vanity.

Suddenly a disturbing thought smote the junior detective.

"Speaking of Miss Hill, sir—you remember she told us
she'd seen Gilbert many times. Surely she too remarked
the resemblance; yet she said nothing about it to us."

"Do you know what I think, son?" O. W. could have laughed at the boy's long face! Corey looked as worried as a woman in a new hat caught in a shower. "I think little Janet kept mum because she *likes* you!"

4

His assistant having departed for the gardener's cottage, Mr. Wimble made his way to Miss Allen's private sitting room on the second floor of the house. In answer to his knock the door was opened by a woman who introduced herself as Marcia Allen.

Forgetting for the moment that the murder had interrupted a fancy dress party, the detective was somewhat startled to find Miss Allen in the garb of Queen Elizabeth. A tall, proud woman of thirty, Marcia carried the costume off exceedingly well; and Mr. Wimble reflected that, in an age when females dressed as scantily as the law allowed, it was rather a relief to see a woman wearing a few clothes for a change. The full sleeves, the voluminous skirt, the high ruche around her neck, were of the finest materials; and there was such an astonishing display of jewelry down the front of her gown that at first Mr. Wimble thought the gems false. However, their faultless beauty, the dazzling light that played in them when Miss Allen moved, assured him of their genuineness.

Upon making known his identity, Mr. Wimble noted that Miss Allen eyed him with marked circumspection. He smiled slightly.

"Your scrutiny recalls to my mind something my sister Portia once said. Portia is a great lover of dogs; there are always several to be found in her sitting room. One time someone remarked in her presence: 'I like dogs well enough—in their place!' 'But,' retorted Portia, 'who's to determine their place?'"

The gleam in Miss Allen's eye as she countered this sally was rather one of intelligent understanding than of cordiality.

"Who's to determine what a private detective should look like—is that it? I'll admit I had a preconceived notion of a man of your profession. I stand corrected."

Mr. Wimble's quick glance had taken in the other occupants of the room: two men and a woman.

"Inspector Clancy told you it wouldn't be necessary for me to interview any of you tonight?"

One of the men replied; of the four he alone was not in fancy dress costume. "We didn't like to leave Miss Allen until after the—Mr. Gilbert was taken away."

"As for me," came the shrill voice of the woman, "I wouldn't have missed meeting a real detective for anything!"

Miss Allen introduced this woman as Mrs. Katharine Wells, the two men as Hugh Osborne and John Dwight. As John Dwight and the detective shook hands they exchanged smiles which, under less tragic circumstances, might have expanded into laughter. Though Dwight was some twenty-five years the detective's junior, his were the same Humpty Dumpty proportions as Mr. Wimble's.

"My nickname's 'Dumpling'," said Dwight.

"And I'm called 'O'. You'll agree there couldn't be a rounder nickname than that!"

Miss Allen said: "These costumes we're done up in seem rather indecent in the face of what's happened, but I was giving a fancy dress ball tonight."

"I don't believe Kitten's costume could be considered decent in the face of any circumstances," said Osborne.

Finding herself the center of attraction, Katharine Wells proceeded to engage in a number of minor setting-up exercises apparently under the impression that in justification of her pseudonym she was being kittenish.

Katharine Wells was a small woman in the late twenties, dainty as a figurine in Dresden china—and as hollow. Her facial prettiness was marred by an expression of discontent and querulousness. She affected mincing ways and made the error so prevalent among small women of believing that men liked baby talk. Her undisputed claim to beauty lay in her figure. Though smaller than the accepted standard it was perfectly formed; a fact, judging by her choice of fancy dress, of which Kitten was not unaware.

She had chosen a pirate's costume—if the low cut of the shirt, the brevity of the shorts, indicated anything, a pirate who plied tropic waters. From the top of her boots to the end of her satin panties stretched a generous patch of bare leg.

Despite the exposure Kitten's appeal, like that of the unclad chorines at the Folies Bergères, was pictorial rather than biological. This was because, though her vanity fed on attention, she was inordinately cold.

Kitten returned Osborne's observation in kind. "What about you and your own legs?" Osborne had come dressed in the gay trappings of a toreador.

"An old Spanish costume!" he told the detective.

Hugh Osborne, a year or two older than Kitten, was in appearance a type familiar to the American public, a type however less often encountered in real life than in magazine advertisements. He had symmetrical features, was immaculately groomed—even his rented costume fitted him perfectly—and looked as if all his life his share of trouble had been below par. Though Hugh Osborne was conspicuously not a man of parts, his personable appearance, intrinsic wit and verve made him universally popular.

Of the four, it was John Dwight who arrested the detective's attention. He was younger than the others—perhaps twenty-six or seven—though his corpulent figure gave him a look of greater maturity. The detective's first impression of him was that Dwight was a young man who recently had been shocked to the roots of his existence. Gravity did not become his round, freckled face, with its pug nose and dimples. His generous mouth, now so sternly set, was built for laughter. His plump hands, spasmodically opening and closing, were not those of a person habitually nervous.

In the high-pitched voice that she supposed sounded childlike but which in reality resembled the cry of a lapwing, Kitten entered upon her self-appointed task of entertaining the detective.

"You should have seen Dumpling's costume, Mr. Wimble. It was a wow!" Obviously Kitten's sense of delicacy was completely obliterated by her belief that, no matter what the circumstances, she was cast for a frivolous role.

While apparently paying the strictest attention to the garrulous Kitten, O. W. intercepted the look that passed between Marcia and Osborne.

"Clever of your wife, Dumpling," said Osborne, "to realize that with your red hair and buxom figure you'd make an ideal Henry VIII."

Kitten gave vent to a series of giggles. "Considering Henry's reputation for cutting up, it wasn't so inappropriate of Dumpling to come as—"

Marcia interrupted her sharply. "It's getting late, Kitten. I imagine Mr. Wimble would like to get down to business." Mr. Wimble strongly suspected that Miss Allen realized he had been "down to business" from the moment of entering her sitting room; hence her endeavor to derail Kitten's train of thought—a suspicion that was confirmed when she deliberately changed the subject.

"I understood there were two detectives, Mr. Wimble."

"I've sent my assistant, Mr. Webb, to the gardener's cottage to take charge of a girl there named Marie Hawkins."

The name conveyed nothing to Miss Allen until Mr. Wimble described the girl.

"Oh, yes," she then remembered. "Blanche, the gardener's wife, was supposed to have helped here tonight but was taken ill. Her cousin—this Marie—happened to be visiting at the cottage and offered to take Blanche's place."

"Marie may have committed the crime!" Kitten piped up excitedly.

"Nonsense!" exploded Dwight. "A *woman* couldn't have done it!" In the young man's indignation O. W. detected an atom of anger.

"Why not?" he ventured.

"Sensitiveness in the first place. That sort of thing's just not a woman's job. And lack of strength in the second. Physically a woman's not cut out to do violence."

Kitten laughed with the hint of hysteria her laughter was never without. "Dumpling judges every woman by his wife. When will you make up to the fact that all those 'headaches' of Chiquita's are due to boredom and not ill health? Not that Chiquita probably didn't have a legitimate headache tonight,"—Kitten's voice was becoming acid—"for she certainly didn't look bored the last time I saw her."

"Nevertheless," said Dwight curtly, "Chiquita is not a strong woman!"

"Rot!" ejaculated Marcia. "No weakling could have given Chiquita's performance at the Oakland Horse Show." At an expression of pain on Dwight's face she broke off contritely: "Sorry, Dumpling! I forgot."

Osborne spoke. "I don't wonder Chiquita had a headache with that king's ransom on her head."

Dwight explained to the detective: "Mrs. Dwight was dressed as Diana, Goddess of the Moon. She wore a crescent

of jewels in her hair. She looked very beautiful." It was
plain to everyone in the room that he was remembering
how beautiful his wife had looked.

"Goddess of the Moon?" shrieked Kitten. "We were
taught at Miss Perkins'-on-the-Hudson that Diana was
Goddess of the Chase. What did that quiver slung over
Chiquita's shoulder and the arrows she carried have to do
with the moon?"

Marcia explained that Diana was Goddess of both the
Moon and the Chase.

Kitten protested: "If you ask me, the chase seemed to
interest Chiquita tonight more than the moon."

Again the detective caught the interchange of glances
between Marcia and Hugh; and again Osborne filled the
breach.

"I think Chiquita's jeweled diadem interested Gilbert
more than her dart."

Kitten turned her narrow face toward Marcia's display
of jewelry. "Oh!" she said, with a look she believed expressed tolerant amusement but which in reality showed
malicious satisfaction. "Now I know the reason for the
Family Jewels!"

"Check!" retorted Marcia tersely.

"Where is Mrs. Dwight now?" inquired Mr. Wimble.

Dwight replied, with undue eagerness the detective
thought: "She went home with a sick headache directly
after dinner."

Kitten corrected him. "Not *directly* after dinner, Dumpling!"

"Directly after dinner." There was no acrimony but decided firmness in Dwight's voice. "Kelly will corroborate
my statement."

"Well, I like that!" shrilled Kitten.

With a swift glance at Osborne, Marcia put in: "Ugly
as sin, that chauffeur of yours, Dumpling."

"Just when," drawled Osborne, making a wry face at Marcia, "did you gather the impression that sin was ugly?"

But Kitten clung to cues. "The idea of saying that, when every last one of us spent a full half hour in the library after leaving the dining room!"

With a savage glance at Kitten, Marcia backed up Dwight's statement. "The coffee we had in the library was part of dinner."

Perhaps Kitten's chief fault was that she liked to hear herself talk. Being male, O. W. found this type sufficiently distasteful socially, but in the detective business he encouraged chatterboxes.

"Of course," she tittered, "you could easily have been mistaken about the time, Dumpling, considering your condition. You're surely a riot when you're tight! The way you ran around threatening to take Gary's life if he didn't stop flirting with Chiquita was *too funny!*"

A short silence, tense with varied emotions, filled the room—broken finally by Hugh Osborne's pungent comment: "Kittens will be cats!"

As yet unaware of the slip she had made, Kitten's small features screwed up in indignation. When realization dawned on her she darted a troubled glance toward the detective. Mr. Wimble had the sort of face that inspired nervous persons with confidence. Kitten's anxiety vanished.

"It isn't as if I'd said anything in front of the police!" she vindicated herself.

To Hugh she said pertly: "I guess I'm the pal who needs legal advice now, Lawyer Cook!" Her words were pregnant with some secret significance. The detective's rapid survey of the facial expressions of the others showed a preponderance of distaste.

"You need an alienist to examine your head; that's what you need!" snapped Marcia. It was obvious that her nerves were reaching the breaking point.

Kitten assumed an air of injured innocence. "Just why is everybody picking on me, I'd like to ask? I don't know how it is in your finishing schools out here in California, but at Miss Perkins'-on-the-Hudson we were taught the Art of Conversation. 'Conversation is a Ball that must be Kept Rolling!' Miss Perkins used to say. I'm sure I've done my best to keep the ball rolling tonight!"

"At last I know where Kitten's going when she dies," announced Osborne wearily. "Into a medium's cabinet. She'll become one of those Voices named Pink Dandelion that tell what dear departed Papa wants Mama to do about that fresh plumber!"

Kitten began to cry—in the manner, O. W. observed, of a woman remembering her mascara. She sounded like a Pomeranian with indigestion.

O. W. patted her small hand with its pointed, varnished fingernails. "Everyone's on edge tonight, Mrs. Wells."

The vigilance of the others became less patent. It was evident that, in her endeavor to keep the conversational ball rolling, Kitten had been in a fair way of making some definite disclosure incriminating John Dwight. Their relief was born of her more immediate concern of weeping without shedding tears damaging to her makeup. They were reckoning without Mr. Wimble, however. Completely shattering their feeling of security, he asked:

"Just what was your fancy dress costume, Mr. Dwight?"

"I came as a butcher," replied Dwight heavily.

Immediately O. W. stored in his memory for future use the observation that Dwight's costume had been a convenient one for a man to choose who might wish to arrive at or depart from a fancy dress ball in a hurry.

Marcia laughed. It wasn't a musical sound; laughter so forced couldn't be. But O. W. knew that because she had managed it Marcia Allen was both a brave woman and a true friend.

"It was like Dumpling to impersonate a butcher," she said. "He's always been so fond of animals."

5

"May I ask you a few questions before you retire?"

She frowned. "Mr. Wimble, the police have made it very clear to us that everyone who was in the house at the time of the murder is under surveillance—virtually under arrest. It would hardly be to my advantage to run away. Need we proceed further tonight?"

The detective became stern in his manner.

"Miss Allen, your attitude toward me has been antagonistic ever since I entered this room. I understood from Janet Hill that you wished my assistant and me to handle the case. We postponed our trip East expressly to oblige you. If our presence here is in any way distasteful to you, kindly say so and we will go at once."

Miss Allen flushed. "In other words, I forget that I'm an employer—and a hostess. My excuse is that I'm tired. I've been under a terrific strain this evening. Can't your questions wait till tomorrow morning?"

A bowl of red roses stood on the table. As Mr. Wimble leaned over to smell them he said: "I do some of my best thinking at night."

"I consider that an odious remark, Mr. Wimble," returned Miss Allen crisply. "I assure you that I wish to use what remains of this night for rest—not thinking up lies with which to meet your queries tomorrow!"

HELEN BURNHAM

"Your nerves certainly are frazzled," replied O. W. suavely. "What I meant was that the time is short and I have as yet but few facts to go on; if you could supply me with additional ones I could employ to better advantage the hours remaining before I turn in."

Miss Allen's mind seized on one of the detective's remarks. Had she been less weary and nerve-racked she might have recognized it as bait.

"What do you mean: the time is short?"

"I must leave for the East in a week."

"What if the mystery is not disentangled within a week?" It was apparent to the detective, that she was hanging on his reply.

"Then I must give up the case."

Marcia was so relieved by this statement that, Mr. Wimble did not have the heart to tell her that he never yet had failed to solve a crime mystery within seven days. Undoubtedly she was not familiar with the detective's pseudonym, or if so it had failed to impress her. Though, his initials were O. W., his title of "One Week" had not been idly bestowed.

With her relief a degree of friendliness warmed Miss Allen's voice, though as yet there was no evidence of that open hospitality for which Californians are renowned.

"I really am desperately tired; Mr. Wimble. Giving a big party's always a hard job; and then this tragedy on top of everything else—"

"I shall not keep you long, Miss Allen. Of course motive is the kernel of a crime. Can you tell me why anyone should have wished to kill Mr. Gilbert?"

Apparently Miss Allen had anticipated this question. She made the mistake of answering it too promptly and in a manner of speaking that, lacking spontaneity, sounded as if she were reciting some story she had already rehearsed in her mind.

"Gary hadn't a very strong character. I think he led a pretty conventional life after coming to San Francisco two years ago, but before that I shouldn't be surprised if he had lived a more adventurous one. He spent the greater part of his life on the Continent with his Aunt. I met her once in Paris. She was a vain, silly woman, living a hand-to-mouth existence from what I could tell. There may have been secrets in Gary's past. I often thought there were, I could get him so infrequently to talk about his life abroad. He seemed to attract women of all classes." A troubled expression swept across her face. "Please understand me, Mr. Wimble. That girl Marie, the cousin of my laundress—I don't mean to accuse her especially; but it has occurred to me that some jealous woman might have followed Gary here tonight."

"Was there anyone here tonight of whom some woman could rightfully have been jealous?"

"Yes." Marcia's head was lowered so that Mr. Wimble was unable to read her facial expression, but judging from her manner up to that moment he was willing to wager that her face was not testifying to any grief for her fiancé. "Gary Gilbert and I were going to announce our engagement tonight. That's why I gave the dance." A bitter laugh escaped her. "What a sardonic sense of humor Fate has! When Gary and I were planning the ball, he kept referring to this evening as the night he was to be led to the slaughter." She broke off with a twisted smile. "I begged for a short interview and here I am making use of my woman's prerogative to chatter on and on about entirely irrelevant matters."

"No one was aware that Mr. Gilbert was your fiancé?"

"No. We had kept it a secret. I knew I'd be in for a lot of ragging. Everybody'd got used to me as an old maid. Besides," she added in some embarrassment, "there's always talk when a plain rich woman marries a handsome poor man."

"Gilbert may have told someone of your engagement?"

"Maybe, though I doubt it. He was very close-mouthed about his affairs."

Mr. Wimble asked her to tell him what had taken place at her house that evening from the arrival of her guests till the discovery of Gilbert's dead body.

"My guests arrived a little before six;—all but Dumpling. We dined early tonight because of the ball. Dumpling was visiting a sick friend—not a friend exactly—one of his charities. His wife begged me not to wait for him so we went into dinner without him. Nothing untoward happened during the meal."

"Gilbert hadn't begun flirting with Mrs. Dwight during dinner then?"

"Well, yes—he had."

"Pardon me, Miss Allen. I mean no offense. But was Mr. Gilbert a man of breeding?"

Marcia's quick smile betrayed her sense of humor.

"Isn't it Michael Arlen who said: 'A gentleman is a man who is never unintentionally rude'?" She became serious. "Despite the age we live in, Mr. Wimble, I'm a bit old-fashioned in my ideas. Gary was of the modern school. He meant to maintain his freedom even though married. I think his flirtation with Chiquita tonight was a gesture on his part to warn me that I still had time to break the engagement if I didn't approve of the contract."

"I understand," replied Mr. Wimble, reserving for his own thoughts just what it was he understood. "Please go on."

"After dinner I announced that everyone was to amuse himself till the dance began. That's the way I entertain as a rule. I find people have a better time if left to their own devices than if something is planned for their diversion. I myself went upstairs for a nap. I was in my room when

Rosie, my maid, rushed up to tell me that Dumpling had discovered Gary's murdered body in the library."

O. W. tried a new approach. "What time had Mr. Dwight arrived?"

At this question Marcia's nervousness clearly mounted, but resolutely she swallowed down her qualms and answered, all her wits alert.

"He arrived when the rest of us were having coffee in the library. Rosie brought him something on a tray."

"Would you say that relations among your guests tonight were amicable?"

"Perfectly. That is—" She broke off in some distress. "This sounds more like gossip than testimony, Mr. Wimble."

"I assure you I shall not take it in that spirit."

"Well, Chiquita was annoyed because Dumpling was late and they had a few words. At least Chiquita had the words. Dumpling just listened, as he invariably does. Dumpling isn't the quarreling kind." O. W. did not miss the tenderness in her voice.

He said gently: "To my way of thinking, Mr. Dwight was well embarked on a quarrel with Mrs. Wells tonight on the subject of his wife's headaches."

The jewels decorating Miss Allen's dress sparkled as her bosom heaved in agitation. But Marcia Allen was not a woman to be shaken out of her wits by signs of danger.

"Perhaps I had better qualify my statement. It would be impossible for Dumpling to quarrel with Chiquita. He is madly in love with his wife. To him Helen and Aspasia and Cleopatra and Juliet are just names; Chiquita's the real article." Her voice grew vibrant with bitterness. "In Dumpling's eyes, compared with Chiquita, the Virgin was a *Borgia!*"

Mr. Wimble put his next question insinuatingly. "In fact he'd go to any extreme to protect his wife's honor?"

The detective's shot told. Marcia had to force herself to present a show of composure.

"Mr. Wimble, you mustn't take that threat of Dumpling's seriously. He had seen men flirting with his wife before. She's almost unbelievably lovely, you know. Even if flirting weren't the accepted thing in our set, Dumpling just couldn't expect men not to lose their heads over Chiquita."

She went on defiantly: "Why, Dumpling Dwight wouldn't kill a fly. He's the kindest man in the world. We grew up together. I know. When we were youngsters, every kid in the neighborhood used to run to Dumpling with their broken dolls, sick puppies and bleeding noses."

"A drunken man might kill a fly."

Marcia laughed shortly. "I don't know who started Kitten Wells' nickname, but I'm quite sure someone did it in a spirit of irony. The name is so much more applicable to her catty character than her kittenish ways. A man who'd been drinking an hour or so previously would have shown more signs of it than Dumpling did tonight when you saw him, don't you think?"

"A shock will sometimes sober a man."

"And a horseshoe will sometimes bring a man good luck," retorted Marcia. "I know a man who once found a horseshoe and nailed it over his door for good luck. One day when he was standing in the doorway the horseshoe fell down and broke his crown. Dumpling was only pretending to threaten Gary."

"With the butcher knife?"

Marica's gaze met the detective's without faltering. "Yes. Why not? It was handy. For that matter I think it was the butcher knife that suggested the farce to him. It was a former butcher of theirs he'd been visiting, a man named Jenkins. Not having time to go home and dress, he'd borrowed an apron and the knife from Jenkins. If you knew

Dumpling, you'd realize that he'd feel under obligation to play the clown with the butcher knife."

"The fact remains that he pretended to be intoxicated."

"Why not? He thought it made it funnier."

"Why does Dwight consider it his duty to be the life of the party?"

"Pagliacci," said Marcia briefly. "Clowning to hide a breaking heart.

"Can you imagine how Dumpling feels when he looks into a mirror? I can." She laughed raggedly. "Mirrors certainly have a way of letting anyone beyond the city limits of Hollywood down! It's a part of being in love to imagine yourself beautiful and fine and heroic in the eyes of the one you love. I'm sure that in his day dreams Dumpling fancies himself Helen's Paris, Aspasia's Pericles, Cleopatra's Antony, Juliet's Romeo." Her voice sank almost into a whisper. "And then to look in a mirror and see his own dear, roly-poly self!"

O. W. was not the kind of criminal investigator who would allow a lump in his throat to interfere with his work.

"May I ask to what you referred this evening when you expressed regret for reminding Dwight of 'Chiquita's performance at the Oakland Horse Show'?"

"That has no bearing on the case."

"Miss Allen, may I assure you that any questions I put to you during my stay here will not be prompted by idle curiosity but by a sincere wish to find the murderer of Gary Gilbert?"

Marcia said without further remonstrance: "You must have read in the papers of the terrific fire that occurred in the stables during the recent Horse Show in Oakland. Dumpling owns a splendid stable. He had several gorgeous horses entered in the Show. They were all lost. That cut Dumpling up badly, but what nearly drove him mad

was that one of his stablemen was burned to death trying
to save the horses. Dumpling feels responsible, has been
dreadfully broken up about it. My reference to Chiquita's
riding at the Show merely recalled the tragedy, that's all."

"Dwight has been brooding—acting strangely—of late?"

Marcia instantly caught his meaning. "Suffering doesn't
make Dumpling murderous. It makes him kinder."

Mr. Wimble picked up the thread of the interview.

"You last saw Gilbert alive when you and your guests
were having coffee in the library?"

"Yes."

"What did you do when Rosie told you of the murder?"

"I hurried downstairs."

"Immediately?"

"Yes."

"Without waiting to don your Queen Elizabeth costume?"

"I already had it on."

O. W. looked mockingly skeptical. "Surely you didn't
take a nap in that rig?"

Marcia cast an admiring glance at the detective. "You
warned me that you did some of your best thinking at
night. Your bedtime must be sometime off, you appear so
extremely wide awake at the moment. I didn't take a nap
as I'd planned. When I got upstairs I found a letter from my
sister in Hollywood which I decided to answer right away.
When I got downstairs everything was in confusion. Someone rang up the police. Wing, I think. Later that little Miss
Hill telephoned and suggested my sending for you."

Mr. Wimble took the crimson doily out of his pocket.

"By the way, Miss Allen, just where was this before you
gave it to the policeman to wrap around his flashlight?"

"Under the library lamp. No," she reflected, "I don't
believe it was. That's where it belongs but I don't seem to
remember moving the lamp. It must have been lying on

the table. At any rate, I wanted to keep my guests from entering the grounds. I suppose the bare flashlight would have done as well, but one automatically thinks of red to indicate danger. Being red, the doily suggested itself."

A knock sounded. At Miss Allen's command the door opened and a Chinese servant shuffled into the room, carrying a tray on which were a glass of milk and some graham crackers.

"Missy's bedtime."

"My guardian angel," Marcia smiled at the detective. Her face was full of affection as she turned toward the Chinaman. "This is Mr. Wimble, Wing, the private detective who is going to find the murderer for us."

A guardian angel in parchment, Wing, brown and brittle. O. W. had the feeling that if he were to touch him the old fellow would crackle. The fingers that held the tray were like twigs. The expression on the Chinaman's face was inscrutable—the network of wrinkles traced by time as hard to read as the faded writing on old parchment.

All evening fear and strain had been attacking the walls of Miss Allen's control. Suddenly they began to crumble. As her lips quivered, the tall, proud woman became a little girl, sad, frightened, lonely.

Swiftly O. W.'s eyes sought Wing's. He must not infringe on the right of the old retainer to comfort the girl. The Chinaman made no move.

The detective stepped over to Marcia, gently raised her chin. "Come now, Miss Allen," he said kindly, Holding the glass to her lips, "drink your milk."

As keen as was the defective's hearing, he was unaware when Wing left. Later, when Marcia had conducted him to the room he was to occupy during the investigation, he found on the table by his bedside a tray on which stood a glass of milk and a plateful of graham crackers. In his modesty, Mr. Wimble took this to be a custom of the house.

6

Mr. Wimble slept fitfully that night. It was not the case that interfered with his sleep. Had O. W. possessed the sort of mind that went to pieces over an investigation he would not be enjoying the success he had earned solving crime mysteries. The reason Mr. Wimble did not sleep was because he found it so inordinately quiet in Thousand Oaks. In New York O. W. lived in an apartment overlooking one of the city's busiest thoroughfares. The multisonous hubbub of urban night was his lullaby: the clangor of street-cars, the grinding of brakes, the tooting of horns, the thundering of elevated trains, the laughter of night-blooming revelers. To others in Marcia's house at Thousand Oaks, there may have sounded numerous distracting noises: the chirping of crickets, the croaking of frogs, the calls of small animals, the rustling of leaves; but to O. W. the night was as quiet as a tomb.

Shortly after five he was awakened from a cat nap by what sounded like a cannon going off in his room. Despite his rotundity, Mr. Wimble was light on his feet. So it was not his build that kept him from bounding out of bed. The years had taught the detective the wisdom of stopping, looking and listening. Therefore, when the cannon exploded, O. W.'s first act was cautiously to open his eyes. Upon seeing what it was that had awakened him, the knoll

formed by Mr. Wimble's round paunch in the center of his
bed shook under the pink counterpane like a mound of
strawberry jelly. A tiny bird was perched on the window-
sill, chirping at the top of his small lungs!

"All right, young feller!" chuckled Mr. Wimble. "Have
it your own way. It's high time I got up and looked around
outside anyhow."

Taking pains not to disturb the household O. W. went
downstairs into the library. Though he was accustomed
by this time to the vagaries of Murder, as he entered the
room it seemed incredible that a heinous crime could have
been committed in so tranquil and elegant a place. The
body had been taken away. The telltale traces of blood on
the rug and chair had been removed. Only the faint smell
of flash powder smoke reminded O. W. that the night before policemen, reporters and photographers had milled
through the library on their respective errands in connection with the murder of Gary Gilbert.

Suddenly a sound so muffled that it might have been
the sigh of Gilbert's ghost caused the detective to whirl
toward the door.

"Yes?"

Miss Allen's aged Chinese servitor entered. He was
bearing a well-filled breakfast tray which he set on the
table in front of the detective.

O. W. beamed his pleasure; "You are a mind reader, I
see." Removing the lid of the coffee pot he inhaled the
aroma of its contents. "As well as an excellent cook." The
library clock, the tone of which Corey had found so lugu-
brious, struck six.

O. W. said in some anxiety: "I trust I didn't get you
up?"

"It is my custom to arise early," the Chinaman replied
in his schoolroom English. As the slits that were his eyes
became thin glistening lines, O. W. realized that Wing

was at least trying to smile. "An old man borrows from his nights to make longer his days."

"Great country, California!" reflected O. W. "Paradise for climate and philosophers for cooks!"

Mr. Wimble was in the habit of wasting precious little time during the solving of a crime mystery; but after his breakfast when he stepped out on to the library porch he could not resist lingering a moment to view the marvelous panorama spread out before him.

Below him stretched the East Bay cities: Oakland, Berkeley, Albany, Richmond—variegated beads strung on the long length of San Pablo Avenue which ran through them all and which showed white at intervals like the bits of slack thread so common to necklaces. Beyond the cities lay the Bay, blue under the spring sky, already astir with craft. And across the Bay was San Francisco, where hills and buildings vie with one another in scraping the sky.

O. W.'s contemplation of the glorious vista was interrupted by the sound of footsteps. A figure, from all appearances a turbaned sultan in trousers, was coming down the driveway. The detective recalled that, with the exception of those who had been invited to dinner, Miss Allen's guests last night had been denied admission to the grounds. Had one of them, celebrating instead at some night-club, become befuddled and decided to show up at Marcia's after all?

To Mr. Wimble's astonishment, as the sultan approached, he heard his own name called.

"O. W.!" The turbaned potentate was his assistant Corey Webb!

Mr. Wimble was not easily startled. In his long career as a private detective he had found himself in many situations demanding steady nerves. But his aplomb certainly received a jolt when he saw swathed in head bandages the young man he had left hale and hearty only a few hours before in the gardener's cottage.

His first agonized thought was: "How can I square my-self with Dolly?"

His throat was dry as he shakily inquired of Corey what had happened.

His chief's anxious solicitude warmed the younger man's heart, but his principal emotion at the moment was an overwhelming contrition. "I'm beastly sorry to have startled you, sir! I haven't been in an accident."

Mr. Wimble looked for a place to sit down.

"Jan—Miss Hill's responsible for the bandages," explained Corey, dropping down on the steps beside his chief.

That he had forgiven the lad for frightening him was manifest in the good-natured raillery with which the detective countered his assistant's explanation. "I suppose you tried to kiss little Janet good-by last night, whereupon she—pushed you in the face I believe is how she expresses what she does to gentlemen who get fresh."

The bit of Corey's face that was visible through the bandages turned a vivid pink. Of course it was a warm morning and bandages are not known for their cooling qualities.

"This is a disguise," announced the junior detective with what dignity he could muster. The older man's arm slid with a fatherly gesture about his assistant's shoulders.

"Tell me about it, son."

"That French girl, Marie, is very anxious to recover a portrait of herself from Gary Gilbert's rooms. She offered to pay me for impersonating Gilbert, going to his hotel and retrieving the portrait." A laugh escaped him. "You ought to have heard the volley of French oaths she fired at Miss Hill!"

"What did Marie have against the charming Janet?"

"Well, Miss Hill pointed out the impracticability of the scheme to Marie. Everyone in the hotel would know by the papers that Gilbert was dead. Marie insisted I could bluff it through. Miss Hill said it would put me in a most compromising position to be found in Gilbert's rooms except on official business and that, furthermore, I was not the sort to let chivalry get the best of my commonsense." As Corey forgot to talk Mr. Wimble knew the lad was remembering Janet. What a little "mountie" the child was, thought O. W.; took her no time at all to get her man!

Corey came to with a start. As he stole a glance at his chief, that beloved imposter pretended he hadn't noticed the pause.

"Then Marie let loose," Corey continued. "That girl's tongue is a veritable machine gun. She had ammunition in two languages. When she'd exhausted her supply, Miss Hill fired back. All she said was: 'Hussy!', but I swear she got more feeling into that one word than Marie into all her hot invective."

"By the way, son, how did Marie go about trying to persuade you to get that portrait for her?" Again Corey's beautifully shaped nose turned crimson. O. W. managed to hold back his chuckle. "They say French girls are great vamps. I dare say Marie's not a bad-looking sort when she's not falling into swoons on front porches."

"I don't care for those dark-haired, flashing-eyed girls myself," said Corey carelessly. O. W. recalling the pale blonde beauty of Miss Janet Hill again had difficulty leashing his chuckle.

"Well, how did the argument come out?"

"I placated Marie by promising her I'd think it over. Of course I wanted your advice. I told Miss Hill I intended seeing you about it. She suggested this disguise. You see, I'd let her know that because of my resemblance to Gilbert you wanted me to keep under cover for the time being."

According to O. W.'s mother, there were fewer jealous wives in the days when handsome husbands went in for beards. The detective wondered if it had occurred to Miss Janet that, as well as a disguise, head bandages provided a pretty good Keep-Off sign. He made no mention of this to Corey. He felt that the boy had been sufficiently teased for the moment.

The detectives discussed the matter of Marie's request while examining the grounds. To a casual observer their inspection would have looked like a leisurely pre-breakfast stroll; but Corey, acquainted with his chief's powers of observation, knew that Mr. Wimble's keen glance was recording with the relentlessness of a camera everything he saw.

As they sauntered over the estate Mr. Wimble gave his assistant various instructions. Corey was not yet so adroit at the detective game that he could pay attention to two things at once; so in listening to his chief he missed seeing the crumpled piece of paper that immediately attracted the senior detective's attention.

The evening before, in discussing with Janet Hill the fascinating profession he had chosen as his life work, Corey had told her that it was surprising how few tangible clues a detective found on a case to help him. Monsieur Bertillon's acolytes rarely discovered thumb- or footprints to facilitate the investigation. Only novices in crime, in which case of course the services of a private investigator of Mr. Wimble's prestige were not solicited, left such incriminating articles as caps, gloves, buttons and locks of hair around to help identify them.

"O. W. says that a scrap of conversation is the best clue there is. Some stray remark, something held back, different intonations of voice, often help the trained investigator to unravel an apparently inextricable mystery."

But occasionally a tangible clue presents itself, something flagrantly in keeping with violence. In this instance, the rumpled paper that Mr. Wimble picked up near the summer-house gave every appearance of having some bearing on the Gilbert murder case. It was a telegram. The message was intact, though all other information was obliterated by a dark stain.

MARCIA KNOWS ALL STOP BEWARE OR SOME GREAT HARM WILL OVERTAKE YOU

CARA

The dark blotch that hid the address was obviously a blood stain.

7

When Mr. Wimple and Corey came within view of the house, O.W.'s keen eyes detected Wing on watch inside the screen door of the kitchen. The moment their footsteps sounded on the walk the old Chinese stepped out on to the porch. Though he could not possibly have missed seeing them he appeared oblivious of their presence. His brittle body was enveloped in a full-length white apron and the clawlike, fingers of his right hand curled around a bread knife. Through an association of ideas Corey's mind immediately recalled the fact that on the night of the murder John Dwight had worn a white apron and carried a knife.

"*What the—!*" Corey suddenly whispered to his chief. With his left hand the Chinaman was holding aloft by the scruff of its neck a black and tan puppy.

To Webb's astonishment O. W. remarked in an ordinary tone of voice: "I must ask Miss Allen if the bird that woke me up this morning were a linnet."

Corey understood that he was to conduct himself as if nothing unusual were happening. "There are linnets about," he returned conversationally. "I saw one as I was coming to meet you. Chestnut brown, with its forehead and foreneck crimson."

They were abreast of the porch when Corey clutched his chief's arm. Certainly Mr. Wimble's young assistant could not be blamed for this lapse from the casual. If appearances could be relied upon, a blood-curdling scene was about to be enacted on the back porch. Yet as Wing raised his knife O. W. looked as unconcerned as if what was about to occur were intrinsically as much a part of the California morning as its glorious sunrise.

A noise like an ill-bred diner at his soup found vent through the Chinaman's lips. Simultaneously Corey sprang up the steps.

"Hey!" he yelled. "What's the big idea?"

To Corey at least the Chinaman's facial expression was unfathomable. "The ribbon of Mitzi is too tight." Wing spoke in the stilted manner of a foreigner who has learned academic English. His voice was low and passionless. "The life of a puppy is no longer than the length of his collar."

Corey in his alarm had snatched the dog from the Chinaman's grasp. He noticed that the pup's ribbon was indeed too tight and that the knot looked stubborn. "Well, then, cut it like a human," he sternly admonished. He had been too badly frightened to be able as yet to appreciate the farce of the situation. "There's no sense going about it as if you meant to murder the animal!" No foreman on important construction work ever oversaw a job as meticulously as Corey watched that aged Oriental free Mitzi of her cervical decoration. A bit to the young man's disgust, when he had set Mitzi down, the puppy waddled over to Wing, nuzzling against the Chinaman's leg.

From the foot of the steps Mr. Wimble chuckled. "Did you think Wing was preparing the Sunday roast, son?" But Corey still felt there was something queer about the affair.

When O. W. introduced his assistant and Miss Allen's cook, Wing bowed with old world courtesy. Though skeptical, in case he might have misjudged the Chinaman,

Corey tried to make amends by saying what he had learned never failed to conciliate a resident of California.

"Fine weather you have out here!"

Wing's reply may or may have referred to Corey, but as he spoke his eyes were on the young man's bandages. "The sun is not warm if winter is in the heart."

On their way to the gardener's cottage, the senior detective discerned signs of excitement in his assistant's face. He suspected what was on the boy's mind and felt gratified that Corey was learning to observe. Young Webb was still a bit too prone to build up theories on faulty premises, but experience would lend incisiveness to his reasoning. On the whole Mr. Wimble was proud of this lad who had been in his employ only a year.

Immediately they were beyond earshot of the Chinaman Corey spoke. "O. W.! Do you think that old Chink's quite right in the head?"

"I see nothing wrong with Wing's head," returned O. W. ingenuously, "nor, judging from his histrionic demonstration on the back porch, with his heart."

Corey gaped in amazement.

"You think, sir, that Wing was merely putting on a show for our benefit?"

"I'm afraid those bandages of yours act as sort of blinders, son. Wing was on the lookout for us; he didn't begin his performance till we had front row seats, as it were; he fairly purred with gratification when your interference proclaiming the success of his ruse; and," O. W.'s voice became affectionately mocking, "I'm sure that if a few moments previously Wing had been eying Mitzi with murderous intent she wouldn't have rubbed up quite so lovingly against his shin."

There was one good thing about head bandages, Corey decided; they kept a fellow from looking as sheepish as he felt.

"Guess I haven't much understanding of human nature, sir."

"I'd hardly call Wing's willingness to hang for somebody else typical of human nature," returned O. W. dryly. "From my experience I've found that more fellows are disposed to let their friends hang for them than vice versa."

Which set Mr. Wimble's assistant to thinking. In trying to implant in the detectives' minds his own predilection for sticking knives through hearts, just whom was Wing shielding?

Upon reaching the cottage the detectives met the gardener starting out on his day's work. They had made the acquaintance of Michael the night before—a blinking-eyed Irishman in a woolen nightshirt aroused from slumber by his nonplused spouse.

Michael Maloney was a phlegmatic individual some forty-five years of age. His tanned skin and the brown corduroys he affected gave him the appearance of being a part of the soil. His back was crooked as if from too many years of bending over his flowers. Except when directly questioned he maintained a consistent taciturnity, due perhaps to a disinclination to converse on any subject but gardening or perhaps to the fact that he had a loquacious wife. When he did talk his brogue was marked.

Mr. Wimble greeted the Irishman with his customary geniality that made the day just a bit brighter for anyone coming in contact with him. Michael grunted a response, but his shuffling feet, the fact that he did not lay down his garden implements, plainly demonstrated his desire to be on his way.

Corey, to whom the attitude of the Native Sons and Daughters of the Golden West was a huge joke, saw an opportunity to twit the gardener. "I thought the flowers grew by themselves in 'Sunny' California!"

Michael was impervious to jollity. "Roight ye are, sir-r. But so do the weeds an' th' wee bugs."

Mr. Wimble said: "I may wish to question you about the murder later on."

Michael scowled. "I've me gardhen to attind to!"

Suddenly a scent sweeter to him at that moment than the fragrance of Michael's rarest bloom assailed Corey's nostrils. Voluptuously he sniffed. It was the aroma of frying bacon.

"Lord bless me sowl!" ejaculated Michael. "Blanche towld me t' call Misther Webb t' breakfast!" As he cast a nervous glance toward the cottage, it was evident that though Michael lorded it over the garden a feminine ruler wielded the scepter in the cottage. "I bether be gettin' t' me plantin' at th' pond." He added grudgingly: "Thot's where ye'll be findin' me if ye want me."

Mr. Wimble was not to escape Blanche's despotism. Despite his protestations that he had already breakfasted, she insisted that he sit at the table with Corey.

"From Mr. Webb's speed removing his bandages so he can tackle that bacon," laughed O. W., "I don't believe you'll have enough for two!" But Blanche was not to be circumvented. The detective suspected that Wing and Blanche were rivals and that she wished to acquaint him with the superior merits of her cookery. He also suspected that his appreciation of the meal would put her in a tractable frame of mind, always desirable in a witness.

Blanche Maloney, née Feuillat, was of a race that looks upon cooking as an art. In France it is considered an honor for one's cognomen to be bestowed upon a dish. Though no little renown has accrued abroad to Chateaubriand because of his divers literary works, in his own country you will first hear his name as applied to a steak. French history tells of a cook committing suicide because the

fish he'd ordered for his master's dinner failed to arrive in
time. No scientist ever applied himself more zealously to
research than a *cordon bleu* to his quest for a new flavor.
Long before "specialists" were heard of, more than one
French chef was known to have devoted his entire lifetime
to the perfection of a single delicacy.

Assuming cooking as numbering among the Muses,
Blanche served the detectives one of the most artistic
meals they had ever eaten. At first as she waited on the
two men, her mien was solemn, owing to the gravity of
Saturday night's events; but Mr. Wimble's pleasant eye and
hearty manner soon won her over to a good humor. In
fact, when after his fifth *brioche* O. W. said: "A few of your
breakfasts, Blanche, and I'd be fat!", she went off into a
gale of wholesome laughter.

Blanche was a woman nearing forty. With that fatal
tendency of even the most chic French women, after thirty
Blanche had begun to fatten until now in structure she
resembled a mound of multi-sized bubbles. From the knob
of brown hair on top of her head to the cushions of fat
over her insteps she was orbicular. She had a jolly round
face, round, slightly protruding brown eyes and a blob of
a nose. Her generous breasts were round; her still more
generous hips were round. Having lived in America since
infancy she spoke with no trace of a French accent.

Blanche was by nature a chatty person. O. W. had a way
of directing conversation without visible effort, so that by
the time breakfast was over he had learned considerable
about Blanche's connection with last night's affair.

Though Rosie habitually waited on table at "the house",
when there were entertainments Blanche helped. She was
to have helped last night.

"Mike and I had our supper early as Miss Allen wanted
me up to the house by six-thirty. Just as we were sitting
down to the table, who should arrive but my cousin!"

Marie had seemed strangely excited, and upon being questioned had admitted having been oppressed all day by the feeling that Blanche wasn't well.

"She fairly gave me the willies, looking at me like I was on my last legs! I wasn't feeling any too good last night but," virtuously, "I ain't a woman to let my health interfere with my duty."

Upon hearing that Blanche was due at "the house," Marie had offered to take her cousin's place. On several previous occasions Marie had acted as extra maid at Miss Allen's, borrowing suitable attire from Rosie. Fortunately Marie had left a note for her husband saying that she intended spending the night with Blanche.

Blanche didn't care much for Marie's husband, a man some years older than Marie by the name of Henry Hawkins. Henry was of English descent and in him Blanche found all the Anglo-Saxon traits frowned on by those of Gallic temperament. Her main complaint was that Henry was "heavy"—took life too seriously, was afraid Marie would have a good time. She had often wondered what a girl so vivacious and fond of fun as Marie could have seen in a self-righteous stick like Henry. Perhaps Henry's adoration of Marie had something to do with it. The man certainly was mad about his wife. And jealous! Marie didn't dare even to thank the postman for bringing the mail.

"Not that Marie ever gave Henry any cause for jealousy. She wouldn't *look* at another man. Not if Rudy Vallee himself came serenading beneath her window!"

Like most persons who like the sound of their own voices Blanche preferred talking about herself; so her conversation swerved back to her own somewhat negative role in the tragedy.

It was funny how active she was on her feet for a heavy woman, she said. She got tired before she knew it.

"It ain't easy serving refreshments at a big party. I'll admit when Marie offered to take my place I jumped at the chance to get out of doing it."

At about seven Kelly, the Dwights' chauffeur, had come in to play cards with Michael. Kelly was fond of Mike, was in the habit of visiting the cottage often. He admired the purity of her husband's brogue, he had told Blanche, his own having suffered from his many travels. As Kelly seemed intensely interested in the subject of gardening, he had no difficulty in getting Michael to talk. Sometimes, Blanche said, the chauffeur would repeat a word after Mike as if trying to recapture the dialect of his childhood.

At about nine o'clock Kelly had gone home and the Maloneys were in bed at nine-thirty as usual.

Blanche terminated her recital by naively inquiring of Mr. Wimble if he would like to interrogate her. The detective gravely replied that he probably would have some questions for her later but that at present he wished to have a chat with Marie.

The investigation took Corey that morning to "the city"—the designation of the East Bay dwellers for San Francisco. So when O. W. interviewed Marie Villette Hawkins he was unaccompanied by the young man she had found so indifferent to her wiles the night before.

Marie was still sulky and plainly showed the effects of a sleepless night. Though not at her best, the French girl bore a marked beauty—rather animal than otherwise, for though her features and form were perfect there was no evidence of spiritual beauty in her face, no mark of superior intelligence. Blanche had stressed Marie's liveliness and fondness for fun; no doubt the girl's gaiety was her chief allure but of course the murder temporarily had crushed her high spirits. Marie spoke English with only a slight accent and with but a few pardonable provincialisms.

As the girl paused for a moment by the door, moved toward a chair, went to the window, O. W. was struck by the grace of her various attitudes.

He asked pleasantly: "Are you anyone's model at present?"

Marie swung toward him, startled. "Nobody knows about me being an artists' model. That I do not tell."

"Your husband wouldn't approve, I take it?"

"He would not." She added in surly loyalty: "Henry has his reasons."

"I have no intention of revealing your secret," returned Mr. Wimble smoothly, "but I disagree with you that you don't tell it. You pose too much for a keen observer not to guess at once."

Marie regarded him sullenly but with some respect.

Mr. Wimble opened the interview. "Why were you so anxious to get into Miss Allen's house last night?"

"I wasn't!" snapped Marie.

"Come now, Marie. I guessed that you were an artists' model. What's to prevent me from guessing that you were mighty anxious to be present at Miss Allen's party last night?"

"Guess what you like!" Her tone was insolent.

Though Mr. Wimble had but a week in which to complete his investigation, this arrant waste of time did not in the least disturb his equanimity.

"Very well. You came here last night with the express purpose in mind of taking Blanche's place at Miss Allen's. So that your cousin would offer no objection, you convinced her that she was too sick to go herself."

Marie looked alarmed but offered no comment.

Imperturbably O. W. continued his inquiry. "Did Mr. Gilbert tell you he was coming over here or did you read of it in the paper?"

"I didn't come to see Gary! I came to see my cousin."

"Oh, you knew Mr. Gilbert well enough to call him by his first name?"

The girl flushed, in anger as well as chagrin. "How can I help knowing his first name? That is all you hear around here. Gary Gilbert. The Murder of Gary Gilbert."

O. W. smiled ruefully. "You still don't put much faith in my guessing powers, I see. My assistant is loyal, Marie. He has told me of your request that he rifle Mr. Gilbert's rooms."

Marie's eyes were shot with venom. "Mr. Webb would have done what I asked, too, but for that little hell-cat he had with him!"

"It wasn't very clever of you to try to vamp young Webb," observed Mr. Wimble softly, "when he'd just met the Loveliest Lady."

"I wasn't trying to vamp him!" Marie's voice soared to a scream. "Vamping's not my lay! I never tried to vamp a man in my life. Never! Do you hear? Never!"

Her sang-froid completely shattered, with an impassioned *Zut alors!* she surrendered to a crying spell.

When her sobs had somewhat subsided Mr. Wimble made a simple experiment. "Does Henry like red noses?"

Marie's retort came swiftly: "Henry, he would love me any way I looked!" But a fresh torrent of tears told the detective what he wanted to know.

"I'd hate to see your marriage go on the rocks, Marie." Another paroxysm of sobbing seized the girl.

"I might be able to help you, if you'd tell me what was wrong." There was pleading in the detective's voice when next he spoke. "I should think you'd take any chance there was rather than lose Henry." He was gratified to observe that she was listening to him. "Come, Marie, why don't you tell me what's troubling you?"

"I thought you were the good guesser!" she sniffled. O. W. felt encouraged. You don't joke with a person you don't trust.

"No," he smiled, "only a good bluffer."

So after a raid on her handkerchief Marie took the detective into her confidence.

"I read in the paper that Gary was coming over here. So I left a note for Henry saying Blanche was sick and I was coming over to stay all night with her. I wanted to see Gary. He had a painting of me. I had to get it back." Her voice became a wail. "I would have got it, too, if somebody hadn't done him in!"

Controlling herself, she went on: "Fortune, she played in to my hands last night. I heard Gary and Miss Allen talk about getting married. I knew at last I had a weapon to use against him. I could threaten that unless he gave me the painting I'd tell Miss Allen what I knew about him."

"Blackmail's dirty work, Marie."

"Dirty!" she echoed vehemently. "I'd clean put garbage cans with my bare hands it it'd help me keep Henry!"

"What scandal did you know about Gary Gilbert that would have turned Miss. Allen against him?"

The agony of returning Mr. Wimble's steady gaze became too great. Marie's eyes fell. In anguish her fists pounded each other. Piteously she gulped in an endeavor to speak. No word came.

Mr. Wimble said gently: "I'm sure, Marie, that to Henry Hawkins you've been everything a man would want his wife to be."

Her words fairly tumbled over themselves then. "The life I led in Paris as an artists' model was not decent. I know. But a girl she must eat. I was too young when I was sent out into the world—and too pretty. The men— A young girl she is starving. A man offers her food." She

shrugged expansively. "What would you? Life is sweet.
I did try to get work. Modeling was all I could find. I
met Gary in the studios. He also was a model. We were
so poorly paid. You cannot imagine! Neither of us had
enough for food and lodging both." Again she shrugged.
"What would you?

"While Gary and I were living together an artist, Ger-
ardin, painted us. He called his picture 'Day and Night'.
I understood that an Italian art collector in Paris by the
name of de Palermo bought it. Two years ago I learned
that Gary had it.

"I met Gary one day in San Francisco. I had lost track
of him. I had never loved him; he was without character.
I was sorry to learn he was in America. He brought back
the old days in Paris I was trying to forget. A few days
after our meeting I got a note from him saying it would be
to my advantage to call on him. I was frightened. I went
to his hotel. He showed me the painting. I asked for it; I
offered to buy it from him. He refused." The girl's shoulders sagged. "After that I paid him every month to keep
him from showing the painting to my husband.

"Henry knows I was a model in Paris, but to him I am
an angel. He thinks I posed in furs and picture hats. He'd
leave me in a minute if he knew I'd posed in the nude before men.

"I saved as much from my housekeeping account as I
dared without arousing Henry's suspicions, but it wasn't
enough. I posed on the sly for an artist in 'the city'. Every
single minute I was posing I was afraid the door would
burst open and in would come Henry. When I was late
with the payments Gary would write. Once Henry found
one of Gary's letters. Fortunately the note sounded only
like an invitation to visit him. I had to tell Henry that
I had known Gary in Paris, had met him lately in San
Francisco. I tore the letter up and promised not to see

Gary. But Henry didn't trust me. Once he followed me to Gary's hotel. Luckily for me I saw him in time; instead of going to Gary's penthouse rooms I went into the roof lounge and was ordering tea when Henry found me. And one time Henry and I passed Gary on the street. After that it was worse. How could I be true to him, Henry wanted to know, when a man as handsome as Gary wanted me?"

A sudden palm smote the girl. "I guess I'm not presenting my husband in a very good light."

O. W. smiled: "When you think what other wives have to put up with, I don't believe Henry's jealousy is so bad."

"That's what I say!" corroborated Marie eagerly. "I'd rather Henry had fits of jealousy than just plain fits." Tenderness sweetened her voice. "Henry's the only man who ever thought me good. To the others I was only good company. Plenty of men have wanted me; only Henry wanted to marry me. And kind! You can't imagine! He fusses over me as if I was a baby. He won't think of letting me get up in the morning till the house is warm. That doesn't sound like much, maybe, but I wish you could have seen me in the old days when I was living around in the studios. Me, I'd be the one to get up and warm the studio.

"Oh, Mr. Wimble!" She was speaking to him but her whole attitude expressed prayer. "If only you could get that painting for me!"

"I've told my assistant to bring it to me," said the detective softly. "You shall have it directly the investigation is closed."

Marie's black eyes glowed. O. W. had not bought her gratitude. He had been genuinely moved by her story. At the same time he felt that because of her gratitude her ensuing testimony could absolutely be relied upon.

Taking Blanche's place at "the house", Marie had spent as much time as possible maneuvering without success to see Gilbert alone. Most of her loitering had been done in the hallway outside the library. Arranging things on a refreshment table there over, which she was to preside had given her an excellent excuse for being in that vicinity. Slightly before eight she had been joined by a stout young man wearing a white apron.

At this point in her story Marie giggled. "I took him for a waiter and began joshing him. Then I found out he was Mr. Dwight, one of the guests. He wasn't a bit sore, though. I liked him fine. While we were there together we heard Gary talking in the library; then a woman's voice that Mr. Dwight told me was his wife's. I said: 'A lady with such a musical voice must be beautiful!' Then Mr. Dwight told me how lovely 'Chiquita' was. But when he knocked on the door nobody answered. 'Guess they went out while I was talking,' he said and tried the door. It was locked. He looked sort of troubled. 'Think I'll join my wife in the garden,' he said and went away. I decided I'd look for Gary in the garden, so I slipped out the front door."

Marie had kept close to the house so that in the shadows of the bushes she would not be seen. She had been about twenty yards away when a woman in white, accompanied by a man in uniform, had stepped through the French windows on to the library porch.

"The man spoke to the woman in a low voice—I couldn't make out the words but he sounded as if he was giving orders—and then went back inside. The woman staggered down the steps, sort of like she was sick or maybe tipsy. She was walking away when Mr. Dwight came around the back of the house. 'Chiquita!' he called and joined her. When they were out of sight, thinking the man in the uniform was Gary, I started for the library. Only a few steps had I gone when I was stopped by a girl's voice behind me. 'Who are you?' I was so startled! You can't imagine! The girl was in an aviator's suit and if it hadn't been for her voice I'd have taken her for a man, she was so big and ugly. I told her I was an extra maid hired for Miss Allen's party. 'Well, you weren't hired to patrol the grounds!' she said and ordered me back to the kitchen. I only pretended to go. I hid in the bushes. I heard the girl call softly: 'Michele!' and saw the uniformed man on the porch again. *'Get into the car!'* he called back and ran down the driveway. They were no sooner out of sight than Mr. Dwight came running up the steps and into the library. I listened a minute for Gary's voice. I heard nothing. So I went back to the kitchen."

She had been in the kitchen with Wing and Rosie when a few minutes later John Dwight had rushed in with the news of the Gary Gilbert murder.

After two breakfasts Mr. Wimble felt that a walk around the grounds wouldn't do him any harm. The sound of voices raised in argument directed his footsteps toward the pond. Arriving there he saw a man in heated conversation with Michael.

As the men became aware of the detective's presence, swiftly the one unknown to Mr. Wimble picked up some garden tools and without a backward glance hurried off toward the strip of woods behind the house. Scowling, the gardener watched him go.

"You seem none too pleased with yonder gentleman," observed the detective.

Michael thereupon entered upon an awkward explanation to the effect that he had hired the man to clear out the underbrush in the wood but that, owing to the murder, he had considered it expedient for the fellow to return another day.

"But he said I'd promised 'im th' wur-rk and he reefused t' go!"

For Michael to have made the crime his excuse for putting the man off was inconsistent with his earlier intimation that mere murder was insufficiently important to postpone gardening. What suspicion Mr. Wimble entertained that Gardener Maloney was lying, however, he chose to let ride for the moment.

8

Perhaps not even Mr. Hearst himself fully understands why human beings are so interested in crime. It may be that the habitués of the half-world as they pore over lurid accounts of murder, banditry and the drug traffic eagerly picture themselves as the human monsters perpetrating the atrocities. Inversely it may be that the Best Families, in these democratic days when a royal prince is at best only a traveling salesman, like to read of crime in order to tone up their sense of superiority. For though according to police records Murder hoots at social position, no one numbering among the Four Hundred would as much as dream of himself in the role of murderer, even after midnight suppers of caviar, whipped cream and watermelon.

Whatever their appeal, newspaper scarelines are as keenly interesting to those whose names grace the Society Columns as to those whose names editors consider news suitable only for the sections devoted to Vital Statistics. There is something fascinating about victims, whether of earthquake, confidence men, famine, lockjaw or murder.

To Marcia's crowd the murder of Gary Gilbert was by far the most thrilling thing that had ever happened among them. They'd had fires, elopements, burglaries, jiltings, nervous breakdowns, divorces and suicides before—but never a murder! It became their one topic of conversation.

Unanimously they expressed regret that the crime had not been timed a couple of hours later, when the fifty odd guests Marcia had invited to her ball would have been present. The sales of mystery yarns at the local book stalls went up by leaps and bounces. Gentlemen who prior to that exciting event had been bond salesmen, importers, bank presidents, lawyers, landlords and dentists became private detectives overnight.

And everyone who had even a bowing acquaintance with Marcia Allen felt it incumbent on himself, if not to call on her, at least to telephone occasionally to ask for information, more often to offer advice.

As Mr. Wimble neared the house Miss Allen stepped out on to the front porch. Marcia, in a simple white dress, looked less imposing than in her Queen Elizabeth garb. She was the sort of woman, however, who would have appeared dignified in overalls. Her face, relieved from plainness only by her fine gray eyes, was pale; but her manner was calm. O. W. saw that she had a pair of pruning shears in her hand.

"Cutting posies?" he asked.

"No, telephone wires. Since daybreak the phone hasn't stopped ringing. Reporters, friends, acquaintances. Inspector Clancy is sending some men over to keep people off the grounds."

For the ensuing few moments Marcia's conversation took on the tone of a hostess'. Had Mr. Wimble slept well, she inquired with hospitable solicitude? Had Wing served breakfast at the hour Mr. Wimble liked it? Marcia usually lunched at half-past twelve. Was that satisfactory to Mr. Wimble? Knowing that he wanted to see them, she had invited Mrs. Wells, the Dwights and Mr. Osborne to luncheon, she said.

At this juncture an anxiousness crept into Marcia's manner, which she endeavored to hide from the detective by clipping a dry leaf from a Virginia creeper climbing up one of the porch pillars.

"Mr. Wimble," she asked, with fair success at sounding casual, "in the investigation of a case did you ever come across a murderer who enlisted your sympathy?"

"Yes, indeed; many times."

"You have been tempted to let him go?"

"No. My sympathies have never carried me quite that far. I have always felt the community to be more important than the individual."

"But if the victim had been of no use, a parasite even, and the man who committed the crime doing real good in the community, with all manner of persons dependent on him?"

"When I am put on a case, Miss Allen, it is my duty to deliver the criminal to the police. It is for the Law to determine the degree of his guilt."

Miss Allen clipped several leaves from the vine before continuing. O. W. noticed that her face looked drawn and that she spoke with decided effort.

"Mr. Wimble, I was talking with Inspector Clancy this morning. I feel convinced that, because of your splendid reputation, if you should give up the case the police would not reopen it."

Suddenly Mr. Wimble looked his age. It was strange that a man, who for a quarter of a century had followed a profession bound to bring him in contact with mortals at their worst, should feel sick at heart every time he found a rotten spot in human nature. O. W.'s mother had confided in Dolly Webb one time that she had never lied to her son but once—when she had told the five-year-old O. W. there was an Easter Bunny. Later, upon discovering the Bunny

to be a myth, the chubby little, boy had turned such dis-
illusioned, accusing eyes on his mother that she had never
fibbed to him again.

Mr. Wimble said: "Miss Allen, with no sense of boasting, when I filed my income tax report this year. I was
rather appalled by its magnitude."

Miss Allen's quick intelligence immediately grasped the
significance of the detective's remark. To her credit she
flushed scarlet. "You suspect me of trying to bribe you!"

"Not with money. With flattery. The essence is the
same."

Miss Allen's hauteur of the previous evening returned.
"After all, we were speaking hypothetically."

All at once, with his knack at assuming the other fellow's viewpoint, O. W.'s thoughts turned to Dolly. What
if Dolly, whom he loved as this young woman loved John
Dwight, were suspected of murder? What price his principles then?

O. W. found it singularly easy to smile again at Marcia
Allen. "Of course!" he agreed warmly.

Marcia said impulsively: "I didn't realize that private
detectives could be such gentlemen!"

Mr. Wimble conquered an inclination to smile.

"I'm curious to know just why you employed the services of a private detective."

Miss Allen replied promptly—a bit too promptly.

"I don't like publicity. And of course murder and publicity go hand in hand. Because Gary was my fiancé, because he was murdered in my house, because he has no
relatives in America that I know of, I felt it the sporting
thing of me to take the customary steps to avenge his
death. My idea in employing the services of a private detective was that I thought there would be less notoriety
than if the police were in control.'

O. W. retorted irresistibly: "Are you sure it wasn't because you thought the bunglesome efforts of a private detective would give the culprit a better chance to escape than the scientific methods of the police?"

Marcia Allen possessed a tremendous sense of humor. Under normal conditions she fairly bubbled over with it. A person not so blessed might have shown anger at the detective's thus exposing her finesse. Marcia laughed.

"Now we're even!"

Mr. Wimble felt that had the circumstances been different he and Marcia could have been friends. For the moment at any rate, as their laughter joined, their minds were in complete accord.

The detective's mirth subsided in a sigh of regret. He would have preferred his relations with Marcia to rest on this footing. But duty exempted a remark which he knew would again put Miss Allen on the defensive.

"I'm sorry Mr. Dwight is causing you so much anxiety, Miss Allen."

The key to Marcia's character lay in her steady glance and strong chin. Her reply was controlled, albeit slightly scornful.

"You are too intelligent a man to take stock in circumstantial evidence, Mr. Wimble."

As a man, Mr. Wimble was the kindest person on earth; but he had not earned his reputation as a criminal investigator by being a milksop. For the sake of gaining a detective point he was not above yielding to cruelty.

"On the contrary, Miss Allen, it is usually only in fiction that circumstantial evidence turns out to be a comedy of errors. In crime detection, circumstantial evidence frequently incriminates a suspect. You see, it's not always so easy for him to disprove the fact in issue when the other circumstances which usually attend it are proved."

The despair dulling Miss Allen's eyes confirmed the detective's suspicion.

9

Oral testimony played a conspicuous part in Mr. Wimble's *modus operandi*. A biographer would have said of Mr. Wimble that he was supremely human. The detective himself put it more simply. "I *like* folks!" He was genuinely interested in their jobs, new hats, babies, birthdays, income taxes, cooks, gallstones, gardens, bridge prizes, quarrels, automobile trips, homebrew, reducing exercises, stamp collections and fish stories. And just as a dog will wag its tail at some individuals and bark at others, persons ordinarily as uncommunicative as clams would pour forth their life histories into the sympathetic ear of Private Detective Wimble. Even as a boy, O. W. had been the sort mothers send out to play when a new family moves into the neighborhood. Thus a natural gift for getting persons to talk became one of O. W.'s detective methods.

Though he made extensive use of oral testimony, Mr. Wimble did not take too seriously the actual answers of a witness to his questions. After thirty odd years of criminal detection, O. W.'s knowledge of human nature was vast. He pretty well knew when a man was lying and whether through malice or fear or vanity. Mr. Wimble could not have been the humanitarian he was without appreciating that no individual alive is happier than when shining before his fellows. It was not in the detective's heart to censure a witness for seizing what was perhaps the only chance he'd ever had to emerge from obscurity. But understanding this very human weakness, so baffling to less experienced investigators, O. W. knew how to cope with the otherwise inexplicable subterfuges of a witness, his flights of fancy, his quibblings.

At Mr. Wimble's invitation to be seated Rosie chose a chair as near the door as possible.

"Marvelous day!" observed O. W. It was not that the detective lacked small-talk; he was really impressed by the glorious climate of California.

"No different'n usual," returned Rosie indifferently. Another Californian who took good health and good weather for granted!

A night's sleep had removed the ravages of tears from Rosie's face, and Mr. Wimble saw that Miss Allen's little servant girl was quite pretty. Rosie was twenty-one years old and Celtic in type. She had dark hair and the violet eyes Erin reserves for its prettiest women. Her nose was a bit too small, her mouth a bit too large. Her cheeks were round and pink, and her bare neck and arms glowed with healthy vigor.

Though in a more cheerful mood than when the detective had first made her acquaintance, the girl was still apprehensive. She admitted that only her fondness for Miss Allen prevented her from giving notice. From the timorous glances she darted about her, O. W. judged that dread of encountering Gary Gilbert's ghost rather than any disinclination to testify had accounted for her hesitancy in entering the library.

"Miss Allen's a fine woman," said Mr. Wimble.

"I'll say! She's wonderful! You oughta seen how she took care of me when I was sick!" It was characteristic of the detective that for the ensuing ten minutes he paid rapt attention to the girl's proud account of her recent attack of appendicitis.

"And she don't blow up when I smash a dish or over-sleep in the morning, neither!"

Rosie would have continued in further commendation of her mistress' virtues had O. W. not stemmed the flood of her eulogy by a question.

"Of course Miss Allen is upset right at present, but I'm to understand that usually she is good-natured?"

"I'll say!"

"She is good-natured," his eyelids covered the twinkles in the detective's eyes, *"you'd* say, because she is happy?"

Rosie looked troubled. Mr. Wimble correctly diagnosed her distress.

"I want you to know, Rosie, that anything you tell me will be held in strictest confidence."

The girl did not seem entirely satisfied, however. "I'm scared what I tell you might get somebody in trouble."

"I *like* Miss Allen, Rosie!"

Rosie eyed him in admiration. "How'd you know it was her I meant?"

"Because it was Miss Allen we were talking about."

Rosie's disappointment was evident. Hers was not the mentality to be impressed by reasoning so simple.

Mr. Wimble decided to skip over Miss Allen's unhappiness for the time being.

Upon asking Rosie if she had waited on table Saturday evening the girl replied in the affirmative.

"Anything unusual happen during dinner?"'

"I'll say! Mrs. Dwight acted up like I never saw her before." Apparently Rosie felt no qualms about implicating Chiquita.

"How, exactly?"

"Flirting with Mr. Gilbert, sir. Drinking out of his glass and making eyes at him. The others thought it was funny but it didn't seem decent to me. Her a married woman and Mr. Dwight being so crazy about her he'd sit on tacks if she asked him to, and all! When Mr. Dwight came—he didn't get here till they were having coffee—he looked like it didn't make a hit with him, neither."

"What did he say?"

"Nothing right at first; then Mr. Osborne egged him on. You know that Lawyer Cook who Andy got mixed up with awhile back when he was writing his life story? Well, Mr. Osborne began taking off Lawyer Cook. I can hear him now!" She mimicked Osborne mimicking "Lawyer Cook." "'Now, Pal, if you need a good little lawyer bad just call on me!' Then Mr. Dwight took it up and pretended Mr. Gilbert was making him jealous. Once Mr. Gilbert touched Mrs. Dwight's bare arm—to see what marble that had come to life felt like, he said; and right away Mr. Dwight said: 'Now I ask you, Lawyer Cook, isn't that actionable?' And Mr. Osborne came back with: 'It sure is, Pal!' Of course I didn't get it all, being in and out the way I was."

O. W. harbored no illusions concerning Rosie's method of picking up information. She could not have gathered this much without considerable eavesdropping. It was safe to assume that she knew more. O. W. had a way of allying himself with his witnesses. His manner now intimated that if he had been in Rosie's shoes he too would have listened outside the library door.

He chuckled. "I'd have taken my time over those coffee things!"

Rosie sniggered slyly. "I'll say I took my time! 'Specially when I went in to get the empty cups. Mr. Dwight was just whooping it up then. I forgot the sugar bowl on purpose, so I could go back to the library; then when I went in for the sugar bowl I left the door ajar so if I got a chance later I could stand outside and listen. But you might know Wing would keep finding things for me to do in the kitchen!" Resentment edged her voice. "I noticed he didn't find such a lot for Marie to do. Marie was an extra girl we had in last night. She left the kitchen when the dishes were done. Wing went out once, though."

"Whereupon you scooted for the library!"

Rosie shot a hostile glance at the detective.

"It must have been comical!" said Mr. Wimble gleefully.

"I'll say!" her self-assurance restored. "Mr. Osborne with his Pal-this and Pal-that! And Mr. Dwight carrying on with that butcher knife; he was a scream!" Rosie was actually laughing in the presence of a ghost!

"You *like* Mr. Dwight, don't you?"

"I'll say!" Rosie's face glowed. "He sent me flowers when I was sick. Not out of his garden, either. Store flowers. The most expensive kind you can buy. Orchids!"

With a pang for the caprices of humankind, O. W.'s glance sought the window. Flowers of a hundred varieties tumbled over themselves in the garden: geraniums, roses, sweet peas, hydrangeas, marigolds, pinks, narcissuses, calla lilies, snapdragons. . . . What a treat for New Yorkers, many of whom had never seen a growing flower!

It was obvious to the detective that in Rosie's eyes Dwight's farce had been just that and nothing more. He saw no reason for distressing the girl by asking her if in last night's comedy she had sensed tragedy.

"So you didn't get back to the library!" O. W.'s manner intimated that his regret was because Rosie had been cheated out of entertainment rather than because she had nothing more to add to his investigation.

"Yes I did, once more about eight o'clock."

"You're sure of the time?"

"Yes, sir, because when I was passing through the front hall Mr. Osborne came in and asked me to get Mrs. Wells' coat and I noticed by the dressing room clock it was eight.

I knew it was about time for the other guests to come, so
I made up my mind, if anyone caught me hanging around,
to say I was going into the library to tidy up before they
got there. I guess Mrs. Wells was waiting for Mr. Osborne
in the library because when I got to the hall I heard his
voice. He said like he'd been saying all evening: 'Pal!' And
then," she concluded sulkily, "of course Wing had to call
me back to the kitchen! I wasn't there but a few minutes
when Mr. Dwight came running in to tell Wing that—"
She broke off to glance furtively about her.

"That Gary Gilbert had been murdered?"

"Yes, sir," gulped Rosie. She peered apologetically into
space. Mr. Wimble ought to be careful; ghosts might be
awfully sensitive for all he knew!

O. W. gave her something else to think about.

"What seems to have been troubling Miss Allen lately?"

"Miss Roberta mostly, I think."

"Miss Marcia's sister?"

"Yes, sir. Miss Rob is as different from Miss Allen as
night and day."

"You don't care for Roberta?"

"Miss Rob gives me a pain!" returned Rosie bluntly.
"She's a big girl, homely's a mud fence. Crazy about men,
and I bet one never looked at her twice. She goes to school
in Hollywood and when she comes home she plasters pictures of talkie stars all over the place. Pretends they gave
'em to her, but I wasn't born yesterday! Besides, I caught
her autographing one of them herself once. 'To Roberta
the Fair,' she wrote. The Fair! The *Side Show*'d be more
like it!"

"Roberta and her sister don't get along?"

"Miss Allen gets along with everybody. And then, Miss
Roberta don't stay home much. She's away at school most
of the time or visiting her friends. Bet the only reason

she's got any friend's is because she's rich. Miss Allen gives her a whale of an allowance."

"You said that Roberta was causing Miss Allen some anxiety." Patiently Mr. Wimble steered the garrulous Rosie up the right road.

"I think Miss Rob was in love with Mr. Gilbert. One day when she was home for the spring vacation I overheard her and Miss Allen talking. Miss Allen said something that knocked me for a row. She said: 'I'm going to marry Gary Gilbert, Rob!' Just then Wing called me for something. Isn't that old Chink the *limit?*" she broke off in exasperation.

"He certainly keeps an eye on you," agreed the detective sympathetically.

"He admits it!" returned Rosie disgustedly. "He's all the time reading me something out of a thick book he's got full of those hen scratches the Chinks use for writing—sort of a Chinese 'Science and Health' I think. He calls what he reads to me a 'Truth' and it goes like this: 'My ears hear what you tell me; my eyes believe themselves.' Wouldn't that give you a pain?" She sighed: "But I can't do anything about it because when I came here to work Miss Allen said I was to mind Wing."

"I'll wager you managed to give him the slip that day Miss Allen was telling Roberta about her engagement to Gary Gilbert!" O. W.'s voice dripped honey.

"I'll say! And when I got back to where they were I heard Miss Rob screaming at the top of her lungs: 'It's just like you, Marsh Allen, to rob me of the only man I ever loved!' 'Nonsense!' said Miss Allen. 'You fall in love with every man you look at. I'll bet you winked at the minister who christened you!' They argued for awhile, and then Miss Roberta yelled: 'I'll punish you for this if it's the last thing I ever do!' She sounded as if she was heading for the door I was listening behind, so I had to beat it."

"You overheard further conversations between the sisters?"

"No, sir; that was the only one. Miss Rob went back to Los soon afterwards."

"Please tell me now, Rosie, what else has been troubling your mistress lately?"

Rosie's face reddened. "What makes you think there's something else?"

Patience must be a necessary ingredient of crime detection, O. W. possessed so much of it.

"When I first asked you what had been troubling your mistress, you said: 'Miss Roberta, *mostly*,' which intimated that there was something else."

O. W.'s explanation left Rosie feeling a bit dashed. This Santa Clausy old gentleman seemed to get the best of her without half trying!

"Well, gee, Mr. Wimble, it's none of my business!"

"But it is mine," returned the detective kindly, "so suppose you tell me."

Rosie sulked. Apparently loyalty toward those she loved was the very core of her character.

"Testifying isn't tattling, Rosie."

Rosie frowned in an endeavor to get this observation through her head, deciding in the end to take the detective's word for it.

She continued, though with marked reluctance. "Ever since I been here I've suspected Miss Allen was in love with Mr. Dwight. Mr. Dwight's crazy about his wife, though. Mrs. Dwight's beautiful all right but—I don't know—she's ditzy or something—hasn't got half the 'it' Miss Allen's got. It's plain to see Mrs. Dwight wouldn't wipe her feet on her husband—or any other man for that matter. She's more like a statue than a real woman. Still, Mr. Dwight can't see anyone but his 'Chickie'."

Rosie was not without philosophy. "Men are funny that way.

"About two weeks ago," she went on, "a few days before Miss Roberta got home, Mr. Dwight came over for tea with Miss Allen." As she hesitated, again the slight belligerence that showed she was not without a conscience appeared in Rosie's manner.

O. W. applied the proper salve. "Anyone who waits on persons can't help hearing what they say."

Rosie's ready smile signified the efficacy of the detective's remedy.

"When I went in with the tea," she continued, "Miss Allen was making out like she was kidding Mr. Dwight, but I knew she was more than half in earnest. Mr. Dwight looked sort of blue. Usually he's awfully jolly—kind of put on, I think, because he sure can't be happy married to a statue—but Miss Allen being an old friend I guess he thought he could act natural in front of her. Miss Allen said: 'Sometimes I think you're just a marshmallow, Dumpling!' 'Dare say I look like one,' Mr. Dwight laughed. Miss Allen said: 'Sweet all through but not very tough.' Then I had to go to the kitchen.

"When I got back, something in Miss Allen's voice made me stop outside the door. Did you ever hear Greta Garbo? Her voice is just swell—husky like she has a cold, only of course she hasn't. That's the way Miss Allen's sounded. 'Why don't you chuck Chiquita?' she said. 'You haven't had a moment's happiness since you married her. She'll wreck you, Dumpling.' She sort of laughed. 'Icebergs do cause wrecks, you know. You can make a settlement on Chiquita. She'll be satisfied. It's common property why she married you. Then find another woman. A woman who loves you—wants you—' 'Yes, I know,' Mr. Dwight said. 'I should have married some other woman—some girl in our set—' I heard Miss Allen catch her breath at that. 'Anyone but Chickie,' he said. 'The conceit of me to have aspired to Chiquita!' Gee, Mr. Wimble, I could have cried, my heart ached so for Miss Allen. But she's a good sport, Miss Allen is! She just laughed it off, though I knew she was ready to die. 'Marshmallows never did agree with me!' she said. Then I took the tea in. That's all I heard.

"After Mr. Dwight had gone I went into the library and there was Miss Allen crying like her heart would crack in two. It was just terrible, Mr. Wimble! She wasn't making a bit of noise; just sitting there, the tears streaming down her face. I didn't think she'd want me to see her like that so I tiptoed out. At dinner time I went in to call her, but she said account of her late tea she didn't want any; but I felt it wasn't because of the tea she didn't want her dinner.

"Just a few days after that she told Miss Rob she was going to marry Mr. Gilbert. I'm just as sure as I'm alive, Mr. Wimble, that Miss Allen decided to marry Mr. Gilbert because she knew she didn't stand a chance with Mr. Dwight."

It was not only because he enjoyed their prattle that Mr. Wimble encouraged his witnesses to talk; it was by calculated design. A stray remark often contained an important clue.

"Oh dear," sighed Rosie, and this was a remark O. W. considered worthy of being pigeonholed in his brain, "if someone had to be murdered, why couldn't it have been Mrs. Dwight? As far as I can see she don't make anyone happy, and Miss Allen wants Mr. Dwight so bad!"

Rosie settled back in her chair as if she were talked out. O. W.'s next words had the same effect as if he'd stuck her with as many pins. "Now for the rest of it, Rosie."

"Th—the rest?"

"You said awhile ago that you were afraid what you told me might get someone in trouble. I guessed—correctly you admitted—that you were referring to your mistress. Nothing you have as yet said about Miss Allen would get her into trouble."

Rosie picked at her fingers. "Do I have to tell?"

O. W. glanced apprehensively around the room as if the walls had ears; then he lowered his voice to a portentous whisper.

"You might get into serious difficulty if you don't."

Rosie shivered.

Later Mr. Wimble remarked to Janet Hill that she might do worse than to take a few lessons in reporting from Miss Allen's housemaid. Rosie had a nose for news. With such as Rosie reporting for the Fourth Estate the public would soon know Mrs. Coolidge's private views concerning her husband's "colyum", the probable date of public traffic in beer, what induced Mr. Drinkwater to write about "Uncle Carl." It did not astonish Mr. Wimble in the slightest that Rosie had listened in while Gary Gilbert proposed marriage to Marcia Allen. More often than not good taste flees before a reporter's urge to get his story.

Rosie, ever ready to excuse her eavesdropping, said that the reason she had listened to the proposal was that Gary and Marcia had sounded more like actors on the stage than real people. This contention was not without substantiation.

> GARY: I've brought you a betrothal ring, old
>   dear!
> MARCIA: I suppose I might as well wear it. I'll
>   be paying for it.
> GARY (piqued): I'm at least decorative, Marcia.
> MARCIA (impudently): I deserve a decoration
>   for marrying you.
> GARY: You have a delightful sense of humor,
>   dear thing!

MARCIA: Ditto. I doubt if we could go through
with it if we hadn't. Perhaps we're more
compatible than we realize.

GARY: Mon Dieu! You don't think there's any
danger of your falling in love with me?

MARCIA: With a parlor snake? No, I think not!

GARY (nettled): I trust, Marcia, that we can
always manage to be polite to each other.

MARCIA: I see your point. But right now I
think we should employ plain speech.
You're marrying me for my money. I'm
marrying you—well, let us say because I
want a pet, a parlor snake. You'll find me
generous—with money. In return I expect
you to be generous—with outward respect,
decent treatment of me before my friends.

GARY: I'll never embarrass you, Marcia.

When in the midst of her recital Rosie suddenly burst into
tears O. W. felt no alarm. Rosie was the sort who could
have the time of her life at the theatre weeping through a
melodrama.

"What did Miss Allen say next, Rosie?"

"She s-said—" It was then that Mr. Wimble realized
he was on the point of being introduced to the bugaboo
Rosie was in a mortal funk lest the detective find inimical
to Miss Allen's welfare.

Again O. W. simulated an air of foreboding.

"What did Miss Allen say to Mr. Gilbert, Rosie?"

"She s-said: 'If I find that my parlor snake develops
rattles, I'll—I'll *kill him!*'"

The detective's first impulse was to laugh. He strongly
suspected that the italics were Rosie's. But his impulse
faded before the glaring fact that Gary Gilbert, shortly

after a violent flirtation with a beautiful woman not his fiancée, had been found murdered in the library of the unbeautiful woman to whom he was engaged.

10

Luncheon at Marcia's on Sunday was not a very joyous affair. Luncheon at a house the day after a murder has been committed there could not be expected to inspire hilarity. The guests were Katharine Wells, Hugh Osborne, John Dwight and Mr. Wimble. Chiquita had not come. Dwight apologized to the detective for her absence—said her headache had developed into something more serious, a touch of the flu he thought—there was a slight epidemic again this year.

"No doubt, too," said Mr. Wimble, "Mrs. Dwight is feeling the shock of last night's tragedy."

"Of course my wife feels it, Mr. Wimble, though we didn't know Gilbert very well. But she was spared the full shock of it. You see, having gone home last night before it happened, she didn't know anything about it until this morning when I told her."

As Dwight stumbled through this explanation, it occurred to the detective that the young man was not in the habit of practicing guile.

"I should like to meet your wife sometime."

"We'd be pleased to have you call on us," returned Dwight, "when you've completed your investigation." O. W. felt that a more subtle man would have left the latter part of this statement unspoken.

During luncheon Kitten Wells, in a shimmery figured chiffon of artichoke green, usurped the duties of hostess. Had she been inspired by sympathy for Marcia's harassed countenance, her gesture would have been admirable. But in her whole attitude Kitten seemed impervious to the strain that gripped the others. Kitten possessed few inner resources. Silence to her was like smallpox to others. She was the sort to whom the radio is a boon, filling the house with racket all the day long—and most of the night. She kept parrots for pets. And whenever possible she talked.

Throughout luncheon her high-pitched prattle filled the dining room. She seemed unaware of the resentment she roused in her companions. She asked Osborne if he'd heard about a certain acquaintance of theirs, a Mrs. Josiah Pugh, whose income was reputed to be a dollar a minute, bursting a blood vessel because her nickel hadn't been returned after an uncompleted pay station call. Buttering a French roll, Kitten giggled, recalling a christening she had attended at Notre-Dame in Paris. In that dark, dank place, she said, the round white babies had put her in mind of moth balls. And wasn't it astonishing, she inquired of Dwight who most recently of them had been in France, what a noise the French made eating oysters? It was drinking the juice out of the shells that did it, of course. Over the avocado salad she informed Mr. Wimble that California had legally adopted the alligator pear, renaming it calavo.

It was not that Kitten's mind had ejected the murder. That it had occupied her thoughts was manifested by her earnest query: "What are you going to wear to the inquest, Marcia?"

"For Heaven's sake!" cried Marcia.

Hugh gibed: "Anybody'd think this were a show put on for your special benefit, Kitten!"

"Well, I never went to a party given by a coroner before." Kitten became the least bit dispirited by the lack of applause. She said in a hurt voice: "It isn't as if any of us had really cared for Gary."

Though the others resented it, Mr. Wimble was grateful for Kitten's frivolous twaddle. The meal would have been a somber repast without it. Osborne maintained an outward show of composure, but O. W. had the feeling that if he said "Boo!" the man would jump out of the nearest window. Marcia was clearly distraught. And Dwight hardly touched his food.

Marcia's guests understood that they had been invited to luncheon because Mr. Wimble wished to interview them. John Dwight requested that he be the first to be interrogated. He wished to return to Mrs. Dwight, he said. The detective was glad that Kitten hadn't made the request. Knowing that an interview with her promised entertainment, O. W., much as a child keeps his choicest sweet till last, preferred interviewing Kitten after the others.

"You're pretty fond of that wife of yours, aren't you, Mr. Dwight?"

Dwight's round face was remarkable for its sweetness of expression when he smiled.

"I saw Chiquita first when she was eighteen. I was at her father's house, buying some horses from him. She had been boarding at The Little Convent of the Flowers—had just come home. I fell in love with her then, though we weren't married till several years later." The look on Dwight's face, the inflection of his voice, betrayed his adoration of his wife.

The detective said: "I cannot understand why you wish to harm Mrs. Dwight."

In his amazement the young man's mouth became an O.

"Surely you recall your *Hamlet,* Mr. Dwight. Don't you think you're protesting your wife's innocence a bit too much?"

Dwight's upper teeth closed down on his lower lip.

"I assure you that I am anxious to protect her only from the notoriety, Mr. Wimble, and any annoyance."

"Unfortunately your wife is a suspect." At this announcement Dwight's features seemed to disintegrate like a drunken person's.

"Everyone who was here the night of the murder is a suspect." O. W. was glad to see Dwight's features become more positive.

It would have been logical for Mr. Wimble to say next: "My boy, I have a fairly good idea what you're up to. Why don't you tell me the truth?" But he felt that if he startled the young man to such an extent Dwight would drop dead at his feet. So biding his time, he changed his tack.

"There's one thing certain," he said. "Miss Allen will never forget her engagement party of last evening."

Dwight showed his astonishment.

Mr. Wimble turned chatty. "Miss Allen told me that she had planned to surprise her guests by announcing her engagement at midnight."

An ejaculation escaped Dwight. "Jove! Hugh Osborne, the old fox!"

Mr. Wimble corrected him. "It was Gary Gilbert Miss Allen was engaged to."

"Gary Gilbert! Gary and Marcia? Are you sure?"

"Why otherwise should Miss Allen have assumed the responsibility for my detective investigation? You don't seem to approve of her choice."

The knuckles of Dwight's hands gleamed as he clenched his fists. "Gilbert was a skunk. But Marcia!" Dwight's thoughts now centered on his friend's distress. "She must be feeling this terribly. The poor kid! What rotten luck!"

"You've admitted that Gilbert wasn't much of a man, Mr. Dwight. Perhaps in the last analysis his untimely death will prove to be Miss Allen's good luck. She'll probably get over this in time and marry some man more worthy of her."

"Yes, that's so. Osborne's been pretty faithful."

"Or—some widower might come along."

As Dwight struggled for self-control O. W. busied himself plucking an imaginary thread from his coat sleeve. He *liked* folks; he hated to see them suffer.

Again he relieved the strain by amplifying his remark.

"Miss Allen's not so young as she was. She won't find many single men hanging around."

O. W. later confessed to Corey Webb that he had been in a cold sweat throughout his interview with the corpulent John Dwight. A younger and vainer O. W. had once consulted a doctor about his figure and been warned that dire results attended shocks on a heart weakened by obesity.

The detective took still another tack.

"I think you can appreciate, Mr. Dwight, that appearances are strongly against you in particular."

As the young man nodded, curiously the expression on his face was not one of apprehension.

"Naturally you will do all you can to help me prove that the evidence against you is false?"

Dwight smiled rather wanly. "Naturally."

"I should like you kindly to tell me just what happened from the time you arrived here last night to the time I took charge."

"I was late getting here. I had been to see a man who was sick—a butcher named Jenkins."

"Mrs. Dwight was a bit annoyed with you for being late?"

Dwight flushed, though he squared his shoulders with a show of indignation.

"Chiquita is always so punctual herself, of course my delinquency in that respect rather disconcerts her at times." As he continued, from the shade of unconscious pleading in his voice Mr. Wimble judged that Dwight was repeating something he had already said to his wife. "I realized when I was sitting with Jenkins that the time was flying but I hated to tear myself away. It's downright pitiful how frightened the old chap is of death. Of course I could hire a nurse to stay with him but it's a friend he needs right now. He's not so sick as he is plumb scared. When I heard the clock strike half-past six I simply had to break away. My costume for Marcia's fancy dress party was at home and I hadn't time to get it, so I borrowed an apron and a knife from Jenkins. He lives over his shop and had them handy. When I got here dinner was about over; they were having dessert. We went into the library for coffee— Chiquita, Marcia, Kitten, Hugh, Gilbert and I."

Up to this point Dwight's manner had been sufficiently frank as to cause no suspicion; but from now on he was ill at ease, noticeably unable to recall readily the sequence of events in the library. O. W. found it necessary throughout the remainder of the interview to prompt him.

"I understand that you weren't quite yourself last night, Mr. Dwight."

"I wasn't drinking," returned Dwight quickly. "That was part of the horseplay."

Mr. Wimble smiled. "Inferring that Miss Allen was not breaking the law last night?"

Dwight replied simply: "Telling you that Chiquita Dwight's husband is not a drunkard."

"Yet you were pretending drunkenness. Why?"

For a moment Dwight hesitated, then replied with marked hesitancy: "Gilbert began carrying on with Chiquita. I'm the sort of chap—well, that kind of thing is always my cue to play the fool. I pretended jealousy, taking to drink—all that."

"Sufficient cause had been given you to feel jealousy, I'll warrant."

All at once dignity gained a signal victory over Dwight's avoirdupois.

"Mr. Wimble, your remark infers that Chiquita in turn was carrying on with Gilbert. At the risk of being considered a fatuous, lovesick fool, I must tell you, sir, that Chiquita is as aloof from that sort of thing as a little girl."

In fancy O. W. saw Dolly, adorable and young, as he had known her when he was this boy's age, smiling at every man she knew but with eyes as innocent as a child's. Young Dwight certainly had a way with him!

"How long did your buffoonery continue?"

Dwight smiled ruefully. "Till the others tired of it. When I'm playing the donkey, at the first yawn Marcia always finds something for me to do somewhere else. Last night she carried me off to the conservatory to look at some new plants."

"You took your butcher knife along with you?"

"No; I left it in the library—on the table I think. That knife was rather a villainous affair to use as a toy. Jenkins is a conscientious workman. I had already decided to beg a less dastardly one from Wing."

"You returned later to the library?"

Dwight avoided O. W.'s eyes; suddenly recollected that he was doing so; finally in his endeavor to appear nonchalant fairly glared at the detective.

"Yes. I found my wife there. She was alone. She said she'd asked Gilbert to leave her as her head was aching fearfully."

O. W.'s heart warmed to the young man as Dwight interpolated: "Chiquita said their mock flirtation wasn't any fun without an audience.

"As my wife's head was aching so badly, I advised her to go home."

"You drove her there?"

"That was my intention, but as we neared the car we met Kelly, our chauffeur. He'd come to put the lights on. So he drove her home."

"While you—?"

"I returned to the library. The light was rather dim. I turned up the lamp." He took out his handkerchief and mopped his forehead. "Gary Gilbert was lying on the floor—as you saw him."

"How long had you been away from the library?"

"Possibly ten—fifteen minutes."

Mr. Wimble took the red doily from his pocket. "Did you happen to notice this anywhere in the room?"

Again Dwight's handkerchief was pressed into service. "Yes, I think I did—on the floor near Gilbert's body."

"You notified someone of the tragedy?"

"Yes. Wing. It seemed the natural thing for me to go to Wing." The tone of Dwight's voice became affectionate. "The lawyers who handle my business affairs contend that I ask them for too little advice. That's because Wing supplies me with all I need. He's the wisest man I know. Wing notified the police—took entire charge till they arrived."

O. W. veiled the mischief in his eyes. "When you informed Wing of the murder did he offer you any advice?"

Though as he replied the young man's voice was grave, the detective felt that Dwight was not inappreciative of the joke. "As a matter of fact he did. He said: 'Silence is as deep as the sea; speech as shallow as a brook.'"

Mr. Wimble grinned. "I wonder if Wing is aware that detectives are sometimes deep sea fishermen?"

He put his final question to young Dwight: "Then the last time you saw Gary Gilbert alive was in the presence of the others when he was flirting with your wife?"

"Pretending to be flirting with her. Yes."

Before interviewing the others O. W. decided to take a
breath of air, so he was in the garden when Dwight drove
away from Marcia's. It came to the detective that it was
pleasant having an assistant to relieve him of some of the
work. His interview with John Dwight had tired him. Marcia had asked him if a criminal ever enlisted his sympathy.
If this young man were proved the murderer, he had the
detective's sympathy in advance. Mr. Wimble *liked* John
Dwight!

As John's car drove by, O. W. caught a glimpse of the
Dwights' chauffeur. Though immaculate in a well-tailored
uniform, the man was one of the most unprepossessing
individuals O. W. had ever set eyes upon. What he noticed
first was that the man's mouth seemed put in at an odd
angle. As the car came closer he saw that a scar extending
along the chauffeur's cheek from his right temple to his
jaw stretched his mouth to the right and pulled it upward,
giving the man a sinister expression. His face was further
marred by an unhealthy pallor and bushy black eyebrows
under which his slightly bulbous brown eyes peered forth
as from in ambuscade. Marcia who had been seeing John
off, when the car had gone, joined the detective.

"Hardly an Adonis, that driver of Dwight's," observed
O. W.

"A plug-ugly if there ever were one," agreed Marcia.
"We tease Dumpling about him—say he hired Kelly because by contrast he himself appears positively handsome."

11

When interrogated by Mr. Wimble Hugh Osborne's demeanor differed radically from John Dwight's. Whereas Dwight's manner had been ill at ease, his gaze shifting, his memory lacking, Osborne's aplomb left nothing to be desired. Not even when hard pressed by the detective did his unruffled appearance destroy the illusion that he was on the point of posing for a *Saturday Evening Post* color-page advertising what the well-dressed man should wear.

During the interview an interesting, though by no means admirable, phase of Osborne's character manifested itself. Mr. Wimble discovered the man to be a gossip of the first water. That Osborne was an excellent raconteur, with a flair for the epigrammatic, did not conceal the fact that his anecdotes merely provided convenient vehicles for the carrying of petty scandal.

O. W. opened the interview with a query about the man Osborne the night before so unmistakably had been trying to shield.

"Young Dwight's pretty well thought of, isn't he?"

"Dumpling's generally considered a hot sketch."

"I gather that the Dwight's aren't particularly compatible."

Osborne shrugged. "Chiquita made no bones of the fact that she was marrying Dumpling for his money. But he keeps bucking the tide like a salmon—the poor fish!"

"From all accounts he seems extremely fond of her."

Osborne replied with studied insouciance: "Dumpling would rather fry in Hell with Chiquita than fly in Heaven with any other woman."

"Last evening when Dwight arrived late for dinner, was Mrs. Dwight's annoyance more noticeable than usual?"

"Yes, I think it was." Osborne seemed to be recalling the scene with relish. "Of course Chiquita's acrimony is always a matter of implication." With elaborate unconcern he added: "Chiquita never says a word you could put your finger on."

It was not Mr. Wimble's practice to withhold from witnesses that until they could prove their innocence he considered them under suspicion. Therefore, it was as much to his credit that by his beaming good nature he was able to make this man wish to cut a figure before him as it was to Osborne's that his self-possession enabled him to glitter in the presence of one who might eventually send him to the gallows.

Mr. Wimble asked: "Why was Mrs. Dwight more put out than usual last night?"

"Chiquita has no sense of humor, at least where Dumpling is concerned. She hates his clowning. You see, the crowd had planned a joke on Dumpling. We'd got wind of the fact that he was coming to Marcia's ball as Henry VIII, so six of the girls had fixed it up among themselves to impersonate Henry's wives. We hadn't meant to acquaint Chiquita with the plot, but when we heard he was at the butcher's our anxiety was so marked we let the cat out of the bag. It's a trick of Dwight's to leave his hostess up in the air while he goes off to fill somebody's hot water bottle! When he finally did show up in the butcher's rig, Chiquita wouldn't let him go home for the royal purple. I think that gave Dumpling the idea Chiquita rather fancied him as a butcher and led to his subsequent tomfoolery."

"Then you didn't sense an undercurrent of malice beneath Dwight's buffoonery with the butcher knife?"

Charity toward his fellow man does not characterize the gossip. He is one who, lest his anecdote suffer, will tear a man's reputation to shreds. O. W.'s hint of malevolence on Dwight's part ordinarily would have sufficed to provide the motif for the fabric Hugh Osborne would weave of the incident. Perhaps the one potion that will purge a man of baser impulses is love. The evening before Mr. Wimble had witnessed the splendid support given Marcia by Osborne. O. W. felt reasonably sure that this morning love of Marcia Allen biased Hugh's reply.

"Lord, no! Dwight never bore rancor toward anyone in his life. Little Friend of All the World—that's Dumpling!"

Mr. Wimble said guilelessly: "I understand that you played a part in Dwight's little act last evening."

Osborne's eyes narrowed. It was the first time during the interview that he had seemed on guard.

O. W. sighed: "Mrs. Wells' mimicry last night of Lawyer Cook was so clever one can't help but wish she had looked elsewhere than to Calliope when choosing a model for a speaking voice."

Osborne returned with some derision: "Not being possessed of a detective's acumen, of course I can't follow your reasoning. It is beyond me why from Kitten's quoting a radio star you should deduce that I played a part in Dwight's burlesque with the butcher knife."

"You were annoyed last night when Mrs. Wells addressed the phrase to you," returned Mr. Wimble amiably, "and concerned just now when I asked if you'd enacted a role in Dwight's little piece."

An ugly expression flitted across Osborne's mouth. "It so happened that I did enter into the spirit of Dumpling's travesty last evening—caricatured legal counsel and counterfeited that 'Pal' you recognized."

Perhaps every detective must be an actor. Mr. Wimble's voice was grave as he replied: "Thank you for telling me. It has saved me from the necessity of having my conjecture verified by the others."

Incredulity showed in Osborne's face. "It isn't possible that my fun of last evening has any bearing on your investigation!" Evidently he preferred appearing as Boswell than as co-star.

The detective grinned. "Yes—and no!"

O. W.'s infectious grin was enough to dispel the direst of qualms. Prompted by a query now and then from the detective, Osborne returned to his habitual occupation of relator. Whenever possible he converted his replies into anecdotes, and Mr. Wimble could not but wonder what success Osborne would have in a courtroom where answers are restricted to yes and no.

O. W. asked if Gary Gilbert had been a man with many enemies.

"Perhaps I can best answer your question by saying that to my knowledge he was a man without a friend. Take this tragedy, for instance. Aside from the morbid curiosity aroused by Gilbert's violent death, not a soul so far has shown the slightest interest in him but Marcia, and I doubt if she would have if she hadn't been engaged to him."

Mr. Wimble was surprised to learn that Osborne knew of the relationship existing between Marcia and the dead man.

"Miss Allen told me she had not mentioned her engagement to anyone."

Osborne said quietly: "I didn't need to be told in words, Mr. Wimble."

Sympathy for this man welled up in the detective's heart. Except for his gallantry last night in standing behind Marcia to the point of falsehood, O. W. had found

Hugh Osborne's character reprehensible. Unrequited love is an oppressive burden. Might not such a load crush a man's finer impulses? The detective's mind traveled back to the time a young O. W. had gone through the agony of seeing the girl he loved become interested in another. It hadn't been necessary for Dolly Corey to tell him in so many words that she was engaged to Sim Webb. And except for the sweet tact of Dolly herself mightn't that young O. W. have become as bitter and waspish as Hugh Osborne? But at least Osborne had the consolation of knowing that Marcia had not loved Gary Gilbert as Dolly had loved Sim Webb. Marcia's manner belied any deep regard for the murdered man; Hugh's own spoken inference that circumstances rather than affection had led Marcia to instigate detective investigation proved that Osborne knew love hadn't been her reason for becoming engaged to Gary Gilbert.

"A dearth of friends, perhaps," said Mr. Wimble, "but surely, considering his looks, there must have been a host of women in Gilbert's life."

"He treated women like dirt beneath his feet. Found them too easy to get, probably. Kitten Wells' experience is typical. She was introduced to him one night at the Bohemian Club. Men's club but occasionally they invite women to their plays. When Kitten saw Gilbert she fell flatter than a boarding-house mattress. She maneuvered all evening to get him alone. Finally she managed to inveigle him into the darkened auditorium—not a light in the place but the gleaming eyes of an imitation owl on the speakers' rostrum. Kitten was agog with excitement—thought her Big Moment had arrived. Well, there was a loud smack—someone turned up the lights—and there we were, fifteen or twenty of us, giving Kitten the merry ha-ha. Kitten saved her face by pulling a 'swoon'—the sort prescribed by Miss-Perkins-on-the-Hudson for girls too dumb to think their way out of tight places—and then took to her bed for a week.

"To make matters worse, the little goof demanded a public apology from Gilbert. So he invited the same crowd to his rooms and put on the richest comedy I ever witnessed. 'My dear Kitten,' he said—you'd have sworn Gilbert's contrition was the real thing—'I'm sorry I offended you the other night. I was drunk. It was not my intention to kiss the *stuffed owl,* Kitten!'"

Osborne summarized his appraisal of Gary Gilbert. "He was a male butterfly. There was nothing to him but his decorativeness." Osborne assumed the air of indifference the detective by now recognized as the harbinger of a *bon mot.* "I've always thought *flutterby* a more appropriate name than butterfly. That's the way Gilbert was with women: fluttering by. None of them could pin him down. When I saw his body lying on the floor last night, that knife stuck through him, my first thought was: 'Somebody's pinned down the Butterfly at last!'"

"Kitten Wells?"

Osborne's want of concern by no means meant that his wits were not alert. "Considering that Kitten spent the entire evening in my company, I could hardly have suspected her of committing the crime."

The detective became thoughtful. Had Hugh Osborne related that cruel story about Kitten Wells with no ulterior purpose than to appear amusing? If it had been his intention to build up a suspicion of Kitten in the detective's mind, why then had he immediately pulled it down by establishing her alibi? Or was it just Osborne's bad luck that, in contriving his own alibi, he must perforce at the same time construct Kitten's? Surely Osborne appreciated the importance of making known his whereabouts at the time of the murder. Last night Marcia had suggested to the detective that a jealous woman might have been responsible for the crime. Why not a jealous *man?* Osborne was admittedly in love with Marcia. And Marcia had been engaged to Gary Gilbert.

"Just where were you at the time of the murder, Mr. Osborne?"

What Osborne lacked in depth of intellect he made up in quickness of wit. With a slight grimace he replied: "At the time the murder was *alleged* to have been committed, I was in the summer-house by the pond with Kitten Wells, testing my will power. You've heard Kitten's vocal fireworks. It seems that among her other attainments, Miss-Perkins-on-the-Hudson was a voice culturist. I'm proud to say I passed my test one hundred per cent. I listened to Kitten for a solid hour without pushing her into the pond."

"When did you last see Gilbert alive?"

"After dinner, in the library. We were all there. When Dumpling began carrying things too far Marcia took him into the conservatory. I could see Chiquita and Gary considered Kitten and me decidedly *de trop* so I took a deep breath and invited Kitten for a stroll."

"In just what way was Dwight carrying things too far?"

A frown corrugated Osborne's forehead. "I'm not so sure I enjoy conversing with detectives. I'm not used to guarding my speech!"

The detective thought: "So I've noticed!" He said: "You are aware of course that circumstantial evidence is strong against Mr. Dwight? I must examine even the most trivial fact concerning his actions last evening."

"Dumpling wasn't becoming dangerous when Marcia led him away; he was merely becoming tiresome. To tell the truth, I think Marcia's done much to foster Dumpling's reputation as a wag. She has a knack at giving him the right cue when only a speedy exit will save his act from being a flop."

"I am to understand that you and Mrs. Wells were together from the time you left Gilbert and Mrs. Dwight in the library until the body was discovered an hour later?"

"The body was discovered before Kitten and I returned to the house. Everything was in confusion when we got here. We'd decided to come in upon noticing several cars driving into the grounds—thought the other guests were beginning to arrive."

"You don't recall having left Mrs. Wells during that hour?"

Mr. Wimble, like any strategist, always took into account the element of chance. It was at this point in the interview that chance lent him a hand.

It seemed to the detective as he put the question that his witness looked puzzled. Osborne may have been trying to recall whether or not he had quit the company of the chattering Kitten, but the fellow did not impress Mr. Wimble as one who had trouble with his memory. Throughout the interview, at intervals from an adjoining room, the high-pitched twittering of Kitten Wells had reached them. As Osborne hesitated now before replying, her shrill voice again penetrated the library. O. W. saw Osborne glance thoughtfully in the direction from which the sound came. This simple act as much as told him that, if Osborne and Kitten had come to any agreement as to what answers they would make to certain of the detective's questions, through some oversight the possibility of this particular one had been overlooked. O. W. made speedy use of his opportunity.

"I intend putting the identical question to Mrs. Wells," he said, and the pleasant way in which he delivered the remark camouflaged its sting, "without giving you an opportunity to coach her."

Osborne recovered his poise. Indeed, no one but a criminal investigator so keenly alert to facial expression and voice inflection as O. W. would have realized that at any time during the interview the man had lost it.

"Though it slipped my mind for the moment, as a matter of fact I did leave Kitten alone for a short interval. As you observed last evening she was rather scantily attired. California nights are cool. I went to the house to get her a wrap."

"At what time?"

"I don't know exactly. Roughly between seven-thirty and eight."

"You entered by way of the library?"

"No. I skirted the rear of the house, entering by the front door. There is a dressing room off the main hallway where the ladies leave their wraps."

"Anyone see you go into the house?"

"Yes, the maid Rosie. It was she who found Kitten's coat for me."

"You went out again via the library?"

"No, the same way as I'd gone in. I didn't go near the library." O. W. recalled Rosie's testimony that she had heard someone in the library, presumably Hugh, say "Pal!" a short time after giving Osborne Kitten's wrap. But as it was not Mr. Wimble's habit to think out loud, for the present he abandoned the subject.

He said, watching Osborne with intentness: "So Mrs. Wells may have pinned down the Butterfly after all!"

Osborne was in a corner. O. W. had discovered a flaw in his alibi. And yet, whereas another man's collar would have begun to wilt, his handkerchief to show soil from a perspiring brow, Hugh Osborne's alarm manifested itself only in a fleeting sneer across his lips.

"Perhaps," he replied. "Kitten has a fondness for killing things that fly. Her husband fell in his airplane—after getting all his affairs in order."

O. W. championed Kitten to the extent of protesting: "Many persons don't quite trust the air—take the precaution of making out wills before going up!"

"It's my conviction that Kitten drove Dicky Wells to suicide."

O. W. had the feeling that Dicky Wells' suicide provided the theme for one of Hugh Osborne's anecdotes.

"Strikes me you're a cynical young man," he observed bluntly.

Osborne shrugged. "If a cynic is one who sees life as it really is, then I am." Mr. Wimble felt that Hugh was less impressed by his cynicism than by the pungency of his epigram.

O. W. said softly: "Poor Kitten!" His sympathy did not lie in the fact that little Katharine Wells was the butt of Osborne's cynicism; O. W.'s business had to do with the investigation of the Gary Gilbert murder. He felt sorry for Kitten because his conversation with Hugh had supplied her with a motive for the crime and the time in which to commit it.

He chuckled suddenly as he imagined what Kitten's venomous little tongue might do to Osborne's unhealthy alibi.

Osborne was regarding him curiously.

"I just recalled a bit of verse that amused me," explained Mr. Wimble. It occurred to the detective that he was feeding Osborne out of the younger man's own dish. "Perhaps you know it:

"'The man recovered of the bite;
"'The dog it was that died.'"

12

To all intents and purposes Kitten Wells had been looking forward with eagerness to being interviewed by the detective. Mr. Wimble was surprised, therefore, when Kitten entered the library, to see that she was nervous. In her agitation her fingers kept gathering up little bunches of her dress. As the green chiffon mounted, O. W. rather sternly surmised that the new styles with their trailing skirt lengths were far from satisfactory to a woman as leg-conscious as Kitten Wells.

At no time did O. W. relish the distress of a pretty woman; but a chattering Kitten would be of far more value to the investigation than this perturbed, reticent one. So the detective made it his business to put her at ease.

He teased: "Is it because we're alone that you are afraid of me?" He could tell by the coquettish tilt of her small head that she was pleased.

Kitten said petulantly: "Marcia's enough to scare a person to death with all her warnings! Don't tell Mr. Wimble this! Don't tell him that!" She added, with no consciousness of her overwhelming egotism: "I didn't kill Gary Gilbert, so why should I watch my step?"

Mr. Wimble became confidential. "I wish the others would stop watching theirs. If everyone would come out and honestly tell just what he knows, it would be a lot easier for me."

"I hear you're a perfectly frabjous detective, Mr. Wimble!" Kitten was getting back into form. Soon the floodgates of her tongue would be let down and her torrential garrulity released.

O. W. said deprecatingly: "The police do most of the work. I merely act as sort of a consulting engineer. I couldn't get very far without official photographers, fingerprint and medical experts, you know."

"And witnesses who'll talk," added Kitten importantly.

"You display remarkable discernment, Mrs. Wells." O. W. realized that he would get farther with Kitten if he plied her with compliments.

Feigning modesty she lowered her head. As she smoothed her dress the defective noticed that she took pains to leave her legs exposed. Aside from Marlene Dietrich's, O. W. had never seen legs so assiduously featured as Kitten's. He felt tempted to turn Kitten over his knee. Later he felt rather ashamed of the impulse, she offered him such a ripe, juicy clue.

Kitten pouted. "I don't care what Marcia says. I'd rather talk in a nice friendly way to you than be yanked into a horrid old courtroom and forced to testify." She said with arch mysteriousness: "I have something very important to tell you, too."

"I am anxious to hear it," returned the detective, playing up to her bid for interest.

Kitten clapped her hands.

"Oh, but I'm going to save that till last. Like dessert."

O. W. wondered if she would have acted in a like manner had the murdered man been anyone for whom she had cared.

"When I run out of questions, in other words." He had no wish to antagonize this little magpie. "Well, to begin:

last night in the summer-house did you remain where Mr. Osborne left you when he went back to the house for your wrap?"

"Oh, but you're getting too warm!" squealed Kitten like a child playing a game. "You mustn't ask me that yet!"

O. W. humored her. Even systematic crime detection had sometimes to capitulate to the caprices of woman-kind. So he switched her thoughts to another track.

"Miss Allen is going to great pains to divert suspicion from John Dwight, isn't she?"

Kitten's voice rose on a high note that soared like a bird. "I told Marcia she was putting it on too thick!" She went on in the slightly sneering tone some women employ when speaking of other women's love affairs: "Of course everybody knows Marcia's crazy about Dumpling. You ought to have heard her light into Hugh last night when he spoke slightingly about Dumpling. It was when Dumpling was cutting up with the butcher knife." She giggled at her pun. "Isn't that rich?" she screamed.

"Best I've heard in years!" replied O. W. giving an excellent imitation of a man indulging in side-splitting laughter.

Kitten finally stopped giggling to continue: "It was when Gary and Chiquita were carrying on their flirtation. I heard Hugh say to Marcia: 'Dwight's Sleeping Beauty seems to be waking up.' Marcia agreed that Gary was doing himself proud as the Prince. Then Hugh said: 'I don't recollect in the fairy-tale that the Sleeping Beauty ever had a nightmare.' Marcia didn't get that, so Hugh explained. 'Isn't Dumpling acting the jackass?' Marcia was wild!"

Occasionally O. W.'s investigation demanded his tak-ing a witness into his confidence.

"Miss Allen gives every appearance of suspecting her friend Dumpling of the crime, however."

Kitten nodded. "I asked Marcia this morning if she thought Dumpling had done it and I wish you could have heard her!" O. W. wished he could have. "The way Marcia yelled 'No!' it was as if her mouth had exploded. She does think Dumpling did it, though."

Carefully, so that the heel of her green suede slipper would not make a runner in her stocking, Kitten crossed one leg over the other. O. W. wondered, like so many before him, why a silk-stockinged leg was considered so much more alluring than a bare one.

"So do I think Dumpling did it," announced Kitten.

Perhaps the memory of Marcia's recent hectoring occurred to her, for she then took particular pains to sweeten her accusation. "They don't hang a person when there are extenuating circumstances." O. W. did not consider it essential to inform her that sometimes when a man escaped hanging for first degree murder he was sentenced to life imprisonment for second degree murder.

"You think his jealousy of Mr. Gilbert warranted Mr. Dwight's killing him?"

"I certainly do!"

"Come now, Mrs. Wells—"

"Why not Kitten?" Archly.

"What I was about to remark, Kitten, was that flirtations are not so rare in your set that the one between Mrs. Dwight and Gilbert would call for murder."

Kitten smugly informed him: "If you ask me, I think Chiquita and Gary had been carrying on for some time. The other day I happened to have luncheon at the hotel where Gary lived. He occupied a penthouse on the top. I was lunching in the roof lounge. There's a balcony off the lounge and from it you can see over to Gary's house. While I was standing there I saw Gary admit Chiquita's chauffeur. Gary was all smiles when he saw him. I'll bet anything Kelly was carrying notes between Chiquita and Gary."

"That was the important news you had for me?"

"Oh, no!" chirped Kitten. "I know something far more exciting than that!"

"I've about run out of questions."

From Kitten's small throat issued laughter that sounded like the practicing of a vocal scale by someone lacking an ear for music.

"Well, then—listen!"

"I'm all ears."

Kitten giggled. "More chin than ears, I'd say!" O. W. chuckled. He appreciated a good joke even when on himself. Indeed, he preferred little Katharine in a jocular mood to little Katharine in the throes of making a conquest.

Kitten leaned forward and announced in a trenchant whisper: "Mr. Wimble, whoever murdered Gary Gilbert tried to kill me!"

As O. W. assumed an expression of amazement, he felt precisely as if he were feeding a cube of sugar to a circus pony. Kitten herself was so thrilled by the disclosure that she allowed her dress to slip down unforgotten over her knees.

"The attack on you occurred while you were waiting for Mr. Osborne to return with your wrap?"

"Yes. It seemed awfully dark and still after Hugh left. All at once I thought I heard a sound. I spoke but nobody answered, so I decided it was a bird on top of the summer-house roof. I heard the noise again, but when I spoke, there was still no answer. 'It must be a bird,' I thought. Then all at once, there came the sound of someone running toward me. I stepped outside the summer-house. In the moonlight I must have been clearly silhouetted. 'Hugh?' I called. Whoever had been running stopped dead still. It was awfully creepy. 'Is that you, Dumpling?' Just as I said that, I heard a rock whiz past my ear and land with a terrific bang on the roof of the summer-house. Then without a single word Dumpling ran back to the house."

"You are sure it was Dumpling?"

"Of course I couldn't see very well, but he didn't throw the rock until I mentioned his name. Doesn't that look funny to you? I was a wreck when I realized what might have happened. If that rock had hit me, if it hadn't killed me on the spot the force of it would have pushed me into the pond and drowned me."

"You should learn to swim," said Mr. Wimble gravely.

"Marcia often gives swimming parties," babbled Kitten archly. "Perhaps you'll stay long enough to teach me?"

O. W. asked, somewhat hurriedly: "From what direction did the—rock come?"

"From the house. Dumpling must have been halfway between the house and the pond when he threw it."

"What did you do after—your narrow escape?"

"I was too petrified to move. Fortunately in a few minutes Hugh came back."

"From the same direction as the rock?"

"No. He came around the pond. I asked Hugh if he'd thrown anything at me but he only poked fun at me for being afraid of the dark. 'But I saw a man standing right over there!' I protested. 'It's no news to me that cats see in the dark,' he said. There's no use arguing with Hugh. He considers everything you say a foil for one of his jokes. But the minute I saw Gary Gilbert lying dead, I knew that but for the grace of God I'd have been the murderer's second victim."

"You know then that the stone was hurled at you after Gary Gilbert was murdered?"

A puzzled frown made ridges between Kitten's plucked eyebrows. "Oh, I see what you mean." Her forehead

smoothed. "I should have said the murderer's *other* victim.
You detectives are so technical."

Mr. Wimble reflected that it might be amusing to wax
technical to the extent of inquiring of Kitten where the
man had picked up the rock. The grounds of the Allen
estate, with the exception of the driveway which was of
concrete, were covered with lawn. But to bother Kitten
with technicalities when she had just handed him so lus-
cious a clue would have been ungrateful.

Suddenly, somewhere behind the house a shot rang out.
With a frightened cheep, Kitten precipitated herself into
the detective's arms.

"I'm afraid he's missed you again," observed O. W. dryly.

Kitten's teeth were chattering. "That was a sh-shot!" If
it had been an imp of Hell calling to his mate she couldn't
have been more terrified.

Mr. Wimble patted her quivering shoulders reassuring-
ly. "Someone shooting squirrels in the wood, likely."

At a sharp knock on the library door Kitten's arms went
around the detective's neck.

"Mr. Wimble!" It was Marcia calling. "I think you'd
better come. Something's happened."

O. W. got out of the room with remarkable speed considering the fact that the timorous Kitten was clinging the
while to his arm.

Marcia led the way to the front porch where Hugh
Osborne had assumed temporary control till the arrival
of the detective. Obviously there had been a capture. His
arms pinioned on one side by Miss Allen's gardener, on the
other by a uniformed policeman, was a sullen-faced individual whom O. W. instantly recognized as the man he had
seen that morning in conversation with Michael.

Mr. Wimble addressed the policeman. "I'm Wimble,
the detective on the murder case. What seems to be the
trouble?"

With his free hand the policeman touched his cap. "My name's Murphy, sir. Headquarters sent me over this morning to keep people off the grounds. I was on guard at the front gate when I heard a shot over in that patch of woods behind the house. I thought I better investigate so I started over. I almost got there when out ran this guy, Hell bent for election, this here gat in his mitt. I yelled to the gardener and together we caught him."

He drew a revolver out of his pocket, handing it to the detective. A rapid examination showed Mr. Wimble that one of its six cartridges had been discharged.

"Were you shooting squirrels?" piped up Kitten. The eyes the prisoner turned on her were so full of venom that Kitten, whom Marcia had kindly unhooked from the detective's arm, made haste to step beside Mr. Wimble. She seemed less afraid of firearms when there was a possibility of their being used in her defense.

"Careful, Kitten!" cautioned Osborne, characteristically claiming the limelight. "The man may make game of you!"

O. W. gave his attention to the gardener.

"You'd better come clean this time, Michael. You know this man. Who is he?"

"He's Henry Hawkins, me wife's brother-in-law."

"Marie's husband?" Michael nodded.

"Hawkins put you up to the lie you told me this morning?"

"Yes, sir-r." With a wrathful glance at his wife's brother-in-law, Michael turned toward Miss Allen. "I don't care what innybody does if they'll jus' lave me alone so's I can attind to' me gardhenin'!"

Marcia and the detective exchanged a smile.

O. W. said to Michael: "I don't believe you're needed here any longer. You may get back to your work if you like." The gardener departed with alacrity.

O. W. next addressed the culprit. "What have you to say for yourself?"

"I killed a man. I been laying for him in the woods since daybreak. He came there a few minutes ago and I got him." He added with intense satisfaction: "He's deader than a door nail!"

From O. W.'s elbow Kitten shrilled: "Did you try to hit me with a rock last night?" The man tossed his head as if to rid himself of a mosquito buzzing about his ear.

"And what's more," screamed Kitten, "I'll bet you're the man who murdered Gary Gilbert!"

"Pipe down!" snapped the man. "I just now got done telling you I shot Gary Gilbert, didn't I?"

"Thinks Gary Gilbert's twins, this egg does!" observed Murphy with elaborate sarcasm.

"I think the man's *crazy* if you ask *me!*" shrieked Kitten.

"Shut up, everybody!" demanded Hugh suddenly.

The others were so startled by Hugh's departure from calm indifference to startled wonder that momentarily they could not follow his glance for looking at him. When finally they were able to tear their gaze from Hugh's face they saw an O. Wimble no one had ever seen before. The detective's small blue eyes were gleaming like points of steel; his mouth was set in a thin, straight line. His face was drained of all color.

Fascinated, the others watched him. Grimly the detective cocked the revolver Murphy had handed him. As he raised his head, the prisoner fell a step backward before Mr. Wimble's red hot fury. When the detective spoke it was so quiet on the porch that, as Hugh Osborne afterward put it, you could actually hear the vines growing.

"For the first time in my life," said O. W., and his voice carried chill to all who heard it, "I feel inclined to take the law into my own hands."

"O. W.!" There came the *clop clop* of heels on the concrete driveway. "O. W.! *Corey's safe!*"

In another moment little Janet Hill, breathless from haste, was at O. W.'s side, whispering that his young assistant whom Henry Hawkins had mistaken for Gary Gilbert was all right.

"He's safe, O. W. dear! Not even scratched!"

The detective said shakily: "Take charge till I get back, will you, child? I'm off to the bushes. I'm afraid I'm going—to be sick."

13

The day following the murder of Gary Gilbert turned out to be one of the most memorable in Corey Webb's life.

To begin with, he was intrusted by Mr. Wimble with the investigation of the murdered man's rooms. Corey had been a bit skeptical about appearing in Gilbert's hotel, but Mr. Wimble had felt that Corey's resemblance to the dead man in all probability would go unnoticed. In the first place, there was the psychology of the thing to help him; everybody believed Gary to be dead. Then, too, Corey's resemblance to Gilbert was not marked except in profile. O. W. believed that, with smoked glasses as his disguise in lieu of the bandages and with his hat pulled well down over his eyes, his assistant would be immune from fainting females.

Corey enjoyed the deference shown him by Riley, who accompanied him to the hotel. He realized of course that Riley's esteem was due to "One Week" Wimble's reputation; but even second-hand glory was gratifying. Corey prayed that his performance as an assistant detective at the penthouse would be such as to do his chief credit.

It was Riley's official badge that procured for them entrée to Gilbert's rooms. The manager of the hotel presented a formidable front until the two men were able to establish their identity. Once he had explained his attitude they felt his lack of warmth to be warranted. From the moment the extras had appeared making public Gary Gilbert's tragic death and giving among other details the place of his residence, the hotel had swarmed with sensation seekers. With one accord they asked to be shown Gary Gilbert's rooms. This, the manager dourly informed Corey and Riley, they were unanimously refused. Of course they tried by every conceivable trick to get there. Only one man, however, had succeeded in reaching the roof. But this, said the manager, was Smitty's story.

Smitty was a bellhop. What differentiated him from his neatly uniformed associates was his ambition, a state of mind advertised by a dreamy quality hovering in his blue eyes, an expression suggestive of a hankering after bigger and better things.

Smitty was on the long watch, coming on duty at six-thirty in the morning. Upon reporting to the bell captain on Sunday morning, he was told that under no circumstances was anyone to be allowed on the roof. Already scores of persons had called, claiming to be relatives of the deceased and requesting to be shown his effects. Were Smitty found responsible for conducting anyone to the penthouse, or if he failed to do his utmost to frustrate any attempt to enter it, he would lose his job. A conscientious manager was taking every precaution to check further notoriety.

Smitty had been on duty about half an hour when a call came from the seventeenth floor which he was sent to answer. As he stepped into the elevator he noticed that it held a solitary male passenger. But what occupied his attention was the expression on the elevator boy's face.

This lad was a German Swiss named Ernst Lanker. He was liked around the hotel for his sunny disposition; but now his face was the epitome of gloom. Out of respect for the occupant of the elevator Smitty could not very well inquire of Ernst what ailed him.

Considering the fact that the man had entered the car only a few minutes previously, Ernst put an extraordinary question to his passenger before starting the elevator.

"Vill you be geddingk oudt, zir?" he pleaded.

"I'm going up," was the gruff response. "Seventeenth."

Ernst cast an entreating glance toward Smitty.

"Seventeenth," said Smitty, whereupon Ernst sighed in semi-relief. The hotel was seventeen stories high.

At the specified floor Smitty stood back to allow the passenger to pass him. He noticed that Ernst was huddling against the wall like a frightened animal.

The man walked briskly down the hallway. Smitty followed. It was a blind corridor.

"What number you looking for?" Smitty helpfully inquired.

"I can read."

"There's no stairway to the roof from here," announced Smitty cheerfully. It was easy to see what the gent was up to.

The man took a twenty-dollar bill out of his wallet.

"Look here, boy! I want to visit that penthouse on the roof. I'm a private detective."

Smitty thought: "If this yegg's a dick I'm Siamese twins!"

The self-styled private detective went on to say that he was at the hotel on behalf of a beautiful young married lady who'd been indiscreet enough to write some incriminating letters to Gary Gilbert. All he wanted to do, he said, was to get into that penthouse and retrieve the letters, and what was more the beautiful lady would be so grateful that, in addition to the twenty, she was bound to come across with a swell present for Smitty.

"Well, how about it, boy?"

Smitty was married and had a family. Times were hard. That twenty looked mighty good. "Lindy took a chance," he thought. Not that he was any Lindy—but neither was the chance so big. He guessed that Ernst had been offered the money; but Ernst did America the great compliment of being scared out of his wits he'd be deported. Upon taking out his citizenship papers, Ernst had been warned that unless he followed the straight and narrow he'd be sent back to yodel among the Alps. Once he became one of Uncle Sam's adopted nephews, he might go to Chicago if he liked and set up a brewery, but in the meantime he must watch his step—which in the present instance meant prohibiting souvenir hunters from paring off samples of Gary Gilbert's penthouse with their pocket knives.

In a very few minutes Smitty's brain had hatched a plan. Smitty was a quick thinker. Bellhops have to be. The amount of a tip often depends on rapid thinking. Putting his plan into action Smitty led the pseudo-detective to the service elevator.

The elevator operator was dubious. "Orders was not to take anyone up."

"Cut the stalling, Pat!" Smitty pulled a blank laundry list from his pocket, waved it before the operator's eyes and returned it to his pocket. "An order from the office to take this guy up to padlock the penthouse door."

Smitty thought he caught a look of approval on the dick's face but he couldn't be sure, the man had such an ugly map—dabs of charcoal for eyebrows and a scar shining like a road in the moonlight the whole length of his cheek.

"Better wait," Smitty told Pat when they had reached the roof. "Won't take a minute."

"Neat work," exulted the dick as he and Smitty made their way to the penthouse.

"Got a pass-key?" asked Smitty.

"Sure! Always carry pass keys in my line." Smitty had his own ideas about that guy's line, confirmed when for no reason at all he put on his gloves.

Smitty remarked that the man knew just which way to cross the roof to reach the penthouse.

As they neared the house Smitty gave a warning whisper: "Sh!"

His companion stopped short. "What's eating you?"

"Thought I heard someone inside," returned Smitty. A deep scowl added to the general ugliness of the man's face. Evidently he hadn't counted on any such obstacle.

"Soft pedal!" he ordered briefly and Smitty proceeded on tiptoe. Unfortunately the curtains of the penthouse were drawn so that they could not hope to see into the rooms. The best they could do was stand outside the door listening.

Suddenly a peculiar grunting came from within the penthouse.

"A dog, maybe," suggested Smitty. He got a kick in the chin which he took to mean that he was to shut up. There was an expression on the man's face right then, Smitty said, before which a dog would have dropped dead in his tracks.

"Gossakes, fellers!" from the interior of the penthouse. Unmistakably a man's voice. "Wish Headquarters would send over our relief. I want my breakfast."

"Cheese it!" hissed Smitty. "The cops!" But the man was already cheesing it; in fact the service elevator had dived into the depths by the time Smitty reached it.

At this point in the narrative the manager of the hotel voiced an opinion: "I think Smitty earned that twenty, don't you?"

Corey and Riley eyed each other in bewilderment. As far as they could see, luck rather than any foresight on the bellhop's part had routed the intruder.

Smitty laughed. "There wasn't no cops in that there penthouse till I went in and telephoned down to the front office for the house detective. If vaudeville ever comes back, I hope to go on the stage. You see," with a modest grin, "I'm a bit of a ventriloquist."

Before accompanying Riley to the roof Corey telephoned Janet Hill. After stating his business he invited her to luncheon. She accepted. Having been a woman-hater for so long, as Corey emerged from the telephone booth he thought his quickened pulse was due to the fact that he was about to enter Gilbert's rooms.

However, with the ability of the male to concentrate on the subject at hand, during the time he and Riley spent in the penthouse Corey was all detective. His business there was twofold: he was to collect whatever clues revealed themselves; and he was to recover the portrait which had so distressed Marie Villette Hawkins.

The interior of the penthouse was arranged on the order of the hotel suites; consisting of a living room, bedroom and bath; but its furnishings were far more luxurious. If Gary Gilbert had possessed shady companions, the air of refinement permeating his living quarters belied the fact. There were a good many letters in his desk but no legal papers such as a will. It was possible that he had maintained a safe deposit box downtown, though Corey came across no keys of any description. There was no safe in the room. After opening a few of the letters, Corey concluded that they were largely social: bids to various functions, acknowledgments of flowers and candy, one or two personal notes. He set Riley to reading this mail in the hope of discovering something of importance, while he searched for the portrait. He made a careful survey of the room without unearthing a single clue. Riley, leaning

back in his chair after his tiresome task of perusing countless bids to parties, suggested looking for a secret drawer
at the bottom of a handsome rosewood cabinet that stood
against the wall. Turning rather hastily toward the piece of
furniture in question so that Riley wouldn't be a witness
to his blush, Corey tinkered with the bottom of the cabinet. To his gratification, and a bit to his chagrin as Riley
had made the suggestion, he discovered a secret drawer. In
this drawer he found a small notebook and the portrait.
Being human, Corey looked first at the portrait.

"Whew!" was his reaction.

"Baby!" was Riley's.

It was a study of a man and woman in the nude. The
models without question had been Marie Villette and Gary
Gilbert. The bodies were beautiful, vitally alive. There was
no doubt that the artist had been a master. The drawing,
the composition, the coloring, were excellent. But, as the
voice of that most graceful of birds, the sea-gull, sounds
like a piece of sacking being torn across, so did the artist
who had painted that picture possess an evil mind. By a
greater man, even though a lesser craftsman, the painting
might have been executed to portray the lust of all ages—
terrifying in its stark reality, but gripping in its sincerity.
But the artist who had used Marie and Gary as models
had succeeded in being only obscene. Even the most delicate touches stamped the thing as lewd. No wonder Marie
wanted the painting! Corey felt half tempted to destroy it
on the spot lest there be any slip-up in its reaching her.

14

Within the city of San Francisco lies a smaller city called Chinatown. The main artery of this quarter is the far-famed Grant Avenue. What Bond Street is to London, the Rue de la Paix to Paris, Fifth Avenue to New York, Grant Avenue is to Chinatown. Though Chinatown's byways abound in shadows and are silent save for the shuffling of slippered feet, color and sound pervade its highway. The brilliantly lighted show-windows of the Avenue's enchanting length of bazaars boast the treasures of Bagdad: shimmering silks, rare embroideries, Satsuma ware, gleaming lacquer, brasses, cloisonné, porcelains, ivories, jade, carvings of teak, camphor and sandal wood, porphyry, twinkling crystal, clear as water.

San Francisco's Orientals, deriving their chief revenue from the tourist trade, welcome you. They are well aware that you will not be able to resist their shops. You are also invited to hear the Four Truths at their temples, the pagoda roofs of which lend to the quarter's skyline a lacelike quality; you may even take away little idols of gold and terra cotta to worship as your own—in exchange for a coin or two, of course. You are urged to sit in high-benched discomfort at their theatres, to listen to the metallic crash of Eastern music at their celebrations of the Full Moon. They are particularly glad to have you visit their eating houses,

where almond-eyed maidens in colorful native garb serve
you jasmine tea in little cups without handles and titter
at your clumsy attempts to manipulate *chow mein* with
chopsticks.

Across a teak wood table in The Garden of the Lotus Tree,
much to her amusement Janet caught Corey eyeing askance
the bowl of "Mandarin's Delight" she had suggested he
order as typical of the Chinese dishes.

With his eye on the lemon-skinned proprietor of the
restaurant, Corey whispered: "Do you suppose they really
use rats' tails in their cooking?"

Janet giggled. "Silly! Those are the ends of beets!"

Corey felt immensely relieved, though, had lunching
with Janet Hill actually meant getting around a mess of
rats' tails, he would have done so without flinching. Corey
was happy. He was so happy that he wondered what up till
now he had found worth living for.

He could think up dozens of reasons why Janet was the
most wonderful girl in the world. For instance, she had
the rare ability to make up her mind at once. When he
had telephoned her that morning to tell her he had a good
human interest story for her, she had said: "Thanks. I'll
be right over. Whom do I ask for?" And when he'd added
an invitation to luncheon she hadn't been like the other
girls he knew, trying to make out she was the most popular
woman in town: "Well, I did have a date—rather important—still I *might* be able to break it if you'll coax hard
enough." Instead she had come right back with: "Oh, lovely! I'll meet you in the lobby at twelve." Another reason
Corey thought Janet had it over other girls was because
she hadn't thrown a fit at his remark about the rat tails.
Janet was a good sport and such a charming companion.
She made Corey feel the way Bernard Shaw must feel when

he makes a speech in England; she laughed at his jokes whether they were funny or not.

Still further reason for his crush was the gratitude she had expressed for the tip. Just like Janet not to take it for granted that, because she was a pretty girl, it was her right to have things passed to her on a silver platter!

"It was lovely of you to put me on to that story of Smitty's!" Janet's blue eyes sparkled. "Guess what my City Editor said to me when he'd read it!"

Here was Corey's chance. "I'll bet he said: 'Janet, you have the laughingest eyes!'"

Janet's giggle brought Corey to with a start. "If you could see Dunk you'd never accuse him of poetry. He has a face like a doughnut that's been dunked. That's how he got his nickname. No, when he'd read my article he said: 'Hell, kid, you can write!' I said: 'Hell, Dunk, I always told you I could!'" Janet's eyes sent an intimate little smile across the table to Corey: "And to think it was you who gave me my chance!"

Corey's recollection that he had made Smitty's story the excuse to invite Janet to luncheon caused him a slight pang of remorse.

"No such thing! It was your writing that did it."

Janet clasped her hands in a gesture of delight. "And guess what?"

Corey's heart sank. "Dunk asked you to marry him," he guessed hollowly.

"Dunk's married and has seven youngsters! You're a swell guesser!" she gibed. But Corey was a much happier young man.

Janet said impressively: "Dunk's assigned me to the Gary Gilbert murder case! Isn't that lovely?"

Lovely? It was Dreams Come True! It was the Maker letting an angel in a blue beret out of Heaven to work on the same job as a common, garden-variety junior detective!

However, Corey managed to speak without singing the
words. "If you're coming back to Thousand Oaks with me,
I won't have to go on guzzling tea for the sake of delaying
our parting." He later confided in Mr. Wimble that he had
downed ten cups of the accursed stuff.

After a business call at the head office of the Western
Union Telegraph Company, Janet and Corey proceeded
down Market Street to the Ferry Building. Before boarding the boat Corey bought Janet a gardenia. He wanted to
say: "It's white and pure and fragrant just like you!" But
he dared not risk Janet's raillery. So he contented himself
with: "Your tailor-made coat calls for a tailor-made flower."

Crossing the Bay they fed popcorn to the gulls that
followed the boat. Corey hurled the popcorn over the rail
as if he were pitching for Babe Ruth. He wanted to turn a
hand spring on the deck. He wanted to give a college yell.

Corey had always hated his kind of good looks—today
more than ever. A sensible girl like Janet would prefer a
he-man shock of straight hair to the kind that lay in the
sort of miniature mountain ranges one Monsieur Marcel
had made his fortune copying with a curling iron. She undoubtedly considered a freckled pug nose far more attractive than the classic one he had inherited from Dolly. He
remembered with anguish that, though he could conceal
his cheek dimples by refraining from mirth, he was a victim of the dimple that dented his chin. He wished he had
buck teeth. Inwardly he blessed Mr. Wimble for suggesting the dark glasses. At least they hid the degrading fact
that his eyelashes curled all over the place.

Dan Cupid had Corey Webb on the spot!

It appeared that Janet had ideas of her own concerning
the spectacles. Climbing the hill to Miss Allen's, she requested Corey to remove them.

Corey eyed her breathlessly. "Why?" Maybe she didn't
mind a fellow's having lashes like mops after all!

"'Eyes are the windows of the soul,'" quoted Janet elf-ishly. "Maybe I want to see into your soul. Can't, through those storm windows."

Corey glanced rather wistfully at the trees bordering the road. He was in exactly the right mood to climb one.

Suddenly from Janet: "Oh, we've come up the wrong road!"

Corey stooped to pick a buttercup. The exertion must have been excessive, it made his face so red.

Janet chided her blushing squire. "Corey Webb! You came up this way on purpose!"

Corey bent over to select another buttercup.

"Shame on you for taking the longest way round!" Janet's voice became reproachful. "And Mr. Wimble probably waiting impatiently for your report!"

"Sorry!" lied Corey.

Janet scanned the landscape. "These woods adjoin the Allen estate. We'll climb the fence," she decided.

Though frustrated in his attempt to have Janet by himself for a longer period, Corey couldn't but admire the dexterity with which she scaled the fence. He placed his hands for her as if she were about to mount a horse; lightly she used his palms for a step and jumped over the fence as expertly as a lettered pole vaulter.

Together they walked through the woods.

"Isn't it lovely in here!" exclaimed Janet.

As a light breeze stirred the tops of the eucalyptus trees their leaves reflected the soft silver sunshine of late after-noon. Corey's rollicking mood had left him. In the cool quiet of the woods, he longed in some way to distinguish himself before this slim, young Janet in the blue beret, to do something worthwhile, to make a noble gesture.

All at once an incredible thing happened. Janet delib-erately thrust her little foot in his path and tripped him!

As he fell on his face Corey saw a huge object heading toward him; simultaneously there came a roar that sounded as if two locomotives had crashed into each other head on.

Almost before he struck the ground Corey felt Janet kneeling beside him.

"Fake dead!" Her words cut into his consciousness like knives.

Next came Janet's wailing cry: "Oh, he's dead! He's dead! You've shot him! He's dead!"

Through Janet's screams Corey heard the sound of someone running.

And then he had Janet on his hands. Or perhaps she had him on hers. He wasn't quite sure. At any rate, as the sound of the footsteps died away, they were in each other's arms, Janet crying her eyes out. Corey didn't know just what had happened; but holding Janet in his arms was the sweetest sensation he'd ever experienced—he knew that.

After awhile, when both Janet's little handkerchief and Corey's large one looked ready for a clothes-wringer, Janet calmed down sufficiently to brush some dirt from Corey's face and to tell him what had happened.

"All of a sudden I saw a man standing in the path. He had a revolver in his hand aimed at you. The look on his face—I could tell he meant to shoot you. So I tripped you. Oh, suppose he'd killed you!" A fellow couldn't very well see a girl shuddering like that without doing something about it, so Corey put his arms around Janet again and held her close. Of course, he told himself, it wasn't because he'd almost been killed that she was acting this way; girls always did break down when the danger was over. He certainly was glad Janet wasn't one of those consistently sensible girls. Janet had the good sense to be sensible at the sensible time! A girl who could jump fences like a man and joke about rats' tails might very well have been the kind to save a fellow's life and then laugh it off with: "Well, that's that!"

All at once Corey discovered that somehow or other his cheek had begun to press against Janet's. Then he found that both his and Janet's cheeks were moving—his east, Janet's west.

A kiss was in the process of construction!

"Oh!" said Janet.

"Oh!" said Corey, his face crimson. How rotten of him, taking advantage that way of a girl who'd just saved his life!

"Oh!" repeated Janet, jumping to her feet. "We're letting that fiend escape!"

Corey attempted to arise.

"No!" cried Janet, holding him down. "You've got to stay here and pretend dead till I'm sure it's safe for you to leave the woods. I'll go."

Corey squared his jaw. "Who do you think I am, letting the girl I l— letting you go trailing thugs?"

Janet wasn't so bad at jaw squaring herself. "I think you are O. Wimble's assistant," she said sternly, "and that you are going to obey your chief's orders to the letter." And O. W. had told him under no circumstances to approach the house!

"O. K.," sighed Corey.

For a moment Janet stood looking down at him. Suddenly she bent over and lightly touched his cheek with her fingers. Of course it may have been that there was still a bit of dirt clinging to his face; but, even if he'd had the courage to ask, Janet was gone before he could open his mouth, running toward the house as fast as she could.

Corey was glad to be alone. A man doesn't want anyone around when he's praying for the girl he loves to say, "Yes."

15

Mr. Wimble had as many reasons for sending Corey to Hollywood to interview Marcia Allen's sister as a small boy has for staying up beyond his bedtime. Two of these reasons emanated from his heart and were the only one's he did not disclose to his young assistant.

O. W.'s major reason for sending the boy to the southern city was to remove him from the danger zone; the detective didn't believe he could hold up under another attack on Corey's life. His second heart-reason for getting Corey out of town was that he was anxious for Dolly to meet Janet. For O. W. had hatched up several pretexts for sending Janet to Hollywood with Corey.

The detective had encountered no opposition from the *Globe* to Janet's taking a leave of absence. Hadn't Miss Hill been assigned to the Gilbert murder case, the City Editor rather testily had inquired? If the case entailed a visit to Hollywood, then to Hollywood Janet must go. Little Janet was becoming popular on the *Globe*. Her story "Ventriloquist Routs Ghoul" had gone over big. Her succeeding story "Jealous Husband Shoots Ghost" had gone over bigger.

Janet more than did justice to Henry Hawkins' tragicomedy of errors. Her account of the shooting was so ludicrous one could hardly read the words for laughter.

The dour-faced Dunk publicly complimented Janet on her covert advertising campaign. Hearstian, no less, that passage! If Mr. Hawkins would only contract the habit of reading his *Globe* daily, Janet wrote, he would be spared a lot of embarrassment. It seemed that Saturday's edition had acquainted Henry with the fact that Mrs. Katharine Wells and Mr. Gary Gilbert intended spending the week-end at Marcia Allen's. Upon reaching home that evening Henry had found his wife's note informing him that she had gone over to Thousand Oaks to stay all night with Marcia Allen's laundress. Thereafter, Henry's eyes had been good for nothing but seeing red, whereas if he'd given his Sunday *Globe* a break, he'd have realized not only that his plans for putting an end to Gary Gilbert had slipped through his fingers but that he'd been spared the likelihood of a noose being slipped around his own neck. This much of her story Janet presented in a manner to tickle the reader's risibility. But when she wrote of poor old Henry, so in love with his sloe-eyed spouse that it crazed him to think of her basking in the sunshine of some other man's admiration, Janet's portrayal was so full of pathos that many a reader felt an unfamiliar pulling at his heartstrings.

Janet had not prepared her story without some prompting from Mr. Wimble. She had understood all along, of course, that it was not to be revealed to the general public that Mr. Wimble's assistant was a young man greatly resembling in appearance the late Gary Gilbert. And she had agreed with the detective that there was no need to share with the *Globe's* subscribers the full details of the reconciliation of Marie and Henry, an event which, contrary to the creed of most newspaper reporters, Janet felt belonged to the Hawkinses and nobody else.

Henry had been pretty badly frightened upon learning that he had come within an inch of shooting an innocent man. Fanatically Henry believed that to kill a man who in his estimation deserved death was not murder. But when apprised of his mistake he had gasped: "But for that little girl's presence of mind I'd be a murderer!" And when he had cooled down and for the first time given a thought to consequences, upon being reminded by O. W. that an attempt on a man's life was a criminal offense punishable by imprisonment in the state prison, he had become as putty in the detective's hands.

So Janet wrote up her story as though the victim of Mr. Hawkins' target practice were the ghost of Henry's own jealous brooding. And Henry found nothing wrong with her interpretation. Better a clown than a convict!

Of course O. W. disclaimed any credit for the reconciliation. By this time he was reasonably sure that Marie wasn't guilty. It didn't seem plausible that, if she had committed the crime around eight o'clock, the girl would have waited until ten before attempting to escape. Nevertheless the detective took it upon himself, by solemnly informing Henry that Marie was suspected of the crime, to impress on the man his wife's need of him. He pointed out to Henry how Gary had presumed on his slight acquaintance with Marie in Paris to force his attentions on her in San Francisco. O. W. inferred that Marie was a victim of persecution rather than a party to an illicit relationship, and Henry groaned to think how instead of coming to his wife's rescue he had spent his time nursing his own unjustifiable jealousy.

O. W. made no mention before Henry of the portrait. This subject was brought up only when Marie and the detective found themselves alone.

Contemptuously Marie eyed the unrolled canvas.

"Do you know, Mr. Wimble, when I was running around naked in the artists' studios I didn't think anything of it; but somehow, as I look at this picture, I get Henry's point of view. It does look rotten, doesn't it?"

Apparently Marie was a better artists' model than artist. But O. W. thought it best not to enlighten the young
woman to the extent of explaining that it was not her unclad form that characterized the painting as bawdy. The
way things stood now Marie never again would be tempted
to pose for another artist. This, considering her husband's
tendency to turn green at the slightest provocation, would
make for their greater marital felicity.

O. W. promised that as soon as his investigation was
completed he would burn the painting, whereupon greatly
to his embarrassment Marie fell to her knees and kissed
his hand.

Before sending Corey to Hollywood O. W. had a talk with
Marcia.

"I'd like to ask you a few questions about Roberta, Miss
Allen."

"Roberta?" Marcia's surprise was genuine.

"Your sister is connected with the crime—indirectly let
us hope."

A bitter laugh discharged itself through Marcia's lips.
"She would be! What is it you want to know about Rob?"

"The truth," replied O. W. innocently.

"Go ahead! Ask your questions. I'll probably tell the
truth." Marcia's facial expression was more friendly than
she realized. "You have a way of taking the wind out of my
sails."

O. W. smiled. "I suspect that your thinking boat's
equipped with a motor as well as sails."

He put his first question. "Your sister is not a general
favorite?"

"I'm sorry to say that Rob's a difficult child."

"From what I can gather she's jealous of you." Marcia
nodded. "On Gilbert's account, you think?"

"Heavens, no! Rob never saw Gary." Marcia interrupted herself by a short laugh. "To tell the truth, I took particular pains not to let Rob meet Gary. I intended marrying him, you know, and I was afraid she'd scare him off. Rob has—romantic notions."

"Why then is she jealous?"

"This is rather intimate family history, Mr. Wimble, but perhaps it will clarify matters if I go into it. Roberta is not my own sister. She is the daughter of my father's second wife, who left Dad to run off with another man when Rob was a baby. Rob takes after her mother. Dad never told Rob the truth; he thought we'd have better control over her if she didn't know. The trouble between Rob and me is largely financial. When Dad died he left all his money to me. I make Rob a generous allowance, but she feels she's entitled to part of Dad's estate. The foolish child would have it given away to some man in a week! She makes all sorts of threats as to what she's going to do about it when she comes of age."

"Leaving Gilbert out of it, do you think she's involved in any love affair?"

"A dozen probably," lightly from Marcia. "Rob has a remarkable capacity for falling in love. After all, she's quite young."

"Do you know anybody who calls her Cara?"

"Cara? That's Italian, isn't it? No. I don't believe I do."

"Gilbert possibly understood Italian, having lived abroad so long?"

"As a matter of fact Gary did not understand Italian. I asked him once. He spoke French fluently, but not Italian."

O. W. showed her the telegram he had found near the summer-house, its stain blotting but all but the message proper.

MARCIA KNOWS ALL STOP BEWARE OR
SOME GREAT HARM WILL OVERTAKE
YOU

                                    CARA

Marcia's eyes became enormously intelligent. "Is this your method of accusing me of the crime, Mr. Wimble?"

The detective's eyes became slits as he laughed. "The motor's running now."

"Which means nothing," retorted Marcia. "If it serves your purpose you'll manage to stall the engine."

"Just for that," chuckled Mr. Wimble, "though my detective maxim is 'See everything; hear everything; say nothing!', I'll answer your question." His voice sobered. "Despite the fact that your alibi is a bit shaky, in your frequent manifestations of despair, Miss Allen, I have sensed no grief at all for the loss of your fiancé. What possible motive could you have had for killing Gary Gilbert but jealousy? And where there is no love there is no jealousy."

Marcia made a little moue. "Are you cross because you must eliminate me from your list of suspects, or because you're disappointed that I'm the sort of woman who could marry a man without being passionately in love with him?"

It was clever of her to have caught the note of censure in his voice, O. W. thought. "You're a saucy child!" he returned severely. "And a true woman—answering a question by asking one!"

But Marcia persisted. "You do think it's best to go on through life alone, without companionship, without children, if you can't marry the—the *only one*, don't you?"

O. W.'s faithful heart cried: "Yes, yes—a thousand times, yes!"

But his mind reproved: "Is that sound advice to give a young woman whose every move is motherly?"

"Look here, Marcia Allen!" he said brusquely. "I'm running a detective, not a matrimonial, agency. We were discussing Roberta's telegram."

"You are sure Rob sent it?"

"My assistant has traced the sender through the Western Union Company."

"If Rob sent that wire of warning to Gary, she must have had some inkling of what was going to happen to him. Great grief!" she broke off in horror. "You don't think the child could have—"

"Murdered Gary Gilbert? She hated you. It would have been the perfect revenge. A person tallying with your sister's description was seen in the garden outside the library the night of the murder; someone so familiar with the servants that she questioned the presence on the place of one she failed to recognize. A large, masculine-looking girl, she was, dressed in an aviator's costume. I wired Roberta's school; she was missing for several hours on Saturday night."

Marcia's face was white. "Rob does know how to pilot an airplane. I've refused her one, but several of her friends own 'planes."

"Roberta's telegram was addressed to the Dwight's chauffeur, Miss Allen."

Marcia sighed her relief. "Then that throws an entirely different light on the whole thing!" She eyed the detective reproachfully. "Why did you torture me?"

"Why did you try to hide from me that Roberta was carrying on an affair with Kelly?"

Marcia flushed. "After all, I think of Rob as my little sister. Honestly, though, I didn't know Kelly called her Cara. Rather silly for an Irishman, isn't it? No doubt Rob supplied the endearment herself. Rob has enough sentimentality in her system for her swains and herself both."

"Do you think Kelly cares for your sister?"

Marcia clucked her tongue. "Of course not! He was only amusing himself as a man will when a girl throws herself at him."

"You and Roberta quarreled about Kelly?"

Marcia made a wry face. "I'm afraid Rosie has been eavesdropping again." Once more O. W. felt himself warming in admiration of Miss Allen's perspicacity. "Rob and I did have words, but I began them on purpose. I'd caught her making eyes at Kelly, so I threatened to have Dumpling dismiss him if it didn't stop. I knew Rob would repeat my threat to Kelly and that he would sensibly decide his job was worth a whole lot more to him than a few kisses from Roberta. Judging from the wire you just showed me, apparently that is what did happen. Of course Rob would couch even a public telegram in melodramatic terms. She's like that."

Mr. Wimble became thoughtful. "Do you think a good scare would help your sister any, Miss Allen?"

Marcia artlessly returned: "I'm quite sure that if you frightened her sufficiently she would tell you all she knew."

His laughter shook the detective's round body. He *liked* Marcia Allen!

As if repenting of her fun Marcia proceeded to give Mr. Wimble some valuable information: "Rob has more than her share of vanity. She'd loathe being stigmatized as a murder suspect. She's terribly talkie-struck. She often tells me how Scandal ruins the careers of the stars." Marcia made a face at the detective. "Is it your practice to stick accusations on to folks like mustard plasters?"

O. W.'s official reasons for sending Corey to Hollywood were numerous. They had to be to satisfy his young assistant he wasn't being packed into the life-boat with the women and children.

"Marcia says Roberta is a very difficult young lady to handle," Mr. Wimble warned him.

Corey looked worried. "I'm not so good at handling girls." As the boy blushed O. W. wondered just what had taken place in the wood after Janet had saved his life.

Mr. Wimble said guilelessly: "That's why I think little Janet Hill had better go along."

He continued rather pleadingly; he didn't want the lad to consider him a darn old matchmaker. "Janet knows Roberta, you see. She can introduce you. Roberta's probably not the breed of girl who takes kindly to detectives. Then, too, there might be another story for Janet." He felt himself foundering before Corey's gaze.: "Two heads are always better than one," he lamely concluded.

"Janet could stay with Dolly!"

Something in the breathless way Corey stated this fact made O. W. suspect that the boy hadn't heard a word he'd uttered after his announcement that little Janet had better go along.

16

The inquest was held on Monday morning. Prior to attending it O. W. paid two calls, both on medical men.

The first call was the outcome of a note delivered to the detective the previous evening by a messenger boy:

> Dear Mr. Wimble:
> I wish to certify that Mrs. Dwight's physical condition is so serious as to render her unable to attend the inquest to be held tomorrow morning in connection with the murder of Mr. Gary Gilbert.
>> Yours very truly,
>> Hayward J. Bruce, M.D.

Upon being shown into the elegantly appointed waiting room of Dr. Hayward J. Bruce, Mr. Wimble breathed a sigh of relief. He had been so afraid Dr. Bruce would turn out to be a back-street medico, furtive-eyed, susceptible of bribery, issuing prescriptions for liquor, performing doubtful operations, signing his name to false certificates. The marked refinement of the room, its evidence of culture, placed a stricture on any suspicion O. W. may have entertained that Hayward J. Bruce was a quack.

When ushered into his presence, O. W. saw that the appearance of the doctor did nothing to belie his good taste. Dr. Bruce, some sixty years old, was tall and spare, with clean-cut features. His face was remarkable for the decision of his mouth and the astuteness of his brown eyes. In manner Dr. Bruce was reserved to formality, a man O. W. decided little given to banter, though the detective later discovered that Bruce could have his joke as well as another.

There were times when Mr. Wimble dallied over conversations; but he could see at a glance that there was nothing of the over-the-back-fence gossip about Dr. Bruce.

Producing the note Bruce had sent him the detective said: "I thought I'd have a talk with you before presenting your note at the inquest this morning."

The doctor's surprise if not sincere was at least well acted. "I think that what I intended to convey is quite clear."

O. W. grinned. "Quite!" he agreed.

Suddenly to his utter astonishment Hayward J. Bruce, M.D., found that he was picturing himself and this benevolent little gentleman with the absurd name and absurder profession facing each other over a chess game, cigars between their lips, sherry glasses at their elbows.

It was with difficulty that he resisted the infectiousness of O. W.'s grin.

"Come, Mr. Wimble," he said crisply, "We are both busy men. Let's get to the point."

O. W. pushed the doctor's note across the desk that separated them. "You intended me to introduce this at the inquest, did you not?" The physician nodded.

"Perjury is a criminal offense, Dr. Bruce, punishable by law." Bruce gave no sign that he recognized the truth of this observation. He waited for his visitor to continue.

"I believe," said O. W. cheerfully, "that your note has told me more than I'd learn if Mrs. Dwight were to testify at the inquest." Apparently the matter had not occurred to Bruce in just this light; a faint expression of sheepishness showed that he felt he had been weighed and found wanting.

"I take it you are questioning my professional skill, Mr. Wimble."

"Let us say, rather, your veracity."

"I think," said Bruce tartly, "that I have the right to request your justification of that remark!"

O. W. indicated by a shrug his willingness to explain.

"I am a great lover of flowers, Dr. Bruce. You must admit that the flowers hereabouts are worthy of note. This morning I went for a stroll. My rambles led me by many beautiful gardens. Finally I drew up before a particularly charming one—a riot of color and fragrance. The pansy beds especially interested me. I never saw so many pansies before in all my life. I stood staring at them across the hedge. All of a sudden I burst out laughing. There was I staring at the pansies—and every single pansy in the bed staring back at me for all it was worth!"

Had Dr. Bruce's office nurse been present she might have suspected that Mr. Wimble had come to the wrong physician. Dr. Bruce was not an alienist. But the detective had not been in his office five minute before Bruce himself had realized that he was in the presence of a perfectly healthy and exceedingly keen mind. He waited with interest the denouement of Mr. Wimble's horticultural tale.

"All at once I heard a giggle. I raised my eyes, and there stood a young woman—one of the most beautiful young women it has as yet been my good fortune to look upon. I didn't blame her for her ridicule. I must have looked comical standing there grinning at the pansies. When I told

her why I was amused you ought to have heard her laugh.
She agreed it was as funny as it could be.

"We had a little chat. She was gardening. She always
gardened, she said, when there was anything troubling her.
She was going at it with a vim, too, when I left—digging
and pruning. As I walked away I heard her chuckling to
herself. I knew she had caught the pansies staring at her as
they had stared at me."

"Well?"

"While we were standing there talking together the
butcher boy passed through the yard." O. W. smiled reminiscently. "More freckles than the sky has stars, and two
teeth out in front! As he went in the lad called: 'Howdy,
Mrs. Dwight!'"

There was a moment's silence; then Dr. Bruce tossed
across the desk to the detective the note he had written
swearing to Mrs. Dwight's inability to appear at the coroner's inquest that morning.

"I have no intention of altering my original statement,
Mr. Wimble."

Gravely O. W. placed the affidavit in his wallet.

"How long have you known these two young people,
Dr. Bruce?"

The rigidity of the doctor's features became less apparent as he replied. "I saw John into the world and have been
his physician ever since. Not that he's a gold-mine patient
by any means! There's never been anything the matter with
him—except his heart. It's too big. I have known Chiquita
only since their marriage."

O. W. patted his wallet pocket. "You must care deeply
for John to have taken the risk."

"Mrs. Bruce and I were never blessed with a son of our
own," replied Bruce simply.

His eyes looked straight into the detective's. "I have
never known John Dwight to do a mean, low thing. Mr.

Wimble, I don't know John's reason in the present instance, but whatever he asked of me I should do willingly,
without question."

O. W. said softly: "I *like* young Dwight!"

Throughout the interview Hayward Bruce's spirit had
felt dragged down. At Mr. Wimble's declaration of regard
for John a feeling of comfort stole over him. His relief
prompted him to make a confession to the detective that
otherwise his austerity of manner would have kept a closely guarded secret.

"I am not running nearly the risk you suppose. I happen to be personally acquainted with the coroner. We were
boyhood chums. It wouldn't occur to Paul Channing to
doubt my word."

"Dr. Bruce," said Mr. Wimble earnestly, "the police are
working on this case as well as I. Were I to contest your
affidavit at the inquest this morning, suspicion would
immediately surround John Dwight and his wife. I intend
letting your statement concerning the state of Chiquita
Dwight's health go unquestioned. May I ask—not in return for this but because you trust me—that you use your
friendship with Coroner Channing on my behalf?"

Coroner Channing was a man who revered his office. He
had a passion for doing his best by the county, was tireless
in the performance of his duties, had never been known
to shirk and, having been elected by the people for the
purpose of serving the people, did not use his office for
the exploitation of himself. But what was most important, Paul Channing was an intelligent man. He welcomed
constructive suggestions. Therefore, even without his old
friend Hayward Bruce as intermediary, he would have
been glad to consider Private Detective Wimble's proposition. But Bruce's letter of introduction proved of value in

that it induced the coroner to lay aside other matters and devote the hour preceding the inquest to Mr. Wimble.

Obviously Gary Gilbert had been killed by the butcher knife which had punctured his heart. And yet on the night of the murder what had kept the detective occupied for hours tracing on innumerable scraps of paper the geometrical designs that always accompanied his professional pondering was the small scratch he had discovered on the body of the deceased. It was this second wound—in the nature of an incision about half an inch wide and three-quarters of an inch deep in the breast three inches above the death wound—that featured on Monday morning in the pre-inquest conversation of Coroner Paul Channing and Private Detective O. Wimble.

As a result of this conversation considerable information was withheld at the inquest that otherwise might have been divulged.

A suicide hypothesis was advanced but adjudged shaky inasmuch as no incriminating finger-prints had been found on the handle of the weapon.

The verdict was that, to the best of the jury's knowledge, Gary Gilbert had been stabbed to death with a butcher knife on Saturday evening at about eight o'clock by an unknown person evilly disposed, the knife penetrating the chest wall directly over the cardiac region. As no great force would be required to inflict such a wound, it remained undetermined whether the murder had been committed by a man or a woman.

17

The fact that she was serving in a house where a murder had been committed made Rosie Ryan the envy of the neighboring servant girls. Rosie's desire to carry dramatic accounts of Mr. Wimble's detective procedure to her friends, together with her natural propensity for eavesdropping, might have proved a nuisance to the detective had not Wing unexpectedly come to his assistance.

Early in the investigation O. W. had realized that he was being watched by the aged Chinaman. Wing was like a Broadway columnist in his ability to know what was going to happen before it took place. No matter at what hour or how quietly the detective left his room in the morning, when he reached the library he found his breakfast, piping hot, waiting for him on the library table.

When he was deliberating Miss Allen's suggestion that he use the library for his business office, Wing hitting the nail of his qualms on the head had said: "I shall protect you from Rosie." This the Chinaman had managed successfully to do by the simple expedient of keeping Rosie occupied in the kitchen whenever O. W. was in the library.

Rosie was sufficiently sharp to see through Wing's ruse.

"I'll bet you're in cahoots with Mr. Wimble!" she pouted. She was emptying the library waste-basket at the time. "Look here!" Triumphantly she salvaged a slip of paper. "If that isn't Chinese writing I'll eat my hat!" The paper was covered with the geometrical designs Mr. Wimble was in the habit of penciling when thinking deeply,

"I will provide baking soda when the war begins," announced Wing serenely.

"War?" Rosie's brow wrinkled. "What war?"

"The war between Rosie's belly and Rosie's hat."

"You go jump in the lake!" retaliated Rosie. Whereupon Wing quoted her a Truth on the respect due their elders by young people.

Though Wing's vigilance prevented her from eavesdropping, it was Rosie's job to empty the waste-basket. So when the Gary Gilbert murder case was finally solved and Mr. Wimble had departed Eastward, there wasn't a servant girl for miles around who didn't possess a sheet of paper covered with little geometrical drawings. Such is fame! At that, Mr. Wimble's scribbled designs were as decipherable as the autographs of most famous men.

On the day following the inquest O. W.'s pencil was hard at work. Propped up before him was a book on horticulture, opened at a chapter entitled "Pansies"; but the detective's eyes were not on this book. A keen observer, however, would have noted that the angular, five-sectioned pattern his pencil was tracing over and over again could by a stretch of the imagination be called a pansy. Therefore there was probably some connection between the chapter on pansies and the detective's thoughts.

Upon learning that Chiquita and John Dwight were expected to luncheon, O. W. had searched among the bookshelves for a volume on horticulture. Knowing Chiquita's interest in pansies, it would not have been inconsistent with O. W.'s character for him to have studied the subject in order to be able to discuss it intelligently when he met her at luncheon. Although forever after his thoughts of her were to be connected with pansies, O. W.'s present interest

in the book on flowers had nothing to do with Chiquita
Dwight. For Mr. Wimble did not believe that Mrs. Dwight
intended accepting Miss Allen's invitation. Yesterday the
news had been spread that Chiquita was too ill to attend
the inquest; she would hardly give the lie to the announcement by appearing today at Marcia's luncheon.

The detective did believe, however, that Chiquita's
husband would come. Marcia Allen and John Dwight
were friends. O. W. had noticed at the inquest how Marcia's white, drawn face had worried Dwight. The young
man would feel under obligation as a friend to stand by
during this trying period. O. W. also counted on certain
of Dwight's mental processes, natural at such a time. He
certainly wouldn't want Mr. Wimble to think he was afraid
to face the detective on the case. Dwight would be curious, too, to know how the investigation was progressing;
moreover it would be to his advantage to know.

At about half-past eleven O. W. left the library by the
French windows. In his hand was the book on plant pro-
duction, open at the chapter dealing with pansies. An
automobile had turned in at the front gate and was coming
down the driveway.

Leisurely, apparently oblivious of everything but the
open book, O. W. strolled up the driveway toward the
approaching automobile. As the car neared him O. W.,
still ostensibly perusing the volume, descried a uniformed
driver at the wheel, John Dwight beside him. A covert survey of the driver's visage, ugly as a Hopi clay doll's, told
Mr. Wimble that the man was Kelly.

O. W. heard Dwight say: "Stop a minute, Kelly! That's
Mr. Wimble, the private detective."

Looking up then, O. W. beheld Kelly eying him in un-
concealed astonishment. Kelly apparently was another person who'd borrowed his notion of criminal investigators
from the late Sir Conan Doyle. Mr. Wimble had supposed

that by this time the different detectives of current fiction—some dapper dandies, some hardboiled unyielding
inquisitors, some drunken reprobates with keen minds—
had prepared laymen to accept without question anyone
pointed out as a private detective. O. W. surmised that,
hatless, book in hand, he probably looked to Kelly like a
retired old gentleman pleasantly occupying himself before
his midday meal.

Dwight smiled as he greeted the detective. "The title of
that book can't be 'How to Become a Detective!' You look
too contented to be studying anything."

Mr. Wimble replied with apparent frankness: "It's a
book on flower culture. I must confess that California is
getting under my skin." He smiled in self-mockery: "You
make me feel like a schoolboy, Mr. Dwight—a schoolboy
playing truant."

"'All work and no play—,' you know," rejoined Dwight.
"I'm sure you're not neglecting the job. Marcia says you
don't go to bed till all hours." He flushed; perhaps he was
wishing he had not let the detective know how eagerly he
and Marcia were following the case.

Mr. Wimble peered into the tonneau. "Mrs. Dwight
isn't with you?"

"No; she's still feeling seedy. The doctor thought it
best for her not to come out yet awhile."

Marcia had discovered Dwight's arrival and was waving
from an upstairs window. O. W. waited till the automobile
had driven around the house, then hurried across the lawn
to the summer-house. By the edge of the pond in front of
the summer-house there grew a bed of variegated pansies.
Here O. W. paused. Farther on, screened by the thick
foliage of some intervening pepper trees, he could hear
Michael busy with his spading.

It was among these pansies that on Sunday morning
Mr. Wimble had found the blood-stained telegram. As he

now assumed a squatting position before the pansy bed, to all appearances he was replacing the crumpled telegram where he had found it. A wide-awake observer, however, would have remarked that the paper the detective dropped among the blossoms was merely one resembling in color and size the telegram. He would also have been immediately aware that in squatting the detective was hidden by the adjacent bushes from anyone coming toward the summer-house from the direction of Miss Allen's residence.

In California, where a householder may have a splendid lawn merely by throwing seed on the ground and watching it grow, lawns are used for carpets. Therefore O. W. did not hear the approaching footsteps until they were well-nigh upon him. When he did hear them he noted that the walker came neither stealthily as if bent on some secret errand nor boldly as if daring anyone to question him, but naturally and whistling. There was a peculiar quality to the whistling, as though, the whistler had a twisted mouth.

"I beg your pardon, sir!" The Dwights' chauffeur was naturally surprised, though not unduly startled, to see Mr. Wimble kneeling beside the pansies. O. W. thought he also detected some amusement in Kelly's voice.

"Hello, there!" returned O. W. with a creditable pretense of absent-mindedness. He seemed unaware that, the summer-house on one side, the pansy bed on the other, he was blocking the chauffeur's path.

But as he turned the leaves of his book the detective was keenly aware of many things. As he knelt there, O. W.'s eyes were on a line with the chauffeur's hands. He saw that Kelly's fingers were well manicured and adorned with several rings, one of which was an exceptionally handsome carved onyx.

"Jove!" exclaimed Mr. Wimble, looking up from his book. "Did you know that the pansy was one of the earliest cultivated flowers?"

There is one thing about hobbyists. You may ridicule them, envy them, sympathize with them, marvel at them— but you're never indifferent to them!

"The pansy's a native of Europe, I've always understood," said Kelly. He spoke with a pleasing Irish accent.

"Europe?" O. W. thumped his thigh. "Then that explains what this book says about the three principal strains being named after French horticulturists." He was as eager as a child putting together the pieces of a jig-saw puzzle. Excitedly he turned back several pages. "I don't seem to find it, but it said that most important strains were named after three Frenchmen. Cassier was one but I found no mention of the other two."

"Bugnot and Trimardeau, I believe." The absence of surprise in O. W.'s manner may have been due to the fact that Blanche had already apprised the detective of Kelly's interest in gardening. O. W. recalled also that Blanche had mentioned Kelly's many travels which no doubt accounted for the Irishman's excellent French.

"Thanks. I'm glad to know."

O. W. said conversationally: "Dare say the gardens across the Atlantic are pretty fine!"

Kelly's face became the least bit more prepossessing as he recalled the beauty spots abroad. As he spoke he seemed to be talking to himself rather than to the detective— about something often in his thoughts.

"Oxford, with its rows of neat little gardens! Paris in spring, when to drive along the boulevards under the new green leaves of the chestnuts is like driving through the heart of an emerald! And the Riviera!" He smiled down at the detective. "They say that God created the rest of the world for human beings, the Riviera for Himself!"

"I believe you're a poet, Kelly!"

Kelly shrugged. "I appreciate Beauty. But I remain the chauffeur. In my brain is the itinerary for the ideal automobile trip."

"A honeymoon trip perhaps?" smiled the detective.

The man's face flushed suddenly; his eyes seemed afire. "Perhaps," he repeated.

With the chauffeur's polite assistance the detective arose from his squatting position before the pansy bed.

"You don't mind writing those names down for me, do you?" he asked.

"Not at all."

Mr. Wimble tucked the book under his arm, took out his fountain pen.

He said carelessly: "You might write them on that scrap of paper you picked up from the pansy bed."

The chauffeur grinned. "Now you're behaving like a detective!" O. W. noticed that Kelly's fingers fumbled considerably in getting the paper out of his pocket; it was partially unfolded when he handed it to the detective.

Kelly acquitted himself of any possible defection in acquiring the ball of paper. "Michael's finicky about the appearance of his garden."

The detective smiled. "I'll take care to be less untidy in future." He attempted to smooth the paper. Apparently Kelly had no interest in it now that it was no longer littering his friend's pansy bed.

"Too rumpled to write on," decided O. W., thrusting it between the leaves of his book.

"I have a card," said Kelly. As he groped for it a rabbit foot charm fell out of his pocket.

The detective stooped to recover the token, "What an interesting looking object!"

"It's a luck charm. I've carried it since I was a kid." Kelly took it from the detective, eying it anxiously, blowing off any possible dust that may have clung to the fur.

O. W. smiled. "Bring you any?"

"Considerable," returned Kelly soberly. O. W. had the feeling that he had been reproved.

Using the detective's book as an impromptu desk Kelly wrote on the card the names of Messieurs Bugnot and Trimardeau. Carefully, as though he feared smearing the wet ink, O. W. picked up the card by one corner. He waved it in the air for several moments before placing it in his wallet.

Mr. Wimble was a most amiable gentleman. Kelly found himself warming to the detective's admiration of his onyx ring. He extended his hand to facilitate O. W.'s examination of it. The ring was a signet, a crest engraved on the stone, the device representing a chimera, with a motto in Latin underneath.

"I ran across it in a junk shop once. I have a lot of fun pretending it's the crest of my family." A grin spread his ugly features. "Imagine Mick Kelly with a crest!"

The sound of Michael's spade reached the two men. If it had been Kelly's plan to visit his friend, O. W. forestalled it.

"That reminds me," he said, with a benevolent air of reproaching the chauffeur for being so entertaining as to make him forget his work, "I have business with the gardener."

Touching his cap Kelly went off the way he had come. O. W.'s business with Michael had to do with the Dorothy Perkins roses that climbed over the summerhouse roof.

18

Corey Webb, respecting the fact that it was his chief's forte, to solve crime mysteries within a week, suggested that he and Janet fly to Hollywood. For which he deserved a medal, Corey suffering so from airsickness during airplane rides.

Mr. Wimble was proud of his pseudonym but not to the point of cruelty. Rather than cause his assistant any unnecessary suffering the detective would prefer allowing the investigation to extend beyond seven days. An ulterior motive entered into his acceptance of Corey's suggestion. O. W. was an inveterate traveler. During his lifetime he had taken innumerable sea voyages. He had witnessed many a steamer romance, begun during a smooth moonlit sea, shattered when a sudden storm had sent one or both of the cooing doves to the rail. Janet had told him she was immune from *mal de mer*. But O. W. had seen his young assistant in the clutches of airsickness. Under no other circumstances—unless he snore—does a man cut so sorry a figure as when "casting bread upon the water in a way he hadn't oughter." After seeing him through a bout with Nausea, if Janet still retained any regard for Corey, ten to one she would remain true to him for life.

So Corey and Janet proceeded to Hollywood by air. During the journey Corey thanked his lucky stars that the roar of the motors prevented conversation. Called upon to converse with Janet Corey felt he couldn't have got beyond the weather. From the way he felt inside he feared his complexion was pea-green and yellow; so he kept darting anxious glances at her, but was gratified to observe that she apparently found nothing amiss with his facial color scheme. At intervals he forced himself to smile at her. It was not only from politeness that he did this. When Janet returned his smile he felt better.

He tried to focus his thoughts on the murder case. O. W. had gone over with Corey all of his findings to date; that is, Mr. Wimble had given his assistant the gist of the various interviews so far conducted. He had not, however, shared with Corey his conclusions. Mr. Wimble wished his assistant to do his own thinking. From the evidence submitted Corey was trying to deduce just why someone had seen fit to murder Gary Gilbert, Once the motive for a crime could be established the investigation proceeded more easily. In this case the motive was tantalizingly obscure, a state of affairs that was affording the newspapers another chance to make game of the police and which, in consequence, would have caused that organization considerable worry except for the fact that with One-Week Wimble on the job they felt that the last laugh would be theirs, being gratefully aware of course that Mr. Wimble always shared his spoils with the police.

Between his pea-green and yellow smiles at Janet, Corey built up several hypotheses, only to tear them down again upon an examination of the facts. As his theories crashed Corey began to hate himself for an inefficient detective. He would have felt elated could he have guessed how sorely at that moment the motive question was troubling his chief.

A muddy purple was being infused into his pea-green and yellow smiles at Janet when the 'plane landed. As Corey, clinging to Janet's arm, staggered dizzily from the

landing field his initial impressions of Hollywood recurred to him.

Hollywood. A town with hennaed hair, ginny breath
and five carat diamonds. Hollywood—where the women
would rather have beards than hips; where the majority of
the men are so beautiful one thanks God for Joe E. Brown;
where the Lost Tribes can be found directing talking pictures; where Cupid discards bow-and-arrow for machine
gun. Hollywood, Kingdom of It: that neuter pronoun
made sex-conscious by Elinor Glyn. Hollywood—where
you can't tell a lady evangelist from a movie queen. Hollywood—where the signs in the beauty shops read: Women
and Children First.

And yet Corey felt the drama of entering Hollywood,
Shrine of Feminine Pulchritude, in the company of the
most beautiful girl in the world.

Dolly was there to meet them. She had come in response to two wires: one from her son, one from her old
friend O. W. The latter had caused her no little alarm:

AM SENDING COREY AND JANET TO
HOLLYWOOD ON THE GILBERT CASE
STOP PLEASE LOOK AFTER JANET SO
THAT COREY WILL LOOK AFTER HIS
WORK

"Oh dear!" Dolly had sighed. "First it's teething, then
measles, then girls!"

But the minute she saw Janet solicitously steering the
wobbling Corey through the crowd her alarm lifted. She
ran forward, a vision of such heart-shaking loveliness that
several of the incoming passengers breathed: "Which star
is that?"

"Oh, you poor child!" she cried, her eyes on Janet. "I'm
sure my bad air-sick boy has just ruined your trip!"

Corey saw the most beautiful girl in the world look up into the eyes of the most beautiful woman in the world. Then they did something utterly inexplicable to him. Without saying a word they threw their arms about each other and began to cry.

"Hey, there!" the male in him uppermost. "I'm not as sick as all that!" Which cleared the air. Laughing, Dolly and Janet separated.

Behind his back Dolly winked at Janet when Corey discovered that he was still too sick, however, to leave the landing field without holding on to Janet's arm.

Before interviewing Roberta Allen, Dolly, Janet and Corey held a council of war.

"Rob's boy-struck," said Janet. "It may be best for Corey to carry on a flirtation with her." Corey looked as if he'd sooner drink hemlock.

Dolly had what she thought a better idea. "Is Roberta a very attractive girl?"

Janet tittered. "She's a Polly Moran model in a stylish stout size."

"In that case," decided Dolly, "I think that if Corey were to show his preference for you, Janet, Roberta would boast of her own conquests."

Corey heartily approved of this plan. "It's that mysterious 'Michele' in the uniform we're anxious to get a line on."

"You and Janet might even pretend you're engaged," suggested Dolly. At which Corey made a remark that sounded like something boiling too fast. Though his words were incomprehensible, Dolly understood the look dawning in his eyes. When she was Janet's age, she had seen the same sort of a look in O. W.'s eyes and said "No" and in Sim Webb's and said "Yes."

She sprang to her feet. "We'd better be starting now, I think." She wasn't going to have Corey proposing to the girl he loved before a third party. Showed how little experience the young idiot had had with women!

They drove to Roberta's school. Janet had telephoned the head mistress and received permission to invite Roberta Allen to tea with her friends the Webbs.

Janet went in alone to get Roberta. She found that the three years since she had seen Rob hadn't improved the girl's appearance. Roberta was large and looser jointed, with proportionately long arms. She had deep-set eyes of an indeterminate color, a nose like Dante's and a thin mouth. Her self-assurance was that of queens—royal and movie. What saved her from complete ridicule was the way she wore her clothes. She had a natural flair for style.

She greeted Janet cordially enough but showed no enthusiasm for the tea party. "Three women to one man's not so hot!"

"But wait till you see the man!" Perhaps Janet didn't realize quite how feelingly she said this. She noticed that Roberta brightened. However, Roberta intended to reserve judgment until after she had met her host.

"Remember I'm used to Hollywood sheiks!"

She snickered. "You ought to have heard the girls cheer when I announced I had a tea date. They're having their fencing lesson this afternoon. They simply loathe fencing with me."

"Why?" Janet politely inquired.

"Because I'm so good." Roberta possessed the self-esteem of a horse. "I learned outside the school from an Austrian talkie director I know. The girls are scared stiff I'll run them through."

Suddenly Janet had a vision of a butcher knife run through a man's body. "Come on!" she said hurriedly. "The Webbs are waiting."

Corey was at the wheel of Dolly's car. When Roberta saw him her surrender was unconditional.

"I'm going to sit on the front seat," she announced without waiting to be introduced.

"I wish she *would* sit on the front seat," Janet whispered to Dolly as Roberta jumped in beside Corey, "instead of on his *lap!*"

As he drove to the hotel where they were to take tea, Corey savagely and with an exceedingly red face reflected that Roberta's friendships with the opposite sex must depend on the ability of the parties of the second part to conceal what they really thought of the girl.

Upon arriving at the hotel Dolly giggled up at her tall son: "How about a nice cup of hot tea, darling, to cool off?"

During tea several unsuccessful attempts were launched by the others to get Roberta to talk about the murder. She admitted having read of it in the papers, but as the victim had been no friend of hers she wasn't interested.

Dolly expressed regret that Roberta's sister had become involved in such an affair.

"Oh, Marsh likes attending to somebody else's business," was the most they could get out of her.

Devoting all her time to Corey, Roberta was downright rude to Dolly and Janet. Apparently her association with the gentle Marcia had done nothing but thinly whitewash a character inherited from her mother.

After several leads, frustrated by that young man himself, Roberta finally managed to announce to Corey that she was going to get him a hearing with an Austrian talkie director she knew.

Corey groaned.

"What's the matter?" inquired Roberta. A waiter was at Corey's elbow with a tray of French pastry. "Can't you decide which piece to take? Here! Have this one." She forked a chocolate eclair and dropped it on to his plate. Next to frogs' legs Corey loathed nothing as much as chocolate eclairs!

He tried holding Janet's hand, conspicuously.

"Three lumps of sugar in my tea, please!" commanded Roberta. As Corey obeyed he wished the sugar were ground glass.

Finally Dolly saw that something had to be done. She turned sweetly to Roberta.

"I have a fitting at five and Janet promised to go with me. *Would* you mind keeping Corey company till we get back?"

"Would the cat mind dining off the canary?" thought Janet bitterly, watching Roberta's face.

"N-need you go right now?" gulped Corey.

"Business before pleasure!" Dolly sternly reminded him.

"Yes, ma'am," meekly replied Mr. Wimble's assistant.

As Dolly and Janet were leaving the tea room Dolly glanced back. "Poor Corey!" she giggled. "He looks like the boy standing on the burning deck."

Yet the ruse brought results.

Left alone Roberta got to work. She started in by telling Corey how easy it was for her to climb out of her window at night. She said she often sneaked out to keep dancing dates. In his mind's eye Corey could see her swinging from tree to tree by her long arms like a monkey.

Corey nipped these preliminaries in the bud by telling Roberta that he was engaged to Janet.

"Gentlemen prefer blondes, you know," he said, insulting in a manner not so original as ardent.

"But ladies don't!" replied Roberta, outdoing him in the fervor of both tone and insult. She looked him over as if he were something on sale. "And as for doll-faced males, I consider them simply *poisonous!*" At the conclusion of this remark she snapped her fingers with such gusto that the head waiter came running.

Corey felt like slapping her face. Instead he said: "I've heard that men with faces like mud fences are very fascinating. Still, I dare say you're too young to know many fascinating men."

"Oh, really!" with elaborate sarcasm. "Well, I happen to know a man who's so fascinating, every time he looks at me I go like *that!*" She wriggled her hand like a fish across the table-cloth. "The man I'm referring to is a Count!"

"A foreigner!"

His tone angered Roberta. "Yes, a foreigner. With more romance in his little finger than an American has in his whole *body!*" With a stupendous sigh she looked into space. "He calls me Cara and kisses my hand."

"The poor sap!"

"Don't you dare call Michele a sap!"

But Corey's further attempts to get Roberta to discuss the murder proved fruitless. When he asked her if her sister approved of the Count she said that she never discussed her grand passions with old maids. Upon his inquiring how long it was since she had seen her sister, she replied that she hadn't been home since the Christmas vacation. He spoke of his trip south by air and asked her if she flew. She answered in the negative. Finally, either because she sensed that he was trying to get information from her or because an engaged man bored her, she refused to talk at all.

When Dolly and Janet returned, Dolly exclaimed: "Good Heavens! Did we go off without introducing you two?"

"What makes me so sore," mourned Corey, when Roberta had been driven to the school and he and Janet were back at Dolly's bungalow, "is that I feel certain the girl was lying to me."

"I guess you're a better detective than a lady-killer, sonny," sighed Dolly and could have laughed to observe how pleased Janet looked.

"I'll be hard-boiled next time," decided Corey. "I'll treat her rough!"

Janet asked quickly: "You're going to see Rob again, then?"

As Corey looked into Janet's eyes he did not know that she was filled with a great pride of him for not giving up; all he was conscious of at the moment was that a sort of holiness was stealing over him, a feeling akin to the way he felt when he entered a great cathedral, dark save for the soft light penetrating the stained-glass windows.

Dolly repeated Janet's question, rather sharply. Heavens! Hadn't the boy the least idea of the time and place for proposals?

"Janet asked if you were going to see Roberta again, sonny!"

Corey's mind returned to the murder case. "I'm going to find out what that femme knows if I have to choke the information out of her!"

Janet thought of Roberta's long arms, her boasted prowess at fencing. "Rob frightens me a little," she shivered.

"Me, too," admitted Corey; "I rely on facial expression to tell me what a person's thinking about. Those gargoyle features of Roberta's get me!"

"Nonsense!" put in Dolly. "There's nothing inscrutable about Roberta. She's man-crazy. You can get whatever tune you like out of her by merely playing on that one chord."

"I've got it!" cried Corey. "Her Count Michele was seen with the beautiful Chiquita Dwight. It's not very noble to make light of a lady's reputation, but all's fair in love, war and the detective profession. I'm going to manufacture an affair between Chiquita and the Count for the purpose of arousing Roberta's jealousy. The elephantine femme's so darn spiteful, I bet she'll tell plenty!"

19

Mr. Wimble devoted Tuesday afternoon to what he called paper work. Rosie, overhearing him using this expression, later informed the recipients of the penciled pages she distributed that they were what the famous New York detective called his "paper work." It so happened that O. W. received a surprisingly large number of telegrams during his investigation of the Gary Gilbert murder. It was Marcia's pleasure to deliver personally these telegrams to the detective.

On Tuesday afternoon she took to the library the third telegram that had arrived for him within the hour.

"Here's more 'paper work' for you, Mr. Wimble."

At the detective's invitation she sat down.

"Do you know," she said, "the sight of a telegraph boy always used to fill me with as much terror as if Satan himself stood at my door; but by the time you've solved this case I believe I'll be as calm when I see a telegram as I am when I see a calling card." A wry smile curved her lips. "In fact, more so than I am when I see some calling cards!"

Suddenly the fun left her face. "I've been tempted several times to steam open the envelopes before bringing them to you."

"Had I feared that possibility I shouldn't have had them delivered here."

Marcia flushed. "You did consider the possibility then?"

The detective retorted: "Such a thought never entered my head, Marcia Allen, and you know it!"

His gaze played like lightning over her downcast countenance. "Miss Allen, why don't you tell me everything you know about this affair?"

Miss Allen sat smiling in silence for a few moments. Though plain in repose, her face was not so when she smiled.

"Mr. Wimble, I acted most disagreeably when you first came here. Though I had asked you to come I felt an unreasonable—a feminine, if you like—antipathy toward you. May I tell you now that I've entirely lost that feeling? I like you immensely, Mr. Wimble." She clenched her fists. "And the irony of it is—"

The detective concluded her thought: "That I may be instrumental in sending to the gallows the person you love best on earth. Is that it?"

Marcia sighed. "Circumstantial evidence is dead against Dumpling, isn't it?"

"It affords the basis for reasonable suspicion of Dwight, I'm afraid."

Bitterness hardened Marcia's voice as she demanded of the detective: "Must every act be measured by the rule of reason?"

"Not necessarily," replied Mr. Wimble kindly. "But in this instance, if we make allowances for human weakness—jealousy, say—that doesn't help John Dwight, does it?"

Marcia brushed her hand across her forehead in a gesture of weariness. "My common sense and my loyalty toward Dumpling are hopelessly interwoven! I know how easy it is to become jealous—to what lengths jealousy might go." Her voice grew tense with feeling. "I've been horribly jealous of Chiquita sometimes—jealous because she has the love of the man I've always wanted—jealous, too, because of her almost unbelievable loveliness. I can appreciate so fully how Dumpling felt Saturday night. Diana and Apollo! Those two were simply gorgeous together! How could Dumpling help being jealous?" She whispered shakily: "Dear old Funny Face!

"And yet to think of Dumpling killing anyone—I just can't!

"Dumpling'd hate having me tell this on him, I know; but it'll help you understand how I feel. Once years ago we went hunting, a large party of us. Dumpling brought down the first deer. That night around the camp fire I noticed that Dumpling looked a bit pale about the gills but I thought it was only fatigue. His tent was next to mine. In the middle of the night I awoke. I heard him tossing. I went to his tent and spoke to him. He was in an awful state, partly delirious. 'Did you see the questioning look in that deer's eyes, Marcia? Not anger. Not fear. Just surprise that I could have hurt it so.' It was the look in Dumpling's eyes that nearly got me. . . . I managed to calm him down before morning. Then I sprang a sprained ankle on the hunting party; and as Dumpling had already got his deer he volunteered to take me back to town. He never went hunting again. Imagine Dumpling killing a man!" A sob rose in her throat. "But oh, Mr. Wimble, *I'm scared out of my wits!*"

It was the impulse of O. Wimble the man to pat Marcia's hand, to reassure her with comforting words; but O. Wimble the criminologist knew that to do so would be to admit to her that John Dwight was not guilty of murdering Gary Gilbert, and he did not as yet know the identity of the killer.

So O. W. chose the next best way he knew of comforting Marcia Allen. He changed the subject.

"Miss Allen, what debt of gratitude does your Chinese cook owe you?"

Marcia darted the detective a quizzical look. "I should like to hear your definition of a detective sometime."

Mr. Wimble assumed a mock pedagogic air. "I'd say a detective was a sort of fisherman. He spots what he considers a likely looking hole and casts there. His bait is thoughtful questions, keen analysis, the ability to move his bait to and fro in a manner to attract response."

Miss Allen wagged a playful finger at the detective. He was glad to see that she had veered from the breaking point which, when she was talking about John Dwight, had seemed so perilously near. "I ask you a civil question and you tell me a fish story!"

Mr. Wimble retorted: "I ask you a civil question and you put me off in the typical feminine manner by asking me a counter-question."

Marcia smiled. "Your assertion that the detective game is like fishing explains everything." She interpolated with friendly sarcasm: "By explaining nothing! How a man can sit beside a mud puddle all day long with a fishing rod in his hand just *knowing* a fish will bite sooner or later is beyond me!"

"It's a secret sense," chuckled Mr. Wimble. "The same that tells a woman down to the fraction of a second when her nose needs re-powdering."

"Did your secret sense tell you that according to the Oriental honor system Wing owes the Allens a debt of gratitude?"

O. W.'s expression was as innocent as that of a della Robbia bambino. "No. I acquired that information from you."

Marcia's quick intelligence, that for a moment had been caught napping, told her that she had walked into a detective trap. She laughed at herself.

"If I tell you the story, will you tell me how you guessed there was a story?"

Mr. Wimble nodded.

"Dad saved Wing's life when I was a child. We were living on a ranch in the Sonoma Valley at the time. There was a labor war on in the Valley. Some of the ranchers were employing Japanese farm hands. Living on almost nothing, ten or more in a room, demanding very low wages, these Japanese were seriously competing with white labor. So the white workers got together with a plan for running the Japs off the land. One group of wandering cowboys— from Texas I believe—who didn't know the difference between Japanese and Chinese, happened to see Wing in the back yard of our place and, detaching themselves from the mob, decided to take matters into their own hands. They'd entertained at tar-and-feather parties before so decided to deal in that way with Wing. The poor old fellow—he was old even then—I think he must have been born old— was half dead with pain and terror when Dad dropped in uninvited on the party. Of course after that Dad's slightest wish was law to Wing." Twinkles danced in her handsome eyes. "There was so much respect in Wing's adoration of my father I've always suspected he regained consciousness in time to see just how it was Dad dealt with the cowboys."

The twinkles disappeared. "How did you read gratitude in Wing's affection for me?"

O. W. recalled the Chinaman's pantomime on the back porch.

"Wing has managed by a clever piece of suggestion to convey to me that he is ready to go to the gallows in place of the murderer of Gary Gilbert?"

"The old goose!" Affection flooded Marcia's voice. "As if Dumpling would allow him to make any such sacrifice!"

"I don't believe Wing would offer his life for John Dwight's," Mr. Wimble gently corrected her. "I think he considers his life as belonging to the Allen family."

Marcia eyed the detective without flinching. "You mean you feel that Wing suspects me of the crime?"

O. W. made use of the conversational trick he had dubbed feminine. "Does the world know that Roberta is not your own sister, Miss Allen?"

Marcia paled. "It seems to be out-of-the-frying-pan-into-the-fire for my emotions," she said with a wan smile. "No, it isn't generally known that Rob and I aren't sisters. Naturally disgrace would attach itself to the Allen name if Rob were accused." A slight acidity tinctured Marcia's voice. "Wing had better stick to his pots and pans!"

O. W. chuckled. "Instead of putting ideas into my head, eh? Wing is wise. Many a man has lost his way by following the other fellow's directions."

Marcia regarded him thoughtfully. "I don't believe you rely on anyone but yourself for directions when you're traveling, Mr. Wimble."

O. W. looked as embarrassed as a schoolboy caught presenting a valentine to a girl. He always felt uncomfortable when anyone paid verbal tribute to his professional skill. He managed an awkward acknowledgment of her compliment.

"That's mighty kind of you!"

Marcia smiled. "Maybe I'm 'bribing' you again to leave Rob alone!"

Mr. Wimble was moved to generosity. "We have as yet found no flaw in your sister's testimony, Miss Allen."

When Marcia had left the room it was characteristic of the detective that he proceeded to fill small scratch papers, which if patched together would have measured about six square feet, with geometrical tracery.

This accomplished he turned his attention to the telegram Marcia had brought in. It was from the Detective Bureau of the New York Police Department and read:

MRS ELMER BOTTLES WAS IN NEW YORK
ON SATURDAY EVENING STOP WAS
SEEN BY THREE RELIABLE WITNESSES
AT AN ALL MICKEY MOUSE PROGRAM
AT NEIGHBORHOOD PICTURE PALACE
IN A GREEN DRESS

The detective sighed. Primarily O. W. was interested in people. He would have liked knowing what there was so astonishing about Mrs. Bottles' green dress that three witnesses considered it worth mentioning. But for the time being, at least, this knowledge must be denied him. For it was Mrs. Bottles' alibi, not her gown, that was important to his detective investigation.

The telegram concerning the whereabouts of Mrs. Elmer Bottles on the night of the murder was the last in answer to nine wires O. W. had sent in his process of eliminating suspects, this of course being one way of arriving at a solution.

The notebook his assistant had found in Gary Gilbert's penthouse, besides being interesting because of the absence of Page 13, was of value in that it contained the names and addresses of eleven women. Marie Villette Hawkins' name was one. The inquiry establishing the fact that Gilbert had been blackmailing Marie, it was reasonable to suppose that the remaining ten women had also been his victims. There was a chance that one of these women had followed Gilbert to the Allen home and murdered him. It was necessary, therefore, in order to clear herself of suspicion, that each of the women listed be able to establish an alibi. According to the telegrams he had received from different parts of the country, nine of them had been able to do so. Marie, of course, O. W. knew about. And the eleventh woman it was his intention to call upon in person.

This woman was a local resident. Mrs. Benjamin Bell of Berkeley. Mr. Wimble turned again to the page of Gilbert's notebook on which her name and address were entered. The detective's assumption that the notebook had been Gilbert's property was based on the fact that the murdered man's name was embossed on the leather cover in gold lettering.

This entry, though varying of course in its particulars, was typical of the others:

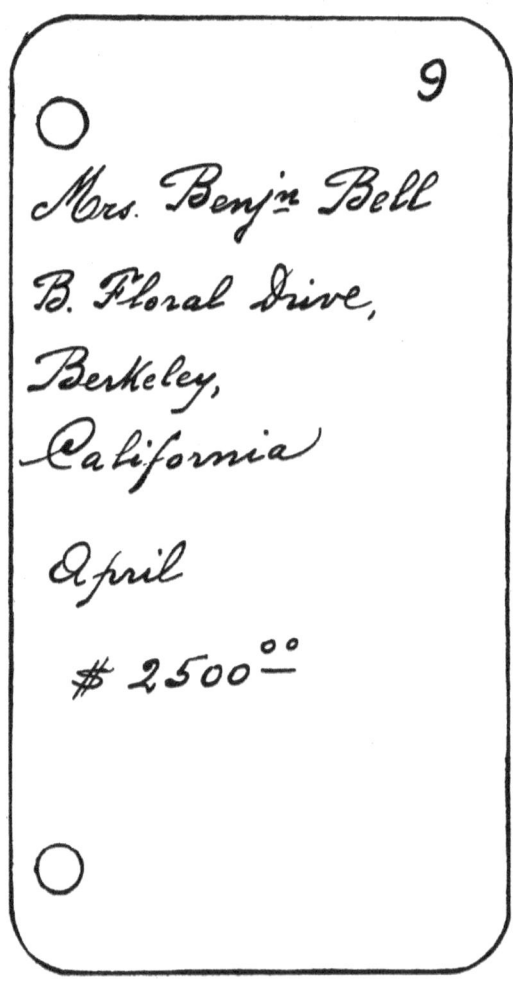

O. W. had taken the precaution of asking Marcia to show him a specimen of Gilbert's handwriting. The penmanship of the letter she had shown him was dissimilar in every respect from the entries in the notebook.

O. W. now took from his wallet the card on which Kelly had jotted down for him the names of the French horticulturists, comparing the writing with that in the notebook.

20

Mr. Wimble realized by this time that Californians were a hospitable lot but he was hardly prepared for the warmth of the reception awaiting him at the residence of Mrs. Benjamin Bell. In answer to his ring a young female servant threw open the door. Stepping outside she darted behind the detective and, with a motion of her apron as if she were shooing a recalcitrant baby chick into a coop, shooed Mr. Wimble into the house.

"Gosh!" she exclaimed, the ejaculation riding on a sigh of relief. "You don't know how glad I am you're here!"

Mr. Wimble said regretfully: "I'm afraid I'm not the person you were expecting."

"Yes you are! You see, I was praying someone would come and all of a sudden you up and ring the doorbell." She declared with satisfaction: "You're him all right!"

O. W. decided that under the circumstances he must be. "Anything the trouble?"

"Plenty!" came her succinct rejoinder as she took the detective's hat. "Mrs. Bell's been carrying on something fierce all morning. Listen!" From an adjoining room came a gust of laughter. "That's her now!"

O. W. had been interestedly taking in the furnishings of the reception hall. The place looked like a museum devoted to prehistoric art, with the same dearth of light

and air characteristic of such repositories. The floor was
littered with fragments of archaic statuary—arms, legs and
torsos. In one corner stood a huge and to Mr. Wimble
exceedingly ugly Canopic jar of terra cotta, its cover in
the form of a human head. On the walls were hung several slabs of Egyptian and Greek relief, the lower jaw of
a mastodon in papier-mâché and an enlarged photograph
of a primitive fossil bird having a long tail of many verte-
brae and jaws with teeth. It occurred to Mr. Wimble that
if the Lares and Penates of the other rooms were similar
to these Mrs. Bell's living quarters were not conducive to
light-heartedness.

"Mrs. Bell's been carrying on like that all morning,"
the girl told the detective, "sitting in there all by herself
laughing her head off."

"Maybe she's reading one of the Boner books."

"No, sir, she ain't reading no books. I got all the books
in the back yard ready to dust 'em. Last Sunday's paper's
in there though. I know because I took it in to her myself when she asked for some paper to empty the carpet
sweeper into." Her tone became as derisive as her station
permitted. "We're having spring cleaning!"

In an age of vacuum cleaners, hardwood floors, sani-
tary furnishings and freedom from the fear that fresh air
is an emissary of his Satanic Majesty, most homes have rel-
egated "spring cleaning" as far into the limbo of pioneer
customs as travel by covered wagon. But Mrs. Bell had
been raised in a small New England town where it was the
practice once a year to inject hell into the domestic scene
by tearing the house to pieces.

"Is Mrs. Bell's husband living?"

Jennie sniggered. "Gosh sakes!" she gasped, when her
mirth was under control. She inclined her head toward
the room where Mrs. Bell was. "Guess the disease she's
got's catching. Do you know Professor Bell?" Mr. Wimble

admitted that he did not. "Then of course you wasn't trying to wisecrack." She giggled. "I been working for the Bells over two years now and the Professor don't know my name's Jennie yet! Ten times already he's said to me: 'Good morning, my good girl! Are you the new maidservant?' That's the way he talks; I mean like somebody in an old-fashioned book." She giggled again. "The census man put the Professor down on his list, though, so I guess you gotta call him living!"

"You haven't consulted him about Mrs. Bell's strange condition?"

"No, sir. You see, he's out of town just now. The Professor ain't so dumb at that! He always thinks up some excuse to get away when we're cleaning house."

O. W. knew that nothing cheers a woman up so much as a chance to talk. He let Jennie chat until her nervousness seemed dissipated, then suggested announcing himself to Mrs. Bell whom, he explained, he had come to see.

"All right, sir; go on in, and if you need help holler."

Mr. Wimble smiled. "You needn't be alarmed about your mistress, 'my good girl.' Mrs. Bell is laughing because she has had good news."

Jennie looked skeptical. "I won a hundred dollars in the lottery once and when I heard the good news I cried!"

"I dare say that in between her laughing spells Mrs. Bell is crying," said Mr. Wimble wisely.

After a brief interval, during which the detective suspected Mrs. Bell to be getting a grip on herself, an unsteady "Come in!" answered his knock on the living room door.

Fortunately Jennie had mentioned to Mr. Wimble the fact that the Bell ménage was now in the midst of spring cleaning; when he came upon Mrs. Benjamin Bell in faded purple wrappings, therefore, he did not think she was a mummy belonging to the relics in the reception hall but was able to identify her as a woman in dust cap and bungalow apron.

One's initial thought on beholding Mrs. Benjamin Bell was that it was too bad she looked like that. Her face was on the side of virtue rather than pulchritude. No cosmetics were there to assist in the job done so badly by Mother Nature. The eyebrows were thick; the nose likewise. The eyes were small; the mouth large. The wisp of hair that straggled down one cheek was straight, thin and graying. The bungalow apron did little for Mrs. Bell's figure, which was flat-chested; broad-hipped and short-legged.

The room appeared as if the guests of a children's party had recently departed. Though the furniture was in a state of extreme disorder, O. W. saw that no antiquities garnished this room—except the furniture itself which was early American and fine. He felt sure that after the cleaning was over and the furnishings rearranged it would be a most attractive and livable room.

Mrs. Bell was the first to speak. "Are you the plumber I telephoned for?"

O. W. chuckled. Considering his unflattering appraisal of her, Mrs. Bell's revenge was rather neat.

"I'm a private detective. I have come in connection with the Gary Gilbert murder case."

Mrs. Bell's mouth fell open. It was a habit she had when agitated. One of the Professor's students once said of Mrs. Bell: "When Beulah's alarmed, she has an expression on her face like the last look of a goldfish before the cat gets it."

"Did B-B-Benjamin send you?"

"I'm not acquainted with your husband, Mrs. Bell." He saw that she was trembling violently. "Don't be frightened. The police have already established the fact that you were attending a lecture at the University on the evening the crime was committed."

"The p-p-police?"

Mr. Wimble smiled in a way intended to eradicate her fear of the police. "Oh, you'll not be molested by the police. That is, if you'll answer the few questions I'd like to ask; and I'm sure you will!"

"What big oaks grow from tiny acorns!" muttered Mrs. Bell.

Suddenly she remembered that she was a hostess. "Won't you sit down, Mr. Wimble?" She smiled at his surprise at hearing his name. "I read in the paper this morning that the detective working on the Gilbert case was a Mr. Wimble from New York. Better let me do that," she broke off as O. W. was about to pluck a chair from a pyramid of furniture in the middle of the room. "I built it."

As she flicked a feather duster over the chair she said: "I should think newspaper publicity would act as a deterrent in the solving of a crime mystery—telling a criminal how the investigation is progressing, supplying him with the name and photograph of the detective working on the case."

"Crooks pretty well know how to read the papers," replied Mr. Wimble. "Such expressions as 'The complaint states,' 'Officer Jones claims,' 'It is alleged,' 'The report has it,' et cetera, may fool the average reader but to the criminal they mean that nobody knows a thing. And as for newspaper photographs," O. W. grinned, "once a police sergeant who was working on the same case I was remarked of my picture in the paper: 'Ain't he the rum-looking guy!'"

Which reminded Mrs. Bell of her own appearance. "If I'd known you were coming I'd have fixed up," she apologized.

A small pang attacked Mr. Wimble's large heart. What could "fixing up" do for a woman so obviously one of Beauty's remnants as Beulah Bell? The futility of her vanity was pathetic to O. W.

"I'm sorry to intrude on your housework, Mrs. Bell. I won't stay long."

"Just what did you come for?" inquired Mrs. Bell. Her anxiety was melting under the warmth of the detective's geniality.

"You were of course acquainted with Gary Gilbert?"

Mrs. Bell folded her hands on her lap. Sitting there in the middle of the sofa, a footstool filling in the gap between her short legs and the floor, she looked as stolid and ugly as a heathen image.

"Please don't cat-and-mouse me, Mr. Wimble! I shall tell you everything you wish to know. Had Benjamin sent you, of course I should have thrown away without a scruple my chances of getting to Heaven—by lying like a fortune teller! Yes," she replied to the detective's unspoken question, "I was fool enough to go to a fortune teller." A short, ironic laugh escaped her. "She told me I'd never be found out!"

New anxiety quickened Mrs. Bell's voice. "Even though he didn't send you, Benjamin doesn't know you're here?"

"To my knowledge, no."

For the fraction of a moment the expression of Mrs. Bell's face remotely identified her with Beauty. "It's lucky I thought up a business trip for Benjamin to take when my spring cleaning time came around!"

O. W. said softly: "You seem very fond of that husband of yours."

"I go fishing with him every summer," smiled Mrs. Bell. "Of a wife's love for her husband there is no greater proof than that."

"Which makes it rather difficult for me to understand your connection with Gary Gilbert."

"Yes," agreed Mrs. Bell, "I suppose it does. However, when I've told you about it I think you'll understand." She then paid the detective what he considered one of the greatest compliments he had ever received. "Do you know, Mr. Wimble, I've been wanting to tell about my—affair with Mr. Gilbert for a long time; but until now I've never met anyone I felt would understand."

"Mr. Wimble," she began after a short pause, "I'm a happy woman. I have a husband whom I adore and who adores me. I am the mother of two splendid sons. I have an independent income. And today my mind was relieved of the only worry I ever had."

"You didn't read about the murder until this morning?"

"No, I didn't. I'm spring cleaning!" Her manner was defensive. "I missed Sunday's paper seeing Benjamin off and I've been too busy since for newspapers. You knew that Mr. Gilbert was blackmailing me?" The detective nodded.

She said suddenly: "It was trying to have fun that got me into this mess!"

Her expression became wistful. "I suppose you can't imagine anyone going through life without fun. Oh, I suppose I had fun as a child. No matter what obstacles are placed in their way children manage to make good times for themselves.

"Mother's early death loaded me with grown-up responsibilities. Father was a paleontologist. He cared more about fossils than fun. I married young—an archaeologist. I'm not criticizing my husband, Mr. Wimble, but Benjamin's mind doesn't run to frivolous things."

She sighed. "It's having to act as an example for Benjamin's pupils that's so wearing. A professor's wife must be so eternally *correct!*

"It was during our sabbatical year that Benjamin and I went to Paris. From the moment I set foot in Paris I felt stimulated. Benjamin felt excited, too, but only because the museums were overflowing with antiquities. We were in the midst of doing all the harmless things tourists do when some of my husband's cronies invited him to Greece to help dig up a bust of Sabazius they'd learned from an ancient papyrus was buried under some ruins there." She shot a mischievous glance at the detective. "Familiar with the gentleman?"

O. W. smiled. Uncomely as she was, her sense of humor saved Beulah Bell from being a bore.

"A deity—of Phrygian origin, wasn't he?"

Mrs. Bell nodded. "Regarded as a form of Dionysus and worshiped in Ancient Greece with orgiastic rites. A gay dog of a god! Ran around with naughty little maenads— blondes likely! Which of course water-logged my credentials as a traveling companion for Benjamin in Greece. Benjamin is old-fashioned in his attitude toward wives— thinks the only time a man's wife should be taken out of her cage is when she's being put on her pedestal." Again an expression of tenderness crossed her face. "I believe I'd rather have it that way than for us to be like some modern couples I've seen, each trying to hold the other up after a cocktail party.

"Well, the result was that Benjamin left me in Paris to amuse myself at the art galleries while he went off on his digging trip.

"I don't know what got into me exactly. Except that I was alone—unwatched for the first time in my life. And excited. It seemed to be in the very air of Paris to have fun. I remember meeting a compatriot of mine. She said to me: 'Do you know, ever since I got to Paris I've felt like doing something wild. Nothing downright bad—not the sort of thing the Sunday Supplements wouldn't write about—but something unconventional!' That's just the way I felt!

"One day my longing got the best of me and I went to a place where there was dancing. I told myself that I was going for tea, but when I got there I saw a woman at the next table drinking something green so I ordered the same thing. I remember saying to myself at the time: 'If

Benjamin should come in here and see me doing this, he'd think it was my double.'" Her voice quivered. "My husband trusts me implicitly, Mr. Wimble.

"Well, there I sat sipping that green, sweet stuff. It tasted good. Nobody seemed to think it odd that I was there. The music was enchanting. And I was having a good time!

"My adventure should have ended there. I'd have been perfectly satisfied. But it didn't. Suddenly a young man approached me, the most handsome individual I'd ever seen. 'Hello!' he said. 'I'm afraid you've made a mistake,' I returned. 'I'm Mrs. Benjamin Bell.' At that he deliberately seated himself at my tables. 'Quite green,' he said, 'but very sweet.' He was toying with my glass, but I knew he wasn't referring to the crême-de-menthe. Of course I was blushing scarlet. A flower girl passed. He selected a pink rose. 'A rose to match the blush on your cheek,' he said."

Mrs. Bell pressed her hands against her flaming cheeks. "I am more ashamed of myself when I remember that moment than any other time during the whole hideous affair. When Gary Gilbert compared the rose to my cheek I said to myself: 'Benjamin would have compared my cheek to the rose!'

"He asked me to dance. I hesitated. After all he was not much older than my own sons. He laughed: 'When in Rome do as the Romans do. When in Paris do as the Americans do.' I thought: 'Why not? Lots of American women dance with gigolos!' I realized by that time of course that his interest in me was purely professional. I knew I should have to pay him for dancing with me.

"During the last dance he said he hoped he'd have the pleasure of dancing with me again. I told him I didn't expect to repeat the experience. 'Afraid some of your compatriots will see you?' He had an uncanny sense of divination. To my shame that is just what was bothering me;

my conscience unfortunately had nothing to do with it. I had had a glorious time. 'Why not let me take you places where you won't be recognized? Places unfrequented by Americans?"

"I went out with him every afternoon for two weeks, sometimes in the evening. Once we had onion soup in a queer little restaurant at three o'clock in the morning. Some of the places we visited weren't fit to be seen in. But nothing mattered to me. I was having fun!

"The day before Benjamin returned to Paris I tipped Gary Gilbert generously and bade him good-by. I remember the little speech of gratitude I made. How he must have been laughing up his sleeve!

"Benjamin and I traveled around France for several months before returning to America. A few days before our departure from Paris I was in the lobby of our hotel addressing some postal cards at one of the writing desks. They were double desks, back to back. I had been there but a few minutes when a man sitting opposite me said in a quiet voice: 'Mr. Gilbert says that you owe him twenty-five hundred dollars.'"

"Just a moment, Mrs. Bell," Mr. Wimble interrupted her. "What did this man look like?"

"He was dark, of medium height, rather heavily built. What I remember about him particularly is that he was the ugliest man I ever saw. He had a scar across his face.

"'I've already paid Mr. Gilbert everything I owe him,' I faltered. 'I know nothing of your business with Mr. Gilbert, madam,' he replied. 'I am merely Mr. Gilbert's secretary. He told me to collect twenty-five hundred dollars either from you—*or the Professor.*' That last terrified me, of course. I promised to have the money for him in an hour. There was nothing else for me to do.

"Needless to say I didn't draw an easy breath till France was behind us. For weeks I was a nervous wreck. My friends teased me about the effect on me of 'Gay Paree'. Some of them even mentioned gigolos. I wish you could have seen Benjamin's face when that came up. He couldn't bear to have me associated with gigolos even in fun. But when months went by without anyone molesting me I began to breathe more freely. After all, I had paid.

"But apparently only the first installment. One afternoon last April when I was entertaining some of the Faculty ladies at tea, my maid announced that 'Mr. Gilbert's secretary' was calling. I don't know how I got out of this room without fainting. He was waiting for me in the reception hall. He seemed to be intensely interested in my husband's relics; I had to speak to him twice before he heard me. 'Mr. Gilbert says the next installment is due,' he said. Of course I paid it. I could afford the money and I couldn't afford to go to the police. I consoled myself with the thought that I'd come up against a very reasonable blackmailer. After all, Gary Gilbert's extortions might have amounted to more than I could pay. I made up my mind then that I was in for blackmail the rest of my life."

"You think Gilbert followed you to California?"

"Naturally that was my first thought; but later upon reflection I decided that it was just coincidence. I had read in the paper that Mr. Gilbert was living in a penthouse on the roof of a luxurious hotel. His expenses there plus his secretary's salary would have cost more than my twenty-five hundred a year. I don't doubt in the least that he had other victims besides me. To my knowledge no one of my acquaintances knew him; I've never mentioned his name for fear someone might."

"You can tell me nothing more?"

"That's all." She smiled. "I hope what I've told you has helped you as much as it has helped me."

21

When Corey called on Roberta Allen the second time, on the advice of Dolly and Janet he went alone. As Roberta entered the reception room of the boarding-school where he awaited her she looked at him, Corey later told Dolly and Janet, exactly as he imagined the reception committee on a cannibal isle would eye a visiting missionary.

"I knew you'd be back," she said.

"I'm here professionally," returned Corey witheringly.

"I suspected what your profession was from the start." Corey wondered if he had been doing the girl an injustice. He was more used to being mistaken by young females for a talkie star than a he-man. He actually managed a smile for Roberta.

"You see," she explained, shattering his remorse into bits, "I've met chorus men before!"

From the bottom of his heart Corey wished he were possessed of adequate facts to enable him to inform this Roberta disease that she was wanted for the murder of Gary Gilbert.

He drew himself to his full height: "I'm a private detective."

"Now I'll tell one!" jeered Roberta.

Furiously Corey produced his credentials. Roberta looked slightly impressed, but the effect of her triumph at Corey's return had not yet sufficiently worn off for his announcement that he was a detective to inspire her with uneasiness.

Corey decided to get down to business. "I am working on the Gary Gilbert murder case."

"I've already told you I was unacquainted with the gentleman," retorted Roberta airily.

Corey thought grimly: "Through no fault of yours!"

He chose to ignore the interruption. "Your companions have testified that on Saturday afternoon you left the school and failed to return till long after the 'Lights out!' gong Saturday night. Your friend Chet Walters, whose name I got from one of your teachers, has told me you borrowed his airplane on Saturday afternoon." Corey saw with extreme gusto that the girl was fidgeting in her chair.

"I flew down to Caliente," she stated feebly.

Corey continued as if she had not spoken. "It has been established that you visited your home in Thousand Oaks at about eight o'clock Saturday evening. You carried on a conversation with Marie Hawkins, an extra maid on duty that night. She heard you call to a uniformed man whom you addressed as 'Michele.' This man told you to 'get into the car'."

Roberta's small-deep-set eyes blinked, more in surprise however than in agitation.

"Well, what of it?"

"Unfortunately for you the hour of your visit coincides with the time Gary Gilbert was murdered."

"I wasn't acquainted with the gentleman!" repeated Roberta stubbornly. She added with her customary self-complacency: "My sister took care we didn't meet; she was afraid of my S. A."

Corey was nearing the crux of his interview. Corey was a cub detective. This business of conducting interviews was new to him. He was worried. His worry showed in his face. Roberta remarked his distress. Characteristically she cataloged his perturbation as concerning herself.

"W-what's the matter?"

Corey pronounced his next words with deliberation. He feared presenting his case from the wrong angle, omitting something, missing his point altogether. This large method of speaking gave to his words a weight which impressed Roberta.

"At your sister's costume party on Saturday night Mrs. Dwight was dressed as Diana, Gary Gilbert as Apollo. Both costumes were of white, cut along the same lines. It has been proved that at the time you were discovered in that vicinity the lights in the library were dimmed." His voice became tense with earnestness. "A person whose intention it was to kill Chiquita Dwight might easily have killed Gary Gilbert by mistake."

Roberta laughed hysterically. "Why on earth should I have wanted to kill Chiquita Dwight?"

"You've admitted being in love with Count Michele." Corey decided that melancholy should accompany his ensuing remark. "It's too bad the Count doesn't return your love."

Roberta showed fight. "Oh, is that so? Well, Michele's mad about me, no less! We're going to get married just as soon as Marsh turns over my money to me. Michele's got some lawyers working on the case now. I give him half my allowance every month to pay them."

"Oh! So it's your money the Count's after?"

"What a poisonous mind you have!" came Roberta's pert retort. But from the way she averted her gaze Corey judged that Roberta had been entertaining a suspicion along these lines.

"What about me wanting to kill Chiquita?"

Corey felt that Roberta would rather be accused of murder than of losing a beau.

"You went to Thousand Oaks Saturday night because you knew the Count was to be there."

"Well, go on!" cried Roberta irritably. "There's no use of me saying anything. You seem to know all the answers."

Before embroidering his plain statement of fact Corey went over in his mind the French girl's testimony. According to Marie, Chiquita Dwight and a man in uniform had come out of the library together. Sending Chiquita away, the man had gone back into the library, reappearing a moment later alone. Roberta from her hiding place among the bushes had called: "Michele!" whereupon the uniformed man had told the girl to "get into the car". Corey felt that he had sufficient material at hand for the embroidery.

"But when you discovered your Count, Miss Roberta, he was with a beautiful young woman."

Roberta began to cry. She did this thoroughly as she did everything else. As the tears dripped down her long nose her face put Corey more than ever in mind of a gargoyle's.

Corey recalled that O. W. was always as kind toward the Polly Morans of life as toward the Janet Gaynors. Perhaps a change of subject would take her out of her grief.

"We found your wire to Kelly warning him that your sister knew everything and would try to harm him."

Roberta's idea of looking haughty was stretching her neck and peering down her nose. "I don't see why my love affairs should be aired in public!"

Corey's reply was Wimblesque. "Oh, but great love affairs are always public! Consider Du Barr's! Catherine the Great's!" He looked out of the window and saw Hollywood. "Gloria Swanson's!"

Roberta was mollified. "That's so!" she returned, proud to be numbered among so distinguished a galaxy.

Corey took advantage of her chastened mood. "It's often occurred to me that if the famous lovers of history had been more confidential their biographers could have made a better job of it." What Corey lacked in subtlety Roberta made up in conceit. She immediately fancied herself a Dulcinea, pausing a moment during the bewitching business of reducing self-respecting gentlemen to lovesick jackasses to grant audience to her biographer.

Self-consciously Roberta entered upon her memoirs. "I am a devotee of love. Often my better sense succumbs to my romantic impulses."

The strain of being literary became too great. After all, Du Barry had probably spoken milliner French. Roberta's correct diction gave way to flapper idiom. "Saturday afternoon I got an urge to see Kelly. So I borrowed Chet's 'plane and flew up. I knew Marsh would throw a fit if she knew I'd flown up, so I didn't let on I was there; had my dinner in town. I went by taxi to the Dwights'. Katie, the maid, said Kelly'd gone to our house so I drove over home to see if I could find him. As I neared the house Wing popped out of the back door, so I ran and hid in the bushes near the library. You can imagine my horror when I saw—" Her voice broke. For the moment a gawky schoolgirl took the place of Dulcinea the sophisticate.

Corey finished her sentence: "Michele and Chiquita!" He felt a twinge of pity. "Skip that part of your story, if you like. Begin with getting into the car."

After a snivel or two Roberta continued. "Just as I was about to get into the front seat I heard voices coming toward the car. Chiquita's and Dumpling's. So I hid in the tonneau. Chiquita got into the front seat. She seemed to be sick or something—acted awfully strange. Dumpling said: 'I'll say you went home with a bad headache.' He was horribly worried about something. He kept repeating over and over again: 'Whatever you do, Chiquita, don't talk!' Pretty soon Kelly came. Dumpling told him that Chiquita was ill and wanted to go home, that he'd put her in front so Kelly could look after her."

Corey was of an age in which parked automobiles have superseded the parlor sofa, but he felt that a crack detective would leave nothing to chance. So he interposed a question. "Why did you choose the Dwights' machine when Michele told you to 'get into the car'?"

"I supposed that was the one he meant. But afterwards I figured maybe he'd seen me drive up in the taxi and thought I still had it. I'd dismissed it at the gate, though."

"Did Mrs. Dwight and Kelly carry on any conversation on the way home?"

"Yes. Kelly said: 'Does Mr. Dwight know I saw anything?' Chiquita seemed in a daze. He had to ask her three times before she heard him. She said: 'No.' Then Kelly said—" The girl's mouth twisted.

Corey forced himself to pat her hand. "Don't cry, Miss Roberta!" Corey was not only a young detective but a young man; he had no experience behind him to tell him that Roberta would react to this treatment by crying as hard as she could.

She calmed down finally. "You ought to have heard Kelly's voice when he spoke to her. Like he was singing waltz music, no less. Simply poisonous! 'I won't say a word, Mrs. Dwight. I swear I won't!' I don't know whether Chiquita heard him or not. The only thing she said the whole way home was: 'My head is splitting!' But Kelly kept talking all the time. 'You must go right to bed, Mrs. Dwight. You mustn't talk to a soul. You mustn't allow anyone to talk to you. You mustn't look at the papers.' Made me sick to my tum listening! You'd have thought Chiquita was a nitwit, no less. Not that she didn't act like one, at that!

"By the time we got to the Dwights' I was spitting fire, no less! Of course Chiquita was a *mess* and he *had* to help her up to the house; but wouldn't you have thought he'd have made *some* sign to me?"

"Perhaps he was merely being cautious. You'd warned him yourself to be careful, you know."

"Cautious my eye! He just *forgot* me!"

"Did you wait for him?"

"I wouldn't have waited for him if he'd been the Prince of Wales! I flew home as fast as I could; that's what I did." She concluded bitterly: "I might have known how it would end—playing around with a chauffeur!"

"Oh, well," Corey comforted her. "You still have the Count."

Roberta eyed him in stupefaction. Then she laughed.

"A swell detective *you* turned out to be! Kelly is the Count. Nobleman impoverished by the War. His real name's Michele. Mick-kay-lee. That's Italian. 'Kelly' is the best Americans can do with the name. Mick Kelly."

22

Through the French windows of the library Mr. Wimble saw a handsome sport roadster turn in at the gate. Swiftly the detective drew the drapes over the center windows so that no one outside would realize they were ajar. The car was moving at a snail's pace and its occupants were earnestly conversing. O. W. had sent for Kelly; he was not surprised to learn that Kelly's employer accompanied the chauffeur.

As the car slid up to the library steps and stopped, O. W. drew back into the shadows of the room. Kelly alighted and Dwight moved over into the driver's seat, making a final remark to the chauffeur as he did so. The noise caused by Kelly getting out of the car prevented O. W. from distinguishing Dwight's words but the young man's earnestness was unmistakable.

He did catch Kelly's reply. "You can trust me, Mr. Dwight. You've been a marvelous employer. I swear I'll keep my mouth shut."

Peering through the windows O. W. saw Dwight lean over the steering wheel and shake hands with his driver, gratitude stamped on his chubby face.

When Kelly knocked, Mr. Wimble was seated at a desk in the far corner of the room opposite the one in which the murder had been committed.

He called: "Come in!", looking up as Kelly respectfully entered, cap in hand. "Oh, hello there! Glad to see you again. Hope you didn't mind coming. Customary formality. I'd like to ask you a few questions—about what happened on the night of the murder and about yourself."

Kelly's ugly features fused in a smile. "I'm afraid I haven't anything very interesting to say on either subject, sir." However he showed no unwillingness to talk and not once during the interview did his gaze falter before the alert, penetrating blue eyes of his interrogator.

Mr. Wimble asked the chauffeur first to describe his actions on the evening of the murder.

At about five o'clock on Saturday evening, Kelly said, he had driven Mrs. Dwight in one of the limousines to Miss Allen's. Then he had gone to the home of a Mr. Jenkins to call for Mr. Dwight. He had waited perhaps an hour for Mr. Dwight, then driven him to Miss Allen's.

"Mr. Dwight was in fancy dress costume?"

Kelly smiled. "Yes, sir; he was wearing some of Mr. Jenkins' clothes. Mr. Jenkins is a butcher."

"Mr. Dwight was carrying a butcher knife, was he not?"

Kelly twisted his cap in his hand.

"I realize how difficult this is," said O. W.

Kelly sighed. "I suppose if I don't talk to you willingly I'll be put on oath and made to. Yes, sir, Mr. Dwight was carrying a knife—and a deadly-looking affair it was, too!"

Continuing his recital, Kelly said that after parking the car he had dropped in at the gardener's cottage, he and Michael being good friends. After awhile Michael had suggested cards. Kelly had agreed, saying that he must first go out and light up the car.

"What time was it then?"

"Between six-thirty and seven, I'd say."

Reaching the car, Kelly had found Mr. and Mrs. Dwight there. Mrs. Dwight had a bad headache and wanted to be taken home. After driving her home—the Dwights lived but a short distance from Miss Allen's—Kelly had returned to play cards with Michael as planned, quitting the cottage about nine o'clock. He had then visited a local dance hall until time to call for Mr. Dwight. Upon arriving at Miss Allen's he had been met at the gate by a policeman, apprised of the murder and ordered to park outside the grounds.

Mr. Wimble asked the chauffeur if he and Mrs. Dwight had carried on any conversation during the drive home.

"A little; not much. Mrs. Dwight had a bad headache."

"You spoke of the crime?"

"The crime hadn't been committed then," the chauffeur reminded him.

The detective turned the inquiry to the man's private history.

"Mick Kelly you said your name was. Irish?"

Kelly nodded. "The Mick of course stands for Michael." The fellow's brogue was pronounced.

"I'd have said you were Italian. I wonder what gave me that impression. Your dark coloring, perhaps; certain attitudes." He did not add: "Your rings; your superficial polish; your superstitions."

"I've lived abroad a good deal." He turned the onyx seal ring on his finger. "It's so much fun feeding the romantic notions of silly schoolgirls, I sometimes pretend to be an Italian count."

With his quick ear for nuance in the voice of a witness, O. W. recognized a trace of swagger in Kelly's. Could it be possible that this man with a face like a satyr's was vain?

"How long have you been the Dwight's chauffeur?"

"About two years."

"You knew Gary Gilbert?"

"Yes, sir. It was Mr. Gilbert who got me my job with the Dwights."

"What sort of a young woman is Mrs. Dwight?"

The ugly face which a moment before had worn a smile of ease lost it abruptly and became acutely vigilant. "Mrs. Dwight has always been kind and thoughtful." He followed this remark with an observation the flavor of which O. W. considered more Latin than Celtic. "I dare say Mrs. Dwight as a woman is quite different from Mrs. Dwight as an employer."

"I presume you had ample opportunity to observe her as a woman when she was with Gilbert."

Kelly's body stiffened. "I'm afraid I don't understand you."

"You didn't know that Gilbert and Mrs. Dwight were involved in a love affair?"

"Whoever told you that lied!" Kelly fairly barked the words. "Gilbert was barely acquainted with Mrs. Dwight."

"Yet Gilbert knew the Dwights well enough to recommend you as chauffeur."

"Mr. Gilbert had met Mr. Dwight in Paris, I believe. I happened to see Mr. Dwight's ad in the paper myself; and I had heard that he was partial to men who had been mutilated in the War." A bitter smile twisted his ugly features; it was easy to see that he did not bear his cross with fortitude. "My face was of more value than Mr. Gilbert's recommendation."

"It may distress you to learn that you yourself are responsible for the rumor about Gilbert and Mrs. Dwight. You were seen several times going to Gilbert's penthouse; and unfortunately gossip placed the obvious construction on your visits."

Kelly said without hesitation: "I had been Mr. Gilbert's secretary in Paris. He frequently called on me to straighten matters out for him."

"When you tried to enter the penthouse the morning after the murder you inferred you were after letters some woman had written to Gilbert."

"And being in Mrs. Dwight's employ it was immediately supposed that the letters I referred to were hers!" Kelly sighed. "I'm afraid I was a bit clumsy that morning though I assure you," with a smile intended to purge his remark of conceit, "that my motive was quite noble."

O. W. caustically observed: "I suppose one might call your efforts to remove your notebook from Gilbert's rooms before the police got there inspired by a noble motive. Had you succeeded it would at least have prevented notoriety attaching itself to the various women mentioned in it."

Kelly's voice was smoothly unangered as he corrected the detective's statement. "It was Mr. Gilbert's notebook I was trying to get."

"Every entry in the book is in your writing, Kelly! You will recall that I procured a specimen of your handwriting Tuesday morning at the pansy bed."

Still the chauffeur maintained his unruffled front. "I see no reason for trickery, sir. I am perfectly willing to tell you all I know." Regret rather than ire characterized his tone. "The fact of my having been Mr. Gilbert's secretary explains my handwriting in his notebook, I think."

"And your 'noble motive' was your desire to keep the book out of the hands of the police?"

"Exactly."

Kelly sat forward in his chair; the earnestness of his words impressed the detective. "Mr. Wimble, I was fond of Mr. Gilbert. Although when we reached San Francisco certain things came up that decided me to seek employment elsewhere, I have many pleasant memories of our association. I should like very much, if possible, to be spared going into details. I hope it will suffice for me to say that I suspected Mr. Gilbert of following certain pursuits of which I disapproved. My disapproval has nothing to do with my loyalty. When I heard of his death I remembered that incriminating little notebook. I tried to get hold of it in order to preserve his reputation."

Mr. Wimble said gravely: "I called on Mrs. Bell yesterday."

Kelly shrugged. "Having come into possession of the notebook, I suppose your call was inevitable."

"Mrs. Bell told me you visited her house last April."

"I was wondering why you asked me to testify." The ingenuousness of Kelly's remark gave him a boyish air. "I have already told you that I used to help Mr. Gilbert out occasionally even after I had left his employ. He sent me to Mrs. Bell's to collect some money owing him."

"Owing him for what, do you know?"

The detective's question deepened the gloom that reference to Gilbert's reputation had settled on the Irishman. "I dislike extremely clearing myself at the expense of Mr. Gilbert's memory." He took a long breath. "While in Paris Mr. Gilbert was an art dealer. As you know, the Bells are interested in antiques. Mrs. Bell's husband, that is; I have a suspicion that Mrs. Bell knows very little about the subject. Mr. Gilbert possessed a segment of crenelated molding reputed to be a relic of medieval times. One day he told me that Mrs. Bell had bought it. Her husband was away at the time, I believe. Apparently the price was more than she could pay at one time, for Mr. Gilbert let her have it on the installment plan."

Mr. Wimble's manner in no way testified to his amazement at hearing this version of Beulah's folly.

"And when did you begin to suspect that Gilbert's business dealings weren't strictly above board?"

"My suspicion grew gradually—small doubts piling on top of one another until they made something formidable that I couldn't ignore. Perhaps the beginning was in Paris when he sent me to collect the first installment due him from Mrs. Bell. She seemed so unduly terrified when I

asked her for the money—as though I were a highwayman.
Mr. Gilbert's idea in bringing me to America with him was
that he intended going into business out here. After our
arrival, however, he kept putting it off. When I questioned
him he said: 'Why should a man work when he can marry
an heiress?' That was my opportunity for suggesting that
I leave his employ. He agreed it would be for the best.
The day he became betrothed to Miss Allen Mr. Gilbert
practically confessed to me what he had been up to. 'I've
passed off many a fake in my time, Mick,' he said, 'but I'm
handing Marcia the biggest of all!'"

"Just what do you think Gilbert was blackmailing Mrs.
Bell for?"

"I suspect Mr. Gilbert of having passed off a counterfeit antiquity on Mrs. Bell."

An expression of incredulity flickered across the detective's face. "Surely the Professor is a connoisseur in such
matters!"

"It's my opinion that the Professor either doesn't want
to cause his wife unhappiness by discrediting her purchase,
or that Mrs. Bell has kept from her husband the price she
paid for it."

A blank expression said to be invaluable during poker
games settled on O. W.'s face as he inquired of the Irishman: "Did Mr. Gilbert ever sell anything to Mrs. Dwight?"

Only a slight twitching of his crooked lips evidenced
Kelly's agitation. "Not to my knowledge, sir."

Rarely did Mr. Wimble share his thought with those he
interviewed. He now chose to vary his usual procedure.

"All through this interview, Kelly, I've had the feeling that
Mr. Dwight must have asked you to protect Mrs. Dwight."

The scar across Kelly's cheek precluded an accurate
appraisal of his facial expression; yet it seemed to O. W.
that suddenly, momentarily, the man was in the grip of a
tremendous excitement.

When he spoke his suavity aroused the detective's admiration. "I'm sorry you've gained that impression, sir. Perhaps my tone has sounded unnecessarily antagonistic. It's only that I resent any discussion of a lady."

Mr. Wimble could feel justly proud of his hands. They were not the hands of a plump person but were slender and long-fingered. When he next spoke he was intently buffing the nails of his right hand on the palm of his left.

"Does your aversion to discussing ladies extend to Miss Roberta Allen?"

"Roberta Allen!" echoed Kelly. "What has Roberta to do with the murder?"

"Roberta has testified that she spoke to you here at Miss Allen's sometime around eight o'clock Saturday evening."

"Roberta spoke to me Saturday evening?" If O. W. was any judge of men he knew that Kelly's surprise was genuine.

Kelly said imperturbably: "I guess it will be easy enough to check up any long distance calls to Miss Allen's Saturday night from Hollywood."

"Roberta claims to have spoken to you in person." If O. W. had expected to see signs of alarm in the chauffeur's face he was disappointed. The Irishman's sole reaction was irritation.

"That kid's imagination works overtime. Roberta had my sympathy for awhile. She came to me with a yarn about her sister refusing to turn over some money that belonged to her. I almost let her talk me into hiring a lawyer. When I saw she hadn't a leg to stand on I gave the money she had given me for lawyers' fees to Mr. Gilbert to return to Miss Marcia."

"Considering your knowledge of Mr. Gilbert's dishonest methods, I wonder that you dared do so."

"I didn't believe such a small sum would attract him. He did give it to Miss Allen; otherwise she wouldn't have known Roberta and I were acquainted. And I'm positive that Miss Allen did know because Roberta warned me by telegram from Hollywood that her sister knew about us and would try to do me some harm."

It occurred to O. W. that he was a hard-shelled old detective not to feel chagrined at thus seeing one of his most choice clues go up in smoke.

"Roberta said she saw you leaving the library on the night of the murder."

If the chauffeur had felt any fear he could not have looked Mr. Wimble so steadily in the eye. "I wrote Roberta that I could not continue to show her attention in the face of her sister's disapproval. I suppose these lies are her idea of getting even."

"Then you weren't in this room the night of the murder?"

"Of course not! And at no other time. I always met Roberta outside somewhere."

Mr. Wimble said: "Those known to have been in this room on the night of the murder have suffered the indignity of having their finger-prints taken."

Kelly's reply was swift and unexpected. "There were no finger-prints found on the knife!" He added with a chuckle: "Lest you suspect me of being an amateur detective, sir, I must tell you that I drove Mr. Dwight and Mr. Osborne home from the inquest."

O. W. arose indicating that the interview was at an end.

He accompanied Kelly to the front of the house where Dwight's car was parked.

"I may need to question you again as the investigation develops," he said chattily.

Dwight and Miss Allen were standing by the car talking together. As O. W. and Kelly approached, the detective saw Dwight flash a questioning glance at his chauffeur, remarked Kelly's reassuring smile.

Before speaking, O. W. sighed. It was hard at times, being a detective.

"I wonder if three could crowd into this two-seater of yours," he said to Dwight. "If you don't mind giving a fellow a lift I'd like you to drop me at the Little Convent of the Flowers on your way home."

The detective saw that the young man's face had turned the color of death.

23

The thick adobe walls of the Little Convent of the Flowers made Mr. Wimble more aware of California's rich historical background than anything he had seen. The building was so old it seemed a part of the rolling brown Berkeley Hills that surrounded it. Vines climbed over it at random, ideal nesting places for birds. The flowers that had given the Convent its name looked as if no attempt had been made to arrange them in patterned beds. Their cheerful disorder charmed the detective. They looked as if they enjoyed growing there.

As O. W. walked up the flagstone walk toward the main building his keen eye perceived signs of activity behind a clump of lilac bushes. Muffling his footsteps he caught the sound of a childish giggle, a whispered admonition: "Hush!", followed by the tart treble: "The enemy approaches. Shoot!" The precaution O. W. took of quickly side-stepping proved unnecessary. The crudely carved arrow issuing from the lilacs fell several feet short of the enemy.

The important business of letting loose the arrow had infringed on the business of keeping within ambush. O. W. caught sight of feathered headgear. So he was being attacked by Indians, was he?

Whipping out his handkerchief the detective fashioned a flag of truce.

"I come in peace, O red brothers!"

There followed more giggling and a whispered consultation; then five small girls in blue and white uniforms tumbled out of the lilacs. One of them wore an elaborate headpiece of chicken feathers. This plump little person the detective took to be the chief of the tribe.

"Greetings, Chief Hole-in-the-Chin," he said with a courtly bow. Quickly the child's hand went to the dimple in her chin; the others giggled.

"It is the custom of our tribe to burn white men to the stake," announced the Chief solemnly.

The captive assumed an attitude of extreme despair.

"Oh, woe is me!" he groaned.

"Oh, whoa is him!" giggled one of the Indians.

The tribe went into a huddle. To the ears of the delighted captive was borne snatches of their conference. "Not when they wave a flag of truce!" "Indians always burned white men to the stake and then danced." "No they didn't; they smoked pipes of peace." "My brother smoked Daddy's pipe once and got orful sick!"

"You could hold me for ransom," suggested the prisoner. Chief Hole-in-the-Chin eyed him with approval.

"Pearls and rubies?"

"Pearls and rubies, or," he said innocently, "a big box filled with chocolate creams and gum drops and peanut brittle—"

The Indians emitted their wildest war whoop. "An' 'lasses chews!" "An' jelly beans!"

It became a chant to accompany their war dance.

"'Lasses chews an' jelly beans! 'Lasses chews an' jelly beans!"

"Children!" A sweet-faced woman in the garb of the Ursulines admonished them from the doorway. It was amazing how quickly the tribe managed to disappear.

"The ransom will arrive tomorrow!" shouted their captive after them. He knew they'd be remembering the ransom the minute they caught their breath.

"It's too bad you met with so barbaric a greeting," said the nun ruefully.

"I'm almost sorry you interrupted us," smiled the detective. "I *like* children!"

She returned his smile. "Did you come to play with the children?"

O. W. reluctantly turned his thoughts to the business that had brought him.

"I am a private detective. O. Wimble. Chiquita Dwight is in trouble. I feel that if I can learn something about her background I may be able to help her."

The Mother Superior was not startled. No doubt during her years of self-sacrificing service she had learned that life's happenings are both varied and strange; and no doubt, too, her brief appraisal of O. W. as he played with the children had told her that this man was one to be trusted.

"I remember well the day her father brought Chiquita here," she said. Her voice was low and mellow. "Chiquita was eleven years old. While I spoke with her father, one of the sisters took her through the buildings. When they returned the child stood before me. 'Where do you keep the men?' she demanded. 'There are no men here,' I replied. 'Then I'll stay,' she said.

"But come," said the Mother Superior gently, "let us sit in the rose arbor and I'll tell you as much of Chiquita's story as I know."

Usually when a man marries a girl someone says: "In Heaven's name what does he see in her?" Or: "What on earth do you suppose makes him seem attractive to a girl like her?" But when Shattuck Geary married Teresa Montez everyone said: "It's a perfect match! They're simply made for each other!" Both were of early California families—Teresa, being Spanish, of one a bit earlier than Shattuck's. He was a tall broad-shouldered young man of thirty, with curling blond hair and eyes the color of the sea. She was a slip of a girl, just past seventeen, with hair as smooth and shining as a raven's wing and luminous black eyes.

They loved passionately, those two—not quite as other people love. When Shattuck was away from Teresa people found him a gay, fun-loving young man, prone to gamble a bit too much, to drink a bit more than was good for him, with occasional sullen spells; but on the whole a likable chap and excellent company. Away from Shattuck Teresa was a mere child—a lovely one to look at to be sure—but with the shyness, the unformed ideas of life, the sudden losses of poise common to young girls. But together they became godlike, as if they were living on a different plane from other people. Their friends got into the habit of leaving them together. Afterwards they were glad they had, because Teresa lived only a year after her marriage. And forever after in telling of Teresa and Shattuck people unconsciously fell into the fairy-tale mode of narrative: "Once upon a time. . . ."

Teresa died giving birth to Chiquita. Something in Shattuck died at the same time. His gaiety and boyishness disappeared; he became quarrelsome and dissipated, tolerated by his old friends chiefly because of their memories of the man he had been, by his new friends only because of his wealth. For a time he took up a hobby: the raising of highly bred horses, a hobby which eventually escaped the bridle path and found its way to the racetrack.

Had Shattuck Geary remembered in the first years of his bereavement that he had a daughter, her sweet shy loveliness might have redeemed his manhood. But at the death of his beloved he had turned the infant over to his housekeeper and forced himself to forget that he was a

father. This housekeeper was not so bad as stupid. When
the services of a nurse were no longer needed she employed a series of inferior governesses in order to pocket
the difference between the low wages they demanded and
the amount Shattuck allowed her for Chiquita's education.
However her avarice might have given way to her honesty
had she realized what the companionship of these self-
styled governesses was doing to the sensitive, over-imaginative little girl in their care. But being of that type of
women who approve of permanent waves for little girls
of five and who consider theatrical troupes of half-naked
babies lisping: "I love you so much, it's a wonder you can't
feel it!" *too cute for words* naturally she did not realize the
harm she was doing.

The various governesses made the wide-eyed child their
confidante. They crammed her young mind with lurid
stories of men's vices, their hit-and-run methods with
women. Before she was eight Chiquita had an unhealthy
notion of the biologic processes.

These women taught the child that life was a battle
between men and women. They said that woman's best
weapon was the possession of money. They hammered it
into her head that without money a woman was lost. They
took her to the movies where the heroines able to bring
the iniquitous clubman to his knees never failed to be
dressed in gorgeous gowns, covered with jewels and living
in luxurious Cecil De Mille houses.

How was Chiquita to know that envy and frustrated desire motivated every word these unwanted women spoke?

One day when Chiquita was eleven, rummaging around
the attic, she came upon one of her mother's dresses. It
was a lovely garment of heavy white satin, with a low neck,
tight waistline and trailing skirt. Though old for her years
Chiquita was still a child. Children like to dress in adult
clothes. Chiquita put on Teresa's gown. Chiquita was more

fully developed than most young girls her age; maybe her Spanish ancestry was accountable. The dress fit her well. In the trunk in which she had found her mother's gown Chiquita had also unearthed a miniature of Teresa. She decided to do up her hair like her mother's.

Chiquita did not realize how superlatively adorable she looked in her mother's dress. Vanity did not enter into the sport of dressing up. Bent on duplicating Teresa's appearance in every detail, it distressed her not to be able to find in the trunk the fan depicted in the miniature. She wondered if there were one in "Daddy's house". Daddy's house was the main section of the great house Chiquita lived in. She and the servants attendant on her occupied the west wing of the house, rooms her father never visited. On several occasions she had seen Shattuck in the distance when his gruff voice and scowling countenance had sent her scurrying behind her nurse's skirts. She thoroughly understood that Shattuck did not wish her to visit his part of the building; in fact, the mere thought of doing so had always horrified her. But she had peered through the windows of "Daddy's house" and knew that his rooms contained many enchanting things.

It now occurred to her that in one of these magic rooms she might find her mother's fan. She decided to go in search of it, a decision somewhat robbed of courage by the fact that an hour ago she had seen her father riding away from the house on horseback.

Quietly she slipped down the stairway, along the corridor leading to "Daddy's house", into his living room. The luxurious appointments made no impression on her; her own quarter of the old mansion was also richly furnished. What did catch her eye was a large glass-fronted cabinet standing in a corner of the room. This cabinet held treasures of many lands—chiefly wedding presents of Shattuck and Teresa.

Her small nose pressed against the glass, Chiquita discovered what she was after: a gossamer lace fan mounted on ivory sticks. The cabinet was unlocked. In a moment the fan became a part of Chiquita's costume.

"Well! Where have *you* been all my life?"

Chiquita's heart thumped as she looked up and saw that a man was watching her, a guest of Daddy's no doubt. At first she was afraid of him. She was afraid of her father and this man looked like Shattuck Geary. He had the same glazed look in his eyes, the same little bags of flesh underneath, the same flabby lips, the same liquored breath.

Then her fear merged into fascination. The man's eyes were full of admiration.

"God! You little beauty!" He came toward her unsteadily. Chiquita saw nothing unusual in his gait; her father walked unsteadily more than half the time. Shattuck's voice was also thick like this man's.

Chiquita remembered the miniature up in the attic. Teresa's pose had been provocative: one hand on her hip, the other holding the outspread fan behind her lovely head. Suddenly the charm of Teresa, the coquetry of her, lived again in her little daughter. Chiquita assumed the pose of the miniature. Her smile was one the most beautiful woman might well have copied.

In fairness to the beast who was approaching he did not realize the child was only eleven years old. The low-cut gown was a woman's; its long skirt made Chiquita seem taller. As he approached he stumbled over a rug. He lurched forward, thrusting out his arm for support. One of his hands came down on Chiquita's bare shoulder. That touch of her soft young flesh went to his head. He caught her in his arms, sliding his hand under her armpit; his lips pressed down on hers in a long, slimy, obscene kiss.

The effect on the child was terrifying. She turned into a Fury. She scratched the man's face, bit his flesh, tore his

clothes, kicked his body. Befuddled by drink, he fell before the child's onslaught. Down she went on top of him,
clawing, pummeling, screaming. . . .

Shattuck Geary arrived before the child went completely out of her senses with hysteria.

"Teresa!" he said, when he had lifted her from the floor.
Chiquita had her mother's features and coloring. Chiquita's face of course was too white for a child's. She had
reached the age when children care more about reading
than anything else; and there was no one to insist that she
go out into the sunshine.

It was the first time Shattuck had spoken his wife's
name since her death. Something in his tone, in the look
on his dissipated face, calmed the child. As he carried her
back to the nursery, she lay in his arms, twitching convulsively but through with struggling.

The next day Shattuck took his daughter to the Little
Convent of the Flowers where she remained for seven
years. Those seven years did much to obliterate that horrible memory—though not as much as the Mother Superior
supposed. Chiquita was always a strange child. She shone
in athletic games; but she didn't care for dolls. It wasn't
that she had no repose; she would sit for hours among
the flowers, whispering to them, softly brushing off their
petals with a fern frond, Chiquita could sit so quietly, the
Mother Superior said, that butterflies would light on her
hand. It was beautiful sight to see the slim, lovely child
sitting there, a butterfly poised on her finger.

For years the sight of even a priest made her blood run
cold.

Chiquita was eighteen when her father came for her.
He needed her at home, he said; and of course a child's
duty was toward its parent. Chiquita protested that she
wanted to become a novice. The Mother Superior advised against this. The Mother Superior watched her girls.

Chiquita's tenderness with the flowers was maternal. The child loved material things. Jewels and fine garments delighted her. She fretted a good deal because the furnishings of the convent were so rustic. Despite the simple life of the convent the Mother Superior felt that if luxury were available, Chiquita would take to it like a duck to water. The child doted on the theatre; had a passion for dancing.

At the time Shattuck Geary discovered that he had a beautiful daughter who would lend tone to his entertainments, his riotous living was beginning to tell on him in more ways than one. Its effect on his health was that he was but a shadow of his former robust self, with periodic heart attacks that left him white-faced, panting, clinging to the arms of his chair. Its effect on his social standing was that even those most loyal to the Shattuck of old would as soon have visited a brothel as the house his home had become—a house, over-run with foul-mouthed men and flashily dressed women. Its effect on his bank account was that one by one his fine horses were being sold to keep him solvent.

Chiquita soon gained the sobriquet of Snow White. No one could deny her beauty, but she was not liked. She was too aloof. No man again attempted to touch her. She was now possessed of womanly weapons that discouraged any such attempt.

And yet during the five years she lived at her father's house she had a good time. She loved the horses. Shattuck was a fine horseman. He taught her how to ride. She enjoyed spending the generous sums of money he allowed her.

John Dwight first came to Shattuck Geary's house to buy a pedigreed horse Geary had up for sale. He happened to see Geary's daughter and came again. Of the so-called friends of Shattuck Geary, John Dwight was the only one who treated his host with the slightest semblance of respect. The others, perhaps realizing that Geary could not much longer keep up the pace he was going, seemed determined to get all they could out of him while there was yet opportunity. They took advantage of his hospitality, some of them actually living in his house for weeks at a time. They borrowed large sums. A number of them actually stole.

Chiquita heard, indirectly because he did not interest her in the least, that John Dwight was an extremely rich young man, with rather unusual views concerning philanthropy. His idea was not to bestow charity on a down-and-outer but to help him help himself. A good man is supposed to be one who gives away a tenth of all he possesses; they said of John Dwight that he kept a tenth of what he had for himself and gave away the rest.

John Dwight's appearance did nothing to suggest to Chiquita that he was anything but an ordinary young man. The fact that he was called Dumpling rather than Jack was significant. He was fat and had red hair. No matter how good a tailor he patronized his trousers always bagged at the knees. He took the adage "Everybody loves a fat man" as seriously as a Commandment. He seemed to consider it his destiny to make people laugh. He never failed to have a joke ready—the kind with burrs.

Chiquita was not interested in Dumpling Dwight. He was a man; therefore a creature to be detested. Moreover, he was a clown, which made him ludicrous.

That the house was continuously fragrant with Dumpling's flowers, that Dumpling was always close at her heels with a wrap if she happened to step into the garden on a cool evening, left Chiquita unmoved. After all, spiders wove attractive webs for the capture of their victims. Chiquita made no distinction between Dumpling and other men; but apparently he found even her rebuffs attractive because his attentions continued.

And yet there was one difference in Chiquita's attitude toward John Dwight. She was not afraid of him!

She was not surprised when Dumpling proposed to her. She knew she was beautiful. She rather hated her beauty because it drew men to her. Dwight told Chiquita that he loved her and that he would be very grateful and humble if she would consent to marry him. He called her "Chickie" and got red in the face. At the close of his proposal Chiquita looked at him dispassionately and said: "I wish that you would not call me Chickie; it is quite abhorrent to me," and left him without another word.

One morning a few months later Shattuck Geary was discovered dead in his chair. After a consultation with her father's lawyers, Chiquita learned that she was penniless.

John Dwight proposed to her again and she accepted him.

On his way back to Miss Allen's from the Convent O. W. was not surprised to hear newsboys calling extras.

"Extry! Extry! All about the Gilbert murder!"

"Poor Marcia!" thought the detective as he bought a paper.

He was still thinking of Marcia when his eyes fell on the glaring headlines:

CLUBMAN CONFESSES MURDER
Gary Gilbert Killed by Knife of John Dwight

24

Mr. Wimble was late returning to Miss Allen's. After leaving the Little Convent of the Flowers he had called at the Berkeley jail to see John Dwight. As he walked up the Allen driveway the detective smiled. He felt much like an errant husband arriving home late for dinner. Yet he knew it wasn't his tardiness that would be disturbing Marcia Allen.

When he entered the house his hostess was nowhere in sight. He was met by Wing who informed him that Miss Allen had retired to her room. He added that the detective's dinner was ready; when Mr. Wimble had washed up it would be served to him on a tray in the library.

He offered Mr. Wimble a choice of desserts. "Would you like strawberries or cantaloupe?"

"It doesn't matter," said O. W. It spoiled his appetite, knowing how that young woman upstairs was suffering.

With an impassible countenance Wing said: "Missy says I am to help you pack your bags."

"Oh, but I won't be going for a couple of days yet," returned O. W. cheerily. "That is," he added with a grin, "unless Miss Allen has decided to throw me out for jailing John Dwight. I'd like to wait for a cable I'm expecting."

Mr. Wimble had not as yet caught Wing revealing his feelings by any readable facial expression; but as the significance of what he had just said penetrated the Chinaman's consciousness Wing suddenly remarked: "I shall bring you strawberries and cantaloupe both!" And O. W. felt that Wing was pleased with him.

After dinner the detective visited the gardener's cottage. He not only had business with Michael, but a note handed him by Rosie had told him that Corey and Janet had returned from Hollywood and were awaiting his pleasure at the cottage.

The youngsters had been watching for O. W. and as he approached Janet came running down the front steps. She threw her arms around the detective.

She had her own way of telling him the most important news in the world. "O. W.," she whispered, "will you give me away?"

Mr. Wimble shook his head. "No, child."

Janet drew back, a hurt look on her heart-shaped face.

"I'll lie like a gentleman!" declared O. W. solemnly.

"Oh, you Charles Dickensy old darling!" cried Janet, giving him a hug.

"So you knocked Corey's misogynous principles sky high, did you, child?" asked O. W. affectionately.

Corey had appeared on the front porch. Janet winked at the detective. "I accepted Corey because I simply couldn't resist having Dolly for a mother-in-law," she said, and thought that O. W. looked tremendously pleased at her joke.

As Janet preceded them into the cottage, O. W.'s arm slid around his assistant's shoulders in a fatherly gesture.

"I feel like a fool, sir," said Corey, "after all the harsh things I've said about girls."

"I don't see why you should," returned O. W. warmly. "Janet's in a class by herself!"

Later Corey made a confession. "O. W.," he said rather sheepishly, "I fell in love with Janet at first sight. Remember that night at the station? I saw Janet talking to one of the gatemen and when I was pretending to see to the luggage, I was asking him who she was."

"I wondered what was responsible for your sudden Doxology to California," returned O. W. innocently. No use embarrassing the lad by telling him that after thirty odd years of practice a private detective doesn't miss much of what's going on about him.

When they had reported the results of their Hollywood trip, Corey was gratified to see his chief take a scratch pad and pencil out of his pocket. He knew by this sign that he had advanced something of importance to the investigation.

"Considering how the rest of her testimony checks up," said O. W. after awhile, "there's no reason to suppose that Roberta was lying about hiding in the Dwight automobile the night of the murder. I feel certain that Kelly knew nothing of her visit, however, that he mistook her call for some other woman's, probably Chiquita's. I felt throughout my interview with Kelly that he was trying to shield Chiquita. In fact I heard him promise Dwight he would. Both those young men know more about Chiquita's connection with this affair than they'll admit."

With a smile the detective turned to Janet. "By the way, were you disappointed when you saw by the papers that somebody else had got the story of Dwight's arrest?"

Janet had indeed been disappointed until reminded by Corey of O. W.'s promise that when he found the murderer of Gary Gilbert she should have the story. This however was a secret between her fiancé and herself.

She replied demurely: "I expect to scoop the story."

It did not occur to anyone of the three that Mr. Wimble would not succeed in locating the true murderer of Gary Gilbert.

"Young Dwight's confession sounded most plausible," Mr. Wimble told Corey and Janet "He gave jealousy as his

motive. He said that when he was threatening Gilbert
with the butcher knife he was so in earnest he thought his
antipathy toward the man must be glaringly evident, He
told me he was so sure his threat would be used against
him that, until everyone began conjecturing who the murderer might be, he had no idea of denying he had committed the crime."

"Yet he took the precaution to efface all finger-prints
on the knife," put in Corey. The senior detective eyed his
young assistant with manifest approval. Corey had been
a private detective only a short time, but he was learning
fast.

"Exactly. I questioned him on that point and he said
rather awkwardly that he'd thought he might as well take
that one chance of covering his trail. He's a rotten liar,
young Dwight He picked up a red cloth from the floor, he
said, and wiped off the knife handle."

"The silk doily the copper at the gate had over his
flashlight," Corey explained to Janet. He turned to his
chief. "Wiping off the knife explains the fleck of blood
on it."

Mr. Wimble added gravely: "Any number of things
might explain why the doily was on the floor and not
underneath the lamp where it belonged."

Which gave Corey something to think about.

"How did Dwight explain the 'Pal!' Rosie heard through
the library door at eight o'clock Saturday night?" asked
Corey.

Again the detective eyed Assistant Webb with approval.

"He didn't. Or couldn't, to be exact."

Janet spoke. "It was Hugh Osborne who said 'Pal!',
wasn't it?"

"Rosie thinks it was," returned Mr. Wimble. "It's clear
enough that Osborne was at the house at the time the

murder was committed. But if he had been near the library surely Roberta or Marie would have seen him. Or some of the others. There seems to have been plenty of activity in that vicinity."

Suddenly from the adjoining room where Blanche and Michael were listening to their radio came the voice of a crooner: *"Would you like to take a walk?"*

As O. W. turned toward them with a grin both Corey and Janet blushed furiously.

"I trust," said O. W. mischievously, "that your thoughts have been on the case."

As they started to protest he chuckled: "Oh, get along with you! California nights are made to order for lovers. Besides, I have a date with Michael."

Janet smiled at him. "I think you're the nicest man I know!"

"Hey!" objected Corey.

Whereupon Janet wriggled her small nose. This proved too much for her young man. He reached over and took her small hand in his. There they sat, totally oblivious of Mr. Wimble, telling each other a number of things with their eyes.

"What is this thing called love?" demanded the radio from the other room.

With a start and a swift guilty glance at Mr. Wimble Corey and Janet drew apart, red to the ears.

O. W. was still chuckling when he joined Blanche and Michael.

Blanche tuned off as he entered. Apparently she was not of the school that expects one to shriek the amenities above the clamor of Station KUKU. Or it may have been that she considered the conversation of a private detective more entertaining than the admonition of a radio announcer to visit your chiropodist twice a year.

Though Blanche had been a resident of America since childhood she still retained notions of old-world hospitality. In her native France no passing guest could leave one's domicile without first being plied with nourishment—preferably liquid.

"I'd like to offer you something, Mr. Wimble." She broke off, fixing an anxious eye on the detective. "You don't wear a—star, do you, sir?" she asked uncertainly.

"I'm not a policeman, Blanche." His eyes twinkled with mischief. "But I'm a very thirsty—man."

"Not that every policeman on this beat didn't strike up a friendship with Mike the minute they found out he had a French wife!" said Blanche with elaborate irony, "But I didn't like taking a chance, on Miss Allen's account. She's in enough trouble as it is, poor dear!"

Before she moved kitchenward, O. W. put a question to the Maloneys.

"Do you and Michael remember what time it was that Kelly left here to go out and light up his car?"

Characteristically it was Blanche who replied. "Why, he didn't go out at all! He probably put on the lights before he came in. It was getting dark then. He sat right down to his card game with Mike. Didn't he, Mike?" she asked in the goading tone typical of the wives of taciturn husbands.

Michael remembered: "Kelly wint out whin we was listenin' t' Amos 'n' Andy."

"That's true. Mike hasn't missed Amos 'n' Andy since they began to broadcast," Blanche told the detective, her voice fraught with pride. "At eight o'clock Mike told Kelly he wanted to stop playing cards for fifteen minutes to listen to Amos 'n' Andy."

"Did Kelly listen in also?"

"No, sir; he said he thought Amos 'n' Andy silly. He said he'd go out and stretch his legs for awhile. I think the real reason was because I was there. He doesn't like me. You see, Kelly's superstitious. One time I opened an umbrella in the house and Kelly said something dreadful would happen. He really was scared—got white. I laughed at him. Kelly don't like being made fun of."

Michael put in a word in defense of his friend. "An' ye broke the crame pitchure th' vurry nex' d'y!"

"Yes, and why?" retorted Blanche. "Because you sat around waiting for something to happen, that's why!" She turned her back on her husband. "Kelly came back after Amos 'n' Andy had finished," she told Mr. Wimble.

"In a quarter of an hour, to be exact?"

"I think so." Blanche looked inquiringly toward her husband.

Michael supplied the information. "I w'ited about five or tin minutes f'r 'im. Don't ye remembher, lass, I played a gime iv solytaire? Faith, an' I won, begorra!"

"And no one could possibly forget so remarkable a feat as that!" smiled the detective.

Blanche sniffed. "He remembers it because I gave him a glass of wine for a prize, that's why he remembers it!" She turned a wrathful gaze on her lord and master. "And I've caught him cheating twice since, trying to win another prize!"

O. W. returned to the investigation. "Did you notice anything peculiar about Kelly's manner when he returned?"

"I'd gone to bed," stated Blanche regretfully. She eyed her husband hopefully.

"I noticed wan thing about 'im thot was unusual," supplied Michael. "He lost a bit iv money thot night an' he didn't growl about it. Kelly don't like it whin I win. He's a bad loser."

O. W. beamed at Blanche. "How about giving Michael and me our refreshments now?"

"Michael and you!" retorted Blanche, while the object of her scorn held his breath. However, she melted under O. W.'s good nature.

"Well, all right," she surrendered. "After all, Mike's worked real hard today pruning the Dorothy Perkins roses on the summer-house."

When she had left the room O. W. turned questioningly toward the grateful gardener.

"Well, what did you find on the summer-house roof?"

Michael's gnarled fingers worked their way into one of the cavernous pockets of his brown corduroy trousers. He drew forth and handed to the detective an arrow. It was a slender, graceful thing about ten inches long of the Grecian type. It was made of silver, except its barb which was of chased gold; and instead of real feathers it was decorated at the end by an arrangement of jewels cleverly fashioned to represent feathers. The arrow looked too pretty to be dangerous.

25

It was with pleasure that Mr. Wimble, waiting in the Dwight drawing-room for Chiquita to come downstairs, looked about him. Outside the palaces of Europe he had never seen so handsome a room. In fact, furnished in the style of Louis Quatorze, it was reminiscent of some of the royal apartments he had visited on the Continent. There was a great deal of gilt, elaborate carving and inlay; but as the room was large, the carpets and draperies subdued in tone and everything of the finest materials, the decorations, which might otherwise have appeared florid, were in perfect taste.

"Really, Mr. Wimble!" A cold voice from the doorway diverted the detective's attention from a beautiful buhl cabinet he was examining. "Now that my husband has given himself up I see no reason for your presence here. Why!" she exclaimed, as O. W. turned his face toward her. "It's the gentleman who laughed at the pansies!" Though she recognized him she was not cordial.

"Laughed *with* the pansies," said O. W. No answering smile met this sally.

Chiquita glanced down at the card in her hand. "I hadn't any idea when Katie brought me this that I had met you before," she said tonelessly.

Mr. Wimble was not like the artist Gibson who believes
that each age produces its own type of feminine pulchritude. In O. W.'s eyes no woman could ever approach Dolly
Webb in beauty; but he was ready to admit that Chiquita
Dwight was singularly lovely. From her Spanish mother
she had inherited her symmetry of features and her dark
coloring; from her Irish father her vitality and grace. Her
body was supple, with a slim length of limb; O. W. judged
that her gait was easy. Her hair was black and lustrous,
brushed smoothly away from her forehead and gathered in
a knot at the nape of her neck. The movements of her eyelids brought into play her amazingly long, curling black
lashes. Under her nose, which was straight and fine, an
exquisite dimple twinkled on her short upper lip. Her
mouth was slightly fuller than the standard conception
of the ideal mouth, her only feature that might be said
to show a faint trace of voluptuousness; though when her
facial expression was not so cold and hard as at present her
large black eyes surely must afford a splendid vehicle for
passion. Her face wore the waxen whiteness of tuberoses.
Because of her perfect physique O. W. felt that she was not
habitually so pale.

Chiquita said: "I am at a loss to account for your—"

"Intrusion?" The detective's half-amused, half-provoc-
ative manner seemingly did nothing to put him in Mrs.
Dwight's good graces.

"I shouldn't express it so strongly. You must realize, of
course, that under the circumstances I am not receiving."

Mr. Wimble said quietly: "I came to return your arrow,
Mrs. Dwight."

Scarcely an appreciable interval of time elapsed between
Mr. Wimble's statement and Chiquita's quiet "Thank you",
yet during that interval various emotions oddly mingling
in her face testified that something prodigious was going
on in her brain.

The thought that came to the detective as he watched her was: "She remains beautiful through her terror."

O. W. had brought the arrow wrapped in paper. Only when he began untying the string of the parcel did Chiquita manifest any sign of emotion.

Trembling, alert, she said sharply: "Don't unwrap it, please!" She pressed her beautiful hands to her temples.

Quickly Mr. Wimble placed a chair for her. "Won't you sit down?"

Chiquita turned her glorious eyes on him. Queer what a softened mood could do to eyes! All at once Chiquita's eyes seemed candid and decent like a child's. He saw now how young she really was.

Chiquita seated herself, motioning for the detective to do likewise. "I hadn't meant to come downstairs," she acknowledged with a half-smile. "But Mr. Dwight has told me so many nice things about you my curiosity brought me." She said impulsively: "Human fellowship is very dear at a time like this."

O. W. sighed as he trespassed on her mellowed mood.

"I've needed your testimony very badly, Mrs. Dwight, these past few days."

"The Law is kinder than detectives apparently. The Law doesn't require wives to testify against their husbands." O. W. remarked that her eyes though still beautiful were no longer the eyes of a child.

"Yes, Katie?" Chiquita addressed a young servant girl standing in the doorway.

"There's a Mr. Bill Smith outside, Mrs., Dwight. He says he wants to see you real bad. I said I thought you was out like you told me to say; but seeing you came down for Mr. Wimble, ma'am, I told Mr. Smith I'd see if you was in."

"Oh, Katie!" deplored Chiquita. "Why don't you try to save me a little now I'm in so much trouble?"

Katie twisted her apron in her fingers.

"I know it was wrong of me, but Mrs. Dwight, ma'am, this Mr. Smith says he's here to tell you something that will save Mr. Dwight." Katie sent Mr. Wimble an appealing glance.

The detective threw out the life-line. "I think we should see this man, Mrs. Dwight," he said in his professional manner. He took Katie's gurgle to denote appreciation.

"Very well, if you think it wise." Wearily Chiquita dragged her lovely fingers across her forehead. It was decided that the detective would receive Mr. Bill Smith. If the man's business warranted Chiquita's attention Katie was to summon her mistress according to a plan the three agreed upon before Chiquita retired to her room and Katie went to admit the caller to the drawing-room.

Mr. William P. Smith, known locally as Bill, was a chap in the early thirties. From his grease-stained clothes and the combined odor of gasoline and machine oil clinging to his person, O. W. judged the man to be a mechanic.

Smith was tall and lank, rather good looking except for a sloping chin. Though upon making the discovery the detective maintained that expression of mild curiosity with which one regards a stranger, he immediately noticed that Smith possessed a most extraordinary pair of hands.

During Mr. Wimble's thirty odd years of detective service he had seen many hands of the quality of Bill's—slender, nervous, tapering-fingered. In fact O. W. had more than once been instrumental in sending the owners of such hands to prison on various pickpocketing, safe-cracking and lock-picking charges.

Though less adroitly, Smith returned Mr. Wimble's scrutiny. As Bill formed his estimate the detective gathered that Smith didn't wholly trust him.

When according to instructions Katie had shown the caller into the drawing-room and shut the door behind her, O. W. assumed the duties of host.

"Won't you sit down? I'm waiting for Mrs. Dwight. She's out."

"You ain't that fancy dick I been reading about in the papers?"

Mr. Wimble laughed. "Do I look like a detective?"

"Not like none I ever seen before." O. W. imagined that during his career Mr. Smith had made the acquaintance of several detectives.

A sudden thought smote Bill, a happy one by the expression on his face. "You John Dwight's dad?"

"Young Dwight and I do look something alike, don't we—in shape?" admitted Mr. Wimble. "No, just a friend of his." This last remark bore fruit.

"I'm a friend of Mr. Dwight's too. Bill Smith."

"Glad to meet you, Smith. My name's Oberon." Which he considered sufficient for the moment. It was his Christian name. O. W.'s mother had been one of those sentimental females who give their offspring just cause for matricide by naming the poor defenseless creatures after their favorite characters in fiction.

Bill was nervous and his nervousness made him talkative. "I'm an automobile mechanic. Run my own shop in Berkeley."

"Followed the line long?"

Bill glanced obliquely down at his hands. "Only about a year. What business you in?"

O. W. was now sure of his ground. "Several." With a grin he handed Smith the watch he a moment previously had filched from the mechanic's pocket. "Among other things I'm supposed to be pretty good at picking pockets."

O. W., whose hands were surprisingly slim and sensitive for so stout a man, had learned pickpocketing from a crook he once had befriended. Picking pockets had become one of his most valuable detective tools, and an amusing indoor sport. An exhibition of his skill at social gatherings never failed to evoke the greatest astonishment. O. W. had anticipated no wonder on Smith's part, however, and got none.

Appreciatorily Bill sized up the detective's hands. "You got the mitts for it, all right. Say!" he broke off, belligerently eying the detective. "What you up to in this joint anyway?"

"I told you I was waiting to see Mrs. Dwight."

"Yeah! In the room what's got the safe in it!" So the man was familiar with the location of the Dwight safe!

"I also told you I was Mr. Dwight's friend," O. W. gently reminded the mechanic. Smith's concern lifted.

"Excuse my suspicions, brother, but you see I think John Dwight's a great guy and he ain't in a position right now to look after his own property."

Mr. Wimble asked dryly: "You aren't here by any chance to look after Mr. Dwight's property for him, are you?"

Smith grinned a bit sheepishly. "You got me straight, brother! I was in that racket myself once. But no longer. Mr. Dwight got me to quit it. He set me up in business. God! To think of a guy like John Dwight in the jug!" Though the weak chin probably accounted for Smith's inability to control his emotions, O. W. felt that genuine regard for John Dwight prompted the tear that trickled down his cheek.

"Hell!" cursed the mechanic. "Why can't that jane get a move on?" An expression of anxiety came into his face. "Maybe she seen me coming and beat it on purpose."

"You have called here before?"

Smith grinned. "Yeah. Pretending to be a book peddler so's to get the lay of the land. I wish you could of lamped Her Royal Highness that day."

"You're not very fond of Mrs. Dwight, I take it."

Mr. Smith made a vulgar gesture signifying his distaste for his absent hostess.

"The way that dame edged away from me when I came up the front steps you'd of thought I had what listerine's good for. She was giving something the flunkey called an 'Al Fresco luncheon' on the front porch. Al's a highbrow caterer what invented eating outdoors. 'My good man,' she says, flashing them big headlights of hers on me, 'the servants' entrance is at the rear!' Me being mistook for a James! Can you tie it? Well, that crack give me the jimjams—see? I got inside the dump O. K. and located the safe; then I pulled a boner. Mr. Dwight came in—see? While he was looking at the book I was pretending to sell I picked his pockets. Like I told you that dame had got me all shaky but I didn't expect the comeback I got from Mr. Dwight. He says to me: 'I guess you're clever all right, but you see I'm ticklish!'

"Now I ask you, Mr. Oberon, what would you have done in a case like that?"

"I'd have called him the better man and given him back the loot."

"That's exactly what I done. Then the two of us had a talk. I guess if I live to be as old as Rockefeller I'll never forget that there talk. Mr. Dwight pointed out how only the big guns like Al Capone make the sort of thing I was up to pay and—no offense he says—he didn't think I had the personality or the training to get by. The little fellows get caught sooner or later, he says to me, and even the Al Capones got their Johnny Torrios.

"Well, you know, I'd never thought of it just that way before. It kinda got me. 'A man's gotta eat!' I says. And then out of a clear sky he sprung this garage gag on me. He says to me: 'I bet you're handy with tools.' He says: 'I wouldn't be surprised if you got so good you could invent something some day—maybe a lock what can't be picked!' Funny as a crutch Mr. Dwight is, ain't he? His idea was for me to open a garage—him to supply the capital, me to pay him back when I could.

"Now I ask you, Mr. Oberon, what would you have done in a case like that?"

"I'd have grabbed the offer!"

"Believe me, brother, that's just what I done! And to think a guy who'd do all that for a second-rate crook is locked up!" He brushed his hands across his eyes. "Hell! Where's that there dame?"

O. W. felt that the time was now ripe to summon Chiquita. He went to the door and called Katie.

"Katie! Are you sure your mistress hasn't returned?" This was the girl's signal.

"Mrs. Dwight just this minute came in, sir. I was on my way to tell you when you called. She said she'll be down just as soon as she takes off her hat."

In a few minutes Chiquita was in the drawing-room. She smiled at O. W. and held out her hand to Smith. Bill shot her a glance of incredulity.

"Guess you don't recognize me, lady."

"Yes I do, Mr. Smith. I'm afraid I wasn't very cordial the last time you were here. You see, you startled me."

"Yeah, I guess it was kind of a shock giving a feed on the front porch and then having a guy show up what looked like he was going to climb it." He glanced down at his soiled apparel. "I don't look so good right now, ma'am, but I was in a hell of—in an awful hurry to get here."

"You wished to see me on business, Mr. Smith?" She glanced at O. W. Smith misinterpreted her look.

"Oberon's all right, ma'am! Him and me's buddies, you might say. What I wanted to see you about, Mrs. Dwight, is a plan I got for getting your husband out of jail."

He expounded his scheme. "It's as simple as falling off a log, Mrs. Dwight. Listen! I goes in to visit Mr. Dwight at the jail—see? I takes Minnie Munn along. Minnie's a dame what runs a restaurant around the corner from my garage. Minnie can be trusted. We're partners, in a way; she advertises free parking space at my place—see? Minnie's a big fat jane and she can screen me from the guards while I picks the lock of Mr. Dwight's cell; and then Mr. Dwight changes into Minnie's clothes and goes out with me—see? We leave Minnie in the cell like she was Mr. Dwight. I got a friend who owns a powerful motor boat. Mr. Dwight jumps into one of my machines and drives to the waterfront where my friend picks him up—see? Mr. Dwight escapes to Mexico. That's all there is to it. Simplest thing in the world."

John had told Chiquita about his friend Bill Smith. She had mocked her husband for his faith in human nature. "Smith's taking advantage of you!" She had prophesied: "He'll never pay you back. He'll borrow and borrow and then one fine day you'll find he's disappeared." But except for the initial sum with which to finance his business, Smith had not borrowed; he was repaying what he owed; and he hadn't disappeared. John had brought Chiquita reports of Bill's interest in his garage, his neighbors, his town—the community's regard for Smith as a self-respecting citizen. And now this man who at last had found his niche in the world was willing to risk all he had gained in order that his benefactor should go free!

"It's a beautiful plan," said O. W.

"There's only one flaw in it," lamented Bill.

"What's that?"

Smith half sobbed the words. "Mr. Dwight refuses to escape!"

Chiquita's gorgeous eyes were suspiciously bright. "It's because he doesn't want you and Minnie Munn to assume the risk."

"Here's why I come to you, Mrs. Dwight. You gotta convince your husband that it'll look like he made his own getaway, that Minnie and me ain't risking nothing. Please, Mrs. Dwight," he pleaded. "You know Mr. Dwight'd do anything in the world for you."

Chiquita struggled to speak in language that Bill would understand. "Do you think in your heart, Mr. Smith, that Mr. Dwight could be—vamped into doing something he considered wrong?"

"Don't suppose he could at that, ma'am," Bill reluctantly admitted. "I'm a great little fixer, all right," he said dejectedly. "Guess I'll go tell Minnie it's all off."

Chiquita extended her hand. "Mr. Smith, you don't know—"

"Cut it, ma'am!" blinked Bill.

Chiquita said impulsively: "I'd like to call on Mrs. Munn!"

"I got my car outside if you'd care to drive downtown with me," offered Bill timidly.

"I'd love to! Wait till I get my hat." At the doorway she turned. "Maybe you can persuade Mr. Wimble to accompany us."

As Chiquita left the room Bill wheeled toward O. W.

"Wimble? Wimble's the name of that dick I been reading about!"

"Oberon Wimble to my friends, Bill. You see," apologetically, "I simply had to learn what you were up to."

This statement had little effect toward placating the irate Bill. He glowered at the detective.

"I ain't forgetting in no hurry that you're the bozo what put John Dwight behind them bars!"

"I'm still on the case," returned the detective pleasantly.

Smith puzzled over this remark for a moment; then his hostility vanished.

"Hell!" he grinned. "Who'd 've thought a year ago that Slick Finger Smith would be chumming with a dick!"

26

Mr. Wimble was prepared to encounter many ludicrous as well as soul-stirring situations during the investigation of a crime. Contact with Minnie Munn brought into high relief both ridiculousness and pathos.

As they drove to Minnie Munn's restaurant Chiquita gave Mr. Wimble an account of her first meeting with its proprietor. She told of it fairly with no attempt to spare herself.

Chiquita came on Minnie Munn one day in her own drawing-room; the woman was waiting for Mr. Dwight, she told Chiquita. Minnie at the time was working in a factory and had come during her noon hour. She was eating her luncheon out of a paper bag.

Eying the corpulent Minnie lolling in one of her Louis Quatorze chairs, Chiquita flared: "John must get an office. I'll not have my home littered up like this!"

"I been eatin' right over the bag, ma'am," from a meek Minnie.

"Parasite!" An apt name for the disreputable humans continually calling on John.

It was obvious that Minnie didn't quite understand the designation—she connected it vaguely with Paris: fast carryings-on and sloe-eyed foreigners selling dirty post cards to American tourists—but it put her on her dignity just the same.

"I may look like somebody out of the circus, ma'am, but I'll have you to know I'm a good woman. Parasite!" she bridled. "No ma'am!" Whimpering a little, "I didn't come here to be insulted."

"What did you come for?"

"A Ford." Still no sign from the arrogant Mrs. John Dwight that she found the plump Minnie in the least degree amusing.

The widowed Minnie Munn, mother of seven, had found getting to and from the factory hard on her poor "dogs". Hearing how charitable Mr. Dwight was, and how rich, she had dared come to ask if he hadn't an old Ford he wasn't using.

From the scornful Chiquita: "Why don't you reduce?" Such easy advice for a svelte creature to give who had her horses, her gymnasium, her swimming pool, her Country Club, her masseuse, her dietician!

Minnie suggested a bit tartly—for what right had this young thing to criticize God's mysterious ways?—that perhaps a person's shape was the Lord's business. Maybe He wanted some folks thin, others fat. After all, there were compensations to being fat. It was almost worth suffering from bunions to have one of the kids bathe her poor tired dogs every night. Blessed kids! Actually fought for the privilege. Once a week each kid had a chance. Seven nights. Seven kids. The littlest one got Sunday because Minnie didn't have to go to the factory Sundays and her dogs weren't quite so all in. Gee, them kids with the little medicine kits they got at school messing around with her bunions! Mrs. Dwight ought to see them sometime. The kids—not her bunions.

By the way, did Mrs. Dwight have any kids? What, no kids! How long had she been married? Three years? Three years and no kids!

Whereupon Chiquita quoted Minnie. Stonily. "After all, isn't that perhaps the Lord's business?"

Minnie retorted dryly: "There are some things folks can 'tend to better'n the Lord, Mrs. Dwight!"

Only John's arrival kept Chiquita from having Minnie Munn shown out of the house. She left them together. Later at luncheon John wasn't hungry, having shared Minnie's paper bag repast. Minnie's doughnuts had won him, he rather boyishly confessed to his wife. The woman really was a born cook. Minnie had read in an old cookbook of her mother's that if a woman wanted her husband to swear *by* her instead of *at* her she'd have to be a good cook. Minnie had taken this advice to heart, with success too, she reckoned, Clarence Munn having sworn many a time that though Minnie might be a yard wide she was all wool.

So it hadn't taken much inspiration on his part, John told his wife, to suggest that Mrs. Munn open a restaurant. It was a business venture, he hastened to assure Chiquita lest she accuse him again of sentimentality; he was sure Minnie would coin money for her silent partner.

"And I suppose," contemptuously, "in addition to putting up the money for the restaurant you gave her the Ford she wanted."

"I did promise her a car, Chickie," said John, uncomfortable before the scorn in her eyes, "but not a Ford. Too small for a woman Minnie's size and seven youngsters. . . ."

It was about eleven o'clock when the detective followed the slender, smartly clad form of Chiquita Dwight into Minnie Munn's restaurant. The hour was one of the dull times in the life of a restaurant—too late for breakfast, too early for luncheon. Therefore, except for a group of University boys, Minnie Munn's visitors found the place deserted.

O. W. liked the looks of Minnie's establishment. While it had none of the white-tiled bathroom appearance of chain eating houses, still there was nothing about it that put it into the tearoom class. From the bottom of his heart Mr. Wimble—and every other male with whom he had ever discussed the matter—detested tea rooms. He hated sitting on an overgrown footstool at a rickety table painted pink in a room that looked like a stage set. He liked less "atmosphere" and more air. He didn't like napkins the size of a child's handkerchief. He liked white napery. He liked he-man portions. He liked waitresses who looked like waitresses—not like the leavings of the Junior League when the June weddings are over.

Minnie's restaurant was clean, roomy, cheerful and, a quality rare in public eating houses, hospitable. The chairs were wide and comfortable; spotless white cloths covered the tables; fresh white curtains hung at the windows.

Bill Smith had told Chiquita and O. W. that they'd probably find Minnie occupying the cashier's desk, but instead they found a young girl about fourteen years old in charge. This girl was a stockily built child with a round solemn face. Her shining cheeks and her stiffly starched pink gingham apron were so clean she looked disinfected.

The child's pale blue eyes became discs of wonder when they fell on O. W.'s companion. Ladies as beautiful and modish as Chiquita Dwight no doubt were rare patrons of the restaurant.

"We're looking for Mrs. Munn," said Chiquita. "Your mother?"

"Yep, that's Mom. She's out in the kitchen right now. I'll call her."

As the child's hand moved toward an electric push button Chiquita put in quickly: "If your mother's busy, we can wait."

"We c'n ask her if she's busy when she comes," decided Pink Gingham sensibly.

"You the cashier, Miss Munn?" asked O. W.

The child glowed under the deference shown her.

"Well, not 'xactly," she replied truthfully. "I'm jus' helping out today because Mom don't feel good. I will be regular cashier some day, though," she added proudly.

Suddenly from the corner where the boys sat came a burst of song. O. W. recognized the air as "Minnie the Mermaid." A quick glance toward the swinging door at the end of the room told him that Mrs. Munn was emerging from the kitchen.

The significance of the tune was obvious even before Pink Gingham explained in a voice swelled with pride: "That's Mom's theme song!"

Minnie Munn as a mermaid was a picture hard to contemplate without mirth. Minnie looked fully two yards in girth. She was dangerously unsteady on her feet. Her gait reminded O. W. of a sailboat in a storm. She, too, had a polished look, as if she'd just taken a bath and put on a clean gingham dress. When she came nearer O. W. saw merry blue eyes sunk in fat cheeks and a wide, good-natured mouth.

As the detective watched the perilous progress of Minnie Munn from the kitchen door to the cashier's roost, suddenly a noise like a fog horn escaped her lips.

"Hey there, Coonskin Coats, soft pedal!"

Her notice of the students immediately brought results.

"Gosh, fellows, we got into a morgue by mistake!"

"'Smatter Minnie? Trouble in the corn belt again?"

"Shut up!" bellowed Minnie.

"Why?" came an aggrieved chorus.

"Might know anybody as fresh as you boys'd be green!" retorted Minnie. "I got company, that's why."

They might not have been so shamefaced had not one of
Minnie's callers been so lovely. With the cheerful two-fin-
gered salute at Minnie they had learned from one of Gary
Cooper's pictures the students subsided into good manners.

Minnie Munn then bestowed her attention upon her
visitors. Her look of inquiry, moving from O. W. to
Chiquita, developed into open-mouthed amazement.

"Laws! If it ain't Mrs. Dwight!"

"You remember me?"

"Guess I couldn't forget you!"

Chiquita flushed. "Not after the way I once treated
you."

"I mean I keep seeing your picture in the rotogravure
sections, Mrs. Dwight."

"I cut that one of you with the horse out," announced
Pink Gingham solemnly. "It was so beautiful."

Chiquita turned to the child. "You mean the horse was
so beautiful?" Her voice was tremulous.

Pink Gingham giggled in embarrassment.

Mom's plump hand went out with a needless but loving
gesture to smooth back her daughter's straw-colored hair.

"Nellie didn't mean the horse." She said to the child:
"Think you can look after things while I take Mrs. Dwight
and the gentleman into the little room?"

"Sure, Mom!" Strange, thought Mr. Wimble, what a
couple of smiles between mother and child can do to two
plain faces.

"We're not interrupting anything?" asked Chiquita.

"No," replied Minnie cheerfully. "I just put some
doughnuts into the grease. My helper can take 'em out.
I got a cook now, you know. The business got too big for
just me alone. But I usually mix up a batch of something
for the boys and girls myself. Mostly college kids away
from home eat here." She laughed self-consciously. "They
tell me nobody's doughnuts can come up to mine!"

The detective said: "I thought something smelled mighty good when you opened that kitchen door."

"I've just remembered," smiled Chiquita, "that I didn't eat much breakfast this morning."

"You wouldn't say Mrs. Dwight was hinting, would you, Mrs. Munn?" chuckled the detective.

"What about yourself?" playfully countered Chiquita.

"Nellie'll bring you a plateful of them doughnuts soon as they're done," declared Minnie heartily.

As Minnie waddled in advance of them, O. W. whispered to Chiquita: "Believe I'll wait out here to remind Nellie of those doughnuts."

"Nothing of the kind!" Chiquita linked her arm in his. "I wish you to come along." It warmed the detective's heart to think she wanted him.

When they had reached the small room adjacent to the main dining room reserved for private parties, Minnie sank into a chair like a loosely packed sack of meal. Seated, folds of fat settling at the base of her neck and above and below her corsets, Minnie resembled a stack of balloon tires.

"Sit down, Mrs. Dwight. Have a seat, Mr.—"

"Wimble." The name conveyed nothing to Minnie.

"Laws! My dogs!" she groaned. "I been on my feet more'n usual the past few days." She broke off with a quick apologetic glance at Chiquita. The detective learned subsequently that, because Minnie had visited the jail so often to look after Dwight, he was teased by the other inmates about his "nurse".

"Why don't you slip out of your shoes, Mrs. Munn?" suggested O. W.

"I got a pair of carpet slippers in that cupboard over there," replied Minnie eagerly. "To tell the truth, when my dogs get too bad I come in here and slip 'em on."

"Believe in being kind to animals, I see," remarked the detective as he brought out the slippers.

A rumble of good-natured laughter shook the plump person of Minnie Munn. "Ain't you a card!"

"Feel like the deuce lots of times," agreed Mr. Wimble. Covertly eying Chiquita he was gratified to observe that she was smiling. Strange how her white, clouded face bothered him!

"Careful of that left one!" admonished Minnie anxiously, as the detective helped her into her slippers.

"You know your bunions all right, don't you, Mrs. Munn?"

Minnie acknowledged the detective's buffoonery by a hearty roar. "Laws! I ain't laughed so much since I heard that Mr. Dwight—" Again her small eyes darted an apologetic glance toward Chiquita.

Chiquita said: "That's all right, Mrs. Munn. I came here to speak of John."

Minnie's round face became wreathed in smiles. "You got him to agree to Bill's plan! I just knew if anybody could do it you could! Well, when do we start?"

Apparently Chiquita dreaded administering the truth. She appealed to the detective. "You tell her!"

Mr. Wimble said kindly: "You know, Mrs. Munn, that Mr. Dwight would be the last person on earth to allow even his wife to persuade him to do something he considered wrong."

"But what's wrong with our plan?"

"Mr. Dwight doesn't want to get his friends into trouble. Haven't you ever heard of accessories after the fact?"

"Sure I have! Mr. Dwight explained all about that to me and Bill down to the jail. But that's when a man's guilty. You see, Mr. Wimble," she said simply, "Mr. Dwight didn't commit that murder."

Beauty assumes many guises. Never to Mr. Wimble had Beauty been more apparent than when this plump, illiterate restaurant keeper expressed her faith in her benefactor.

"Mr. Dwight won't agree to your plan, Mrs. Munn," he said.

Silence followed the detective's words. Minnie finally broke it with a stentorian sigh. "And me and Bill had it down so slick, too! Even practiced picking the lock of my safe when the restaurant was full so's we could open the jail door without getting caught. I didn't know before that Bill was so handy. I told him that for a mechanic he was a pretty good burglar. Of course men know all about machinery. I remember my Clarence; every time one of the kids'd bust a whistle or something my husband could always fix it, good as new."

Minnie suddenly looked old and tired. "Might know John Dwight'd act like that!"

She turned to Chiquita. "Remember the night I sent for your husband, Mrs. Dwight? The night little Willie had croup and I was scared he'd choke to death?" The detective read much in Chiquita's bowed head. "Right after the worst coughing spell he'd had Willie whispered: 'I want that man God created in His own image!' You see, I read to the kids every night out of the Bible. At first the part about God creating man in His own image puzzled Willie. Then, after I got acquainted with Mr. Dwight, all of a sudden Willie stopped asking me what it meant. I didn't know how he'd figured it out in his little head till that night."

Chiquita's lovely white fingers were pressed against her face. A moan came from behind them.

"Oh, you poor lamb!" Minnie turned fiercely on Mr. Wimble. "Why didn't you stop me?" Seeing that Minnie wished to leave her chair, O. W. assisted her to her feet.

This arduous task performed, Mrs. Munn lumbered over to Chiquita. "There, there, lambie!" she crooned.

At this juncture O. W. stepped to the door to receive the plateful of fresh doughnuts Nellie had sent by one of the waitresses. He later assured Minnie that he had smelled the doughnuts the minute they had left the kitchen. Be that as it may, they had arrived and their coming filled an unhappy gap.

Minnie took a doughnut from the plate. "Here, lambie," she said to Chiquita, "eat this and you'll feel better." Chiquita obeyed as meekly as if she were Willie.

"It's good!" she smiled.

"Just like Mother used to make!" recited O. W., and remembered Dolly's gibe: "Like Mother used to make indeed! It's only that everything tasted so much better to you when you were a boy!"

Chiquita covered Minnie's plump paw with her own white fingers. "Mrs. Munn, I told Mr. Smith I was coming here this morning to thank you for your offer to help my husband, but I think the real reason I came—" Suddenly she was shy. "Mr. Dwight asked me please not to visit him at the prison. He couldn't bear for me to see him. You've been there. Mrs. Munn," she whispered, "how does John look? He is all right?"

"Why, you poor little lamb! Of course he's all right." She said not without pride: "If you could've seen him getting away with the apple pie I took him you'd say he was all right! Now, lambie," she said cheerily, "you mustn't worry one bit. In the first place, John Dwight never killed no man!"

"He said he did." It came out rather raggedly.

"Laws! That ain't no sign. Take me, for instance. Once I said a common woman like me couldn't touch Mrs. John Dwight with a ten-foot pole, and now look!" She broke off a particle of doughnut and stuffed it into Chiquita's mouth. "I've actually got you eating out of my hand!"

27

When Chiquita invited Mr. Wimble to return to her home for luncheon he accepted for two reasons: first, because he was in the process of solving the Gary Gilbert murder mystery; and, second, because he was interested in Chiquita Dwight.

All the way home in the car they had hired at Bill Smith's garage the detective found Chiquita entirely out of character. Instead of the cold, reserved young woman she was reputed to be, Chiquita had become a chattering schoolgirl. Being a true Californian her conversation was chiefly geographical.

". . . And these hills at Christmas time, Mr. Wimble! You ought to see them! Veritable fairy-land, then. All these trees in the gardens are decorated. Imagine that, you Easterner, with your ice-bound Christmases! Such lovely decorations, too! Colored lights playing on branches strung with silver balls, trees strewn with artificial snow—all so charming! It's a marvelous show, really. People come from miles away to see it. There's a steady stream of automobiles climbing the hills all night long like a mighty caravan. . . ."

Katie was hovering near the front door when they returned. Chiquita divested herself of her wraps in the entrance hall, running her palms over her glistening black hair without glancing in the mirror.

A cough from Katie halted Chiquita as she was preceding Mr. Wimble into the drawing-room.

"Beg pardon, Mrs. Dwight! Did Mr. Smith's plan work?"

"No, Katie."

Katie turned away with quivering lips. Suddenly she spun around. "I can't *bear* this house with Mr. Dwight gone!" she cried. "It's *dreadful!* Nobody singing in the bathtub any more. Nobody calling me 'Little Buttercup' or 'K-K-K-Katie by the c-cowshed'. And this morning I caught Parker crying." The girl burst into tears. "Working in a place where the butler goes around crying like a baby! It's *horrible!*"

Chiquita put her arm about the sobbing girl. "Katie, dear, you're making it hard for me. Do you think Mr. Dwight would like you to do that?"

"No; he'd *kill* me if—" Chiquita's convulsive shudder stilled the girl's weeping. "Oh!" she gasped.

"I understand, Katie. That just slipped out, like saying of a blind person: 'He'll be glad to *see* you.' You meant that Mr. Dwight wouldn't like it at all if you made it hard for me. So be a good girl now and go see that the table is properly set. We have a luncheon guest."

"All right, Mrs. Dwight." She lingered a moment. "You been just wonderful lately, Mrs. Dwight! All of us appreciate it, ma'am. We was talking about it this morning. Parker said sometimes it takes a terrific jolt for a person to get on to their self." Another gasp escaped her. "Gee whiz! I better get going before I say anything else!"

"Poor child!" thought O. W. "She ought to wear a gag." But he felt that he had learned considerable from Katie's lack of tact.

When Katie had gone off Chiquita braced herself, as if crossing the threshold into the drawing-room required special effort. For once O. W. was in a mood to advocate the use of rouge; Chiquita's face was like marble.

In the drawing room Chiquita stood leaning against the mantelpiece. On it among other choice bits was a photograph of herself in a beautiful hand-carved bronze frame.

"Do you suppose Nellie would like this photograph?" she asked the detective. "It's the original of the one with the horse."

Mr. Wimble felt a tightening in his throat. "She'd dote on it!"

"I believe I'll send it to the child. We bought the frame in France on our honeymoon. John picked it but in the cunningest little shop." The ghost of a smile tiptoed across her lips. "John speaks the most atrocious French. He couldn't make the shopkeeper understand what he wanted. I wouldn't help him out until the bewildered little proprietor almost had a shaving mug wrapped up. Nellie will like the little cherubs on the frame, won't she?"

"Mrs. Dwight!" An agitated Katie trembled in the doorway. "The butcher's here!"

Chiquita's glance at the detective seemed to say: "Having one's husband in jail on a murder charge does confuse things at home!"

"But Katie, Cook orders the meat, you know!"

"It's Mr. Jenkins, ma'am."

Chiquita was puzzled. Apparently she was not in the habit of calling her tradesmen by name.

"He says it's a matter of life and death, ma'am," announced Katie portentously.

The name of Jenkins meant something to the detective, whose mind always pigeonholed isolated bits of information later to be brought out on such occasions as this.

"Isn't Jenkins the sick man your husband was visiting the night of Miss Allen's dance?"

"Oh, yes! How brutal of me not to be carrying on now that John's— Please show Mr. Jenkins in here at once, Katie." The girl fairly flew. Manifestly Katie was impressed by matters of life and death.

Death seemed imminent as Butcher Timothy Jenkins staggered into the room. O. W. sprang to the man's assistance, leading him to a chair which Chiquita made comfortable with some pillows. Jenkins leaned back luxuriously, only then permitting himself an appraisal of the room's occupants.

"Mr. Jenkins!" scolded Chiquita. "Whatever did you come out for? You're ill!"

"I'm a very sick man," he agreed importantly.

Jenkins was a sparely built little fellow in the late fifties, thin of hair, pale of eye, weak of mouth. His choice of a calling was one of those tricks Fate sometimes plays on mortals. Jenkins was the sort of little man one sees distributing handbills and new telephone directories. He didn't look as if he had the strength even to slice bacon, let alone sever legs from rumps. And at present he looked exceedingly ill. His clothes hung to mere skin and bones. His face was gray. Perspiration beaded his forehead. His hands shook.

He fixed his pallid gaze on Mr. Wimble. "You the detective on the murder case?" Mr. Wimble nodded. "I went to Miss Allen's; she said you was here."

"Why did you wish to see me?"

Jenkins cleared his throat. When the room was absolutely still he said: "I came to tell you that I committed the murder."

Jenkins' body jerked spasmodically when Katie screamed. Succumbing to curiosity, after helping the butcher into the room the girl had remained in the background to hear what Jenkins had to say. Chiquita acted as if she had not heard the scream. She made no move to dismiss Katie, in fact did not turn her head from her steady contemplation of the butcher.

Breathlessly Jenkins elaborated his confession. "You see, the papers gave out it was Mr. Dwight dressed up like a butcher threatening Gilbert Gary's life. Well, the papers made a mistake. It was me done it. I'm a butcher."

Mr. Wimble said quietly: "The victim's name was Gary Gilbert, Mr. Jenkins."

A feverish flush mounted Jenkins' thin cheeks. "A sick man's tongue's liable to slip," he said sullenly.

"What was your motive for the crime?"

For a moment Jenkins looked startled. "I—I don't care to tell," he said finally. He added, and his voice bore a triumphant ring: "It was brooding over the wrong Mr. Gar— Mr. Gilbert done me that brought on my sickness."

"Your brooding came to a head Saturday night?"

"Yes, sir. Mr. Dwight had been sitting with me. It was him borrowing some of my togs to wear to her masquerade party that put the idea in my head of going to Miss Allen's house in my shop clothes. I thought if anyone saw me I could say I was one of the guests. It was a plumb easy scheme to carry out. I got into the grounds without nobody seeing me. I crept up the library stairs and into the room without Mr. Gilbert even turning around."

Mr. Wimble asked abruptly: "After you had stabbed Mr. Gilbert in the back, which way did he fall?"

Alarm flickered in the butcher's pale eyes; almost immediately however his assurance returned. "Bless us, man, I didn't hang around to see! I made tracks for the front gate."

O. W. said dryly: "I hope, Mr. Jenkins, that you are a better butcher than you are a liar."

"What's that?" bleated the butcher in a vain attempt to uphold the veracity of his confession.

"Mr. Gilbert was not stabbed in the back, Mr. Jenkins."

The little man's frail body seemed to shrink. Then his pale eyes eagerly sought the detective's. "I was afraid my story wouldn't hold water, sir; that's why I come to you instead of going direct to the police." A smile did the best it could to light up his sick face. "You could coach me, Mr. Wimble."

He chuckled. "Mr. Dwight said to me only last Saturday afternoon when he was sitting with me: 'I'm going to save your life, Timothy Jenkins, if I hang for it!'" The butcher's eyes shone with affection for the young man. "Seems now like the shoe's on the other foot."

Chiquita smiled down at the little man. "Mr. Jenkins, how—can I thank you?"

"You mustn't thank me. I'm not giving away nothing I can use. Why, bless us, Mrs. Dwight!" His pale eyes lit up. "I'm only moving to the Hereafter a few weeks earlier than they're expecting me."

"You're going right upstairs and lie down," declared Chiquita briskly. "That's where you're going. And I intend sending for Dr. Bruce. No more talk about dying—either in bed or on the gallows!"

The butcher attempted to arise, only to fall back dizzily among the cushions, where he lay with closed eyes.

Chiquita spied Katie. "Please call Parker, Katie, to help you get Mr. Jenkins upstairs." Dismally Katie obeyed.

When he felt the strong arms of the butler and the maid lifting him Jenkins opened his eyes. Katie did not veil her contempt. A fine hero to meet his Waterloo in a nest of comfortable cushions! Puzzled at first by her unmistakable scorn, Jenkins suddenly recalled the purpose of his call. Everyone in the room felt the small man's dignity as he spoke.

"Having your doctor here, Mrs. Dwight, will accomplish only one thing; he'll tell you I'm a dying man. You more than any of us must realize what a good man your husband is, how badly needed he is by such unfortunates as me. Say he did kill this Gilbert. All of us makes mistakes at some time or other. Mr. Dwight must have been hard put to it or he wouldn't have done it. I'm sure of that."

Jenkins switched his plea to the detective. "Mr. Wimble, you couldn't've been with Mr. Dwight five minutes without learning what a fine young feller he is. You're a successful man, Mr. Wimble. I been reading about you. One small failure won't hurt your reputation none. If you can't bring yourself to the deceit, withdraw from the case. The police will swallow my lie all right."

A sorrowing smile on her lips, Chiquita looked at O. W. Katie sensed complications. Her appreciation of a servant's position in a household, tottering since Dwight's confession, fell and was shattered as she added her plea to Jenkins'.

"Please, Mrs. Dwight, ma'am, you can always find another butcher. Cook says the new one's just as good as Mr. Jenkins, every bit! But where could you find a second Mr. Dwight, ma'am?"

Everybody in the room was watching Chiquita. They heard her draw in her breath sharply; then saw the convent-raised girl make a sign of the cross. When she spoke her voice was low and sweet; but the effect was of a royal person giving orders of the gravest consequence.

"Katie and Parker, I want you please to carry Mr. Jenkins upstairs to one of the guest rooms. I'll telephone for Dr. Bruce myself."

Silently Katie and Parker made a chair with their hands, upon which Jenkins seated himself. Disappointment was the facial expression of all three.

At the doorway Jenkins twisted his thin neck to look back at Chiquita and the detective.

"I sure made a hell of a mess trying to play God!" he said bitterly in acknowledgment of his defeat.

When they were alone O. W. chuckled: "I have a feeling that Jenkins won't be able to die any better than he can lie. Ten to one Dr. Bruce suggests you give him a job in the garden. He looks to me as if a few weeks of outdoor work would make him fit as a fiddle."

As if she hadn't heard him Chiquita said quietly: "You've known all along that it was I who killed Gary Gilbert."

28

"Mr. Wimble," said Chiquita, "I don't know exactly why your good opinion of me means so much but it does. I should have spoken before. I've been waiting for some miracle to happen, I think." She clasped her hands in the intensity of her feeling. "I want you to believe me when I tell you that, cowardly as I've been, I wouldn't have allowed John to pay for my crime."

"I'm sure of that, Mrs. Dwight. That's why I didn't force your confession."

The girl's beautiful hand sought the detective's in a gentle pressure. "I thank you."

She got up and paced back and forth, as suddenly sitting down again. When she spoke there was a little catch in her voice. "Oh, I've been cruel to him!" She asked pleadingly: "May I tell you about it—before we go?"

"Of course, child!" O. W. felt extraordinarily disturbed. Chiquita seemed so pathetically young!

"Not long ago there was a Horse Show in Oakland. You must have read of the tragedy—the fire that broke out in the stables. My husband lost five gorgeous animals, and one of his men—Martin—was burned to death. When I heard of the tragedy I said: 'Oh! Those beautiful horses!' I thought only of their beauty, their value. John said: 'Poor stupid beasts, running straight for the flames!' I hadn't given a thought to Martin and John—Dumpling—I'm not used to calling him that—didn't remind me.

"One night soon afterward at dinner I noticed that Dumpling looked ill. I asked him what the trouble was. He told me that he had been to Martin's funeral. I didn't know whom he meant. 'Another of your charities?' My manner was so heartless! He told me who Martin was; then I recalled the man. I remember the day Martin came shuffling through our back gate, looking like an animated scarecrow. He went to the kitchen door begging for food. Later John—Dumpling told me that he had hired Martin to look after King, his favorite mount. I thought he was mad—told him so—to trust King with a tramp. 'You ought to have seen Martin's eyes when he looked at King,' Dumpling said. 'And the way he touched the animal—why, there was something godlike about Martin then, Chickie!'"

Her voice faltered. "Chickie's John's pet name for me. I'd never let him call me that. It slipped out sometimes. It's—sweet, isn't it?

"Of course I sneered at Dumpling's sentimentality. He insisted that if Martin's chance ever came to make good he wouldn't fail. I stubbornly insisted that a real man created his own chance to make good.

"Well, when the fire came Martin stuck by King." She covered her face with her lovely hands. "They found Martin's poor charred body beside King's, the scorched halter in his hand.

"When Dumpling told me he had attended Martin's funeral, a wave of shame swept over me. I had been to a bridge tea. I hated myself and my hate made me cruel. I arose from the table. 'I'm not hungry,' I said; 'I had a big tea. I'm going into the music room and try that new song Marcia brought over.' I knew how Dumpling looked forward to dining with me. He smiled. 'Fine!' he said. 'I like music with my meals.' And he kept smiling till I'd left the room. But I'd forgotten my vanity bag and turned back to get it. Dumpling was sitting there—so quietly—his head buried in his arms—I could just feel his despair—

Mr. Wimble said gently: "You were in love with him then."

Chiquita nodded. "I didn't know it then." O. W. had to force himself not to look away from the pain in her eyes.

"Dumpling came to my room Saturday afternoon just after I had finished dressing for Marcia's. I was Diana. My costume was lovely. It was the short-skirted hunting dress of the classic myth, of shimmery white material, and I wore a diamond crescent in my hair. I carried a quiver I had woven of grasses and the jeweled arrow Dumpling had bought for me in Athens.

"When my husband saw me—well, you've seen the sun suddenly burst forth from behind a cloud. His eyes were so full of admiration and pride and reverence you'd have thought I was a real goddess.

"But there was another look in his eyes. The look of the lover. I recognized it—and all at once I was no longer the virgin Diana, Goddess of Chastity, but a woman! For the first time a woman thrilling to the look in her lover's eyes.

"But I didn't trust this new order of things. For so long I had considered myself a nun, had made a fetish of keeping my body inviolate." She said with a low moan of despair: "Oh, Mr. Wimble, how can I hope to make you understand?"

O. W. replied gently: "The Mother Superior at the Little Convent of the Flowers has told me something of your childhood."

Chiquita went on: "Dumpling said: 'Oh, how beautiful you are, Chickie! Your skin is as white and smooth as magnolia petals.' And I laughed at him! Laughed!" A sob broke her voice. "Dumpling will forgive me for that but God never will! 'A fine rehearsal, John,' I said 'Let's not forget to act this scene at Marcia's tonight. I'm sure it will make a great hit!'" She whispered brokenly: "He smiled—but the look in his eyes—

"I was a mad thing that night at Marcia's. You'd have thought flirting with Gary Gilbert was a penance I must do for having fallen in love with my husband. What happened was my fault, not Gary's. When we met he said: 'Another arrival from Olympus!' He was dressed as Apollo. 'Greetings, silver-footed Queen!' He was merely being polite. You can't imagine how astonished he was when I retorted: 'Greetings, Little 'Pollo! How's the Pride of Parnassus?' The others were equally astounded. 'My God!' ejaculated Hugh. 'No; *my* god!' I cried. Marcia reminded us that Apollo and Diana were brother and sister. 'Oh, don't tell me I have to be a sister to this beautiful creature!' I protested. 'Careful!' warned Marcia. 'Apollo was also the God of Pestilence!' I have thought of it since; it was like a warning.

"When Dumpling came and saw what was going on he did the only thing he could do. He made a joke out of it. He played the clown, rushing around with his butcher knife, threatening to kill his rival. But he was suffering. Being a past master in the art of making Dumpling suffer, I knew. But Marcia guessed. She dragged him away finally. Hugh and Kitten were probably disgusted; they went for a walk. That left Gary and me alone. I dare say Gary Gilbert always managed sooner or later to get his women alone. It was amazing how quickly he had the French windows closed, the door leading into the hall locked, the lights dimmed." She paused, reconstructing the circumstances in her mind. "It will be difficult for me to tell what followed, it happened so quickly.

"'You play your part excellently, dear Diana,' said Gary. A new note had come into his voice but I didn't recognize it as a danger signal. You see, Dumpling's consistent kindness, his gentleness, his—restraint, had almost obliterated that beastly memory of my childhood. 'In what way?' I asked. 'Goddess of the Chase, you've bagged your quarry. I am yours, fair Diana!' But before the significance of that remark reached my brain he'd touched on another subject, 'And now, my sweet Goddess, let's sup!' 'Sup,' I stupidly repeated; 'after that Lucullan feast of Marcia's?' 'Must I remind you, adorable Diana, that gods and goddesses sup on nectar and ambrosia?'

"We were standing by the table. I had been toying with my arrow. He took it out of my hand, placed it on the table. If only I had taken to flight like the mythical Diana I could have outdistanced him. But I stood there rooted to the spot, fascinated like a bird gazing into the eyes of a reptile.

"Then he had me in his arms. His mouth closed down on mine. His lips were like the trail of a snail. 'That's the nectar,' he murmured. His hands slid over my body. 'And now, Diana darling, for the ambrosia!'

"'Your actions do not surprise me,' I said. 'According to the mythologies Diana was attended by a hound.' I don't know how I managed to speak so calmly in the face of my white-heat frenzy. Gary laughed thickly; his eyes were a little blood-shot. I could see it was his intention to pick me up, to carry me across the room. My hand gripping the table for support had already fallen on my weapon. As Gary came toward me I stabbed him through the heart."

Mr. Wimble shook her by the shoulders; she seemed dazed. "You must go on, Mrs. Dwight. What followed?"

"It seemed an eternity that I stood there looking down on his dead body. Then, as a feeling of suffocation took hold of me, instinctively I moved toward the windows. I stood pressed against them, stupidly, as they were shut and no air was coming in.

"I felt myself being pushed backward. Somebody was trying to open the windows from the outside, I saw that it was Kelly, our chauffeur. Happening to be passing he had seen what had happened. Gary had not drawn the curtains.

"Kelly was very kind. He said I must get into the car immediately, explained where it was. 'I will do what I can to cover your trail, Mrs. Dwight,' he said. 'In return you must promise to maintain absolute silence.' 'I must tell John,' I said. 'Tell your husband that you have killed Gary Gilbert; nothing more. Your safety depends on complete silence, Mrs. Dwight.' Dully I promised not to talk.

"On my way to the car I met Dumpling. I told him I had killed Gary Gilbert. In the light from the house I could see him staring at me as if he suspected me of having lost my senses. But something in my face frightened him. 'Wait here!' he said and ran toward the library. I knew he hadn't believed me, was going to find out for himself. In a few minutes he returned. He had seen that Gary was dead. 'He—touched me!' I said. Dumpling put his arm about me, led me to the car. 'You had to do it, Chiquita,' he said. 'There was no other way.' He thought of my safety. 'Did anyone see you leave the library?' I remembered my promise to Kelly. 'No,' I said. Then Dumpling, too, hammered into my brain the necessity for silence.

"We had just reached the car when Kelly came."

O. W. interpolated a question: "From what direction did Kelly come?"

Chiquita made an effort to recall this detail in the events of that night of chilling terror.

"From the pond, I think. Dumpling told him I had a headache and wanted to be driven home. He put me in the front seat with Kelly. No doubt he feared I would faint."

"Did you and Kelly carry on any conversation on the way home?"

Chiquita smiled slightly. "It was more like a mono-logue than a conversation. Kelly kept talking the whole way home, but I couldn't tell you just what it was he said. I remember he repeated over and over again that I must not talk. Or read the papers. In fact all that night those two injunctions racked my brain with the insistency of a popular song: 'Don't talk! Don't read the papers!'

"I had no desire to do either. All I wanted was to forget that hideous night. Dumpling helped me. He wouldn't al-low a newspaper in the house, warned the servants against mentioning the crime, refused to discuss it himself. I hadn't the least idea Dumpling was being suspected."

A sob tore at her throat. "Well, the miracle didn't hap-pen. I'm ready to go now."

She seemed so childlike that unconsciously the detec-tive addressed her by her first name. "Chiquita, come here!" Unquestioningly she obeyed.

"Child, the miracle did happen!"

Chiquita smiled wistfully. This kindly old gentleman was referring of course to the redemption of her soul. Chiquita had learned of such matters at the Convent. But the miracle she had been praying for was a marvelous something that would reunite her with Dumpling.

She listened tolerantly while the detective spoke.

"You stabbed Gary Gilbert with your jeweled arrow?" As Chiquita nodded he asked: "Don't you think it rather miraculous for a jeweled arrow to be transformed into a butcher knife?"

Chiquita stared at the detective breathlessly.

"Gary Gilbert died from a wound inflicted by a butcher knife, Chiquita, not a jeweled arrow."

For a moment joy and relief fought for Chiquita's facial expression. Suddenly both fled as fear for John Dwight twisted her lovely features into a distorted mask.

As Chiquita swayed, "No, not that!" cried the detective sharply, inwardly cursing himself for a blunt fool. "I'm still working on the case, child. Don't you understand?"

As realization came to her, for the first time during the miserable days since the murder, Chiquita found relief in tears.

And then—neither Chiquita nor Mr. Wimble knew just how it came to pass—a charming thing happened.

Chiquita afterwards explained it by saying that if she could choose a dad for herself she'd take O. W. without reservations. As for the detective, it came to him all at once that if Dolly had accepted him he might have had a daughter Chiquita's age. At any rate, it happened; and it was a gesture so full of grace and charm that when the detective later told Corey what had occurred he found it necessary to explain to his young assistant as he used his handkerchief that he guessed he must be taking cold.

Katie was the only eye witness.

"I almost dropped dead!" she said in telling Parker of it, "I went into the drawing-room and there was Mrs. Dwight curled up on that detective's lap like a kid, him rocking her."

29

It was the evening of the seventh day of the investigation. But a few hours remained during which O. W. must announce the name of the murderer of Gary Gilbert or forfeit his pseudonym of One-Week Wimble. The detective was in the library awaiting a caller. It had been a busy day and he was tired. He realized that his sister Portia had been right in insisting that he employ an assistant. Not that young Webb had hurt himself by overwork on this case. The lad had been willing enough but his alarming likeness to the murdered man had made it dangerous having him around. Dangerous to himself and dangerous to the investigation.

The boy had expressed his dissatisfaction with the way he had assisted his chief.

"Afraid I haven't been much help this time, sir."

With a smile the detective recalled his reply. "You've helped more than you know, son; if you'd lost Janet I'd have been so cut up I'd have lost the case."

God bless those kids! They'd gone off that morning to get the ring. Janet had come up to the house later to show it to him, her face bright as a new tin pan. The youngster was justified in her pride; Corey had done handsomely by his fiancée. A gorgeous stone it was, a square diamond set in carved platinum.

Corey's chief aid to the investigation was to be given later in the evening. If O. W.'s opinion counted for anything the lad's services were going to prove invaluable.

While waiting for his caller, O. W. went over his longhand version of the cablegram in code he had received from Paris that afternoon.

Marcia had brought him the cable. Though pale, the girl's face had lost its look of suffering.

"You don't seem to mind it much that Dwight's in jail," O. W. teased.

"I'd hate to tell you what I thought about you when I got the news! My brain would have been a good model for a 'Wonder What a Murderer of Private Detectives Thinks About' cartoon. It was only when Wing quoted you as saying that you were still on the case that I came to."

Seriousness aged her voice. "I came to in more ways than one. I used to think I'd rather have Dumpling dead than not have him for myself. I've changed my mind. He's always been dead to me as a lover and—well— somehow the future didn't seem so sweet to me when I pictured going through life without Dumpling for a friend."

Her voice grew tenderly mocking. "How much richer in wisecracks Dumpling'll be after his prison experience! I can just hear his gags! I'm willing to bet he'll refer to himself from now on as 'the jailbird'." She brushed the back of her hand across her eyes. "And of course the first thing he'll do when he gets out will be to supply the prisoners with radio sets and eider-down quilts,"

"Do you know, Miss Allen," said O. W. gravely, "if John Dwight had been guilty I think I'd have been tempted to give up the detective business."

Marcia fixed solemn eyes on the detective. "I haven't much of a flair for pretty speeches, Mr. Wimble, but what I think of you—well, don't be surprised if some day you get a telegram from me reading something like this:

'What does the O stand for? I need the information for the christening of my first son.'"

The detective was touched but appreciating Marcia's aversion to demonstrativeness he lightly countered: "Even if it stands for Oscar?" But the affection in his voice thanked Marcia for the compliment.

"Well, the boy'd probably rise up in righteous wrath some day but—yes, even if it stands for Oscar!"

Marcia had left the library laughing out loud for the first time since the murder.

At about half-past seven Corey Webb reported to his chief for instructions. As the detective looked at his assistant he thought again how handsome the boy was. And again he asked himself if the role he had chosen for Corey to play that night were exposing him to too great danger.

"I think you'd better carry a gun, son," he said suddenly.

Corey laughed. "In just which pocket, sir?"

The detective grinned. "I'll hold the gun myself! Better get along now. Miss Allen is waiting for you upstairs in her private sitting room."

Shortly before eight o'clock Rosie announced Kelly. He entered the library from the hall. The French windows were closed, the curtains drawn. As before, Mr. Wimble was sitting at the desk. A small lamp on this desk was the only one turned on. So except those within the brief radius of light from this lamp the objects in the room were blurred, lacking in detail.

"Come in, Kelly. Sit down."

"You said you might need me again." Courtesy was the keynote of the chauffeur's manner.

For the next few moments the detective was busy shuffling papers on the desk. Kelly could not help noticing that some of these papers were cablegrams, He stirred uneasily.

It was the chauffeur who finally broke the silence. "Bet you were surprised when Dwight gave himself up." O. W.

observed the lack of any prefix. Apparently in Kelly's mind self-confessed murderers did not warrant respect.

"Not particularly. You see, as a rule murderers don't confess unless in a tight corner."

Kelly smiled in acknowledgment of the detective's vanity. "I didn't mean to belittle your efforts, Mr. Wimble. I'm glad Dwight confessed within a week of your taking the case, sir," he added significantly.

O. W. said: "I had no idea you took such an interest in me."

"I admire you exceedingly!" The man's tone was undeniably hearty.

"Blarney!"

"Blarney?"

"Surely an Irishman knows that 'blarney' means flattery!"

Kelly flushed. "I understand that Chinamen—in China —have never heard of chop suey."

Mr. Wimble now gave the chauffeur his full attention. "Kelly, an important dictum in the detective profession is: Keep your own counsel! With no one else's finger in his professional pie a detective is far more apt to find the plum when he is ready to put in his thumb and pull it out. I dare say criminals find that a wise admonition also. However there comes a time when it is politic to break rules. I'm going to do quite a little talking for your benefit tonight. I think if you're wise you'll follow suit."

"You mean to infer—"

"It's not my custom at the eleventh hour of an investigation to indulge in inference," returned O. W. coldly. "From now on, Kelly, I'd like you to understand that for every statement I advance I am able to produce proof."

The chauffeur looked interested but not alarmed. The detective led off.

"As you have already testified, Kelly, on Saturday evening you were playing cards with Michael at his cottage. Although in an endeavor to make it appear that Chiquita Dwight had quit Miss Allen's party early you told me you had left the gardener's cottage between six-thirty and seven to see to your lights, the testimony of Blanche and Michael fix your departure at eight, at which hour the medical examiners have timed the murder of Gary Gilbert.

"Strolling past Miss Allen's library, you heard a woman cry out, through the windows caught sight of Chiquita Dwight struggling in the arms of Gary Gilbert. You sprang up the stairs and into the room." The detective noted with gratification that the chauffeur's finger-nails were digging into the upholstery of his chair.

Mr. Wimble observed stingingly: "I don't imagine your feeling toward Gilbert as you plunged into this room Saturday evening was a sentiment one would find on a friendship-card!"

Steel whets steel. Kelly's voice was caustic as he said: "I understood you had proofs to back up your insinuations."

"Mrs. Dwight has confessed to the murder of Gary Gilbert."

The scar on Kelly's face grew livid as he paled. "She can't have!"

"Your doubt does me little credit as a detective," remarked O. W. blandly. "Did you imagine that the welter of lies and evasions of your former testimony would blind me to the truth?"

"In my country a man does not hesitate to abandon the truth when a lady's reputation is at stake," said Kelly with a feeble attempt at dignity.

"I've always understood that Italians are known for chivalry." Kelly attempted no refutation of this implication; perhaps he felt that he needed his wits for accusations of more urgent consequence.

"Suppose Mrs. Dwight did confess," he demanded. "Women have lied to save their husbands before this."

"You were seen leaving the library Saturday night by two witnesses," continued Mr. Wimble wearily. "One of these was Roberta Allen. She was hiding in the bushes as you came down the steps. She called your name. Apparently you mistook her voice for Chiquita Dwight's. You ordered her to get into the car, which she did. She was hiding in the tonneau when you drove Mrs. Dwight home. She overheard you warning Mrs. Dwight not to talk, to avoid the newspapers."

These disclosures apparently in no way shattered the man's feeling of security.

An inscrutable expression on his face, Kelly said: "My one emotion upon rushing into this room on Saturday evening was hope that I'd be on time to save Mrs. Dwight from harm."

"A fit theme for a bedtime story," observed O. W. with astringent irony, "but for its palpable untruth!"

He took up the thread of the interview: "But before you could reach the pair you saw Mrs. Dwight stab Gary Gilbert."

Kelly gave a typically Latin shrug that said: "Sad but true!"

"You impressed on Mrs. Dwight the importance of holding her tongue," Mr. Wimble continued. "You then sent her to the car while you—"

During this last Kelly had been watching Mr. Wimble intently as if for a clue, but all he could learn was that the detective was in turn watching him.

As O. W. paused the chauffeur put in swiftly: "Would you like me to tell you what next happened?"

"I know!" replied Mr. Wimble briefly.

The chauffeur moistened his lips several times while waiting for the detective to continue. Perhaps never before had his emotions thus been raked over the coals.

"The first thing you did was to remove Mrs. Dwight's arrow from Gilbert's body and wrap it in a piece of paper you found in your pocket. That piece of paper happened to be a telegram recently sent you by Marcia Allen's sister. It was later found and the blood stain-tested, as was that on the tip of the arrow. The telegram fell into the pansy bed as you flung the arrow to the roof of the summer-house. No doubt your original intention was to throw the arrow into the pond. Did Mrs. Wells' voice spoil your aim or did you imagine that the rose vines would break the sound of the arrow falling on the summer-house roof? Too bad Mrs. Wells happened to be there! The water of the pond might have obliterated the incriminating blood stain."

The detective went back a bit.

"You remember the day I got you to write the names of Bugnot and Trimardeau?"

"Your trick to get my handwriting!" Contempt was stamped on the man's face.

"Also your finger-prints. You know of course that finger-tips are always slightly moist so leave their marks on whatever objects they touch? You steadied the card with the fingers of your left hand."

Kelly's contempt dissolved as he hung on the detective's words. Obviously the chauffeur wasn't enjoying this interview as much as he had the first.

O. W. said quietly: "When you took such elaborate pains to wipe off the butcher knife with which Gilbert was stabbed it was careless of you to leave your fingerprints on the lamp."

Kelly's startled glance sought the library lamp which the room's one light had converted into a vague smudge.

O. W. continued: "You will recall moving the lamp to get the doily with which to wipe off the knife handle."

"In removing traces of finger-prints from the butcher knife I meant only to cover up Mrs. Dwight's guilt," said Kelly unctuously.

"To cast suspicion on an innocent man!"

"It is what Mr. Dwight would have had me do." The chauffeur's tone was blandly insinuating.

"Dwight has proved his willingness to hang for his wife," said O. W. bluntly. "I wonder if he'd have been so ready to give himself up if you'd happened to mention the fact that you'd substituted the butcher knife you found lying on the library table for his wife's jeweled arrow?"

A subtle gleam shone in the chauffeur's eyes. "I assumed that she had told him. He has thanked me several times for my assistance Saturday night."

The detective said sharply: "Dwight has been under the erroneous impression all along that his wife stabbed Gilbert with the butcher knife and you know it! Far be it from me to depreciate your cleverness, Kelly," the detective's voice was ironic, "but you were largely abetted by luck in your villainy. There were several persons about Saturday night anxious to learn what was going on in the library; one of these might have caught you. And Dwight in returning to the library to check up his wife's hysterical confession must have missed you only by a few minutes. You were luckiest, of course, after the crime was committed, when Dwight's desire to protect his wife kept from her the knowledge that Gilbert had died from a knife wound—not as she supposed from an arrow wound."

Kelly possessed an animal's instinct for self-preservation. "But Mrs. Dwight killed Gilbert. That's the point."

Mr. Wimble pursued another tack.

"You seem unaware that two wounds were discovered on Gilbert's body: the death wound in his heart and a small cut about half an inch wide and three-quarters of an inch deep in his breast."

The chauffeur swallowed convulsively as O. W. went on with his grim monologue: "It was determined that the smaller wound was inflicted by Mrs. Dwight's arrow, the larger one by the butcher knife. The three-quarter inch stab in Gilbert's breast was not at all serious—didn't even puncture his lung. That's official."

Kelly's breath came hard. "But the arrow's as wide at the base of its tip as the blade of the butcher knife

Mr. Wimble saw immediately what the chauffeur was driving at.

"The arrow prick naturally forced Gilbert backward. Tipping over the footstool behind him he fell, as he did so striking his head a severe blow on the chair in back of him." The detective smiled sardonically. "You believe that Mrs. Dwight, suspecting Gilbert merely stunned, had the pitiless hardihood, the temerity, to pull out the arrow and plunge it into his heart?"

Kelly sighed his relief. "She must have! Gilbert was dead when I substituted the knife for the arrow." He said rebukingly: "Mrs. Dwight must have told you she killed Gilbert."

"Yes; she did." Then, to bring Kelly once more to the brink of the abyss: "But she was mistaken. Gilbert was not dead when the knife was substituted!"

Kelly sprang to his feet. "Gilbert was dead when I stuck the knife into him, I tell you! Dead!"

Mr. Wimble said quietly: "Step over here to the library table, Kelly. The light's better. I have the arrow here. I want you to take a look at it."

Fighting for composure Kelly obeyed.

The detective snapped on the library table lamp.

"You see," he pointed out, "the tip of the arrow is blood-stained only three-quarters of an inch. That proves how deeply it was plunged into Gilbert's body. Even if Chiquita Dwight had stabbed Gilbert in the exact location subsequently, receiving your knife thrust a prick that depth would not have proved fatal. A stab at a depth of three-quarters of an inch would not penetrate the heart, even though the individual be emaciated and the missile used exerted with great force directly over the apex during a diastolic impulse, at which time the heart is nearest the chest wall. That, too, is official."

Kelly's face had become the color of lead. He was gazing at the detective as if O. W. were the arbiter of his fate.

Mr. Wimble said: "It would have been wiser for you to have wiped off the blood stain rather than wrapped the dripping arrow in the telegram."

Doubt and fear engulfed the chauffeur.

"Suppose you're right," he whimpered. "I thought Gilbert was dead! Mr. Dwight'd never let me hang for trying to save his wife."

At this point Mr. Wimble moved aside. Had the chauffeur been less exercised over other matters he would have noticed a salient fact. From the moment of their reaching the table O. W.'s round person had been blocking Kelly's view of the corner of the room in which the murder had been committed.

"*Corpo di Cristo!*" The shocking blasphemy came in a voice charged with fright and horror.

Frantically the chauffeur fumbled in his pockets for his luck charm. He could not find it. O. W.'s nimble fingers had already picked the man's pocket of the rabbit foot.

Further search for the lucky piece proved futile.

"Cristo!" The oath rode on a prolonged sob.

It is not pleasant to witness a man losing control of himself. Mr. Wimble was glad that the role Corey was playing entailed closing his eyes.

What a picture the boy presented, lying motionless on the rug where the ashen corpse of Gary Gilbert had lain, garbed in the same Grecian tunic Gilbert had worn! And how admirably the boy counterfeited death! Marcia, the detective saw, had dusted Corey's face with white powder so that the pallor of the faultless profile turned toward the two men looked indubitably deathlike.

Quivering in every limb, barely able to stand, Kelly clung to the table for support. His tortured eyes were glued on the pale handsome profile of the man he supposed to be a ghost.

Suddenly Corey moved weakly. His long thick lashes swept upward from his cheek. His lips parted. A single word came through them.

"Pal!" he murmured brokenly.

Kelly gave a hideous cry. *"Madonna mia!"*

Then through his chalky lips rushed a torrent of Italian.

"Great Scott!" thought Corey. "He's going to confess in a tongue neither O. W. nor I understand!"

"Gay! Listen!" Even in his anguish Kelly must have remembered that Gilbert had not been conversant with Italian. "Gay! It's Pal speaking! I swear to God I thought you were dead when I did it! I swear—"

Mr. Wimble said briskly: "Get up, son!"

As Corey sprang from the tug, Kelly instantly realized that he had been the victim of a hoax. With an outburst of profanity he bolted for the French windows—into the arms of the policemen secreted behind the drapes.

DETECTIVE TRAPS MURDERER; DWIGHT CHAUFFEUR GUILTY

By JANET HILL

O. WIMBLE, nation-famed criminologist, has again justified his pseudonym "One Week" Wimble by solving the Gary Gilbert murder mystery within seven days of taking the case.

Gilbert's body, stabbed through the heart with a butcher knife, was found Saturday night in the library of Miss Marcia Allen of Thousand Oaks. Pursuing his usual method of sifting all the evidence, Mr. Wimble's conclusions led him to the belief that Michele Palermo, alias "Mick" Kelly, Italian chauffeur of Mr. and Mrs. John Dwight, was the guilty person.

Being a shrewd student of human nature as well as a criminal investigator, Mr. Wimble played upon the superstitious nature of his suspect to bring about a confession. Through a whimsy of nature Corey Webb, Detective Wimble's assistant, bears a marked likeness to the late Gary Gilbert. Thus Webb was able to enact convincingly the role of the murdered man when for

30

O. W. had supplied the copy for Janet's article.

"Early in the investigation," he said, "I established a connection between Gilbert and Kelly. Kelly had been seen in Gilbert's penthouse by Kitten Wells and Smitty, one of the bellhops of the hotel. Both of these witnesses inferred that Kelly had visited Gilbert's rooms on some business connected with Chiquita and Gilbert. Kitten so inferred because she is—" the detective's eyes twinkled, "shall we say—feminine or just over-imaginative? Kelly as much as told Smitty that he had gone there to retrieve some love letters written to Gary by Chiquita. But no such letters were found when Gilbert's rooms were searched. There is a vast difference between a flirtation in the presence of friends and a secret 'affair'. There was nothing in the evidence to justify talk of anything illicit between Gilbert and Chiquita Dwight. Therefore the logical conclusion was that Kelly had visited the penthouse in his own interests."

The detective touched on his habit of filing away apparently irrelevant facts for future use.

"Marie let drop that the portrait she was so eager to get hold of had been purchased in Paris by one Count de Palermo. Guess I'm a curious old cuss. Couldn't help conjecturing how the portrait had come into Gilbert's

"Kelly's" benefit Mr. Wimble reconstructed the scene of the crime. In his terror at being confronted by the ghost of the man he had murdered the chauffeur blurted out the truth.

Stabbed With Arrow

Last Saturday evening Palermo (Kelly) drove his employers to the Allen residence to attend a costume ball. At about 8 o'clock the chauffeur, passing the library windows, saw Mrs. Dwight struggling in the arms of Gary Gilbert. Palermo sprang to the young woman's assistance but upon entering the room found Gilbert supposedly lying dead at Mrs. Dwight's feet. Though in a dazed condition Mrs. Dwight admitted having stabbed Gilbert with an arrow she carried as an accessory of her fancy dress costume. First directing the bewildered young woman to her car, the Italian returned to the library for the ostensible purpose of removing the traces of Mrs. Dwight's crime.

On the library table lay the knife authenticating the butcher's garb worn to Miss Allen's costume party by John Dwight. A diabolical scheme taking root in his brain, the Italian grasped this knife. The substitution of the butcher knife for the arrow and John Dwight would hang for his wife's crime!

But as the Italian bent over the body Gilbert's eyes opened! Upon recognizing the man who had been his friend for seven years, a feeble cry of gladness issued through his lips. "Pal!"

Palermo Stabs Old Friend

But the Italian's iniquitous

plan had now flowered. The plea of a friend should not mow it down! Humane feeling was entirely lacking in this killer, callous to everything but his own malignant designs. Even as Gary Gilbert smiled up at his friend "Pal" whom he thought had come to staunch his wound, Michele Palermo stabbed him through the heart with the deadly blade of the butcher knife!

(Continued on Page 5, Col. 1)

possession. So, knowing that the French police keep an eye on all foreigners within their gates, when I cabled to Paris for information about Gary Gilbert I also asked for any available facts concerning Count de Palermo."

Michele Palermo and Gary Gilbert were at pretty low ebb morally when their paths crossed in Paris—"Gay" handsome as a god; "Pal" ugly as a satyr.

Gary's childhood had been too easy. Upon his mother's death in San Francisco his Aunt Cissy had taken him abroad to live. Gary once said that he had stayed in every hotel in Europe. This was an exaggeration but he had stopped at most of the important ones. Hotel life is not good for a child, especially for a handsome boy like Gary. What petting and spoiling Cissy started, other frivolous women, dashing over the Continent in search of God-knows-what, finished. When Gary was no more than ten Cissy and her women friends used to confess their vices to him. When he was eighteen they got him to escort them dancing and to the gambling casinos. He was a great favorite, being marvelously good looking, with an undeniable charm of manner and, because he didn't expect a woman to be better than he was, with a reputation for gallantry.

When Cissy died Gary went on living as Cissy had lived. But Gary gambled more heavily than his aunt had gambled, and he had not yet learned how to get money from women as Cissy had got money from men. So all at once the small fortune Cissy had left him was gone. He drifted naturally into being a gigolo. But when dancing was work it didn't afford so much fun as when it was play. And being a gigolo altered one's social position. Cissy's women friends were nowhere to be found when he wished to borrow money from them.

He located at last in Paris, got some model work; but he didn't like this work, found it too hard. Nor was he liked by his employers. He was unreliable, broke his appointments, usurped "temperament" that belonged to the artists. He began to find posing jobs hard to get.

It was known in the Latin Quarter that a certain "Count" de Palermo owned a valuable art collection. Gary was actually hungry the night he decided to break into de Palermo's and "borrow" something.

The road on which Michele Palermo had traveled from the time of quitting his father's roof to the night Gary Gilbert broke into his house had been long and devious, the kind on which the traveler is beset by a hundred adventures.

Michele began life in Italy as the son of a gardener. His father had ambition for him; he wanted his son to become the world's greatest gardener. Not having had much schooling himself, he sent his son to school to learn from books about gardening. He afterwards blamed this book learning for Michele's failure to become a good gardener. It wasn't that Michele didn't like flowers. He would stand rapt before the blooms. But the smell of manure and the sight of quartered worms made him sick. Michele left home as soon as he attained his majority.

He spent his time roaming over the Continent, doing odd jobs as he went. He made few acquaintances as he went along, but he could tell you offhand the principal museums and art galleries in any town he had visited and name for you the chief treasures of each. Being so well versed in such matters made him of value as a guide to tourist bureaus. For many years this work was known to be his profession.

He settled finally as a guide in Paris. He wasn't happy in Paris. Italians were not popular there. And at a time when he craved companionship young people avoided him because he was so ugly. Especially girls. This made him shy and morose. He came to hate his ill-looks.

Palermo was in Paris when the War broke out. Like many others he disappeared from the boulevards. After the War he reappeared in Paris, his face terribly mutilated. No one doubted that the deep gash down his cheek that stretched his mouth into a grotesque shape was a War wound. Only Palermo himself knew the truth. He had not seen a day's service in the War. Not for nothing was he acquainted with all the hiding-places in Europe. His wounds were the result of an unsuccessful operation per-formed in Switzerland by a plastic surgeon who had be-guiled Michele with promises of facial beauty. Through all his subsequent bitterness the Italian had the comfort of one realization: he now had a good excuse for being ugly!

By degrees, his love of beautiful things led Palermo to collecting what odd bits of art he could afford. After the War, when hordes of Americans began pouring into Europe with money to spend, it occurred to the Italian that he might profit by dealing in antiques. He might have made a fortune in this business but for a queer quirk in his make-up. Once an object of beauty came into his possession he could not bear to part with it. He began to foist imitations on his customers. He found Americans most gullible. Perhaps having no antiques of their own they were ignorant of how to judge the worth of the articles they bought.

It was while he was an art dealer, ever sensitive about his disfigurement, to make up for his lack of good looks he credited himself with aristocracy by dubbing himself "Count" de Palermo. His clients, particularly the women, gobbled up this counterfeit as voraciously as they did his made-to-order relics.

He did so well financially that he was able to add to his own private collection of beautiful things. But too slowly. Nor did his trade flourish without some trouble from the police. On the night Gary Gilbert broke into his house the Italian was sitting at his desk trying to figure out a new means of livelihood—one that would prove at the same time congenial and so lucrative as to feed his insatiable hunger to possess beautiful things. So he heard Gilbert breaking into the house and was able to get the drop on him.

Gilbert had never seen Palermo before, but the Italian immediately recognized the intruder as the male model for the painting "Day and Night" he had recently purchased. He smiled above his revolver. With his free hand he toyed with his rabbit foot charm. Luck was with him. A plan was taking form in his mind.

Chicken-livered at best, now weakened by hunger and terror, that leering smile deprived Gilbert of all courage. Flinging himself at Palermo's feet, he cowered there, gibbering excuses, pleading for mercy. He promised Palermo anything he wished if only he would not turn him over to the police. Palermo took him at his word.

Flinging aside the revolver, he brought food and poured drinks. Nourished, free from fear, Gilbert became once more "Gay" Gilbert, light-hearted, witty and, with his regular features, fair skin and ease of carriage, astonishingly easy to look at. If he betrayed weakness of character with every other breath Palermo did not complain; it would have been difficult to manage a stronger man.

On that hapless night, though for amenity's sake they gave it a different name, Gary Gilbert became Michele Palermo's tool.

For five years they plied their nefarious trade of blackmail, Palermo supplying the brains, Gilbert taking the risk; Gilbert earning the money, Palermo spending it. And they were not unhappy during those years, these two adventurers. Gilbert liked someone else to do his thinking for him. And as long as Palermo, hearing of a bit of porcelain unearthed by a laborer's spade in Indo-China, had the means to go there and buy it, he was content.

Sometimes, not often, a victim gave them trouble. The pair was none too popular with the authorities. However "Gay" and "Pal" timed their departure from Paris at such periods as the police were making it uncomfortable for them, and by the time they returned the trouble had blown over.

Just prior to Gilbert's return to the city of his birth, Palermo as Gary's "secretary" had gone to the Ritz to collect from a wealthy Jewess of the Bronx who unwisely had succumbed to Gilbert's charms. Negotiating with the Jewess over Benedictine in the Ritz Bar, Palermo happened to turn and saw the glorious *objet d'art* it immediately became his burning desire to possess. The Jewess observed a protracted tremor pass through the Italian's body, sat in silent awe before the ashen pallor of his face. Finally, "This guy's cuckoo!" she thought in an effort to escape from the almost fanatical gleam in his eyes.

In explaining step by step his solution of the crime, Mr. Wimble said: "Of course John Dwight was too avid—and too awkward—in trying to establish an alibi for his wife, to keep her hidden away; and his giving himself up upon learning of my intention to visit the convent was significant. I'll admit I was pretty doubtful of Chiquita at first. I felt she knew as much about the murder as anyone. Yet I could hit on no motive for Chiquita's committing the crime. I visited the convent, learned enough of Chiquita's background to help me construct a motive.

"But by that time the signs of suspicion were pointing toward Kelly. After which the trail led straight to him.

"A study of the man himself helped me to arrive at the truth. I learned that he was superstitious. The missing thirteenth page from his notebook; Blanche's testimony that she and Kelly had quarreled about an umbrella being opened in the house; his rabbit foot charm.

"Kelly was not able to think profoundly. He trusted pretty much to luck rather than to any masterful plan of his own to bring about the results he desired. But he could think quickly. I tried innumerable times to trip him but always he landed on both feet. And often he had me baffled by telling the truth when a less clever man would have lied. He of course was too sure of himself, especially after Dwight gave himself up.

"Kelly's carelessness was evident throughout. It was careless of him to leave his finger-prints on the lamp. It was careless of him to throw the arrow when he knew someone was nearby to hear it land. His gross carelessness, of course, was failing to stab Gilbert in the exact wound inflicted by Chiquita.

"The colossal vanity of the man helped me to pick the grains of truth out of the chaff of lies he unloaded on me. Every time he turned a trick he fairly strutted. If he guessed I knew a certain fact he would benignly out with it before I had a chance to question him. Though he pretended to be self-derisive when telling me that for fun he called himself a Count, I could see it pleased him that he

DETECTIVE TRAPS GILBERT'S SLAYER

(Continued from Page 1, Col. 2)

Michele Palermo was endowed to an overwhelming degree with an appreciation of beauty. Unfortunately he was not content to admire only; he must also possess.

During the Dwights' wedding trip abroad the Italian happened to catch sight of Chiquita Dwight at the Ritz hotel in Paris. Though later he came to regard her as a woman, at that moment through the eyes of a collector of beautiful things he saw her only as an "object of art." From then on it became his "idee fixe" to possess the enchantingly lovely Chiquita Dwight.

Lies Way Into Job

He followed the Dwights to California where he lied his way into their employ as chauffeur. Patiently biding his time for more than two years, the Italian was quick to grasp what he believed his opportunity to acquire the exquisite Chiquita for his own. But for the opportune aid of "One Week" Wimble the scoundrel's rascally plans might have carried.

With John Dwight hanged for murder the hindrance of a husband would have been removed. With the Dwight fortune at his disposal the Italian could have provided the proper setting for the beautiful Chiquita. And with Chiquita's own erroneous belief that she had committed the crime he would have had a weapon with which to threaten her into compliance with his wishes.

could get away with the deception. He was vain about his appearance. He hated his facial unprepossessingness; he was immaculate always; his hands were fastidiously manicured. He was vain of his erudition, vain of his brogue that he so assiduously copied from Michael.

"It is hard to believe that a man who possessed so highly developed an aesthetic sense should be endowed with so under-developed a moral sense. The man did love Beauty. There is no doubt of that. The bit of carved onyx he wore on his finger was superb. There was more than mere admiration in his appreciation of the pansies. His face glowed when he recalled the beautiful scenery of his perfect itinerary. There was ecstasy in his eyes when he pictured the companion of the honeymoon trip."

O. W. discussed the fascinating subject of motive.

"What complicated the solving of this case, of course, was my difficulty in establishing a motive. The more obvious the motive the simpler as a rule the crime's solution. I don't believe I've ever handled a case in which the motive was so obscure. I felt for this reason that the murder must have been unpremeditated, a crime of passion committed impulsively, one in which a scarcely appreciable interval of time exists between the malice aforethought and the actual deed. Even when the net of suspicion was closing tightly around Kelly, I had difficulty in discovering his motive."

The detective smiled down into the lovely heart-shaped face of Janet Hill, flushed with expectancy as she waited to hear One-Week Wimble reveal the Italian's motive for the murder of Gary Gilbert.

"If Kelly had paid more attention to the tenth Commandment, the sixth would not have proved his undoing."

About the Author

Helen Burnham was born in California in June 1896. By the U.S. Census of 1900, her father, Milton, was widowed, and the family (including younger sister Florence) lived in Oakland, California. By 1920, Helen was a "successful writer of short stories and scenarios," and by 1931 she had published her first mystery. At that time she was working as a stenographer at San Francisco's Clift Hotel (owned by Helen's uncle, Frederick Clift). The second mystery followed in 1932. Briefly married, then divorced, Helen continued her secretarial work at the Parker Ranch in Hawaii up through the mid-1940s. At the present time, no further details on her life are known.

COACHWHIPBOOKS.COM (PRINT)
COACHWHIP.COM (EPUB)

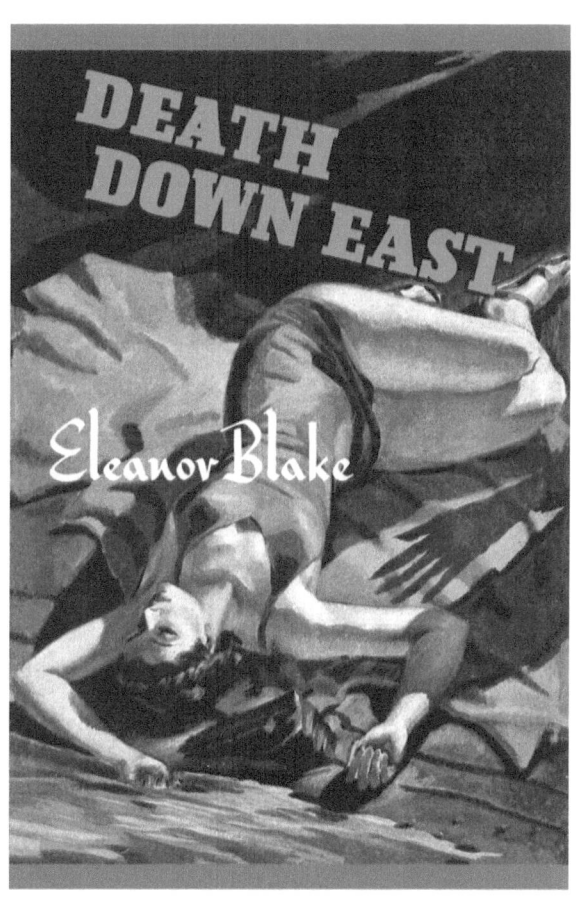

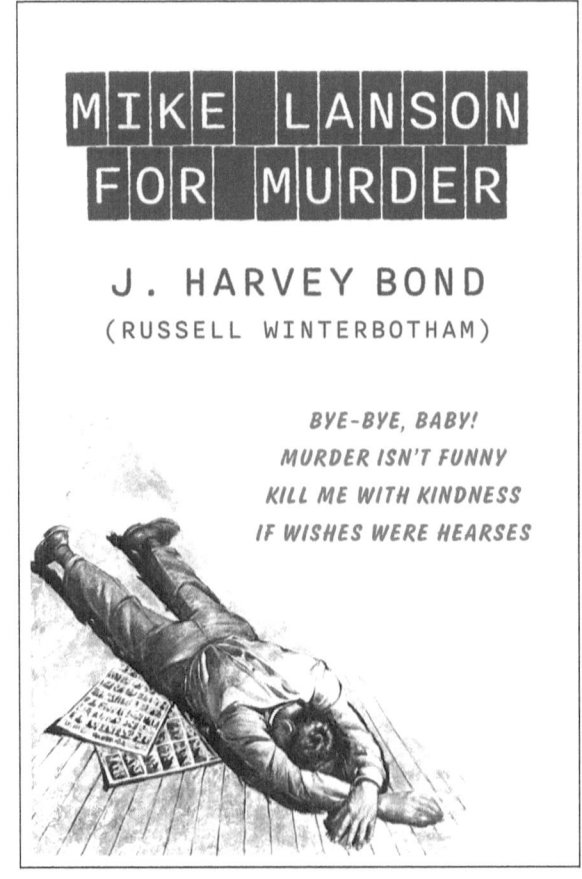

No Face to Murder

EDITH HOWIE

COACHWHIP PUBLICATIONS
ALSO AVAILABLE

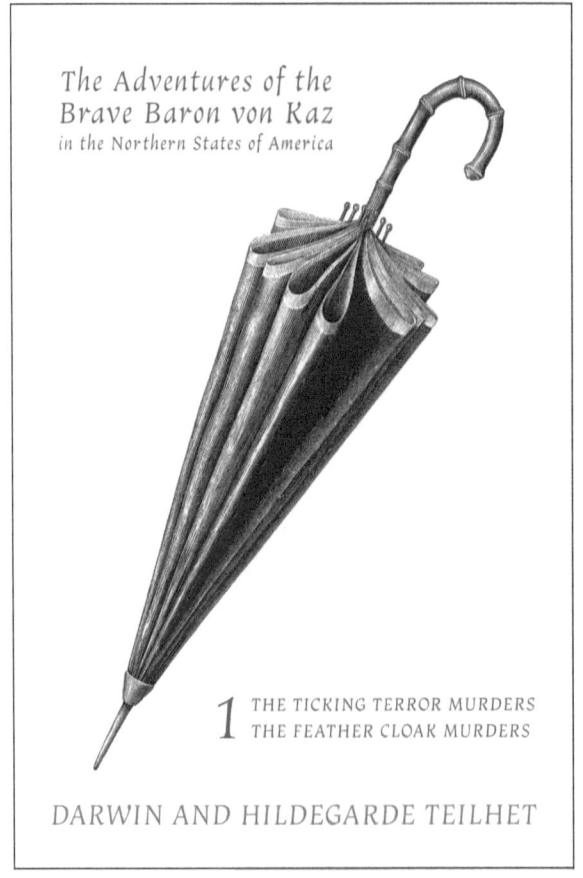

The Adventures of the
Brave Baron von Kaz
in the Northern States of America

1 THE TICKING TERROR MURDERS
THE FEATHER CLOAK MURDERS

DARWIN AND HILDEGARDE TEILHET

MURDER IN THE
FAMILY

NICE
PEOPLE
MURDER

Mary Hastings Bradley

COACHWHIPBOOKS.COM (PRINT)

COACHWHIP.COM (EPUB)

NICE PEOPLE POISON

MURDER IN ROOM 700

Mary Hastings Bradley

www.ingramcontent.com/pod-product-compliance
Lightning Source LLC
Chambersburg PA
CBHW032256020726
47495CB00001B/126